PASSION RUNS DEEP

An impossible situation drives Samantha Delafield to commit a desperate act and forces the orphaned beauty to flee her world of privilege. But her fate takes a shocking turn when she is arrested for petty thievery and shackled to a dangerous criminal.

HEARTS RUN WILD

Nicholas Brogan is a man tormented by his past as England's most notorious pirate. Now a blackmailer's threats have drawn him out of seclusion—and into the hands of the British magistrates. Manacles bind him to a beautiful young hellion who enflames Nicholas with passions he has struggled to suppress—tempting him to care, to want, to feel. And now Nicholas and Samantha must escape together, for their destinies are linked by chains far stronger than the iron that holds them captive . . . and only love can set their imprisoned hearts free.

SHELLY THACKER

HEARTS RUN WILD

An Avon Romantic Treasure

AVON BOOKS ◆ NEW YORK

HEARTS RUN WILD is an original publication of Avon Books. This work has never before appeared in book form. This work is a novel. Any similarity to actual persons or events is purely coincidental.

AVON BOOKS
A division of
The Hearst Corporation
1350 Avenue of the Americas
New York, New York 10019

First Avon Books Printing: April 1996

AVON TRADEMARK REG. U.S. PAT. OFF. AND IN OTHER COUNTRIES, MARCA REGISTRADA, HECHO EN U.S.A.

Printed in the U.S.A.

RA 10 9 8 7 6 5 4 3 2 1

*Dedicated with love
to Claire and Jerilyn,
who gave my soul new wings*

I'd like to express my deepest gratitude to my parents, family, and three special friends: LaVerne Coan, Beth Manz, and Linda Pedder for helping me through the most difficult year of my life. Without your steadfast support, shoulders to cry on, love, and prayers, I could not have endured 1995.

To Rob Cohen and Ellen Edwards for extraordinary patience and understanding. Your gentle guidance helped rekindle my creative spirit and make this book possible.

And above all to my husband, Mark, who held me through the darkness and helped me find the light again. Every day, you show me the true meaning of the words *love* and *hero*.

Love seeketh not itself to please,
Nor for itself hath any care;
But for another gives its ease,
And builds a Heaven in Hell's despair.

WILLIAM BLAKE

Chapter 1

England, 1741

The sun retreated over the waves, stealing away into the darkness until only a blood-red slash remained along the horizon. That last streak of light and warmth held out against the cold weight of night for only a moment. Then it vanished at last, leaving the pirate ship cloaked entirely in blackness and tendrils of fog.

Captain Nicholas Brogan stood alone on the battered quarterdeck, leaning on the rail, oblivious to the chill in the autumn air. He held a Jamaican cheroot clamped between his teeth, its fragrant smoke curling around his beard as he slowly exhaled. He barely tasted the rich tobacco. The glowing tip made a tiny beacon until he ground the cheroot out and flicked the stub into the icy waters of the North Sea. He kept his gaze fastened on the shoreline. *Patience*, he warned himself.

Most of the inhabitants of the small coastal village had settled into their homes for the evening. He had chosen the perfect place. Waited for the perfect night.

He glanced upward, gauging his chances one last time; no moonlight penetrated the clouds overhead. And this remote town employed neither street lamps nor watchmen. No one would notice him. Or even see him.

He wouldn't have to wait much longer. Another

hour, perhaps less. Already a drowsy air had descended along the coast with the fog. The villagers would even now be gathering around their hearths; though he could not see inside the scattered hovels that hugged the shoreline, he could imagine.

He could remember.

Near the light of each fire, a family would share supper and linger afterward, husbands repairing their fishing nets, children playing with toy boats, wives sewing or reading aloud from the Bible. . . .

One corner of Nicholas's mouth lifted in a cynical smile. *Such good, God-fearing people.* As secure in their faith as they were behind the thick daub-and-wattle walls of their thatched-roof homes. So certain that good would always triumph over evil, that God was merciful. That their sins would someday be forgiven.

That Heaven awaited at the end of their lives.

He shifted his gaze away from the town, out over the dark waters of the sea. What panic would erupt, he mused, if they suspected what lurked in the night aboard the small, ragged schooner anchored just offshore, so close to their orderly little town.

But of course none of them could suspect. No one in all of England knew that Nicholas Brogan, scourge of the Atlantic, terror of the Caribbean, despised by every law-abiding, God-loving Englishman, had returned.

Against his will.

The breeze changed directions suddenly, noisily snapping the patched canvas sails, snatching at his cotton shirt, raking through his black hair as if to push him away. Away from this place, from England. From the danger that awaited him.

But he could not turn back. He had no choice.

He would wait one more hour, and then he would go ashore. And break the familiar commandment one more time.

Thou shalt not kill.

A sound behind him interrupted his thoughts—the

sound of booted feet on the ladder that led up from the main deck.

"We could be halfway to Brazil by now," a deep voice, heavily accented with the lilt of the Gold Coast, grumbled from the darkness. "Or Tortuga. Or up to our scuppers in grog and bawds in Hispaniola. I'll bet those shapely little twins we tupped back in '31 still have fond memories of us—"

"Stow it, Manu." Nicholas returned his gaze to the coastline. "I'm not going to spend the rest of my life on the run. If that was what I wanted, I wouldn't have taken such pains to disappear in the first place."

His quartermaster swore under his breath and came to stand beside him at the rail, offering a bottle of rum brought up from the galley. "Then I suppose it's useless to tell you again that this plan is insane."

"It's been useless the last fifty times you've said it." Nicholas irritably waved the bottle away. "No reason to believe it'll work now. This isn't as bloody risky as you think."

"Oh, no, of course not. You've hardly any enemies in England. Merely the entire Royal Navy, every magistrate, warder, watchman, and marshalman in the country, various thief-takers and adventurers who would love to collect the ten thousand-pound bounty on your head, and assorted other friendly types with old scores to settle. You're perfectly safe here."

Nicholas shot him a quelling glance, but the moonless, starless night made it almost impossible for them to see one another. Though he could barely make out the African's angular features, he could hear the concern in his voice. Nicholas shook his head. Even after twelve years, he hadn't grown used to that—someone being concerned about him. Calling him friend.

Nicholas Brogan called no one friend. He trusted no one.

He never had. He never would.

"The man known as the reclusive Mr. James *is* perfectly safe here," Nicholas insisted. "I'm an ordinary colonial, a simple planter from South Carolina. The authorities have no reason to harass me or even *notice* me. I haven't broken a single one of His Majesty's laws. Haven't pilfered a shilling. Haven't bothered a soul—"

"Haven't so much as crossed the street the wrong way on Sunday," Manu chuckled.

Nicholas scowled. "The pirate they knew as Nicholas Brogan met a fiery end six years ago," he declared flatly, absently rubbing his beard, which covered an old scar on his jaw. "He's dead and buried."

"And every person in England believes that. Except one." Manu gestured with the bottle of rum. "Someone out there on that vast island knows you're still alive."

Nicholas clenched his teeth, as if he could somehow bite back the frustration and anger that plagued him. For the past six years, all he had wanted was to find peace. All he had wanted was to be left alone.

But it seemed both would be forever beyond his reach.

Manu had spoken the truth: Someone knew that Nicholas Brogan was alive and living in South Carolina. An anonymous note had arrived by post a month ago. A blackmail note.

The blackmailer claimed to have evidence which he threatened to take to the authorities—unless Nicholas sent the sum of fifteen thousand pounds to a certain pub in York by Michaelmas Day, September twenty-ninth.

It was a king's ransom. Or at least a pirate's ransom.

And Nicholas didn't have it.

This blackmailer seemed to believe the old tales in the penny-post newspapers—stories of the ruthless pirate better known as "Sir Nicholas" swimming in gold and jewels, with buried treasure chests scattered hither and yon on exotic islands.

Nicholas grimaced. It was hell having a legendary reputation.

The truth was, like most pirates, he'd spent what he'd stolen as fast as he'd stolen it. The truth was he'd plied the seas for fourteen years as a buccaneer with hatred burning in his heart and no thought for the future.

Until that day in 1735.

His jaw tightened. Until now, only two people had known he survived that day: Manu, who had pulled him from the burning wreckage, and Clarice, his sometime mistress, who had tended him until he was well enough to leave England.

Manu intruded on his thoughts. "Anyone could've sent that note, Cap'n. Anyone. Clarice might've let her guard down after all these years, let the secret slip. Or . . ." He took a long swallow of rum. "She could be the one blackmailing you."

"Aye," Nicholas said slowly. "I've considered that. But Clarice knows I don't have that kind of money. And if she wanted to do me in, she's had six years. Why wait until now?"

"Doesn't make much sense," Manu agreed. "On the other hand, 'Hell hath no fury . . .' "

Nicholas frowned. If he had to add *women scorned* to the list, the number of people who would enjoy seeing his head on the end of a pike would easily double.

"Cap'n," Manu persisted, "the point is you've no way of knowing who or what you're up against, no friends out there to turn to for help—and a few dozen enemies who'd love nothing better than to kill you."

"And none of that matters a damn," Nicholas grated. "Whoever this blackmailer is, I can't pay. And I don't want the greedy bugger spilling his guts to the authorities. Which leaves only one choice." His mouth curved in a humorless smile. "And it's too late to turn back now, since I've already posted the package."

He'd sent it just before leaving South Carolina—a

package addressed precisely as the note had instructed, containing not fifteen thousand pounds . . . but worthless blank paper.

He'd posted it on one of the Falmouth brigs that sluggishly collected mail along the American coast; it wouldn't reach York until a fortnight from now. Just before Michaelmas. It would look perfect, right down to the South Carolina tax stamps on it.

And he would be at the pub long before it arrived, lying in wait to see who showed up to collect it.

"Aye, Cap'n, you've planned it all carefully," Manu conceded. "You've ample time before he makes good his threat. But if something goes wrong and he doesn't hear from you by Michaelmas Day—"

"Oh, he'll hear from me by then," Nicholas said darkly. "He'll hear from me."

Manu fell silent, as if trying to devise one final reason why his captain shouldn't do what he had made up his mind to do. The African possessed the most annoying ability to do battle with words as easily as he did with pistol and cutlass.

Manu scuffed his boot over the deck planks, the wood scarred by years of grappling hooks, cannon shot, bullets. "You know, Cap'n, I never guessed we'd actually make it this far. Thought for sure our old scow here would sink before we made it a mile out of the Carolinas." He chuckled. "But it seems she's in better shape than either one of us."

Nicholas didn't laugh.

Manu sighed heavily. "Just do me a favor." He set the bottle aside, and Nicholas heard him withdraw something from inside his frock coat. "Take this with you."

Nicholas couldn't see what it was, but he knew. "I won't need it."

"You might. Better safe than—"

"I don't want it."

All trace of humor left Manu's voice. "Has it crossed

your mind that this blackmailer might want your *hide* instead of your money? He might've sent that note *hoping* to flush you out. You might be playing right into his hands. What makes you think you can slip into England, take the bastard out, and slip away without firing a single shot?"

Nicholas swallowed hard. He clenched his fists against the pain that knotted his gut. He started shaking, and hoped to God that Manu couldn't see.

Manu continued in that low, even tone. "You've had a bellyful of killing. I know. I was there. But you can't go ashore tonight without a gun . . ."

Nicholas still couldn't speak, barely heard the rest. Aye, Manu had been there. *But he hadn't seen everything. He didn't know.*

Didn't know what Nicholas had done in winning the revenge he had wanted. Nicholas alone knew the truth, and he had never spoken a word of it to anyone.

He gripped the rail, his fingers tightening with bruising force as he fought to stop shaking, fought the memories that assaulted him.

The faces. The voices. The blood.

And the sound of the single pistol shot that had ended his infamous career.

That sound still haunted his nightmares. Louder than the roar of the storm that had pounded at his ship on that insane day, sharper than the crack of lightning that had struck the mainmast like a bolt from God trying to stop him.

No force of heaven or earth had been able to stop him that day. He hadn't even cared that his own ship was ablaze as he blew Captain Eldridge's Royal Navy man-of-war out from beneath him.

Eldridge's men had swept aboard Nicholas's ship— some fighting his pirate crew, some simply trying to save themselves—but by then they had all known they were about to die together. Nothing could save them from the fire or the sea or each other.

Slashing his way toward Eldridge with his cutlass, Nicholas's only thought had been to take the bastard with him when he died. But the navy men swarmed over him, protecting their commander. In a blind rage, Nicholas hacked one man down, drew his pistol, spun, and fired at the next blue uniform he saw.

And realized too late that it was only a boy.

A cabin boy. Ten or twelve. Too young to know the difference between guts and stupidity.

In that frozen instant Nicholas had felt the rain on his face, so cold. Like a slap from the grave. So icy, deathly cold.

Unspeakable horror held him immobile as he stared into the boy's eyes, watching the lad fall. In that innocent gaze he saw himself at the same age. Saw clearly for the first time what he had become since. What his quest for vengeance had made him.

A soulless animal.

And in the boy's face he saw other faces. Too many faces. So many lives cut short by his hand. So much blood spilled in fourteen years.

A second later an explosion turned the world black.

Days after that, he had awakened to find himself at Clarice's in London—and every newspaper full of stories about his well-deserved fiery end. The admiralty mourned the loss of the heroic Captain Eldridge, and declared the hated Nicholas Brogan dead. Both buried at sea. The bounty on his head was never paid.

As soon as he was well enough to get out of bed, Nicholas had slipped out of the country and left it all behind him. Piracy. England. All of it.

Even pistols. *Especially* pistols. He hadn't touched one in six years.

He did not want to risk unleashing the animal within.

". . . listen to reason," Manu was saying. "And just take the damn thing—"

"Manu, for my purposes, all I need is a blade," Nicholas said slowly, "and I'm carrying several. What do I need with a gun? I'm an ordinary planter traveling to York on a matter of business. No one will bother me." He forced a laugh and raked a hand through the thick black beard that covered his cheeks, the silver-peppered hair at his temples. "And who the hell could possibly recognize me? Most of the coves who knew me well enough to identify me are dead—Falconer went down with his ship, Spears was shot by his own crew, Blake was killed fighting the French, Davison hanged at Execution Dock—"

"And that's exactly where you'll end up if you get caught," Manu countered. "If someone—anyone—figures out who you are, you'll be hanged before you can say 'pieces of eight.'"

"I won't get caught." Nicholas flashed a shadow of his once-infamous sardonic smile. Then he turned to stare at the drowsy little village on the shore, at the glow from the hearths, and repeated it softly. "I won't get caught."

Chapter 2

The unsteady flame of a single torch glowed red on the black iron bars of his cell.

Nicholas closed his eyes with a groan and allowed himself to just lie there for a moment, on his side, letting the cool stone of the floor soothe his stinging cheek. He wanted to sink back down into the numbing abyss of unconsciousness, but the pain kept him awake—pain throbbing in his temples, in his jaw, in his stomach, everywhere. He recognized the sharp, metallic taste on his tongue as blood. His own.

Sounds of human misery assaulted him from all sides, the wretched sobs and moans leaving no doubt about where he was. He coughed, wincing.

First-rate job of it, Brogan. Back in England less than a day, and already you land yourself in gaol.

For something you didn't even do.

He might have laughed at the irony of it, but his bruised ribs brought a stab of pain that choked off his breath in the back of his throat.

Gritting his teeth, he lifted one hand to inspect the damage. His ribs didn't seem to be broken. His left eye had swollen almost shut. His lip felt about twice its normal size. And beneath the thick bristle of his beard, a deep cut along his right cheekbone still bled. He moved his jaw cautiously and discovered to his surprise that it wasn't broken. There was no permanent damage; he would heal.

If he lived that long.

Letting his hand fall back to the stone, he lay there with his eyes closed and muttered curses under his breath, each one hurting his battered lips. He cursed himself. Cursed the blasted local marshalmen who'd jumped him in the darkness, mistaking him for some footpad they'd been hunting for weeks.

Most of all he cursed God for deserting him. Again.

Rolling slowly onto his back, he opened his eyes— or at least his right eye—and glared up at the iron bars overhead. His vision, such as it was, slowly adjusted to the meager, flickering light; he could see that his cell was in the middle of a row of cells, each made entirely of iron bars. Including the ceiling, which was no more than six feet overhead. He wouldn't even be able to stand up straight.

It was like a stall. A kennel.

A sudden knot clenched his stomach. The local lawmen might be bumblers when it came to identifying a suspect on a moonless night . . . but their gaol appeared secure. Alarmingly secure.

He fought the unease rising within him. He'd survived worse situations than this. Much worse.

At present, however, he couldn't remember any one in particular.

He closed his eyes and exhaled a long, slow, steadying breath, telling himself he was in no immediate danger. They didn't know his true identity. They had no reason to suspect.

But in rural areas like this, even those charged with minor crimes—even accused footpads—had to wait for the arrival of the assize judge to have their cases heard. And the assize judge only visited from London twice a year: summer and winter.

Which meant his honorable lordship wouldn't be arriving for several months.

Long after Michaelmas Day.

Nicholas flattened his palms against the floor and pushed himself up to a sitting position, gritting his teeth to force back another groan. His injured ribs ached and his swollen eye throbbed and the haze of pain made it difficult to think—but he bloody well had to find some way to escape.

Turning his head, he realized that the back wall wasn't made of bars, but of wood. He reached out with one foot and kicked it experimentally. Solid wood. A good ten inches thick. No escape there.

Grimacing, he let himself fall back against the bars behind him, wiping blood from his face as he surveyed his surroundings more thoroughly. The gaol was half-empty, his nearest neighbor two cells to the left. The man lay on the floor, sobbing drunkenly, telling the rambling tale of his sorry life to anyone who cared to listen.

Nicholas looked away. The gaol's stale air made breathing about as pleasant as trying to inhale some reeking liquid, but beneath the sour smells of sweat and fear, he caught the lingering scent of horses. It seemed this place had once served as a barn. Or a stable. The heat only intensified the—

He stilled as a shudder rippled through him. A memory.

The stifling air. Couldn't breathe. Darkness. Bodies crushed together in the hold. Father! Why did you kill my father? The lieutenant with a hot iron in his hand. Someone crying. An orphaned boy. Crying. Begging. "Please don't. No! Please. Don't—"

The scream. Agony. The smell of burning flesh . . .

Nicholas shook his head, blinking rapidly, caught off guard by the vivid, unwanted images. He steadied himself with a hand on the floor, sweat running down his face. The sting of it against the cut on his cheek made him reach up—and the roughness of his beard yanked him firmly back to reality.

He was thirty-eight, not ten.

He was in the custody of rural marshalmen, not the Royal Navy.

Jesus. He had thought those particular memories long ago exterminated. Wiped clean. Obliterated by blood and vengeance.

Almost without thinking, he touched his chest, finding his waistcoat, his cotton shirt buttoned to his throat. The mark concealed. As always.

Breathing hard, he forced himself to ignore the too-familiar sounds and stench around him, to ignore all the pain inside him. Forced his mind back to the problem at hand.

His fingers closed around one of the iron bars that caged him, his grip tightening until the cool metal bit into his palm.

Escape.

It would be far too fitting, too ironic, for his notorious career to end this way—since this was how it had begun, twenty-eight years ago.

On the day he'd turned his back on God.

He shut his eyes. Perhaps this was the divine retribution he'd been expecting ever since. Perhaps it was fate that he should find himself here, mistaken for a common footpad, a nameless prisoner in the town of . . . bloody hell, he didn't even know the name of this place.

A nameless prisoner in a nameless town, facing a noose for a crime not his own. An ignominious end to a nefarious life.

Fate.

He rejected the idea almost as quickly as it entered his head. Opening his good eye, he stared defiantly heavenward. He didn't believe in fate.

If anyone was to blame for his current predicament, it was him. The knuckles of his right hand still throbbed and stung; he had managed to land a few solid blows and inflict a bit of damage with his blades before the four men had wrestled him to the ground.

If he hadn't resisted, if he had answered their questions civilly, he might have talked his way out of it.

But some old habits died hard, he thought bitterly. When cornered, Nicholas Brogan fought. Instinctively. Viciously.

The soulless animal had been unleashed.

Had he thought he could control it? Thought he could change? It was clearly too late for that; too many years of blood and violence had made him what he was. What he would always be.

Too late. Those two words seemed to sum up his entire life.

A metallic clatter of chains and a groan of old hinges sounded from the far end of the long, dark chamber as a door creaked open. A slash of light streaked across the stone floor. A man stepped inside, an oil lantern in one hand. A ring of keys jangled on his belt.

Ignoring the pleas, curses, and grasping hands that came at him, he moved slowly along the row of cells, heading straight for Nicholas.

Nicholas was about to get to his feet, but decided it would be better to give the impression that he was too injured to be much of a threat. He remained where he was, slouched against the bars at his back . . . ready to take advantage of any opportunity that might present itself.

Even before the man drew near, Nicholas could tell this wasn't one of the marshalmen who'd ambushed him. This man waddled more than walked, puffing at the effort of moving his considerable bulk. He was either the gaoler, or the county magistrate coming to interrogate him.

He doubted the latter; county magistrates tended to be aristocratic popinjays who prized the status of their crown appointments while disdaining the actual work. Rather than sully their lily-white hands, they generally hired others to carry out their duties—a gaoler to oversee the local prison, marshalmen to gather evidence, interview witnesses, and arrest and interrogate suspects.

Some of the hirelings were honest men. Others, like the ones he'd encountered tonight, were worse brigands than the people they arrested. Brutal thugs more interested in bribes and bounties than truth and justice.

"Glad to see yer finally awake, mate," the man wheezed as he came to a halt before Nicholas's cell. "Brought ye yer supper." He set down a metal pail with a clang.

This, evidently, was the gaoler. "I'm not hungry," Nicholas said weakly, trying to sound like an outraged, innocent citizen. "I'd like to speak to the magistrate."

"Makin' demands, are ye?" The man glowered at him. "Yer lucky we didn't hang ye straightaway, after the way ye near spilled Tibbs's guts with yer knife." He set the lantern down behind him.

Nicholas's every muscle went taut. The pail of food was too big to pass through the bars. The gaoler would have to unlock his cell door. "How was I to know they were the law?" He pressed an arm across his midsection with an exaggerated wince, holding his bruised ribs. "I was merely passing through this pleasant hamlet of yours and when I stopped at the stables to hire a horse—"

"*Steal* a horse, more like."

"*Hire* a horse. The next thing I knew, four hulking blokes ambushed me. It was the dead of night. I thought they were outlaws. I simply defended myself."

"They'd been trailin' ye fer 'alf an hour, mate. If yer so innocent, what were ye doin' skulkin' around the roads so quiet-like after midnight?"

"As I told them, I was merely passing through—"

"On business. Aye, a planter from the Colonies just passin' through on business." The gaoler shook his head in disbelief, the rolls of fat under his chin wobbling. "Ye don't fight like no planter, mate."

Nicholas clamped his teeth to stop an oath, chastising himself again for fighting when he should have remained calm and reasonable.

Unfortunately it seemed that old pirates, like old dogs, couldn't be taught new tricks.

"The magistrate don't need to be seein' ye," the gaoler continued. He still didn't reach for his keys. "Ye match the description well enough. Been in all the county broadsheets fer a month. There's a nice fat reward out fer ye. Fifty pounds."

"Really?" Nicholas asked, one eyebrow quirking upward, the irony in his tone completely lost on the gaoler. "Fifty whole pounds?"

"That's right. More'n any of us makes in two years, even split four ways." Instead of opening the cell door, he bent down and withdrew a few items from the pail. "An' now we got a witness what swears yer the one he saw sneakin' away from Lord Alston's house with a sack full of loot a month ago."

"Witness?" Nicholas demanded incredulously. "What witness?"

"Tibbs 'imself."

Nicholas swore. The wounded marshalman was obviously so infuriated, he would say anything to see Nicholas hanged.

The gaoler passed the foodstuffs through the bars— a leg of mutton, a slab of bread, and a tall pewter mug filled with some sort of drink. Nicholas took them one by one, frustration rising in his throat when it became clear the door wouldn't be opened.

This unsavory bunch wasn't going to take any chance of their fifty-pound prize getting away.

And he couldn't bribe his way out. They'd relieved him of his coin purse when they arrested him. Along with the few weapons he'd been carrying.

His chances of making it to York before Michaelmas were narrowing by the minute.

"You've arrested the wrong man," he insisted. "The

assize judge won't give you a shilling for me. Because you won't be able to prove a thing."

"Oh, we'll prove it, mate." The man's tone made it clear they could prove whatever they wanted, that they had done so before. "And we won't be waitin' fer the assizes."

A new sense of foreboding prickled up Nicholas's spine. "What is that supposed to mean?"

"It means this lot 'ere"—the gaoler waved a beefy hand to indicate the half-dozen prisoners held in the other cells to the left and right—"can wait 'til January when the judge comes on 'is usual rounds. But not you, mate. Yer worth too much. We'll be taking ye in now so we can collect straightaway."

Nicholas felt his heart slam against his bruised ribs. "Taking me in to . . ."

"London," the gaoler confirmed with a nod and a grin filled with greed.

Nicholas stared up at him, speechless, struck by a sense of doom that was like a blast of cannon shot. He was done for. *London*. Not just London but the Old Bailey—the venerable courthouse filled with justices and lawmen who had hunted him for years. If any one of them recognized him . . .

He'd be handed over to the admiralty. Strung up at Execution Dock. Drawn and quartered and left to swing from a gibbet cage as a lesson to others who might be tempted to take up the pirate's easy, profitable life.

Either that or he'd be cashed in for fifty pounds and executed as a footpad.

Either way, he wouldn't have to worry about Michaelmas anymore.

He'd be dead before then.

"If ye can prove yer innocent, ye 'ave nothin' to worry about and the judge will let ye go." The gaoler leaned down with a stern expression. "But I don't think yer innocent, mate. And I don't think 'e'll be lettin' ye go."

Not likely, Nicholas thought. *Not bloody likely*. He managed to force only one word past his clenched teeth. "When?"

"The lads will be comin' to collect ye at first light on the morrow." The man picked up the empty pail and his lantern. "Eat up, mate." He nodded to the food Nicholas had set aside. "This may be yer last meal."

With that pleasant prediction, he turned and waddled out.

Nicholas sat very still for a moment after the door closed with an ominous thud and the chain clattered back into place.

He stared into the darkness as the facts of the situation sank in . . . and an image left over from his childhood lessons reeled through his mind.

An image of Hell.

He didn't believe in much of anything anymore, but he still believed in Hell. He had no doubt he would be spending eternity there—and he had no desire to hasten his arrival by even a day.

Somewhere deep inside him an old, almost-forgotten cunning sparked to life, already had him thinking, scheming, planning. He would *not* let the Royal Navy get their hands on him.

He would never let them do to him what they had done to his father.

No, by Hell, he wouldn't let that happen. He was going to escape. Somewhere between here and London, he vowed, he was going to escape.

A half-hour later, the rest of the prisoners had quieted down for the night and the torches had burned low. Nicholas turned his attention to his supper, leaning back against the bars of his cell as he ate, slowly, being careful of his swollen lip. He had to keep his strength up, and the food was edible enough—the mutton not too overcooked, the thick bread reasonably fresh, the mug filled with water drawn from a cool well. There was something to be said for being arrested in the countryside.

He tore off a bite of mutton, thinking as he chewed. Since he alone would be hauled off to London, the marshalmen might take him on horseback or on foot, rather than in a coach or cart.

That, at least, was some small cause for hope. It would give him a better chance to escape.

Finishing the water, he pressed the cool pewter mug against his bruised face with a pained sigh. He still had a chance of survival. Not a great chance, but a chance nonetheless.

Perhaps God hadn't deserted him entirely after all.

A commotion at the door made him sit up straight and set the mug aside. It couldn't be dawn already.

As soon as the door was thrown open, he realized the marshalmen weren't coming to collect him. They were bringing in another prisoner—a kicking, bucking, struggling prisoner that two of them fought to restrain.

" 'urry up, Bickford!" one of the men shouted.

"Let me go, you cretins!" The new arrival accompanied the demand with a string of oaths that would burn the ears of a Barbary sailor.

Oaths made all the more remarkable by the feminine voice that uttered them.

The gaol's awakened inhabitants quickly filled the air with whistles and catcalls.

"Bring 'er 'ere, mates!"

"Give 'em hell, missy!"

"I'll take 'er off yer 'ands!"

Swearing, the marshalmen wrestled her along the row of cells, the gaoler waddling behind, fumbling with the ring of keys at his waist.

"Ow!" one of the guards howled. "She bit me! Bickford!"

" 'old on to 'er, Swinton, 'old on," Bickford muttered.

"It's 'ard to see and these ain't numbered, ye know. I 'ave to find one what fits one of the empty—"

"Unhand me!" the woman cried, lashing out with her heel. "You half-witted, barmybrained gullions, let me *go*."

The second guard uttered a yelp as the girl stomped on his foot. "Just pick one, Bickford! Any of 'em."

"Plenty o' room in my cell!" one prisoner offered.

Nicholas remained silent. He could see her better by the light of the gaoler's lantern—though he couldn't make out much more than a whirlwind of blonde hair, pale yellow skirts, and white teeth.

The first marshalman, Swinton, yelped as those sharp little pearls again chomped on some portion of his anatomy. "Damnation. Bickford!"

The gaoler triumphantly held up a key in the light. " 'Ere's one." He pushed past them down the row and unlocked an empty cell.

One right next to Nicholas's.

"Wait a moment," Nicholas protested. "Can't you put her somewhere else?"

"Sorry, mate," Bickford wheezed, jerking open the door. "Ye'll be safe enough with these bars to keep 'er away from ye."

Swinton grunted in pain as the blonde's elbow connected with his midsection.

"Just watch out fer them teeth of 'ers," the other guard advised, trying to grab a flailing, silk-clad arm without getting his eyes scratched out.

They dragged her toward the open cell, but the girl was now resisting with one last desperate effort, lashing out, twisting.

Swinton finally snapped. "Listen, missy, I've 'ad about enough of you!" He slammed her backward against the bars, knocking the air and the fight from her.

Before she could recover, he pressed up against her, twisting her hair around his fist and giving it a savage yank. His hawklike features burned an angry red and his beady eyes bored into hers. He took her jaw in his other hand, his grip so tight Nicholas could see the marks of his fingers pressing into her soft flesh. Her eyes widened and she gasped in fear.

"Ye should learn to be a bit more friendly, yer ladyship," Swinton suggested in a cruel, unpleasant tone. "We might take pity on ye if ye were to be ... friendly."

All color fled her cheeks—except for bright scarlet around the marshalman's grimy fingers. His other meaty hand came up to grope her breast.

The other prisoners cheered him on.

"That's the way t' deal with a woman!"

"Let's 'ave a look at 'er!"

"Leave some fer me, mate!"

Nicholas glanced away. Turned his back. Help no one, trust no one, care about no one. That was the rule he lived by. A rule that had kept him alive for the last twenty-eight years.

The girl made a strangled sound of shock. Of pain.

Nicholas fastened his gaze to a corner of the back wall. He didn't bother to guess what Swinton was doing to her. He didn't care. He did not care.

" 'Ere now, missy," the marshalman growled. "Give us a kiss. I might convey a good word to the mag—"

Swinton never got to finish the word or the sentence.

Nicholas glanced around in time to see a feminine knee finding its mark with a blow that made Swinton yowl and Nicholas wince. She followed it with a swift, sharp kick to the same vulnerable spot.

Swinton collapsed on his back with the gurgle of a dying man, amid the laughter of his companions and hoots of derision from the prisoners.

The girl's eyes glittered with fury. "Convey *that* to the magistrate, you filthy piece of rotting gutter slime!"

Before the other two lawmen could collect themselves enough to maneuver the blonde hellion into the empty cell, Swinton was on his feet.

"You little *bitch!*"

He struck her, hard. A blow across the face with the back of his fist. The girl cried out, her head snapping sideways. She suddenly went limp, falling.

Swinton caught her but Bickford shoved him aside before he could inflict any further damage. "Come on, Swinton, ye've 'ad yer sport fer the night." He dumped her in the cell, shut the door, and locked it quickly with a sigh of relief.

" 'Er ladyship just don't appreciate yer 'andsome face," the other marshalman commented, still laughing as he turned to leave.

Swinton stood there, shaking with fury, glowering down at her.

"Come along, lad." Bickford walked off, carrying the lantern. "Ye've got an early morning of it on the morrow."

With one last growled curse, and a glare—which he shared equally with the girl and with Nicholas—Swinton turned away and followed his cohorts toward the exit, slowly. Limping.

He slammed the door behind him, and Nicholas heard the sound of a bar being dropped in place, then the heavy clatter of the chain.

The rest of the prisoners, their brief entertainment ended, settled down once more. One man whispered his prayers. Another moaned for a while in pain or simple misery before he fell silent.

Nicholas turned his gaze to his new neighbor.

The girl lay unmoving, her breathing even but shallow. From the force of the blow, she might be badly hurt.

But somehow he didn't think so.

Leaning one shoulder against the bars that separated his cell from hers, he looked down at her.

She was young, no more than twenty-two or twenty-three, he guessed, with a flawless honey-colored complexion framed by a regal mane of tawny hair. A straight little nose that tilted ever so slightly upward at the tip. Thick, dark lashes resting on elegantly high cheeks. It was an aristocratic face. One that should be painted on an expensive cameo, protected in a gold locket, and kept close to some wealthy young lord's heart.

Nicholas frowned. He was supposed to be making escape plans, not ogling fellow inmates.

He picked up the mutton leg from his interrupted supper and took a bite. "You can get up now," he said with his mouth full. "They're gone."

Her even, shallow breathing suddenly stilled.

After a moment, she opened one eye and cast a cautious sideways glance toward the door. Then she opened the other and glared up at him. "How did you know I was faking?"

"Women have fainted on me before," he said sardonically. "One learns to tell a true faint from a display of female dramatics."

She sat up, gingerly touching her bruised cheek, and squinted at him, as if her vision were only now adjusting to the torchlit darkness. Her eyes widened as her gaze traveled from his beaten, bloodied face down over the breadth of his shoulders and chest.

She quickly, warily moved to the other side of her cell, as far away as she could get. Which wasn't far. Her slender back came up against the metal bars with a muted clang. She sat speechless, staring at him as if he were some kind of dangerous animal in a zoological park.

Her expression made him feel every bit as rough and brutish as he must look. She regarded him with a trace of fear in her eyes, and something else . . . a certain disdain, a haughtiness that he had seen before in the eyes of ladies of quality.

It was a look that never failed to annoy him.

And it made him stare all the more boldly back. He
allowed his gaze to roam over her, deliberately un-
dressing her with his eyes.

Every rich, creamy inch of her.

He mentally slipped her lemon-colored silk gown
from her shoulders and admired the delicate line of her
collarbone . . . the generous swell of sweet feminine
flesh below, almost overflowing her lacy bodice . . . her
slim waist. Her skirt had tangled around her legs.
Long, long legs that seemed almost coltish.

He lifted his gaze slowly, lingering over the swell of
her hips, decidedly womanly. He could imagine the
ripe, soft curves hidden beneath the fragile silk.
Curves that would fit perfectly in a man's hands. His
hands.

Honey-colored skin, flaxen hair . . . spun from gold,
she was, burnished and sleek like a treasure plundered
from a Spanish galleon.

And the pirate in him had never been able to resist
the lure of gold.

He felt a stirring, tightening sensation low in his
body, felt his breathing deepen even as he looked at
her, imagining those legs wrapped around his hips . . .

As if reading his thoughts, she quickly rearranged
her skirts with a whispered oath.

He lifted his gaze to hers. This close, he could see
the color of her eyes, sparkling defiantly in the torch-
light.

Gold. She had golden eyes—a light, clear amber
color with flecks of pure gold around the center.

Forget the last meal, he thought with a slow, hungry
curve to his mouth. One night with her would do quite
nicely for a doomed man's final wish.

Another flash of gold caught his eye—something
dangling from a short, pale ribbon attached to the center of her bodice. A strangely shaped medallion, or
locket. Oblong, like a small barrel. Gasping, she

grabbed it in one fist and clasped it against her. As if she meant to protect it from him.

Or as if it had some power to protect her.

He wondered how the devil a pampered chit like her had landed herself in gaol. And where she had picked up the salty language and street tricks she had used earlier.

One thing was certain: if he was any judge of women—and he was—this was easily one of the most beautiful he'd ever laid eyes on. "What did they arrest you for, lady? Caught stealing crumpets at a tea party?"

"What affair is it of yours?" Her frosty tone matched the disdain in her eyes.

He noticed, however, that her gaze flicked to his food with obvious longing.

He settled more comfortably against the bars and finished the mutton leg, noisily cleaning every last morsel of meat off the bone, licking his fingers with a sound of enjoyment. "Just making a bit of friendly conversation." He tossed the bone aside.

He was definitely *not* making friendly conversation. If she was a petty criminal, she could sit here and rot until the assizes for all he cared.

But if the charges against her were more serious—and the reward high enough—they might transport her to London tomorrow. With him. Which might mean going by coach or cart.

She could, in short, cause him trouble.

And more trouble was the last thing he needed at the moment.

"Friendly conversation?" She arched one tawny brow. "I am not interested in being *friendly*." The locket still clutched in one hand, she added under her breath, "Especially not with one of *your* kind."

Tucking the ribbon and its attached bit of metal safely back into her bodice, she looked around, evaluating her surroundings much as he had earlier. She stood up, dusted herself off, and investigated the lock on her cell door, rattling it before checking the wooden wall at the back.

"No use," he advised. "Locked up tight. Looks like you're stuck here until the winter assizes ... unless, of course, you're charged with some serious offense."

She slanted him an irritated glance. "Picking pockets," she mumbled.

Not serious, Nicholas decided with relief.

"Forgery," she added after a moment.

His relief faded a bit.

She sighed wearily. "And burglary."

His mood was worsening by the minute.

She slumped into one corner of her cell, her voice so soft he had to strain to hear it. "And attempted murder."

He gazed at her in astonishment and disbelief. "Let me guess, your ladyship—it's all a terrible mistake and you're completely innocent?"

She laughed, a humorless rasp that sounded harsh enough to hurt her throat. "Innocent?" She closed her eyes and repeated it, as if it were a foreign word beyond her understanding. "Innocent." She shook her head, whispering, "No, I'm not innocent."

The expression on her face held an odd mixture of bitterness and wistfulness.

She hung her head. "And they said something about not waiting for the assizes. There's a rather large reward out on me."

Nicholas exhaled a curse. "Lady," he ground out, "you picked one hell of a rotten time to get yourself arrested."

"Well, pardon me," she snapped, her head coming up. "It's not as if I planned this. So sorry if it's some sort of inconvenience to you."

"Oh, no inconvenience. We'll just be sharing a trip to London tomorrow, in a bloody secure cart—"

"*London?*"

"That's where the judges are this time of year. Where did you think they would be taking you? To the fair?"

"Manchester. Or Nottingham—it can't be London! You must be mistaken—"

"No mistake. You and I are going to London tomorrow."

She paled, looking as if she might truly faint. "Oh, God. Oh, no."

Sinking to the floor, she wrapped her arms around her raised knees and pressed her forehead against them with a small moan.

"Such is the price of crime," he muttered, wondering despite himself what made her so terrified of London.

"You don't need to tell *me* about the price of crime," she retorted, her words muffled by her skirt. "And what about you?" She raised her head. "I suppose you were arrested by mistake and you're innocent of the charges against you?" she mocked.

"As a matter of fact," he said dryly, "I was and I am."

She cast a dubious glance over every battered inch of him. "Certainly." Her voice held both sarcasm and that annoying haughtiness.

"Completely innocent. They jumped me near the stables when I was trying to hire a horse. They think I'm some local footpad they've been hunting for weeks."

She blinked and studied him more closely. Then her eyes widened. "They think you're Jasper Norwell," she declared. "He's the one they've been after. He's very tall and dark and he has a beard . . ." Suddenly she started to laugh. "You're telling the truth, aren't you? It *was* a mistake. You really are innocent."

"I'm so glad you find it funny."

She was laughing herself silly. "You're innocent and I'm not. I can't tell you how funny that is." Just as abruptly, she sobered. Her expression turned serious . . . then oddly thoughtful. "Actually, you're right," she said quietly. "It isn't funny. Not funny at all." She stood and went to the door of her cell. "Bickford!"

"What the devil are you doing?"

"Bickford!" she shouted again. "I demand to talk to someone! A terrible mistake has been made!"

Nicholas couldn't believe his ears—but he wasn't about to stop her. If she wanted to declare his innocence, so be it.

Reason, bribery, and tunneling were useless . . . but this stunning blonde might just help get him out of here.

"Bickford!" she called again.

A jangle of metal at the door was followed by a grunted oath. "What's all the racket?" Bickford ambled through the door.

The girl glanced down at Nicholas, then back at the approaching gaolkeeper. "I'm afraid a terrible mistake has been made—"

How noble, Nicholas thought, smiling at her. How kind. How—

"This is *obviously* the thief who's been plaguing your town, not me." She pointed a finger straight at his nose. "And you already had him in custody before I was even arrested. I'm innocent and your men have made a terrible mistake—"

"You lying little *wench!*" Nicholas snarled, jumping to his feet and immediately regretting it when his head clanged against the barred ceiling, adding a headache to his other pains.

She ignored him completely, appealing to Bickford. "Do *I* look like a thief?" she asked sweetly. "Now look at him—he's obviously dangerous. Just look at those cold green eyes! The eyes of a born miscreant, I tell you—"

"Lady, you are lucky there are solid metal bars between us." Nicholas clenched his hands around the bars as he wanted to clench them around her throat.

Bickford merely looked annoyed. "Bah!" he spat on the floor. "You roused me from me bed fer this, lass?"

"But I tell you *he's* the one who stole the silverware from Lady Hammond's parlor, not me. I saw him myself! I'll swear it before the magistrate—"

"The magistrate is at 'is country 'ouse and can't be disturbed fer the likes of you. And I don't 'ave no say in lettin' prisoners go once they're in 'ere."

"But since you already have the *real* culprit there's no point in taking me all the way to London. If I could just speak to the magistrate—"

"Ye can explain it to the judge in London, missy." With a disgusted shake of his head, Bickford turned away. " 'E'll sort it all out. Now I warn ye—I'll not be listenin' to any more of yer yawpin', so quiet down."

"No, wait!" She strained against the bars, reaching for him.

He kept walking. "Swinton and his men will be comin' to collect ye both in the mornin'."

"Wait!" she cried. "You can't do this! You can't—"

Bickford closed the door behind him and slammed the bar in place with finality.

The girl slumped against the bars of her cell, eyes closed, shaking. "*Damn.*"

"You treacherous, scheming little liar," Nicholas spat each word with sharp malice.

"I can't let them take me to London," she whispered. "I *can't.*"

"So you decided to send *me* to the gallows in your place."

She gave him a glance that almost held a trace of remorse.

Almost.

"It was worth a try," she muttered.

He studied her with disbelief. She was ruthless. Which made her dangerous.

Not qualities he admired in a female.

"Face of an angel," he appraised coldly, "but no heart to go with it."

Her gaze held equal distaste for him. "I didn't see

you leaping to *my* assistance when that guard was trying to . . . to have his way with me."

"I look out for myself, *angel*. If you're looking for some lackwit knight who makes a habit of rescuing damsels in distress, you've got the wrong man. You're on your own."

"That's perfectly fine by me," she shot back. "I'm used to it. I prefer it that way."

"That makes two of us."

They glared at one another silently.

Eyes like stolen treasure, he thought, *the face of an angel, curves that could tempt a saint into sin . . . and a ruthless heart.*

That sense of foreboding prickled up the back of his neck again. A sense that this girl had some part to play in the divine retribution God had in store for him.

That somewhere above, God was already chuckling with anticipation.

Chapter 3

Dawn. It must be dawn by now. Samantha felt as if she had been here for hours. Days. A lifetime. The pounding of her heart marked off each unbearable second, so loud she could hear nothing else.

She sat pressed against the rear wall of her cell, her spine rigid, her gaze locked on the door at the far end of the gaol. The foul air wrapped around her like a thick, musty fog. Her breath came in shallow little gasps.

The guards had said they would return at dawn.

She kept running one hand along a tear in her yellow skirt. Over and over, as if she could somehow repair the damage with only a touch. Of course she couldn't. She knew that. But it was her only good gown. And now it was ruined. Ruined beyond repair. Like everything else.

The torches had burned almost out. Surely it was dawn. A bead of perspiration trickled down her neck.

Any moment now, the massive door would swing open. The marshalmen would take her to London, where Uncle Prescott lived.

Her stomach lurched with nausea. The London magistrates—his friends—would need only one look at her to know the truth. To recognize exactly whom they had in custody. To realize that Miss Samantha *Delafield*, wanted for various thefts throughout the English

33

countryside, was in fact Miss Samantha *Hibbert*, long-lost, wayward niece of Prescott Hibbert. Her uncle would be notified. He would come to collect her.

And then he would have her killed.

Or worse.

After all, Prescott Hibbert was one of the most powerful and respected magistrates in all of London.

And her guardian.

An icy tremor went through her and she dropped her gaze from the door. She drew her knees up to her chest, locking her arms around them. But she could not stop trembling, only became more aware of her heart pounding against her ribs.

He could do anything he wanted to her. And it would all be perfectly legal. No one would help her. No one could protect her. No one would believe the truth.

She swallowed hard. If no one had been willing to believe her when she was sixteen, they certainly wouldn't believe her now. Back then, she had been a naive innocent, newly arrived from the country with her sister Jessica, both of them still in shock over the loss of their parents. But now . . .

Now she was a wanted woman. A criminal. Alone. On the run since that horrible night she had been forced to flee London.

No one would believe a word she said.

And the charge of attempted murder would be more than enough to ensure her execution.

She was trapped. She was . . .

Helpless.

Sam closed her eyes, hating that feeling, that word, more than any other. When she fled the city six years ago—without a shilling to her name, with nothing but the clothes on her back—she had vowed that she would never be helpless again. That she wouldn't be afraid anymore. That she would never be forced to depend on anyone, ever.

Opening her eyes, unwrapping her arms from around her knees, she braced her hands against the cool stone floor and forced herself to stop trembling. For six years she had made her own way in the world—and she hadn't accomplished that by giving in to panic and despair. Or any emotions.

The only way to survive was to keep moving forward, always forward. Away from the past, from the memories, the fear.

The pain.

She took a deep, steadying breath, touching the filigreed needle case pinned over her heart, hearing a voice in her memory. *You're the strong one, Sam.* Jessica's voice. Sweet, kind Jessica, so fragile and pale as she lay in her sickbed, whispering as she pressed the cherished heirloom into Samantha's palm. *You've always been the strong one.*

Sam blinked to clear the hot dampness from her eyes. She would have to be stronger than ever now. This was no time to suddenly change into a feather-witted, fragile female.

Her mind working quickly, she glanced at the distant door, trying to think of some way to escape. There were no weapons at hand. And fighting the marshalmen had failed. And trying to trick her way past the gaoler had only made her predicament worse . . .

Cautiously, for the first time in hours, she slanted a glance to her left, to the man who would be traveling with her—the surly rogue with the black eye, swollen lip, and blood-spattered clothes.

Unfortunately for her, he looked like the type to harbor a grudge.

Lying on his back with his eyes closed, he didn't appear particularly threatening at the moment. In truth, despite the fact that he was about to be transported to London, he seemed rather relaxed, his sinewy frame stretched out comfortably, one arm cocked behind his head. The fabric of his shirt stretched taut over distressingly powerful muscles, the white sleeve making his hair and beard look blacker than sin.

She almost thought he was asleep. But after a moment, as if he sensed her regard, he opened his eyes and looked her way.

His gaze cut into her like ice, sharp and unforgiving. And beneath that cold surface she sensed something more, something fierce sparkling in that emerald glare. Something . . . dangerous, potent. It made her shiver. Even more so than the thought that he might happily throttle her with his bare hands, given half a chance.

And she had no doubt he could do exactly that; his hands appeared just as large and strong and forceful as the rest of him. He looked like a man who *had* throttled people with his bare hands.

The thought sent a shudder down her spine, but she refused to drop her gaze from his, returning his cool animosity in full measure. Never show weakness. Not with a man. Especially a man much larger and stronger than oneself. She had learned that lesson the hard way.

After a moment, the harsh line of his mouth curved upward in an amused expression and he closed his eyes, apparently unconcerned about either her animosity or the trouble he was in.

Sam frowned. Perhaps the rogue thought that because he was innocent of the accusations against him, he could relax and simply explain everything to the judge in London.

Well, *she* wasn't innocent. She was guilty as charged.

And she had no intention of going to London.

A sound outside the door made her flinch. The bar and chains clattered. The hinges groaned.

Faced with the moment she had been expecting for hours, she suddenly felt her stomach drop to her toes.

Bickford stepped inside with his lantern, whistling a cheery tune, ignoring the annoyed curses of the awakened prisoners. The marshalmen followed: one . . . two . . . three of them, carrying ropes and enough guns to do battle with a brigade. A fifth man—a hulking, swarthy beast she hadn't seen before—accompanied them, dragging a large sack along the floor.

Sam lifted her chin and rose slowly, gracefully, as if she were in an earl's parlor rather than a stinking gaol cell. With all the poise her nannies and tutors had instilled, she smoothed her torn skirts and prepared to face whatever she must.

The coarse quintet chortled over some shared joke as they walked toward her.

The rogue in the cell next to hers didn't get up. Didn't move a muscle or do anything . . . but yawn.

Swinton came to stand before her door, an evil gleam in his black eyes. "Mornin', yer ladyship." Like a cruel boy tormenting a caged animal, he raked the butt of his pistol back and forth across the bars.

Sam didn't flinch, didn't reply. She kept her gaze level, her features composed, raising one brow in a purposely haughty expression that usually helped to distance those she wanted to keep away.

"Over 'ere, Swinton." Bickford searched through the keys on his ring. "Let's take care of this one first. On yer feet, mate."

The rogue—it was becoming easy to think of him that way—got up slowly, holding his ribs as if in pain. He stumbled and leaned heavily against the bars, forced to crouch by the ceiling that couldn't quite accommodate his more than six-foot height.

The marshalmen arranged themselves in a half-circle outside his cell, guns pointed at his head and chest. "If ye make one wrong move . . ." one threatened, letting the sentence hang.

"No need for violence," their target said quietly, wincing.

His voice sounded dark and cool, as if it came from the depths of the sea. Something about it brought an odd little flutter to Sam's stomach.

"I still say we should've 'ired an extra 'and or two."

The youngest of the guards couldn't seem to hold his weapon steady. He had a thicket of red hair, wide blue eyes—and a large bruise on his jaw. "Don't ye think? After the way 'e cut up Tibbs last night? There's still time to 'ire an extra 'and or two, ain't there, Leach?"

"Forget it, Tucker," the first man replied. "We're already splittin' the money four ways."

"And I ain't splittin' it five or six," Swinton growled, cocking his pistol with an ominous click. "Get yer 'ands up where I can see 'em, mate."

"Easy, lads." Bickford found the key and fitted it into the lock. "Don't forget 'e's worth fifty pounds."

"The reward don't say nothin' about a few 'oles 'ere and there." Leach cocked his weapon as well.

The rogue didn't move, silently studying the array of weapons facing him.

Then he slowly raised his hands.

Bickford turned the key and opened the door, motioning him to step out. As soon as he did so, the marshalmen closed in around him, Leach and young Tucker grabbing him by the arms. They spun him around and shoved him up against the bars—while Swinton pressed a gun to his temple and Bickford hurried to get out of the way. The portly gaoler retreated a few paces and drew his own weapon.

Yanking the rogue's arms behind his back, they swiftly tied his hands with one of the ropes. Though the bonds looked painfully tight, he didn't flinch. His jaw remained firm, his eyes unblinking.

"Are ye ready there?" Bickford called to the fifth man who had accompanied them inside.

"Aye, Mr. Bickford, sir." The swarthy giant, who had hung back warily until now, came closer and emptied his sack onto the floor. A tangle of metal spilled out with a crash. To Sam's eyes, the debris appeared to be either strange weapons, devices of torture, or—

"Blacksmith's tools," her fellow prisoner said tightly. "What the devil do you need with those?"

His captors chuckled.

"We ain't used to movin' prisoners 'ither and yon," Leach explained. "Usually we just 'olds 'em fer the assize judge."

"But we ain't takin' a chance of ye gettin' away," Tucker said.

The blacksmith plucked one item from the jumble on the floor—a chain made of heavy iron links, with a thick cuff at either end. About two feet long, it looked more suitable for the previous residents of this stable than for a man.

"Wait a moment, mates," the rogue said in a friendly, reasoning tone. "There's no need for that. I told you, I'm an innocent man. I won't give you any trouble—"

"Tell it to Tibbs," Swinton snarled.

Before their prisoner could protest further, the smithy opened one of the cuffs and closed it firmly around his ankle.

Sam felt not one whit of pity as she watched the blacksmith fasten the shackle in place with a heavy metal bolt, driving it home with a hammer. In fact, she felt relief.

If she had to share a journey through the countryside with this rough-looking brigand, it suited her just fine that he have his hands tied behind his back—which might keep them from around her throat—and his legs chained, which might subdue him a bit.

While the smithy checked his handiwork and picked up the other cuff, Bickford came over to her cell and unlocked the door. "Come along, missy."

She obeyed without making any sudden moves, her eyes on the pistol in his hand.

Young Tucker laughed nervously. "Aye, mate, we're goin' to make it *real* difficult for a big bloke like you to get away."

Leach grabbed Sam by the arm and dragged her forward. "And 'er ladyship is goin' to 'elp."

She didn't understand his meaning.

Until she glanced away from the pistol aimed at her head and realized that they hadn't finished chaining the rogue's legs together.

In fact, the smithy was holding the other cuff open.

"Before ye even *think* of escapin'," Swinton chuckled, "think about 'ow this might slow ye down."

Sam gasped, looking up—and up and up—at the blackguard who stood at her side. Her gaze locked with a stunned emerald stare. He uttered an oath.

And in that very instant she felt the heavy iron shackle being clamped around her ankle.

Chapter 4

~~~~~~~~~~⟡⟡~~~~~~~~~~

They jolted over a rut in the road and the cart's wooden side struck Sam between the shoulder-blades. She didn't flinch, barely felt it, part of her too nauseous from the bumpy ride and the merciless mid-day sun, part still numb with disbelief. From the moment the smithy had fastened the iron cuff around her ankle this morning, she hadn't drawn a complete breath.

She felt dizzy. Sick.

Perspiration trickled down her neck and into her bodice, pasting her hair to her skin in hot, sticky tangles. She couldn't reach up to brush it away; with her wrists tied together behind her back, she could barely move. Her arms ached painfully from being stretched in the unnatural position for hours. Her hands had long ago gone numb. The horses' hooves stirred up clouds of dust that stung her eyes. And a sour smell emanated from the moldy straw piled beneath her and around her.

But the worst part of the journey wasn't the heat or the soreness in her muscles or even the band of metal clamped around her left ankle.

It was the searing glare of the bruised, bloodied, uncivilized-looking man who sat across from her.

The man chained to her by eighteen links of iron.

Eighteen. She'd had time to count them. Eighteen

41

solid, black, unyielding rings. A chain thick enough to
hold an unbroken stallion in check. When Bickford had
shoved her up into the cart, he had chuckled that the
shackles were unbreakable, that it would require a
blacksmith in London to remove them.

That news hadn't improved the rogue's mood in the
least. His initial expression of surprise had given way
to an air of surly, simmering resentment.

Every time Sam glanced across the scant two feet that
separated them, she found him looking at her with a
hard set to his jaw and hostility in his eyes. As if this
were *her* fault. As if she'd purposely set out to cause
him trouble.

This time she responded with a glower of her own.
She wasn't any happier with the situation than he was.
Did he think he was the only one who'd been forced to
abandon an escape plan? She had harbored some hope
of slipping away at nightfall—but shackled to six feet of
mean-looking miscreant, she wasn't going anywhere.

Except straight to London.

Turning away from her hostile traveling companion,
she fastened her attention on the open fields around
them. She took a deep breath, ignoring him, ignoring
the queasiness in her stomach, ignoring the fact that
her predicament had taken this appalling turn for the
worse.

Things weren't entirely hopeless. Not yet. She had to
stop feeling frightened and sorry for herself. Had to
keep her wits about her. Think.

Plan.

The journey to London would take at least a week.
Perhaps somewhere along the way, if a wheel broke or
. . . No, she amended just as quickly. She doubted the
cart would be so accommodating as to break down.
The marshalmen had borrowed it from a farmer; built
to haul heavy goods over the deplorable country roads,
it boasted a heavy axle and two solid oak wheels. Nei-

ther would shatter on the deep ruts that scarred the path.

Her bruised *derriere* could attest to the vast number of those accursed ruts. They were like furrows in a plowed field, topped with hard ridges, some more than a foot deep, and she felt every one of them. Along with every stone and pebble.

No, she couldn't center her plan on a wish that the cart might cooperate.

Nor could she hope that one of the guards might get careless. They kept their eyes trained on their captured prey like a pack of wolves, all four bristling with weapons.

Bickford drove, whistling a cheerful tune that set her teeth on edge. He sat on a wooden platform that jutted out from the front of the cart, a blunderbuss in his lap. Young Tucker fidgeted beside him, nervously glancing over his shoulder every few minutes, eyes wide and pistol at the ready.

The lad kept his finger wrapped so tightly around the trigger, Sam feared the gun might go off accidentally.

Leach led the way, riding a few yards ahead, while Swinton had volunteered to follow behind the cart. He didn't say a word, not a single taunt. Didn't even cough on the billowing clouds of choking dust. His silence rattled her far more than the vulgarities he had snarled at her last night. He rode so close, she swore she could feel his breath on her skin. She told herself it was only the humid breeze.

But she could *feel* those bird-black eyes following her, watching every small movement, tracing every bead of sweat that slid down her neck. It sickened her to realize he was enjoying her discomfort, wanted her to suffer.

She couldn't subdue a shudder. Swinton reminded her of Uncle Prescott, in the worst way.

That thought made her throat tighten painfully, but she fought down the terror, wouldn't give in to tears.

She was not going to let Swinton or Uncle Prescott or *anyone* make her feel helpless.

There had to be some way out of this, something she could do before they reached London.

A fly landed on her cheek. She shook her head to shoo it away but ended up with a strand of hair in her eye. Frowning, she rubbed her cheek against her shoulder, frustrated at being so powerless. She managed to get the hair out, but her eye, already irritated from grit and dust, now brimmed with tears.

Young Tucker turned to look her way just as she lifted her head—and she saw a flicker of something unexpected in his freckled face.

Sympathy. Regret.

Almost instinctively, she made a decision.

Instead of blinking the tears back, she allowed them to spill over. A single droplet slid down her cheek, cutting a path through the grime. Then another.

She added a dramatic little tremor of her lower lip. Then she lowered her lashes as if ashamed to have him catch her crying. Just for good measure, she sniffled, softly.

When she slowly glanced up again, blinking, chin quivering, she met the lad's gaze. Tucker's expression was strained, his prominent Adam's apple bobbing up and down. He looked all but ready to leap from his seat and cut her free from her bonds.

Yet a moment later, he abruptly turned around.

She frowned. Duty, apparently, had won out over sympathy. Drat.

A privately amused chuckle drifted over from the other side of the cart. Slicing her gaze that way, she found the rogue regarding her with a mocking grin on his battered lips, his broad shoulders fairly shaking with silent laughter.

Warmth flooded her cheeks. She lifted her chin, looked away, and wished a pox upon him. She wasn't interested in his cynical opinions. It didn't matter that *he* wasn't taken in by her performance.

Because it *did* appear that she had made an impression on the young marshalman.

Every time Tucker glanced her way now, she caught an unmistakable softness in his freckled face. More than that. Pity.

And pity might very well prove helpful.

She slanted another look at the rogue, smiling sweetly. *Laugh all you want, you overgrown oaf. We'll see who's laughing when I'm free and you're still in custody.*

Satisfied with her progress for the moment, she settled back against the cart's wooden side, admiring the clear blue sky overhead. The day didn't seem quite so miserable anymore.

Except for the way her stomach kept growling. She winced at the gnawing hunger. It had been . . .

By the graces, how long *had* it been since she'd had a full meal?

The few hors d'oeuvres she had nicked at Lady Hammond's assembly last night hardly counted. She had circulated through the throng only briefly before making her way toward the silver in the sideboard—because she hadn't had an invitation.

But then, she never had an invitation. Amazing how the right gown and a few airs could gain one access to all sorts of places.

Sneaking into last night's *soiree* had been a foolish risk, though; she should have left Staffordshire a fortnight ago. Four months working one district was too long. But the elegant country estates offered such easy booty, and she needed only another hundred pounds to have enough.

Enough to leave England behind forever. To start a new life. To finally be safe.

Seeing her dream almost within reach, she had been too eager last night, too emotional. Emotion always made her careless. One foolish, amateurish mistake . . .

and Lady Hammond had caught her and immediately turned her in.

For stealing a half-dozen shrimp forks.

As if someone like Lady Hammond would even *miss* a half-dozen shrimp forks.

Sam grimaced. It was so blasted unfair. She could easily do far more damage if she chose to, but she never took more than a trifling amount from any one person. Partly because greed was the fastest way to gain unwanted attention and land one's neck in a noose . . . but mainly because she refused to cause anyone hardship or distress.

Even someone like Lady Hammond.

It was a fine line she walked, but one she would not cross.

Closing her eyes, she tried not to think about food, or her foolish mistake yesterday.

Or her dreams for tomorrow.

The cart lurched and tilted as it rolled southward, but her sleepless night coupled with the thick heat soon made her drowsy. She was distantly aware of the horses breathing noisily, their hooves plodding now as the hours wore on into mid-afternoon. The sun climbed higher, baking the air and everything in it.

A raucous screech startled her awake some time later. She sat up and opened her eyes to find trees towering overhead on the left side of the cart, the road skirting the edge of what looked like a vast forest. A flock of birds high above squawked a warning of the intruding humans.

She sat up straighter, blinking to clear her vision, fully awake now. The leaf-laden branches blocked the sun and she almost groaned in gratitude; her exposed skin had already darkened a shade and the road's grit, like sandpaper, had rubbed every inch of her raw. The cooling shadows felt like a balm.

Her wrists didn't feel quite so strangled anymore,

either, as if the rope had expanded a bit in the humid air.

Everyone else seemed just as worn out by the long day of travel and heat and dust. Bickford cursed wearily as he swiped a fat, lazy fist toward one of the ravens that swooped low over his head. Tucker, her savior-to-be, leaned on the cart's side, his tricorne settled low over his eyes, his freckled cheek resting on the heel of his palm. His pistol lay in his lap.

Even Leach and Swinton slouched in their saddles, looking as sluggish as their horses.

Yawning, Sam glanced across the cart, expecting to find the rogue napping.

He wasn't. He sat pressed against the wood at his back, head down, but he didn't seem to be asleep. He shrugged his shoulders and moved his arms, as if to ease the soreness in his muscles.

The sun glinting through the trees struck glossy highlights from his black hair, and she noticed a peppering of gray. Odd, she hadn't thought of him as being that old; she wasn't sure why, but the impression she had gotten last night was of an almost youthful, utterly male confidence. Boldness. Arrogance. She found herself wondering how old he was.

The wheels crunched through a scattering of brittle leaves, the sound like the cracking of eggshells. Sam returned her attention to the forest. It didn't matter to her how old he was, or who he was, or even *what* he was. She intended to be long gone from here, from him, from her captors as soon as possible.

Perhaps they would reach a town before long and stop for the night. She could plead that a lady must have a bit of privacy. Bickford and the others would be immune to her request . . . but the red-headed lad might be persuaded to fetch a smithy and unfasten the chain. Just for a moment, she would tell him. Just long enough for her to freshen up and attend to the needs of nature.

Just long enough to escape.

She smiled in anticipation.

The road turned sharply east, following the outermost rim of the treeline. She wondered why the path had been cut that way, when it would've been much more direct to go straight through the woods.

Then she realized where they were: in the southernmost reach of Staffordshire. This must be the infamous Cannock Chase.

She couldn't keep her mouth from forming a silent O of awe. Before her stretched the most vast, deep, rugged forest in England—a place filled with poachers, malcontents, and brigands of all sorts. Even in this modern age, when much of the countryside had been parceled off and fenced in, the Chase remained uncivilized, virtually unchanged since medieval days. Because criminals favored it as a base for their midnight forays, law-abiding citizens gave it a wide and wary berth . . . hence the strange turn of the road.

A sound behind her . . . a soft metallic *ping*—drew her attention. She turned to see the rogue sitting up straight, his eyes sharp as he studied the trees beyond her. He wasn't moving his shoulders anymore. He had gone completely still.

And she didn't like the gleam in those green eyes.

She wasn't sure exactly what it was, but she didn't like it.

And what had made that metallic sound? It wasn't the clanking of the chain.

His gaze suddenly cut right. Toward Leach, riding in front of them. Far in front of them. The marshalman had allowed more and more distance to grow between himself and the cart as the day wore on.

Her stomach made an uncomfortable little flip as the rogue's gaze cut left. He watched Swinton now.

Swinton, too, was several yards away.

Her heart started to beat harder. It was almost as if . . . but no, the blackguard couldn't be . . .

Planning something.

Not now. Not in broad daylight. The guards might be tired, but one wrong move and some unfortunate person might end up full of bullet holes.

Like *her*.

He couldn't try to escape in broad daylight. He would have to be insane.

And she didn't think this man was insane. Clinging to that thought, she tried to calm down. Even bruised and bloodied, with his slashed cheek and swollen black eye, he had an air of logic about him. Cunning logic, perhaps, but logic nonetheless. He wasn't a complete brute. An unmistakable intelligence burned in the emerald depths of those eyes, as sharp and keen as his muscles were taut. Beneath that dark beard and unruly tangle of gray-peppered black hair, his face held reason.

Yet even as she grasped at that hope and stared at his angular, tanned features, she saw again what she had first noticed in the dimly lit gaol: an edge of boldness. Recklessness. Last night it had made her feel wary, but now it terrified her.

It wasn't the mark of a young, confident man.

It was the mark of a man who had nothing to lose.

He looked from Swinton . . . to Bickford . . . to Tucker . . . then slowly, almost casually, back toward her. He glanced down at the chain that bound them together . . . then his gaze rose from her iron-encircled ankle, inch by deliberate inch, up over her legs, her body.

A wash of heat flushed her sun-darkened skin. But this wasn't a lustful appraisal like the one he had turned on her last night. No, this was far different— and it stopped her breath in her throat.

He was studying her with some other intent. Measuring her in some way.

And she thought she saw a strange approval in his expression. But before she could react, his gaze cut left again, seeking the marshalman.

Sam sat frozen for a breathless moment. Everything seemed to go still. Even the birds in the forest.

Then one corner of the rogue's mouth curved upward in a reckless little grin.

Her pulse exploded through her veins. He *was* planning something! He was a madman. Absolutely insane! He couldn't try to escape in broad daylight. Not with her attached!

She moved her left foot, rattling the chain just enough to catch his attention. His eyes met hers. She mouthed a single, silent, urgent word.

No.

He lifted a brow, as if in question or affront. She couldn't tell which. Perhaps he wasn't used to encountering the word *no*. At least not from a woman.

Looking past her, into the forest, he yawned and flexed his broad shoulders in a slow shrug, his expression all innocence, as if he had no idea what she meant.

His black eye and slashed cheek ruined any attempt at an angelic countenance. And she wasn't going to be fooled. If there was one benefit to being a thief and a performer, it was that one didn't fall for the performances of fellow thieves.

Or rogues of any sort.

Not even when he settled more comfortably in the hay, looking as calm and unconcerned as a journeyman cobbler enjoying a day's holiday in the countryside.

A half-hour passed and still he didn't make a move.

Perhaps she had read him wrong. It was entirely possible she had misinterpreted that fleeting grin.

Not only possible, she told herself, but likely. She didn't know the man. Didn't even know his name. He could have been privately laughing at their predicament, or at the dozing marshalmen, or . . .

Or he could've been planning something.

And despite his negligent pose, she couldn't shake the feeling that he was *still* planning something.

Something unspeakably dangerous.

Chapter 5

Nicholas kept his arms behind his back and tried to maintain his nonchalant pose even as the last thread of the rope binding his wrists finally snapped, with another soft *ping*.

Needles of pain flooded into his hands and he fought a grimace. Keeping his features carefully neutral, he slowly, experimentally flexed his numb fingers, letting the rope slip from his wrists down into the hay.

An ordinary footpad would've found it impossible to break free from the marshalmen's handiwork, but a man who had spent his life at sea, who knew his way around a knot, who was as familiar with the ways of rope as he was with his own face in the mirror, encountered far less difficulty.

The unseasonably humid weather had expanded and loosened the fibers. And the cart helped as well. Since it was meant to haul straw, not passengers, the bolts that fastened the heavy axle to the bottom hadn't been covered or even filed down. After feeling his way around, he had found a protruding metal edge just sharp enough to help cut through his bindings.

Hunkered down in the hay, he had accomplished that with a minimum of noise, managing to work his way free without notice—thanks to her ladyship. She not only held Swinton's drooling attention but had se-

51

cured Tucker's as well, with her little display of fluttering lashes and pouty lips.

He subdued a smile, knowing it would irritate her to no end to realize she had unwittingly helped him.

Still slouched against the cart's wooden side, he cautiously stretched the burning muscles of his arms while observing her through slitted eyes. The way she had tried to seduce the freckle-faced lad almost made him chuckle out loud again. The role of seductress didn't suit her at all. Despite the street tricks and gutter language she had used last night, there was a sort of . . . innocence about her.

He frowned, wondering where that thought had come from. Perhaps he'd gone mad with the heat. She was an admitted criminal, in chains, on her way to the Old Bailey. Last night she had tried to send him to the gallows to save herself.

She hardly qualified as a paragon of sweetness and virtue.

No matter how alluring her dewy skin, honeyed curves, and gold-glittered eyes, he was too experienced to be led astray. Unlike the featherwit lad, he was as familiar with the ways of women as he was with the ways of rope. And the two had more than passing similarities.

Both could be treacherous. Both tied a man down. Both were best when pliant.

And both could be either helpful . . . or dangerous.

Unfortunately it seemed that this haughty beauty chained to his ankle fell into the latter category. Even her eyes were both lovely and sharp; she had guessed that he was planning something though he hadn't spoken a word or given any signal.

Bloody unnerving, that.

And annoying as well. Though he reclined lazily in the hay, she remained poised, wide-eyed, waiting for him to do something. Her generous bosom rose and fell rapidly, straining against its silky, lacy coverings.

If she didn't relax, one of the blasted guards was sure to notice.

Minutes passed, each like a knife that scraped across his nerves, as he waited for the strength to return to his arms and hands.

He looked past her, studied the woods. Tried to find a suitable . . . aye, just ahead. Perhaps thirty yards away. The forest dipped into a ravine, a steep hill thick with evergreens and underbrush right next to the road. About fifty feet deep.

Perfect.

But with the cart jolting and rattling so slowly over the ruts, it would take ten minutes to reach that spot.

And the girl was a hairsbreadth from giving his plan away.

He tried again to convince her he was spent, weary. Harmless.

He yawned. She remained tense.

He closed his eyes as if to take a nap. She kept breathing so fast and shallow he could hear it.

Damnation, did she *enjoy* making trouble for him? He opened his eyes, tried glaring at her.

Instead of cowering in response, she faced him squarely, just as she had earlier—not backing down, not terrified, not even intimidated.

The chit clearly had no idea whom she was dealing with.

Another ten yards and they would reach the ravine.

He flicked a glance to the right, to the left. Leach and Swinton remained half-asleep in their saddles. Just far enough away. He hoped.

Seven yards.

He looked at the girl again. Gauged the distance between them one last time. He had to take her with him.

He had no choice.

Those golden eyes burned into his. Her small pink tongue darted over her lips. That full, lush mouth formed a silent, imperious command.

Don't.

He smiled in reply. Captain Nicholas Brogan did not take orders from females.

Three yards.

He flexed his hands. Tensed the muscles of his thighs. Gathered every ounce of his strength.

The cart clattered toward the ravine.

The concealing shadows of Cannock Chase beckoned.

One wheel struck a rut—and the crunch of dried mud seemed deafening. The entire cart lurched, unbalanced. Tilted precariously.

And he jumped.

Like a panther. Like a swimmer diving into the sea. He launched himself forward in a headlong leap.

Straight at the girl.

She screamed. Tried to get to her feet, get out of his way. He grabbed her as he came at her. Caught her with both arms. Yanked her hard against his chest as the momentum of his leap carried them straight over the edge.

Time seemed to slow for an endless second. He could feel air all around him. The girl's slender body against his. Her heart pounding wildly. Heard shouts and startled curses erupt. A wrenching groan of wood as Bickford's bulk and the sudden shift in weight unbalanced the cart. Felt muscles straining as he twisted, tried to roll, to aim his shoulder at the ground. Heard the horse's panicked neighing. A scream. The girl, screaming.

The sound of the cart crashing onto its side.

Then the ground rose up. Too fast.

He slammed into the dirt, taking the worst of it, grunting as his bruised ribs hit something hard and unyielding. The girl's scream cut short with a yelp of surprise and pain.

And they tumbled down the side of the ravine.

The forest floor fell away beneath them at a sharp

angle and they fell with it. Trees and sky and grass
blurred in an insane jumble as they plunged down the
slope. Out of control. A spin of legs and silk skirts and
flying blonde hair and jangling iron shackles. The girl
was helpless with her hands tied behind her back.
Nicholas grabbed for branches. Missed. They kept rolling, faster and faster. He could only hold on to her, one
arm locked around her. Rocks and branches and thick-
ets pounded and scraped as if the forest itself were trying to kill them.

Until by some miracle they reached the bottom,
rolled to a stop.

The girl had gone limp in his arms. Nicholas released
her, falling onto his back, feeling as if every inch of his
body had been battered into fragments. He lay dazed.

Until a bullet whizzed over his head.

The report of the pistol shot cracked through the
woods a second later.

"Don't move, ye bloody bastard!" Swinton snarled
from somewhere above them.

Nicholas could hear him crashing through the underbrush, one of the other marshalmen close behind him.

He opened his eyes. Blue sky and branches tilted dizzily in his vision. The girl groaned.

"Get 'em, Swinton!" Leach shouted.

Nicholas could see them, out of the corner of his eye.
Swinton and Leach, charging down the hillside. They
had left their mounts at the top. The animals couldn't
make it down the hill—not through the tangle of low-
hanging evergreen branches and thick underbrush.

He had counted on that.

He closed his eyes, let his muscles go lax. This would
have been an excellent time for prayer. If he believed
in that sort of thing.

Forcing all pain to the edge of his awareness, he used
every ounce of control he possessed to hold his breath
and keep absolutely still.

" 'Elp me, lad! I think me arm's broken!" Bickford's

voice drifted down from the top of the ravine. "Get this thing off me, blast ye!"

Tucker would be occupied above with the portly gaolkeeper. *Good.*

Swinton reached the bottom of the hill first, panting, cursing. "Leach . . ." he wheezed. "I think 'e's dead!"

"Bloody 'ell. After we come all this way?"

"There goes our fifty quid." Swinton kicked Nicholas in the side.

Nicholas didn't make a sound. Remained absolutely lifeless.

"What about 'er?" Leach growled.

Just then the girl moaned softly.

Thank you, Nicholas thought warmly.

Their attention shifted to her—he heard the crackling of leaves as they moved around him, heard Leach's voice grow closer as he bent down. He opened one eye to a slit.

"Looks like 'er ladyship is still—"

Nicholas exploded into action.

He kicked out with his free foot and sent Leach's pistol flying. Jumping to his feet, he attacked Swinton with a vicious right cross followed by a double-punch to the kidneys. Swinton went down before he knew what hit him, dropping his gun with a yowl of pain and surprise.

Nicholas lunged for the fallen pistol. But he couldn't move fast enough—not chained to the dazed, unmoving girl. Leach grabbed him from behind before he could reach it.

A burly arm closed around his throat. The marshalman yanked backward and with his other hand landed an agonizing blow to the ribs, once, twice. He tried to wrestle Nicholas to the ground, snarling curses. Nicholas jammed his elbow backward, high and hard, catching his adversary in the chest.

Leach gurgled in pain but held on. His grip only tightened.

"Tucker!" he screeched. "Get down 'ere!"

The girl came fully awake and sat up with a moan. Blinking, she gasped at the scene before her.

"*Get* . . ." Nicholas didn't have enough breath to complete the command. He fastened his hands around Leach's heavily muscled arm, pulled with all his strength. He could feel blood pumping hot through his veins. But he couldn't break the choke hold. Couldn't get any air. His tortured lungs burned.

And the girl only stared up at him with a look of panic.

Nicholas glared down at her, trying to say it with his eyes. *Get Swinton's pistol. He dropped it right there. Get the blasted thing before he comes around!*

Even with her arms tied behind her, she could keep it away from the marshalmen, kick it out of reach.

But she didn't move. Remained frozen. A useless weight around his ankle.

Nicholas tried to hook his left foot behind Leach's, knock him off balance. But the marshalman kept his legs braced. Unmovable.

"Tucker!" Leach bellowed again. "Where the devil are ye?"

Swinton moved. Growled a curse, lurched to his knees, to his feet, staggering.

He reached down and scooped up his gun.

Nicholas heard the gut-wrenching sound of the pistol being cocked. Felt his only chance to escape slipping away.

No, damn it.

"Shoot him," Leach snarled.

Nicholas gritted his teeth and shut his eyes, forced himself back into the past, into a chasm of darkness filled with tricks learned in a lifetime of fighting at close quarters.

And he used his opponent's own grip against him.

He suddenly bent at the waist, roaring with the effort, lifting one shoulder to toss the marshalman over his head.

Flung through the air, Leach cried out—a wail cut short when he landed with a crunch of bone against rock.

Nicholas dove sideways the second he was free. Threw himself out of the path of the pistol aimed at him.

But he wasn't fast enough.

The explosion of the shot at such close range sounded like a full broadside. The familiar, acrid stench of smoke and powder filled the air.

And he felt a blaze of hot metal rip through his left shoulder, felt the bullet burying deep.

He hit the ground with a hoarse exclamation, falling half atop the girl.

Before he could move, Swinton was on him, a gleaming knife in one hand, the empty pistol in the other, lifted to use as a club.

With a snarl of rage, Nicholas rose to meet him, in pain, *cornered*. The world dimmed to a blood-red haze of fury. All thought, all reason, all human feeling fell away and he knew only one thought, one need. One he had felt before. So many times.

Kill.

He knocked the knife away with a savage chop of his hand and attacked, pounding his enemy to the ground, striking blow after vicious, bone-shattering blow.

It wasn't until he felt someone tugging at him— small, fragile hands grasping desperately at his arm— that he came back to himself.

"Stop it!" She was sobbing. "Stop it! Stop it!"

Nicholas released his victim, straightening, dazed. Breathing hard, he blinked to clear his vision, unaware even of how much time had passed. The girl's hands were free, he realized. She must have used the knife.

Swinton lay on the ground at his feet, beaten bloody, unconscious.

Nicholas staggered backward a step. Even with a bullet in him, he had just brought down an armed man. Perhaps killed him. With no weapon but his fists.

And he had felt, heard, seen nothing. Remembered nothing.

Only now did he feel the agony that seared through his shoulder. Only now was he aware of the blood soaking his sleeve.

Shaken, he turned, staring at the girl.

She let go of his other arm as if it burned her, backing away, her features pale and stricken at the display of brutality. "You're a madman," she whispered. "You are a *madman!*"

Before he could say a word in denial—or affirmation—the chain pulled her up short.

And a blast of grapeshot rained through the leaves over their heads.

He threw himself to the ground, yanking her down with him, and looked at the top of the ravine.

Tucker stood at the edge of the road, reloading Bickford's musket. Beside him, the fat gaolkeeper leaned against the broken cart, holding his arm.

"G-give up, both of ye," the lad demanded in a quivering voice, raising the blunderbuss to his shoulder. "Raise yer 'ands and . . . and no one'll get 'urt!"

Stubborn little whelp. He had been too scared to jump into the fray before. Why couldn't he just stay scared? Nicholas darted a glance around. He had kicked Leach's pistol away . . . there it was. In the leaves. A few yards to the left.

"Come on," he ordered under his breath. Not giving the girl a chance to argue, he slid forward on his belly.

"What are you *doing?*" she whispered in dismay, forced to follow when the chain pulled taut.

He reached for the gun. Leach hadn't had a chance to fire; it was still loaded.

But to his horror, as soon as he picked it up, his hand started shaking.

It had been years since he had held a pistol.

Six years.

The cold weapon burned him like a brand—the weight in his palm, the smooth surface, the sinuous curves. So familiar. Like a long-lost lover. Sleek. Easy. Seductive.

And he couldn't keep his hand steady.

But there was no time to worry about it. He rolled onto his back, aimed . . .

"No!" the girl cried.

. . . and fired.

He missed by a great deal more than a mile. His hand trembled so badly that the shot went wildly off to the left. But the young marshalman fell to the ground with a shout of panic and covered his head.

"Our mates is done for down there, Bickford," Tucker cried. "Ain't it better if we ride fer 'elp?"

"Aye, lad. 'Elp me up."

Tucker obeyed quickly, loading the gaolkeeper aboard one of the horses and mounting the other himself.

"Ye'll pay for this!" Bickford shouted down the hill. "I swear by me dead mother's soul, I'll see ye 'ang!"

With that ominous vow, the two lawmen fled up the road at a gallop.

Still lying on his back, the smoking gun hot in his hand, Nicholas listened to the fading thunder of hoofbeats.

Silence descended. Not even a leaf in the forest stirred.

The girl lay utterly still beside him.

After a moment, a pair of wary golden eyes turned his way. Trembling visibly, she opened her mouth to speak, couldn't. Then she swallowed hard and tried again.

"You almost got us killed," she whispered, her voice dry with fear.

Nicholas flattened his palm against the earth and sat up. "You were already facing a noose, your ladyship. I'd think you might express a little gratitude for the rescue."

"Rescue?" she choked out. "*Gratitude?*"

He ignored her indignation. Quickly, before he might have time to change his mind, he stuffed the empty gun into his belt, at the center of his back where he'd worn one for so many years.

It slid right into place. As if he'd never been without one. Seemed to fit there.

Too easily.

For just a second, he couldn't move. Christ, he could feel it, pressed against him. Hot. Burning. Right through his shirt. Through flesh and bone. Through his body and whatever might be left of his—

"Aye, gratitude," he repeated sharply, standing.

She came out of her frozen panic as if something had snapped. "Well, don't hold your breath," she sputtered, pushing herself up to a sitting position. "I had a perfectly good plan of my own. I was not in need of res—"

He reached down and pulled her to her feet unceremoniously. "Come on."

"Unhand me," she demanded. "I'm not going anywhere with you!"

"My thought exactly."

Hauling her along beside him, he stalked over to Leach's prone body. He bent down and rifled through the fallen man's frock coat, taking a small coin purse. A powder horn. And a pouch of bullets.

"He's dead," the girl gasped, studying the fallen marshalmen. "They're both dead. You killed them!"

"It was them or me, lady," he grated out. "Faced with that choice, I generally choose me."

He moved on to Swinton, stooping to pick up the

discarded knife along the way. He slid it into his boot.

Swinton didn't present any better pickings than the other marshalman, unfortunately. There was as precious little ammunition as intelligence between the two.

But, Nicholas decided, it would be worth one bullet to be rid of the girl.

He reloaded the pistol.

She inhaled sharply. "W-what are you doing now?" Her eyes searched his face. "What do you intend to—"

He flicked off the safety and stepped away from her. Two paces. His hand seemed a bit steadier now.

She looked stricken, her panic returning. "What are you going to—"

He aimed and fired before she finished the sentence.

The sharp burst of noise wasn't nearly as loud as the girl's scream.

The smoke cleared. She was still standing there, her expression utterly stunned. Gulping repeatedly, she looked down at herself and ran her hands over her body, as if surprised not to find any holes.

Ignoring her, Nicholas knelt down to examine the chain, muttering an oath.

The iron was still intact. Not only had the bullet not broken it in two—it had barely left a scratch.

"Well, bloody hell." He scowled.

So much for his perfect plan. Apparently it was going to be a great deal more difficult to get rid of his charming companion than he had anticipated.

He glowered up at her. His shoulder hurt like the devil, he had precious little money or ammunition, and he had to make it to York in a matter of days.

With the law out searching for him in full force.

And now he had to take *her* along.

She stood there, dappled by light that glimmered through the trees, her face whiter than a sheet despite the fact that she had been in the sun all day.

She shook her head rapidly, a leaf falling from her

tangled hair. "You are . . . y-you are . . . absolutely . . ." She seemed barely able to breathe, let alone summon a word to describe him at the moment.

"Insane," he supplied helpfully. Standing, he slipped the gun back into place, fastened the powder horn to his belt, and stuffed the pouches into his pockets. Then he tore off his bloodied left sleeve and wrapped it around his shoulder as best he could. It wasn't bleeding too badly. Yet.

The makeshift bandage would have to do for now. There was no telling how long it might be before Tucker and Bickford showed up with reinforcements.

Perhaps an hour. Perhaps less.

He glanced up at the sun. "Contrary to what you said before, your ladyship, it looks like you *are* going with me." He tested the wind, chose a direction. "So let's go."

Taking her by the arm, he headed into the forest.

Chapter 6

Insane.

The word echoed through Sam's mind, twisted in and around her stunned senses, louder than the lingering report of the pistol shot. The man was absolutely insane. But when he turned and set off, the chain that bound them and his unyielding hold on her arm gave her no choice but to go with him.

He headed into the woods as if the dogs of Hell were howling for his blood, seemingly oblivious to the bullet in his shoulder and the blood soaking his shirt. But the shackles hampered their every step. She couldn't match his stride or his speed. And the jangling chain caught on every rock and fallen branch strewn in their path.

She stumbled alongside him, struggling to keep up. Unable to catch her breath, still bruised and dazed from their fall down the hillside, she remained mute, numb. Tree trunks and swirling shafts of sunlight danced before her eyes in a blinding blur as they fled. She couldn't form a coherent thought, her mind reeling with images of the unspeakable violence she had just witnessed.

The rogue's fists mercilessly beating Swinton into unconsciousness. Blood. Pistol shots. A flashing knife. Leach's lifeless eyes staring skyward.

The brutal pictures ricocheted through her head, sent the world spinning around her just as it had when they plunged down the ravine. In shock, she ran for several minutes before reason finally penetrated her daze. Like one of the beams of sunlight breaking through the trees, it hit her with stunning clarity: she was no longer on her way to London to face the magistrates and her uncle's retribution.

She was in far worse trouble. Racing headlong into Cannock Chase with a madman.

And she was going along like a sheep.

"N-no!" Roused from her stupor at last, she tried to wrest her arm from his grip, stumbling.

He held her up and pulled her forward with him, giving her no choice but to keep moving.

"Stop!" She resisted again, desperately trying to shake him off. Running, gasping, she tried to think of some way to reason with him. To get the shackles off so she could get *away* from him. "W-we should go toward a town—"

"Every town for miles will be crawling with lawmen before the sun sets." He ducked under a low-hanging branch and kept going, his blunt, strong fingers holding fast to her arm.

"But I d-don't think—"

"I don't give a damn what you think." He swept her along with him.

"Well, I don't give a damn what you say! I am *not* going into Cannock Chase with you!" She stopped suddenly, digging in her heels.

And he was moving so fast, she yanked him off balance.

The chain jerked taut, tripped him. He went down face-first and the sudden tug on the shackles pulled her feet out from under her. Arms flailing, she fell backward with a startled cry. And landed flat on her back in a carpet of leaves and pine needles, sending a shower of both into the air.

She could hear the rogue groan a low sound of pain as she lay there gasping for breath, coughing on the cloud of dust that billowed up from the forest floor. Every inch of her felt hurt, pummeled, scraped, aching. Her left ankle throbbed painfully from the sharp pull on the tight iron cuff.

He sat up first, pushing himself to his knees with an oath ... turning to look at her with a thunderous expression on his face.

The instinct to scramble away flashed through her head but he was too quick. He lunged toward her, pushed her down into the leaves.

She screamed, trying to throw him off, but he pinned her with his weight. An icy blast of wild, unreasoning terror swept through her. It closed off her throat, cut off her scream as fresh images of violence and horror flashed through her mind.

Old images.

Memories.

Her home ... the vicious pack of outlaws breaking in ... the serving maids begging for mercy as the intruders fell upon them ... Mama, Papa where are you ... the men laughing cruelly as they tore at the girls' clothes and bared them to their eyes and their lust ... and thrust up into them like rutting animals and then the screams, oh, God, the girls' screams of pain—

Her voice returned in a single, rasping cry of stark panic. "*No!*" She struck at him with her fists, struggled with all her strength. She would never let a man do that to her. Never, never, *never*. "Get off of me! Get—"

"Shut up." He grabbed her wrists, fastened them to the ground on either side of her head, breathing hard, his eyes piercing hers. "Shut up and stop making trouble for two seconds, damn it—"

"Let me go!" God help her, she hadn't guessed until now that he might intend to mete out a fate worse than death. And she had no hope of escape. The way he had her pinned, she couldn't defend herself with a knee or a kick as she had against Swinton last night. "Don't touch me! Take your hands off of me. If y-you so much as l-lay one hand on me, I'll kill you. I swear it!"

He stared down at her, surprise mixing with the anger in his hard features.

Then, slowly, understanding glimmered in his eyes, and he levered his weight off of her a bit. "Don't worry, *angel*." A mocking grin curved his mouth. "That's not what I had in mind. You forget, I saw what happened to the last man who tried to . . . get friendly with you."

She blinked up at him, confused. Was he making light of her threat? Or making a joke?

She kept fighting against his hold.

"I'll let you go," he continued, some of the storminess returning to his expression, "just as soon as you calm down and listen to reason."

Despite his wounded shoulder, he subdued her and held her still, easily. Too easily. She hadn't realized until now how strong he actually was. How much power lay in that lean, muscled frame. And she could tell he was only using a fraction of that strength at the moment. If he chose to take her . . .

Her heart hammering, she froze, paralyzed by the knowledge that she couldn't hope to fend him off.

But oddly enough, as soon as she stopped fighting, he relaxed his hold. In fact, though he had rendered her immobile, though he was obviously furious, he hadn't hurt her. And he hadn't made any move to rape her. Yet.

Taking shallow gulps of air, she did her best to banish the terrifying memories into the dark corner they always occupied in her mind. She had seen lust glowing in men's eyes more than enough times to recognize it . . . and she didn't see it now, in his.

"That's better," he said in a low rumble when she let her muscles go limp.

She tried to ignore the fact that she could feel as well as hear his deep voice.

"Now, your ladyship, I want you to listen and listen

well, because I'm not going to say this again—"

"I-I don't care what you have to say."

"Well, that's too damned bad. Because you and I are stuck with one another." He grimaced. "You don't like it and I don't like it but we're stuck. So until I find some way to break this blasted chain, you're going to *go* where I say and *do* what I say and you're going to—"

"I don't follow anyone's orders but my own." Her indignant retort surprised her as much as it apparently did him. But she couldn't help herself. Despite the fact that her voice trembled as badly as her body was trembling, she meant every word.

"You do now. Because if you try any more tricks like the one you just pulled, one of us is going to end up with a broken leg or a broken neck—"

"I go where I want and I do what I want and I'm not going to let *you* order me around." She immediately felt foolish for blurting that out. She sounded childish. They were chained together; how could she exert her independence when they couldn't even get far enough apart to *argue* at a respectable distance? Her anger bubbled over. "I didn't ask to be dragged along on your mad escape! I had a perfectly good plan of my own."

"Seducing that freckle-faced, craven-hearted boy? You call that a plan?"

She gasped. "I had no intention of . . . is *that* what you thought?"

"Any man with eyes could see that you were offering your favors in exchange for whatever he might care to do for you."

She gaped at him in shock. "That is not true! I was merely going to . . . to encourage him to take pity on me and . . . help me."

"Oh, aye, now *there's* a plan." He laughed. "You'd make him feel such sympathy that he would set you free? And the other guards would do what? Sit idly by and let you walk away? Brilliant." He couldn't stop chuckling. "If it wasn't for me, lady, you'd have been swinging from a rope in London by week's end."

His biting laughter made her cheeks burn all over again. Made her feel foolish. She hated the way he kept mocking her, as if she were some weak, witless, helpless female. "I didn't ask for your opinion, you blackhearted brigand! I can take care of myself. I don't need *anyone's* help, do you hear me? Not yours and not anyone's!"

"Fine. Because I have no intention of offering you any." He closed his eyes for a second, still breathing hard. Despite all his strength and stamina, he was obviously in pain. "We aren't going to get anywhere if you try to go your way and I try to go my way. So we'll both go my way. As long as you follow orders, we'll get along just fine."

"Then I'm afraid we're not going to get along at all."

He opened his eyes and she saw a spark of something dangerous there. "It's not up for discussion, *angel*. There's only room for one of us to be in charge here—and you're looking at him."

Not giving her any chance for further argument, he stood up, pulling her to her feet with the same effortless strength he had used to keep her pinned. She was struck by the way he towered over her. In gaol, he had been forced to stoop down by the low ceiling; standing at his full height, he loomed above her, a massive, solid presence.

She barely came up to his chin, her eyes level with the second button on his shirt.

Her heart kept pounding a fast, uneven beat.

"This time, your ladyship," he said in a commanding tone, "I suggest you keep those pretty little slippers of yours moving."

With one last stern look of warning, he turned and led her into the forest once more.

An hour later, they had ventured deep into the heart

of the Chase. After some awkward stumbles and a lot of practice, they had gradually learned to coordinate their strides despite the chain, avoiding any further painful falls.

But he never stopped. Never rested. They alternately ran and walked, until Sam felt she had reached the limit of her endurance. The knotted muscles of her legs ached with strain and the soles of her feet felt as if they'd been flattened. Her throat burned, raw from the effort to breathe.

This deep in the woods, the trees loomed thicker on every side. Branches caught at her hair. Brambles and underbrush ripped at her skirts. Roots jutted out of nowhere to trip her. The interlacing leaves far overhead blocked the sun almost completely, but the shade no longer felt like a cooling balm, but a cold, clammy shroud.

She couldn't help but think that Cannock Chase more than lived up to its sinister reputation, its shadows a darker black, even the sharp scent of evergreens and damp earth somehow menacing, overpowering her senses. As if the very air here were different. Ancient and wild and not meant for man.

The unsettling impression lingered, though she told herself it was merely fatigue making her imagine it all. Fatigue caused by her ruthless companion.

The words he had spoken earlier kept running through her head. *It was them or me. Faced with that choice, I generally choose me.*

That was painfully obvious. He didn't care about anyone but himself. Every time she tripped, every time she asked to rest, he would tug her back to her feet and order her to keep moving. Pushing her onward. Relentlessly onward. He was pitiless, cold-hearted . . .

As he drove her mercilessly, a new emotion crowded in on the fear and resentment she felt toward him. A simmering dislike.

Even as she had that thought, her slipper hit a patch

of damp leaves and she slid. He grabbed her with both hands, but they both lost their balance and fell.

He muttered a curse. She lay in the sticky, wet leaves, gasping for air, her limbs shaking with exhaustion.

"I . . . c . . . can't," she panted, shaking her head, tears stinging her eyes. "C-can't . . . go . . . any . . . f-further."

This time, instead of arguing or coercing as she had expected, he relented, making no move to get up. She closed her eyes in relief. The noise of their labored breathing filled the silence around them, the only sound for a long time.

When she could finally catch her breath, she slowly sat up, biting her lower lip to stop a groan. She leaned against the closest tree trunk. The rough bark dug into her suntanned arm but she didn't care. Eyes closed, she mopped at the perspiration that trickled down her face, her neck, using a corner of her ruined silk skirt. She raked her hopelessly tangled hair back from her face, tried to comb her fingers through it, gave up.

Opening her eyes, she looked warily at her companion. He still lay on his side in the leaves, eyes closed, features pale and strained. His shoulder was bleeding. Badly. The makeshift bandage he had fashioned from his sleeve was woefully inadequate. Blood stained the back of his shirt red.

Perhaps he would be too weak to harm her.

Please, God, help me.

Her mouth had gone dry. Her pulse kept pounding an uncontrolled race. As if he felt her regard, he opened his eyes and looked up at her.

When their gazes met, her heart thudded harder against her ribs.

Stretched out on the forest floor, with his disheveled black hair and glittering green eyes and bloodied shoulder, he looked like he belonged here in this wild place. Fit in with the other untamed things. A wounded predator. Dark and unpredictable and capable of all sorts of . . . savagery.

His gaze skimmed downward, coming to rest on her legs. He was still breathing harshly. "Come here."

Sam stiffened. His voice sounded weaker than before, but she wasn't taking any chances. Shifting her eyes quickly left and right, she sought some weapon she might use to protect herself. A rock. A branch. Anything.

"I said come here," he repeated impatiently.

When she didn't comply, he reached out and grabbed her foot.

"What are you doing?" She tried to wriggle out of his grasp. "Unhand me!"

"Gladly," he said tiredly—yet he hung on to her, pushing himself up on one elbow. Snagging her ruined slipper with his other hand, he flipped it off her foot. "I'd like nothing better than to unhand you, unchain you, and be *done* with you."

Instead of attacking her, he attacked the shackle around her leg.

Sam gave up her struggle, even though she knew she could kick her way free; one blow to his wounded shoulder and he would let her loose. But he was already in a foul mood and she didn't want to incite him to violence if she could avoid it.

Besides, she realized what he was trying to do. He pulled at the shackle, trying to slide it off over her foot.

Which just might work.

"Maybe if we had some kind of . . ." Glancing around, she took a handful of slimy mud from beneath the leaves and smeared it over her skin.

"Come on," he muttered under his breath, pushing the cuff, turning it, swearing at it. "Come on."

Sam tried to help but he clearly didn't want her help. Holding her bare foot with one hand and the iron cuff with the other, he turned both at different angles, trying to coax the cuff past her ankle bone.

"It's too tight and it's bolted on," she said finally,

exasperated at being manhandled. "It's not going to come off."

With a short, expressive oath, he released her. Lowering himself back down into the leaves, he tossed the muddy slipper into her lap. "Perfect," he growled. "Of all the lady thieves on the run in England, I have to get myself shackled to the one with big feet."

Sam scuttled backward, as far away from him as the chain would allow. Which wasn't nearly far enough. "I'll thank you to keep your opinions to yourself."

Her tone was frosty, but she feared that even her haughtiest drawing-room airs couldn't conceal the fact that her cheeks felt hot. Scalding. She rubbed at her ankle, wiping away the mud and the unexpected warmth that lingered from the touch of his callused fingers on her bare skin.

Grabbing her slipper, she put it back on. Her foot and her ankle ached with soreness, felt cool from the gooey muck. She couldn't understand why they also . . . tingled.

She decided that the unfamiliar sensation must come from the hours of unaccustomed physical exertion.

"It's not my fault that the shackles are so tight." She glared at the man stretched out on the ground, adding in a mutinous whisper, "And I do not have big feet."

"Doesn't bloody well matter now," he grumbled. "Short of a convenient bolt of lightning from above or a blacksmith, it looks like there's no way for me to get free of you." Opening his eyes with a pained expression, he peered at the lengthening shadows, almost as if he were measuring the sun in some way. "Two hours of daylight left. You ready to press on, Lady Bigfeet?"

She ignored the sarcasm, every muscle in her body aching at the words *press on*. "No." She groaned. "No, I'm not. Can't we stop? Can't we rest just for a—"

"Not unless you're eager to wind up back in gaol." He pushed himself to a seated position. "As soon as word spreads about a pair of dangerous fugitives on the loose, two marshalmen killed, and rewards offered, every lawman and bounty hunter in the north of England will be on our trail. By morning, if not sooner. And if they use dogs . . ."

He let the sentence trail off, running a weary hand over his face.

Sam felt a surge of fear. Dogs. *Dozens* of men hunting her down. Skilled, experienced men.

And they would know right where to start looking. The young guard Tucker would show them.

Her throat tightened. The rogue was right. They had to keep going. Put distance between themselves and the point where they'd disappeared into the forest. Much more distance.

Yet her fear mingled with anger at his apparent nonchalance. "Didn't you consider any of that before you decided to take a flying leap out of the cart? Didn't you think that far ahead? Didn't you think at all?"

"Aye, I did," he retorted, "but I wasn't counting on your charming company, *angel*. I planned to be long gone by now. You are slowing me down." He reached up to unfasten the bandage knotted around his shoulder. "But before we go any further, you'd better take a look at this damned wound."

She felt like spitting in his face. One minute he was insulting her, and the next he expected her to see to his comfort? "If you think I'm going to lift one finger to help you," she said in a low, even voice, crossing her arms over her chest, "you'd better think again."

He clenched his jaw, wincing as he unwrapped the blood-soaked cloth. "Listen," he said tightly, beads of sweat sliding down his face, into his beard, "if you think you're in trouble now, just try to imagine what would happen to you if I pass out from loss of blood. Or if I die."

She had barely started to contemplate the pleasant possibilities when he demolished every single one.

"You'd be stuck here with one hundred and eighty

pounds of dead weight chained to your ankle." His eyes pierced hers. "Helpless as a trussed-up Christmas pigeon when the authorities come looking for you. If their dogs don't get you first, their guns will make mincemeat out of you. When dealing with fugitives who've killed two of their fellow lawmen, they tend to let their bullets do their talking for them."

The violent image stole the air from her lungs. "But *I* didn't kill those marshalmen!"

"I doubt you'll have time to explain that."

They stared into each other's eyes for a long moment, the truth swirling between them like one of the hot beams of light from the dying sun.

Then he said it aloud.

"If I die, you die," he put it plainly, his stark words all the more powerful for their lack of embellishment. "If I live . . ."

For some reason, it took him an extra moment to finish that sentence.

"You live."

Mute, shaking, she tried to control the fear and disbelief and resentment careening through her. He was insufferable. Arrogant. Cold-hearted, uncivilized, utterly self-interested.

But he also had a point. As unavoidable as it was true. If they wanted to survive . . .

They were going to have to work together.

She returned his glare, wrestling with her temper and her pride and the thought of trying to rein in the independent streak honed by years of fending for herself. "It's bad enough that I already look like your accomplice," she hissed. "If I help you, that will *make* me your accomplice."

Not saying a word, his eyes still on hers, he withdrew Swinton's knife from his belt.

Her heart thudded in her chest. *Dangerous*, she thought. She had forgotten to add *dangerous*. That word described him better than any other.

But he couldn't kill her. To save his own neck, he couldn't kill her.

Though that didn't mean he wouldn't hurt her.

Even as she thought that, he flipped the knife with a nimble, almost invisible flick of his wrist, catching it by the blade.

And then he held it out to her, the hilt extended like some kind of bizarre olive branch. "But you're smart enough to know that what I'm saying is true, aren't you, angel?"

His voice was deep, quiet, and for once, devoid of any mockery.

She hesitated, her gaze flicking from his jewel-green eyes to the silver gleam of the blade in his fingertips.

Then she reached out, slowly, hesitantly, and took it.

As her fingers closed around the hilt, another thought flitted through her head. She had wanted a weapon . . . and now she had one.

As if reading her mind, he stopped her with only two words. "I wouldn't."

The mildness of his tone made his meaning all the more clear. It was a quiet reminder—as if she needed one—that she didn't dare attack him, and couldn't hope to defend herself against him. Not even with a blade.

Swallowing hard, she tried to tell herself that everything would be all right. As long as the chain bound them together, they had to keep each other alive and well. Once they found some way to get the shackles off, they would go their separate ways.

For now, she just had to endure his presence and make the best of a bad situation. Because her very life depended on it.

Holding up the knife, she lifted an eyebrow. "So what am I supposed to do with this?"

"Get the bullet out," he said curtly, as if it should be obvious.

Her jaw dropped. "Are you . . . joking?"

"You don't see me laughing, do you?" Turning his back, he started unbuttoning his shirt and waistcoat.

"B-but I can't . . . I don't know how. I've never—"

"Well, there don't appear to be any physicians on hand at the moment. I don't have any choice and I don't have any time. I have to keep moving."

She noted with exasperation that he kept using the word *I*, as if she didn't exist. As if she were nothing but an annoying appendage at the other end of the chain.

As for performing surgery on him, the very idea made her stomach lurch with nausea. She had no medical experience whatsoever. The closest she'd ever come was fixing a broken arm on one of Jess's porcelain dolls when she was twelve.

However, she was quickly learning that it was useless to argue with him once he'd made up his mind about something.

Uneasily, her hand shaking, she edged closer to him, whispering a prayer.

"Never mind asking for God's help," he muttered under his breath as he finished unbuttoning his red-stained garments. "I think it's safe to say He's not interested in the least."

He slid the waistcoat off and then removed the shirt, unsticking it from the wound with a quick yank and a stifled curse.

Sam looked away, covering her mouth to hold back a cry. There was so much blood! A wave of dizziness made the forest tilt crazily for a second. Squeezing her eyes shut, she gulped and took several quick, shallow gasps of air.

"You're not going to faint on me, are you?" he asked over his shoulder.

"No," she insisted.

"Then hurry up and get on with it." He stretched out on his stomach, bunching up his shirt and using it as a pillow on his crossed arms. Almost as an afterthought, he grabbed a stick from the forest floor and placed it between his teeth.

Sam's mouth felt dry as she looked down at her stoic patient. But when she tried to move into position, the chain jerked taut. "I can't reach it from here. The chain isn't long enough."

He bent his right leg, allowing enough slack for her to get closer.

Blinking rapidly, taking a deep, steadying breath, she inched nearer and sat at his side. Determined to prove that she wasn't the weak, witless female he seemed to believe she was, she screwed up her courage and lifted the knife.

But when she bent over the wound, she couldn't go on. It was an actual hole, small and perfectly round, just to one side of his shoulderblade. "It . . . it looks deep. And . . . w-we don't have anything to dull the pain."

He spat out the stick. "I'd love nothing better than a nice bottle of rum right now. Do you see a pub anywhere?" His voice had taken on a flat wearyiness, as if he didn't have much strength left. "Just get it over with, your ladyship."

"But I don't even know what I'm looking for."

"A piece of lead. Shouldn't be hard to find." He put the stick back between his teeth, talking around it. "The bone'll be white."

Another wave of dizziness assaulted her. He didn't say anything more. Just turned his head and closed his eyes, his muscles taut with strain.

Steeling herself, she lifted the knife again, whispering a prayer, despite what he'd said earlier.

Then she gingerly went to work.

Chapter 7

He had fainted. Sam tossed the metal fragment aside with a shudder and dropped the knife into the leaves. His entire body had gone slack when she finally got the bullet out.

"Thank God," she whispered. How could anyone endure what he had just endured? She had tried to be as quick as possible, and the bullet hadn't been as deep as she'd feared at first, but it had still taken her an agonizingly long time.

Her head swam dizzily, her empty stomach heaved, and she felt as if she might faint herself. She had managed to brazen her way through the frightful task, but now that it was over, all the strength and resolve flowed out of her, leaving her trembling like one of the branches that swayed overhead. She closed her eyes and swallowed hard, trying to breathe normally.

Blindly, she felt around for the scrap of her petticoat she had used to clean the knife, snatched it up, and wiped her hands on it. She bit her tongue to distract herself from the rush of nausea. "I'm sorry."

"Sorry?"

His voice was so soft she barely heard it. She went still, stunned that he was still conscious. Then she had to think for a moment, not sure what she had said.

"Sorry for hurting you," she managed at last.

His battered left eye flickered open and a weak version of his cynical grin tugged at the corner of his mouth. "You're not the . . . first female to . . . lay into me with a blade, angel," he whispered.

Closing his eyes again, he lay very still.

She set the scrap of fabric aside, still trembling, unsure what to make of his comment. Or his condition. He must be in terrible pain; despite the way he had remained stoic and unflinching throughout the ordeal, his muscles taut, he had groaned once or twice—and toward the end, he had snapped the slender branch between his teeth. Cleanly in two.

But from the marks on his back, it was obvious he had indeed encountered other blades in his life. And perhaps bullets as well. Looking down at his prone form in the late afternoon sunlight, she could see many scars, pale against the deep bronze of his skin.

Including row after row of long, thin marks straight across his back. Perhaps she was mistaken, but it looked as if those had been caused by a lash. They lay beneath some of the others, stretched into uneven squiggles, faint, faded . . . as if they had happened when he was very young.

Who *was* this man?

She hadn't dared ask before, but now the question hammered at her temples like a headache. Her gaze shifted to the unbreakable chain that bound them together, and she had to press her palms against the cool, damp earth to steady herself.

Who *was* this man with the cold eyes and unsettling strength and scars that bespoke years of pain? She knew he wasn't the footpad that the marshalmen had believed him to be. But she didn't know anything more about him.

Except that he had been willing to risk his life to escape from the law. His life, and hers.

She couldn't blot from her mind the image of him beating Swinton with his bare hands. The way he had killed so brutally. Mindlessly.

Yet those same hands had shaken when he held the pistol. And his aim at poor Tucker had been miles off the mark. As if he'd never held a gun before in his life.

Who the devil was he?

Abruptly she turned away and busied herself tearing another strip from her petticoat for a fresh bandage.

Because some instinct warned her that she didn't really want an answer to that question.

"Are you going to be all right?" She fought to keep her voice even.

"Aye."

That single strained word didn't sound very convincing. And he was bleeding, much worse than before. "I . . . I think I should try to close the wound somehow."

"Give her a knife and she thinks she's a doctor," he muttered weakly.

She ignored him, thinking, looking around at the meager resources available—leaves, sticks, puddled water. Nothing. Less than nothing. "I could . . . what is the word? Cauterize it. With the flat of the knife. If I build a fire—"

"No," he said sharply, lifting his head. "Don't be a fool. The smoke would . . . lead them straight to us."

"But if I can't stop the bleeding, you won't be able to keep going. And then where will you—I mean where will *we* be?"

"I'll be fine." He struggled to push himself up, talking through clenched teeth. "I'll just have to—"

"I could stitch it."

That shut him up for a second. Balanced on one elbow, he blinked at her.

Then the mocking glimmer that she was learning to hate flared in his eyes. "Yet another brilliant idea, your ladyship. And what are you going to use?" he asked between ragged breaths. "A twig and a blade of grass?"

She stared back at him with regally cool silence. Then

she turned her back, not bothering to explain, and reached into her bodice.

And unpinned the small gold needle case from the place she always kept it, over her heart.

It was the only bit of her past she still owned. The only remembrance she possessed of her home, her family . . . her mother. She wore it every day to keep it safe from prying eyes and greedy hands. Untying the ribbon knotted around it, she unraveled the necklace and slipped the fine gold chain over her head.

The cone-shaped pendant slid down between her breasts, the richly engraved surface, burnished by generations of wear, gleaming in the sunlight. She opened the exquisitely fine clasp at the top with one fingernail, and took out a needle. One of her mother's silver lace-making needles.

Turning around, she held it up triumphantly.

He didn't even have the decency to look surprised, much less apologetic. "What sort of locket is that?" he asked, staring.

"It's not a locket, it's a needle case. Haven't you ever seen a lady's needle case before?"

His eyes met hers. "Haven't spent much time among the quality."

"Oh." She was silent for a moment. "I see."

The lame reply made her feel foolish, and in truth she didn't see at all. Most ladies of gentle birth—even those of the lesser aristocracy, like herself—wore a needle case at one time or other. What kind of life had he led, what kind of world did he come from, that he could be unfamiliar with so common an item?

A life and a world, apparently, far different from the one she had been born into.

His gaze slid back down to the dangling bit of gold, the expression in those green depths not admiring or curious but simply . . . covetous. That was the only word for it. Sam had to subdue an urge to reach up and cover her pendant.

Not to mention her decolletage. She could feel his regard as surely as if he touched her with his calloused fingers.

That strange, tingly sensation coursed through her again, unnerving her so badly she almost dropped the needle held between her thumb and forefinger.

"Now then," she said briskly, trying to distract both him and herself. "All I need is some good strong thread."

He looked up at her with a dubiously raised brow. "Don't tell me—you're an expert seamstress as well as a thief, forger, and attempted murderess?"

She shrugged. "Something like that."

If he could be mysterious, so could she. She wasn't about to tell him the truth.

Besides, even if he believed her, he would only laugh at her again. And she had had quite enough of that.

Concentrating on the task at hand, she cast a critical eye over his clothes—the discarded shirt and waistcoat, his snug black breeches. Plain, homespun fabrics, which would have been sewn with plain, homespun cotton thread.

She glanced down at her own garments with a disgruntled frown, realizing she was going to have to decimate either her ruined gown or petticoats a bit more. Made entirely of silk and fine lawn, edged with lace she had made herself, all had been sewn with the best silk thread, which would be stronger and more suitable for this particular purpose.

The gown was already beyond repair, spattered with mud and torn in a dozen places, her beloved lace ripped and drooping. She told herself a little more damage wouldn't matter.

Sighing mournfully, she lifted her needle and began to unpick a seam in her sleeve, using a light touch, carefully removing the thread stitch by stitch. In a matter of minutes, she had an ample supply of pale silk spooled around her thumb.

Feeding one end through the needle, she glanced at her patient. "I'm ready. I'm afraid this is—"

"Going to hurt." He lowered himself back down into the leaves. "What a surprise."

Sam bit back a reply as she positioned herself beside him again. She was doing her best to help him—and her only reward was a constant stream of sarcastic comments. He had to be *the* most irksome man she'd ever met.

Perhaps he was entitled to be unpleasant because he was in pain. Perhaps. She held her tongue and her temper, took another deep, steadying breath, and went to work.

The stitching progressed fairly easily, since the wound was relatively small. She just couldn't believe she was using one of her mother's heirloom lacemaking needles to close a bullet hole.

The thought brought a sudden rush of memories, of a life so sweet it seemed to belong to someone else. Of a drawing room, a fire on the hearth, three women gathered around it in overstuffed wing chairs, silver needles flashing, voices filling the room with laughter, a man seated nearby smoking a pipe and smiling indulgently, content merely to watch them . . .

No. Blinking furiously, she fought the tears, refused to let herself give in to the weakness. She didn't dare remember. All of that was gone. Forever. The love, the laughter. Gone. It was futile to long for the life she had once lived.

There was only now. Today. Survival.

And this stranger, this maddening rogue, whose life had been tangled up with hers by a trick of fate and bonds of iron.

He didn't flinch even once, didn't make a sound as she worked. As if he were made of iron himself.

"All done." She finished the stitching and tied off the thread, then cleaned the needle, using the scrap of fabric she had torn from her petticoat. She placed it safely back in her needle case. "It looks like this will stop the bleeding."

She reached for his shirt, intending to make another bandage of the ragged remains.

But his hand shot out and he snatched it away from her. Pushing himself up to a seated position, keeping his back to her, he pulled it on, slowly, being careful of his new stitches.

She sat back on her heels, frowning. "You're welcome."

He remained stonily silent.

Fine. So he wasn't big on gratitude.

She decided to make one last attempt at being civil. "I suppose we have to call one another something," she ventured. "You may call me Miss Delafield."

It wasn't her real name; it was the one she'd chosen after leaving London. She'd taken the name of the first parish she'd come to.

It was the traditional way that orphans were named.

"I'm not of a mind to be sociable," he muttered.

Irked to the limit of her patience, she stood up and stalked around to stand in front of him, the chain clattering. "Surely you must have a name. You could always make something up. Or would you prefer that I call you something simple like—"

He hadn't finished buttoning his shirt.

Her eyes locked on a scar in the center of his chest. "—Beelzebub."

The word died on her lips, a shocked whisper, as she stared at that mark.

He'd been branded. With the symbol of a pitchfork. A three-pronged pitchfork, burned right into his chest, right over his heart.

Her legs went weak, threatened to crumple beneath her. She couldn't catch her breath. Her mind reeled. She recognized that mark. Knew what it meant. Everyone in England had heard the horrible tales. Nannies still used them to frighten children into behaving.

He was a survivor of one of the prison hulks. Derelict navy vessels that had been anchored in the Thames. Stuffed with the worst offenders to relieve prison overcrowding. The men aboard had been treated like animals by their navy overseers.

But that had been . . . Good Lord . . . more than two *decades* ago. Riots in 1720 had ended with most of the hulks at the bottom of the Channel. Scores of prisoners and guards dead. Dozens of the worst offenders on a rampage in London. The experiment had never been tried again.

Depending on how old the rogue was now . . .

He would've been only a boy.

By God's sweet mercy. She slowly lifted her gaze to his face.

He remained utterly still, his hands frozen over a button in the middle of his shirt, his expression unreadable, his features pale and strained from the surgery.

But the eyes boring into hers blazed, hot with some emotion she could not name.

She blurted the question in a frightened whisper before she could stop herself.

"Who the devil *are* you?"

His lips thinned to a grim line. She thought he wouldn't answer her.

But after a heartbeat he did.

"Someone you're better off not knowing."

His cool tone sent renewed fear sliding down her spine like a single drop of ice water.

He finished buttoning his shirt with studied casualness and put on his waistcoat.

Sam swallowed a gulp of air past her dry, tight throat. *Someone you're better off not knowing.* It was an understatement. It was a warning. She didn't dare ask any more questions. She already knew far more than she wanted to know about this man who was chained to her by eighteen unbreakable iron links.

He would kill without conscience. He cared about no one but himself. And he had evidently learned those traits—and God only knew what else—in one of the most vile gaols in the history of England.

And for the moment, her life depended on him.

Her gaze still locked with his, she remembered a lesson she'd learned very early when she'd been forced to turn thief.

Keep their eyes busy, and your hands can get away with anything.

Kneeling, she picked up the scrap of her petticoat she had set aside earlier. "Can't leave anything behind that might help the lawmen track us," she said calmly.

Using the same hand, she picked up the knife from where she had dropped it in the leaves, slipping both the blade and the fabric into the deep pocket of her skirt.

He didn't appear to notice, struggling to get to his feet. He studied the sun, a red streak just visible along the horizon through the trees.

"There's still daylight left." He braced one hand against a tree, breathing hard, and glanced down at her. "Might as well put it to good use."

She still crouched in the leaves, her heart beating so hard she couldn't speak for a moment. "Yes."

"Then let's keep moving." A shadow of that cynical grin curving his mouth, he extended a hand to help her up. "After you, Miss Delafield."

Like masts in a harbor, trees towered around them, tall and silent. Nicholas guessed that he and his newly quiet companion had been walking for another hour, perhaps more. He couldn't be sure. He was losing track of time, his senses blunted by loss of blood, exhaustion, pain.

The bullet wound in his left shoulder throbbed and burned. He hoped he wasn't getting blood poisoning, he thought with a flash of black humor; he didn't want to die while he had a length of pretty lemon-colored silk stitched into his hide.

That was no way for a notorious ex-pirate to make his grand entrance into Hell.

The entire forest seemed quieter as night approached. Or maybe it was just the incessant clanking of the accursed chain that made everything else seem muted by comparison. The dying sun cast lengthening shadows across the forest floor, the low light swathing everything in a smoky haze, including the slender figure walking a pace ahead of him.

Miss Delafield.

Nicholas stared at her back, not sure what bothered him more: the throbbing ache in his left shoulder, the clatter of the shackles as they trudged through the woods, the unaccustomed, unwelcome feeling of weakness that made him want to drop to the ground and sleep . . .

Or the fact that he had let her keep the knife.

He couldn't puzzle out *why* he had allowed her to keep it. He had no reason to indulge her. It didn't make sense. Bad enough that she was impulsive and headstrong and nervous around him as a cat on a storm-tossed brig. Now she was armed as well.

Grimacing, he tried to tell himself there was no harm in it. Let her think she had outwitted him. Let her have some sense of security, however false. It might make her less argumentative, less troublesome, and he was all in favor of that.

He shifted his gaze away from her stiff back and squared shoulders, away from that tangle of flaxen hair that tickled generous, swaying hips.

One thing was clear, even to his muddled senses: this lady thief was having a strange effect on him. One that no woman had ever had before. One he didn't like.

It must be some form of lust, he decided, intensified by the enforced nearness and the fact that he had been so long without a woman. The mere touch of her hand on his bare skin had been enough to make his blood run hot. And when she had hovered over him, her breath warm against his shoulder, her lacy sleeve tickling his back, the desire that shot through him had tormented him worse than the bullet.

Even now, he couldn't seem to keep his eyes from straying back to her. A familiar impulse deep within made him long to touch her, to feel handfuls of that tawny hair flowing through his fingers like molten gold, to reach out and pull her body hard against his and . . .

He blinked to clear the image from his vision, stunned as if one of the towering trees had fallen on him. Where the devil were these thoughts coming from? He couldn't fathom it.

Even the name she had given earlier kept whispering through his mind in an undeniably alluring way. *Miss Delafield*. It suited her. Simple, elegant, graceful. And probably false.

So why did he feel glad that she had said *Miss*? Miss instead of Lady Delafield. Or Duchess Delafield. Or ordinary Mrs. Delafield. She could be lying about her unwedded status, but somehow he didn't think so. What man would put up with her stubborn ways and sharp tongue long enough to marry her?

He forced his gaze to the ground, forced his attention back to the problem at hand. Escape. Move forward. One foot in front of the other. Whoever—whatever—she really was, it didn't matter. None of it mattered. Not her name, not her tempting golden curves, not the unsettling effect she seemed to have on him.

Because she had seen the brand on his chest. From the look on her face, she had clearly recognized what the brand meant. Even if she couldn't identify the specific ship, he couldn't risk that she might mention the mark to someone. To anyone.

And that meant he might have to kill her.

His gut twisted in a sickening knot even as he contemplated the idea. Never in all his thirty-eight years, even at his worst, had he ever harmed a woman. Even aboard ship, he had forbidden his men to misuse women captured at sea—a thoroughly unpiratical rule that had earned him his nickname, "Sir Nicholas." Ruthless enemy of the Royal Navy, plunderer of merchant vessels, chivalrous toward ladies of any rank who fell into his hands.

But this particular lady was different. He couldn't afford to feel chivalrous or anything else toward her. Not if he wanted to keep his neck out of a noose.

Only a handful of prisoners had survived the riot aboard the *Molloch*, the Royal Navy prison hulk that had been his home for eight years. And Nicholas Brogan was the most infamous. He was bloody well certain the authorities would know the ship's name, if ever Miss Delafield had the chance to describe the brand to them.

And he could just picture her doing so. Especially if it would save her own pretty neck. *It was a pitchfork, your honorable lordships, burned right over his heart, with three prongs, pointing downward. I'm willing to testify, if you could find it in your mercy to drop the charges against me . . .*

Aye, she would do it. In the wink of one of her lovely eyes. Just as she had tried to sacrifice him to save herself last night, in gaol.

Clenching his jaw, he lifted his gaze to her once more, muttering oaths under his breath. It was bad enough that he had to consider her fate while they were chained together; now he also had to consider her fate once they managed to get the chain off. He cursed the wound and the weakness that had made him too slow in buttoning his blasted shirt.

But most of all, he cursed God for throwing her into his path. For placing an innocent at the mercy of a soulless animal.

For forcing him to make a choice he did not want to make.

A surge of hot, bitter guilt choked him. He blinked hard, seeing again the image that tormented him so often: of a young boy's accusing eyes ... of that innocent face in the midst of a blazing, sinking pirate ship ... of the pistol shot that rang out, echoing through his memory again and again.

After that night, he had vowed to never take another life. He had dared hope that six years as a law-abiding citizen might have changed him.

But that hope had died today with Swinton and Leach, had been left shattered in the clearing with their broken bodies. The beast within him hadn't been conquered; it had merely been lying dormant. Waiting for a chance to leap forth and kill again. Blindly. Mindlessly.

He could not control his violent nature. Couldn't trust himself.

And now he was wearing a pistol again. Tucked neatly into his belt at his back. Already, it had become such a natural part of him that he barely even noticed it.

A man like him, he thought with a bitter glance heavenward, shouldn't be allowed within a hundred miles of anything or anyone innocent.

Miss Delafield came to a sudden halt in front of him, freezing like a startled deer. "Look!" she whispered, pointing into the distance. "What is that?"

Nicholas stopped beside her, trying to throttle his chaotic thoughts, squinting into the shadows. "I don't see—"

He saw it before he could finish the sentence. Several yards ahead on the left. A flash of light that winked on and then off.

"Damnation." He grabbed the girl, yanking her with him as he jumped behind a fat evergreen, the chain clattering.

Had it been a lantern? A torch? Could their pursuers **have** closed in already? Burrowed deep into the prickly **branches**, he waited for a shout or a gunshot. He could **feel** the girl trembling beside him, her shoulder pressed against his.

But he heard nothing. Not so much as a single footfall. After a moment, he chanced a quick look, glancing at the spot where the light had appeared. And he saw it again.

But this time he realized what it was. "It's nothing." He heard the relief in his own voice. "Just a ray of sunlight striking some sort of glass."

"Glass?" she whispered. "What sort of glass could there be out here in the middle of Cannock Chase?"

"I intend to find out. You stay here and I'll—" He cut himself off, realizing the order he had started to give was impossible.

"Wherever you go, I go, remember?" she asked dryly, moving her foot to rattle the chain.

How could he have forgotten?

Easily, he thought with a rueful grimace. It was damned contrary to his nature—not to mention bloody inconvenient—to be one half of a pair. "Let's at least try to keep it quiet, your ladyship." Crouching down, he stepped out of the evergreen.

Then slowly, cautiously, together, they moved in for a closer look.

Chapter 8

⟨~~~∽◯◯∽~~~⟩

Only when they came within a few yards of the unsteady light did Nicholas realize what he was looking at. The glass was part of a window, in a structure of some kind, so well-hidden by fallen trees and underbrush that its walls appeared to be part of the forest itself.

He chose a vantage point behind a nearby stand of bushes, drawing Miss Delafield down with him as he hunched over to study the place. "A woodsman's cabin, perhaps." He kept his voice barely audible. "Or a criminal's hideout."

"Do you think it's . . . occupied?"

Nicholas didn't answer at first. He weighed the risks of encountering the occupants against the lure of shelter, a place to rest for the night, perhaps even food. "No one seems to have noticed us yet. And God knows we've made enough noise." He shot a glare at the chain.

"Well then . . ." She bit her bottom lip, eyes on the cabin. "I say let's go and see what's inside. I'm tired and thirsty and starving and . . ." She gave up trying to speak, shaking her head with a weary sigh. ". . . tired."

That one word seemed to sum up the entire accursed day. Even in the deepening forest shadows, Nicholas could see the strain on her pale, dirt-smudged features,

95

noticed that the stubborn set to her chin, the determined stiffness in her spine had all but disappeared. He felt just as exhausted. Their pace had slowed to a weary trudge; they wouldn't get any further before nightfall. Couldn't.

And whatever—or whoever—waited inside the cabin couldn't be much worse than what they'd already encountered this day.

Reaching behind him, he drew the pistol tucked into the waistband of his breeches. There was no sense trying to do this politely. No chance of passing themselves off as travelers lost in the forest. Not with both of them dressed in ripped clothes, covered with blood, and chained together.

"Follow me, Miss Delafield," he whispered, focusing his gaze on the ramshackle cottage.

"You're not going to shoot anyone, are you?"

He hesitated a moment, asking himself the same question. "Not unless they shoot at me first."

Rising in a half-crouch, he began inching forward. The girl picked up the chain to keep it from dragging noisily between them. As they crept closer, Nicholas found himself struck by an eerie sense of how familiar it felt—sneaking up on some unsuspecting target, a pistol in his hand, a fellow outlaw by his side.

Though this was the first time that the fellow had ever been a female.

It took only seconds to reach a fallen tree a few paces from the door. They knelt behind the trunk, side by side, waiting. Listening. All he could hear was his rough breathing, and hers.

He didn't hear or see any sign of life in the cabin. No firelight. No smoke. No movement. From what he could make out in the last glimmers of daylight, it looked unoccupied.

Constructed of hand-hewn wood instead of the usual wattle-and-daub used by peasants, the place boasted riches that didn't belong here in the murky depths of

Cannock Chase: a thatched roof, a solid-looking door with iron fittings, glass windows, now cracked and broken. Perhaps some foolish nobleman in a past century had built it as a hunting cottage.

Whatever the intended purpose, it looked as though the little shelter had been abandoned for years. The forest had almost reclaimed it. Ivy and other greenery dripped down the roof and clung to the walls, competing with grass and weeds that rose in a tangle two feet high even in front of the door.

Still, the air of abandonment might have been created by guile rather than by chance; he had the distinct impression that the concealing trees on two sides had been felled not by nature, but by man.

By a man who had reason to hide.

Nicholas cocked the pistol and turned to look at his fellow outlaw. She was trembling, her quick, shallow breathing making her lace-trimmed bodice rise and fall rapidly, but she clenched her jaw and nodded, urging him to proceed.

The lady had guts, he had to give her that. She might be one stubborn, aristocratic pain in the arse, but she had guts.

Rising, he ducked around the fallen tree and led the way to the door. Swiftly. Stealthily. Take the opponent by surprise and minimize casualties.

It all felt hauntingly familiar.

They reached the door. He lifted the latch. Hinges creaked as he pushed at it and then he was inside, dropping back from the spill of light, pistol sweeping the interior in a single smooth arc.

An animal's screech split the air. Something small and furry exploded out of a corner.

"A wolf!" the girl shrieked, flattening herself against the door jamb as the creature darted past her.

Chuckling, Nicholas flicked the safety on the gun, satisfied that they had just chased out the only occupant. "That, Miss Delafield, was a squirrel."

She unglued herself from the wall. The waning light slanting in through the open door and cracked glass windows illuminated twin spots of color high in her cheeks. "That was no squirrel," she insisted archly, dusting off her sleeves.

"Fine, a wolf." Looking around the cabin, he couldn't subdue a grin. "Smallest wolf in the history of England."

She muttered something unladylike under her breath and changed the subject. "This place is much larger than it looked from outside."

Returning the pistol to his waistband, Nicholas nodded as he studied their surroundings. Whether woodsman or noble, the previous owner had outfitted the place with all the comforts a man could ask, though the fine furnishings were now buried beneath layers of dirt, cobwebs, and scattered leaves that had blown in through the broken windows.

A table and chairs with curving, spindly legs filled one corner, beneath a rack that held dangling iron pots, a kettle, cooking implements. A brick hearth took up most of the adjoining wall, and a trio of fishing poles had been left leaning against the mantel, amid a jumble of baskets and woven fishing creels on the floor.

Most appealing of all was the bed opposite the hearth, made of hand-hewn wood topped with a fat straw mattress and moth-eaten blanket. A four-poster draped with silk in a Grosvenor Square boudoir couldn't have looked more welcoming at the moment.

Resisting the urge to sink down on the bed and slip into unconsciousness, Nicholas turned his attention to a cupboard on the wall beside the door. A locked cupboard.

"I wonder what was so important that he had to lock it up," he murmured, moving toward it, the girl trailing along, shackles jangling.

"I could—" She sneezed, waving a hand in front of her face to ward off the dust particles that spun around them in a musty whirlwind. "I could probably open the lock."

"Right." Nicholas chuckled. "With what? Your magic needle?" He yanked on the cupboard door, coughing when he got a faceful of dust for his efforts. Despite its age, the lock didn't give. "Damn."

His companion had already turned her attention to the dark corner next to the cupboard. "*Food,*" she breathed, lunging in that direction.

Nicholas felt the tug on his ankle and gave in for the moment, following her. Now that his eyes had adjusted to the darkness, he noticed a set of corner shelves that held a collection of dust-covered jars, all the same size.

She grabbed one. "Oh, please let it be something to eat." The jar appeared to hold some sort of thick liquid. She tugged at the lid.

"Hold on, your ladyship," he warned. "There's no way to know what the devil is in there—"

"I don't care as long as it's edible." Her stomach growled noisily as if on cue. Struggling with the lid, she shot him an accusing look. "At least *you* arrived at the gaol last night in time for supper. Which you didn't deign to share."

He remembered enjoying his meal shamelessly, the way he had teased her by licking his fingers one by one. "I pride myself on timing." Taking the jar from her hands, he unfastened the lid, lifted it, and took a sniff.

A breeze drifted through one of the cabin's windows and caught the jar's sweet aroma, the scent overpowering in the stale air.

"Honey!" she said ecstatically. "Perhaps this was some sort of beekeeper's cottage."

He was about to replace the lid when she reached over and dipped two fingers into the jar, lifting a drippy, golden mass of the sweet liquid to her mouth. Closing her lips around her fingers, she suckled, utter-

ing a sigh that turned into a moan, her lashes drifting
downward.

Nicholas froze, the cabin dissolving from his vision,
the open jar almost sliding from his fingers. All exhaustion and pain faded from his consciousness and he
could only see, hear, feel the image before him: her lips,
her soft moan of pleasure, his heart suddenly beating
too hard, a blaze of heat burning through his body,
tightening every muscle below his belt.

He had to shut his eyes, struggled to breathe. She
had acted out of hunger, not seductiveness. She didn't
even realize the effect she had on him. Didn't know
that she had just taken vengeance for the way he had
tormented her last night.

Complete, swift, painful vengeance.

He managed to open his eyes at last, but she hadn't
noticed his distress. Her golden gaze bright, she was
looking at the shelf. "I wonder if he kept any other
foods here besides honey."

"Maybe a nice roast beef." Nicholas shoved the jar
and lid into her hands. "We can search later. I want to
look around outside while there's still enough light."

He turned on his heel. Not arguing for once, she followed him out the door, content with her jar of honey
for the moment.

The jangling chain and the sound of her licking her
fingers played on his nerves as he walked the perimeter
of the cottage. He tried to block her tantalizing little
sighs from his mind, examining the shelter with an eye
to security.

Someone at some point had artfully concealed the
place with brush, branches, and those carefully felled
trees. He doubted any beekeeper would've gone to
such trouble. The cottage had clearly been used as a
hiding place, probably by some previous outlaw. He
wondered briefly what had become of the fellow, then
told himself he didn't want to know.

The important point was, a lone man or even a group

could walk right past the place and never see it. If not for the sunlight striking the windows, he certainly would have missed it.

Actually, he reminded himself, he *had* missed it. Miss Delafield had spotted the cottage. His normally sharp gaze had been focused elsewhere at the time.

On a rather lovely derriere.

He stalked around the corner of the cottage, clenching his jaw, annoyed by the way his mind kept circling back to that subject.

"Sunrise and sunset will be the most dangerous." He spoke the thought aloud, trying to distract himself. "But I can cover the glass with something to keep the sun from reflecting off it. Once that's done, and provided you keep quiet, I can go completely unnoticed here."

"*We*," she corrected absently, still eating.

He shrugged, then regretted it when his shoulder burned like the devil. At the rear of the cottage, he stopped, satisfied with his perusal. He—*they*—had a secure place to sleep for the night. That was all that mattered at the moment.

Unfortunately, he couldn't afford to rest here any longer than one night—not if he was going to arrive in York in time for a certain pressing appointment.

The waning daylight glinted off something metallic in the shadows behind the cottage and he stepped closer to investigate. It was an axe, left imbedded in a stump next to a stack of firewood.

"That might prove useful," he murmured, grabbing the smooth handle. He jerked the axe loose and ran an appreciative hand along the blade; it was still sharp, despite having been left out in the elements for months. He glanced at his companion.

She had already finished half the jar of honey. Looking up, she blinked at him, as if only now realizing how oblivious she'd been to him and to everything for the last five minutes. "Useful?" she asked uneasily, her gaze sliding down to the axe in his hand. "Useful for what?"

He looked at the chain stretched between them, and a hopeful grin tugged at his mouth. "Stand very still, Miss Delafield."

He hefted the axe with a quick, forceful movement and struck the chain—and she jumped despite his warning.

But the glancing blow only earned him a jolt of agony across his shoulders. With a scrape of metal on metal, the axe blade bent. Though it wasn't rusted, it wasn't up to the job.

The accursed chain remained solid. Untouched. Unbreakable.

"Damn," he growled. He really *would* need a blacksmith to get the blasted thing off. He tossed the axe into the woodpile. Turning, he started to lead the way back inside.

"Wait," she protested, lagging behind. "I have to . . . I . . ."

He stopped and turned to face her. "What is it now?"

The day's last light chose that moment to vanish, leaving them in the gray darkness of early evening.

"It's . . . I . . . that is . . ." She sighed, made an uncomfortable little grumble, and he could hear her putting the lid back on the jar. Her tone abruptly became brisk. "We've been on the move all day and there hasn't been time to . . . to . . . heed the call of nature."

She said the last five words all in a rush, so quick it took him a minute to decipher what she had said.

"Oh." He shook his head, not sure whether he was amused or annoyed. He wasn't used to considering anyone else's needs but his own. And he certainly had no experience in considering the delicate sensibilities of a woman.

It was damned inconvenient.

When he didn't say anything more, she filled the silence with another rush of words. "There's a deep thicket right there." If she was pointing, he couldn't see. "And a rain barrel in the corner where I could wash off some of this grime and mud. I thought if you could . . . I mean . . . perhaps give me a bit of privacy."

Her maidenly nervousness and innocence kept taking him by surprise. Perhaps because they seemed so at odds with everything else about her. "That's going to be rather difficult." He moved his foot, rattling the chain just as she had done earlier.

He could practically hear her turning scarlet. "Well, you don't have to make this any more difficult than it already is. We need to face facts here. I've waited as long as I can, and at least it's dark out now and—"

"Enough, your ladyship." He held up a hand, willing to do anything at the moment to stop her from arguing. All he wanted was to go back inside, fall into the cabin's moth-eaten bed, and sleep. "Go and take a few minutes for your evening toilette. I'll try to avoid intruding upon your feminine sensibilities."

He let her lead the way to the thicket. He even turned his back. Not that her feelings mattered to him in the least, of course; he merely wanted to avoid any further argument.

He couldn't, however, resist one last quip.

"Be careful," he advised quietly, grinning. "Might be a wolf hiding in there."

An hour later, he had yet to get anywhere near the bed.

Darkness cloaked the interior of the cabin, not even a splinter of moonlight breaking through the woolen blankets he had tacked up over the windows. Only the flickering glow of a single stubby candle, burning in the center of the table, illuminated their meager supper.

His chair leaned back against the wall, Nicholas bit off one last mouthful of salt beef, lifted the bottle in his hand, and took a long swallow of whiskey. He let its heat spread through him, dulling the pain in his shoulder.

Miss Delafield had indeed managed to open the lock on the cupboard. It seemed needles weren't all she carried in her needle case; a specialized lock pick nestled in there amongst her lacemaking tools.

The cupboard hadn't contained any *roast* beef, but it had offered up some *salt* beef. Along with smoked pork, a sack of sugar and another of coffee, some raisins and dried figs, a variety of jellies and marmalades sealed in tins, three small wheels of cheese preserved beneath heavy layers of wax and enclosed in round wooden boxes, a bag of hard peppermint candies, and a basket of nuts.

Not to mention two bottles of aged Scots whiskey.

And a tightly sealed box filled with biscuits. Which were tough as hardtack and a little green around the edges, but he was willing to overlook that. Hell, he had lived on biscuits like these for years at sea.

All in all, it made a banquet fit for a fugitive.

Or rather two fugitives, he reminded himself.

He set the bottle on the table, wiped his mouth with the back of his hand, and wolfed down another biscuit. Miss Delafield flashed him a frown.

All evening, her displeasure had been clear even in the dim light; she didn't approve of the whiskey, the biscuits, or his table manners. She sat across the table from him—as far away as the chain would allow—and daintily dipped pieces of smoked pork in an open jar of honey.

Nibbling at one, she studiously ignored the way he was picking his teeth with a splinter of wood that he had chipped out of the table. "I still say we might risk a *small* fire in the hearth," she suggested.

"I'm not going to swing at Tyburn just because you want some coffee." Nicholas jerked his head toward the door. "I have no intention of alerting every lawman out there."

She looked up. "You think they are?" she asked uneasily. "Out there, I mean. Already?"

He paused a moment, watching the candle's glow warm her pale, freshly scrubbed features. Then he flicked the splinter of wood to the floor. "Aye," he confirmed quietly.

She glanced down at her meal, silent. And didn't eat any more.

Apparently she'd lost her appetite. He picked up another biscuit from the pile in the center of the table, gulped it down in three bites, and followed it with a long swallow from the bottle. She didn't ask what made him so certain about their pursuers. He wasn't sure he could explain if she did.

All he knew was that he could feel them out there. Marshalmen and thief-takers, fanning out through the forest, hungry for blood and bounties. He could feel them with every throbbing ache in his wounded shoulder. With the certainty of a man who'd been hunted for years.

Too many years.

He shoved that thought aside. He didn't want to live that way again. Wouldn't. If all went as planned, within a fortnight he'd be finished with his business in York and he'd never have to run again. He'd be free.

The trouble was, nothing had gone as planned since he set foot back on English soil.

Miss Delafield put the lid back on the jar of honey, then dabbed at her lips with a serviette she had improvised from another piece of her petticoat.

Nicholas watched her with amusement. There couldn't be much left of that petticoat.

He instantly regretted the thought. Because it led him straight to an image of her legs. Long, pale, silky . . . and almost bare now beneath her skirt.

His throat went dry. His hand tightened around the bottle of whiskey and his body suddenly felt too hot. She remained blithely unaware of his discomfort, neatly tying shut the sack of dried beef, sweeping nut-shells off the table with her hand, closing the box of biscuits.

His gaze followed her every move, lingering over her smooth skin, her slender fingers. During her toilette outside, she had washed with water from the rain bar-rel, scrubbing away the day's sweat and mud, and now she almost seemed to glow in the candlelight, warm and fresh and golden.

Tangles of damp hair clung to her neck ... and her bodice, the long strands curling around the soft femi-nine swell hidden by gown and corset. He suddenly longed to reach out, cup her in his hand, feel the del-icate textures of her hair, the silk, the warm curve of her breast against his palm—

He wrenched his thoughts back to reality, clutching the bottle tighter, clenching his other hand into a fist. He willed the mad impulse away. Damnation, it felt like he'd been knocked on the head with a belaying pin. Thrown overboard. Like he was drowning in an ocean too deep to fathom.

He blamed it all on exhaustion and pain; that was the only rational explanation for the way his thoughts kept careening out of control.

Miss Delafield stood, reaching across the table to gather up the sacks and baskets. "We can't carry all of this with us. I suppose we might as well put some of it back for whoever else might happen along."

She seemed oblivious to his torment. As always. "How thoughtful of you," he said caustically.

She shot him a frown, but he was already getting to his feet, welcoming whatever distraction he could get at the moment. He followed her over to the cupboard, carrying the bottle with him.

He thought it best to keep his hands full.

When they reached the cupboard, he leaned his un-injured shoulder against the wall and watched her re-place the leftover foods neatly on the shelves. The complicated lock that she had opened earlier still dangled from the latch on the cupboard door. He plucked it free with his left hand. "You picked this monster pretty easily, Miss Delafield. Like you've done it before. Frequently."

She glanced at him and on this side of the room, so far from the single candle, there was just enough light to make out a gleam in her eye. A sharp look that held both affront and accusation. Somehow he sensed what she was thinking: when they had first approached the cottage, he had led the attack with gun drawn, coolly, easily. As if he'd done it before. Frequently.

She might be thinking that, but she didn't say it.

Interesting, he thought with a growing, grudging sense of what he couldn't believe was respect—the lady not only had guts, she was smart as well. Smart enough to know when to hold her tongue.

She turned back to her work. "I'm good at what I do."

She said it simply, tonelessly. Without pride. Without apology.

Without any emotion at all.

He lifted the bottle and took a long swallow of whiskey, watching her as she closed the cupboard door. "How did you come to be a thief?"

The words spilled out before he could stop them. Too late, he realized that the liquor was not only dulling the pain in his shoulder but loosening his tongue. He didn't want to venture into these waters; didn't want to know a thing about her. Didn't want to think about her any more than he already did.

Her hand still on the cupboard door, she turned to stare at him. He stared back, almost as surprised as she was. Curiosity about another person was utterly unlike him. He had kept to himself, thought only of himself for years. Decades.

But, he reasoned a moment later, he *needed* to find out all he could about Miss Delafield. She had seen the brand, knew one of his most carefully kept secrets. He had to evaluate just how much of a threat she might be.

"How did you come to be a thief?" he repeated quietly, casually.

He thought she might tell him to go to hell.

Instead, she told him something else entirely.

"There weren't any other choices available." She shrugged and finished closing the cupboard, locked it.

He all but snorted in disbelief. "There are always choices for women like you."

She turned to face him. "Really? And what sort of woman am I?"

"Well-born. Cultured." *Beautiful.* He avoided adding the word *beautiful.*

The smile that curved her mouth held equal parts derision and irony. "Yes, I suppose most people assume that." She crossed her arms under her breasts, her hands clenched into fists. "But I'm living proof that being well-born doesn't guarantee anything."

"So why turn to theft? I thought you were a seamstress." He avoided glancing at the pendant that rested between her breasts.

"There aren't any positions available these days, except among the aristocracy in London, and I . . . had to leave London," she said cautiously. "Rather suddenly. Several years ago. I won't go back."

Standing there in the flickering candlelight, chin raised, she looked very small and vulnerable and defiant. He thought her too naive and trusting for telling him so much. For telling him anything.

And he urged her to tell him more. "There had to be safer ways to earn a living."

"You mean as a governess or servant? One needs references for that." She shook her head. "I didn't set out to become a thief. I didn't *choose* this life."

She turned away abruptly only to be brought up short by the chain. If she had thought to flee, it was futile; she couldn't even take another step unless he moved.

And he didn't move. He still leaned against the wall, waiting.

Beneath that cascade of tawny hair, her shoulders rose and fell rapidly. After a moment, she lowered her head, staring at the floor. "I didn't . . . have anything. Not even a shilling. I tried to find work. I tried." Her arms tightened around her waist, her voice falling to a whisper. "And I was so hungry."

Nicholas didn't say a word. Couldn't. The strangest, most unfamiliar feeling crept through his midsection and he couldn't do anything but stare at her straight, stiff back.

He'd felt that same hunger and fear, as a boy.

"Then one day I stole some food from a vendor's cart. It wasn't much. An apple and a loaf of bread. I ate it all in a few bites." She tilted her head back, looking up into the darkness. "But I was so scared I threw up."

She laughed—a harsh laugh that sounded like it must hurt her throat.

Then she continued, with an almost eerie calm. "The second time, it became a little easier. And the third time . . . and the fourth." She turned to face him again, the defiance returning to her expression. "Because it felt good not to be hungry. It felt *good*. That's how I became a thief." Her breathing returned to normal, though her fists were still clenched. "And there's something else. I learned a long time ago that there are two kinds of people in this world—predators and prey." She looked straight into his eyes. "I was the latter once, for too long. I won't be again. Ever."

It sounded like a warning. That he was facing not prey, but a fellow predator.

The threat made the unpleasant, squishy sensation in his gut evaporate. "When you first found yourself in trouble, why didn't you choose the most obvious means of support?" he demanded sarcastically.

She shook her head, not understanding.

"The one most women choose. Marriage."

She laughed again. "I didn't receive any offers of that sort. Plenty of less savory offers, but no honorable ones. Men from the circles I grew up in wouldn't think of marrying a woman like me."

That surprised him more than anything else she had said. "And what sort of woman are you?" He fired her earlier question back at her.

Her cheeks reddened, whether with suppressed fury or something else he couldn't tell. "Tired," she said flatly, her voice devoid of emotion. "I'm a tired woman. And it's late and all I want to do is go to sleep."

He stared at her a moment longer, then nodded, sensing he wouldn't learn anything more tonight. The full weight of his own fatigue pressed down on him stronger than ever. "We'll leave at daybreak."

He turned and led the way back to the table, where he corked the bottle. Bending down, he tucked it into the pack of provisions he had secured earlier; he had taken one of the fishing creels and loaded it with foodstuffs and a few useful items scrounged from the cabin's shelves. A length of rope woven through the top and bottom of the creel would allow him to carry it on his back, while leaving his hands free. He checked the sheepshank knots he had secured it with.

"Where exactly *are* we going?" she asked, meeting his gaze as he rose. "You haven't just been running through the woods randomly. You're going in a specific direction. Where?"

"You have a pressing appointment?"

"I just want to get to my room in—" She cut herself off, her eyes narrowing warily. "I want to get home. I need to go there to . . . get my things. So I can leave England. There won't be anywhere in the country that's safe for me now. Not with the law after me."

"Well, Miss Delafield, I'm afraid that unless your room is in York, you're once again out of luck." He reached down to the table and picked up the candle. "I have a pressing matter of business there and I don't have time for side trips."

"York?" she sputtered. "But that's the opposite direction from—" She stopped herself again. "I don't want to go to York. And I have no guarantee that something won't happen to me when we get there. Or long before."

"You also have no choice," he reminded her, moving his foot until the chain pulled taut between them. "And unless you want a rematch of our wrestle in the woods, you'll accept that I'm in charge and do as I say until I can get us safely to a blacksmith."

Some part of him—*damn* him—hoped she would opt for another round of wrestling. Though it would be different this time.

The thought of just how different he would make it heated his blood.

But the fury emanating from her slender form was far hotter. "I do *not* care for the way you keep making all the decisions."

"Too bad. Get used to it." He walked over to the bed, slipped his pistol from his back, and laid it carefully on the floor close at hand. He placed the candle beside it. Then he sat on the mattress with a weary sigh. "Get some sleep, your ladyship. We have a lot of ground to cover on the morrow."

She was silent for a moment.

But only for a moment, unfortunately.

"And where am *I* supposed to sleep?" she asked indignantly. "On the floor?"

Something small and mouselike scrabbled across the hearth, the sound of its claws terribly loud in the night.

"Wouldn't recommend it," he said dryly.

He could hear her breathing, rapid and shallow. "A gentleman would let me have the bed."

"Unfortunately for you there's not a gentleman to be found for—oh, I would wager, at least a hundred miles. *I* have no intention of giving up the bed. You can share it or take the floor." Leaning down, he extinguished the candle wick between his thumb and forefinger, plunging them into darkness. "The choice, Miss Delafield, is yours."

Chapter 9

Samantha lay on her side atop the covers, clinging to the very edge of the bed. Her stomach felt like knotted fire. All her senses had become unnaturally, uncomfortably sharp; the cabin's utter blackness rendered her blind, which intensified every sound, every scent, every second of time that dragged past.

Her breath came fast and shallow as she waited for the man next to her—just inches away—to fall asleep.

She could *feel* him watching her in the darkness. Could feel his cold, hard gaze tracing over her shoulders and back. Or was that only her imagination? Perhaps he was asleep. Perhaps he had slipped into unconsciousness some time ago.

Yet he hadn't moved, not from the moment she had climbed into the bed, more than half an hour ago.

At least it *felt* like half an hour. Had it been only minutes? She could hear his breathing, as unsteady as hers. Every inhalation and exhalation sounded deafening in the stillness.

He shifted his weight, and she heard not only the creak of the bed ropes but the soft rustle of his garments against the rough blanket. She could feel the heat of his body radiating toward her. And his scent—a spicy, heavy muskiness mixed with the freshness of the rainwater he had splashed himself with earlier. He seemed to fill the very air she breathed.

Blast the man! She shut her eyes, tried to shut him out. Tried to stop trembling. How was it that he managed to play on her nerves without even saying a word?

She silently cursed the rogue for keeping her awake. After everything she had endured this day—after being carted through the steaming countryside, thrown down a hill, shot at, and run ragged by this madman chained to her ankle—she should be dead to the world by now. Every bone, every muscle, every bruised and aching inch of her body cried out for the healing relief of unconsciousness.

She tried to tell herself there was no reason to feel tense. He hadn't made any move toward her. Hadn't so much as touched a single hair on her head.

Still, her fingers tightened reflexively around the knife in her right hand. She had quietly slipped it from her skirt pocket before getting into bed. The hilt felt cold and solid and at least a little reassuring against her palm.

But she couldn't relax. Thoughts kept whirling through her head.

Thoughts of her unpredictable companion.

But he couldn't be much of a threat at the moment, could he? After all, he had been bruised, battered, shot at, and run ragged today too. Not to mention the fact that he'd been wounded, lost a great deal of blood, and had a bullet dug out of his shoulder. He was hardly in any shape to . . . to . . .

She opened her eyes again. Her stomach felt queasy. Her head was spinning. Perhaps it was all the honey she had eaten earlier, but she didn't think so.

It was the fact that she had never slept beside a man before. Ever.

If not for the accursed shackles, she wouldn't be sleeping beside one now. The chain wouldn't reach far enough for her to sleep on the floor. She had tried. Then she had suggested rolling up the blanket and placing it between them, but he had only laughed at her again.

Blackguard.

Staring into the darkness, she knew it was ridiculous to think that a blanket would protect her virtue. If he wanted to make any unsavory advances, a tattered length of wool wouldn't stop him.

Nothing would stop him.

She clutched the knife tighter as the old images sprang to mind unbidden, clawing their way out of the darkest reaches of her memory. Images of what men did to women.

Her throat closed off. She couldn't seem to breathe. She dug her fingers into the wooden side of the bed, struggling to hang on, to force back the visions of blood and terror. But they only became stronger, more vivid. *The outlaws yelling, grunting with lust as they thrust into the helpless maidservants, again and again, the girls fighting, screaming . . . screaming . . .*

The screams tore through her head.

And the cold blade of another memory sliced through her. Of a place where she had thought herself safe. Of a night when the lock on her door hadn't been enough to protect her, when her Uncle Prescott had forced his way inside, had very nearly . . .

No. Digging her nails into her palm, she forced herself to forget, forced the fear away. Uncle Prescott was in London. She would never let him close enough to have another chance to hurt her. She would never let *any* man near her.

If the rogue so much as touched her, she would fight to her dying breath.

She wasn't a naive girl of sixteen anymore. She was older, wiser, armed with the truth about men and their lust. Armed with a knife—and the many tricks she had learned while living in the streets for six years. She could protect herself.

Gradually, her breathing slowed as the old memories

and the fear they brought began to recede.

Closing her eyes for the third time in the past hour, she tried to put all the troubling thoughts aside, tried to find the sleep she so desperately needed. But the late summer heat made the cabin sultry, even in the darkness, and no breeze, not even a whisper of fresh air, managed to slip through the fabric tacked over the windows. The uncomfortable warmth made her all the more aware of the smooth, cool blade clutched in her hand.

And the rough iron shackle around her ankle, binding her to this man.

Just when she despaired of ever getting a moment's rest, a soft sound came from behind her.

A snore.

Finally! The object of all her worry and dread was peacefully asleep. She frowned, not sure which she felt more—resentment or relief. For the moment at least, she could relax her guard.

Still, she could sense his large, male presence so close. Too close. By all the graces, when she awoke this morning, she had certainly never expected to end the day in bed with a man!

A man whose name she didn't even know. A dark stranger with cold eyes that had seen too much and hands that could kill far too easily.

She shivered despite the summery heat. The sooner she got away from him, the happier she would be. They would find some way to get the shackles off. They had to. And then she would go straight to her flat in Merseyside, grab her hidden cache of money, and leave the country.

For six years she had saved every shilling she made; whenever she finished her work in a particular district, she visited Merseyside and added to her stash. Two hundred pounds wasn't much to show for all the risks she had taken as an outlaw.

And it wasn't nearly enough to get her where she *really* wanted to go.

But it would be enough for passage to one of the colonies. Or perhaps France. She would just have to be practical. Settle for what she had. As before, as so often in her life, the choice wasn't hers to make; it had been made for her. She had to leave England as quickly as possible. Marshalmen had been killed, and the law wouldn't rest until the culprits had been tracked down.

She had to run and keep running and just be grateful that she was still alive.

Exhaustion—or perhaps it was despair—began to pull her downward toward unconsciousness, and she finally let it take her. But even as her eyes drifted closed, she wondered whether she would ever find peace.

Would she ever be safe? Would she ever be able to stop running?

A moment later her muscles began to go slack.

And when the knife slid from her hand and hit the dirt floor with a soft thud, the sound did not wake her.

Nicholas groaned, pulled awake by pain . . . and by a soft scent nearby, like sun and rain, like delicate honey sweetness and lush earth.

Her scent.

Opening his eyes, he found himself unable to see her or anything else. Impenetrable darkness still filled the cabin. How long had he been asleep? A couple of hours? All night?

He lifted his head, shifted his weight—and instantly regretted it, gritting his teeth to bite back a curse as pain burned a hole straight through his shoulder. By *hell*, it felt worse than before. Probably because his muscles were stiff from a night on the thin mattress.

At least he hoped that was why.

He lay down again, settling into the same position, on his side. He hadn't been able to sleep on his back or stomach, not without some part of him touching some part of Miss Delafield, which seemed guaranteed to send her into fits. Having endured enough of her sharp tongue for one day, he hadn't broached the possibility.

The lady had the damndest knack for causing him pain and suffering, he thought with a glare in her direction. Sometimes she managed it without even trying.

After a moment, the fiery agony in his shoulder subsided to a dull throbbing, provided he remained still. So he did his best to remain still. Dawn would come soon enough, and he would have no rest after that; better to steal as much of it as possible before then.

He lay listening to a breeze that rattled the cabin's broken windows, to the rustling of the trees outside . . . to the soft breathing of the woman beside him.

He scowled at the way she reclaimed his attention so easily. Obviously he had been without a female for far too long. That was the only logical reason for this one to seize his awareness like a grappling hook digging into a ship's deck.

He clearly couldn't allow his thoughts to drift, since they seemed to keep drifting in one direction. Annoyed, he resolutely turned his mind to a more useful purpose: the puzzle he had been trying to unravel for weeks now.

Who the devil was blackmailing him?

He had lain awake more nights than he cared to count trying to find an answer to that. But now it seemed more pressing than before—because the blackmailer was closer than before. Whoever the bastard was, he was here, in England, at this very moment. Somewhere.

But who?

Nicholas could name a score of enemies who had once wanted him dead, but most of them were six feet under. Including his two most hated adversaries, Eldridge and Wakefield, the men he had sought vengeance against for fourteen years. They were burning in Hell. Sent there by his hand.

And anyone who knew him, even his enemies, would know that he didn't have fifteen thousand pounds. In fact, anyone even passingly familiar with the realities of piracy would know that.

So it had to be an outsider, a stranger, someone either so naive he didn't realize that Captain Brogan might show up to silence him . . .

Or so powerful and protected that he didn't care.

Perhaps, as Manu had said, it was someone *hoping* Captain Brogan would show up.

Which led Nicholas right back to the beginning: if it was a ruse, a trap, it could be anyone. Anyone.

He stared into the darkness, willing an answer to come, only to find more questions instead.

If this cove wanted his blood, why go to the trouble of blackmail? Why not just come to South Carolina and kill him? Why alert the quarry that someone was on the hunt? Merely for sport?

What kind of twisted mind was he up against?

Unfortunately, that didn't narrow it down at all; he had known his share of twisted minds in his day.

Who was it? Who the devil *was* it?

Frustration and impatience roiled deep in his gut, tormenting him as much as his wounded shoulder. The hell of it was, deep down he knew that he would get no answers. Not until he reached the pub in York.

If he could get there—traveling on foot, wounded, chained to a stubborn female, with half the lawmen in England hot on his trail . . .

And he had to get there by September twenty-ninth. Which gave him a little less than a fortnight. He'd been in England four days now. At least he thought he had; it was all starting to blur together in his mind.

He grimaced. If he were a gambling man, he wouldn't bet a single shilling in his favor. Not even a counterfeit shilling. The odds were a hundred to one at best.

Then again, he wasn't a gambling man. Never had been.

What he was was a washed-up ex-pirate. With nothing to lose.

At that thought, his grimace slowly curved into a sardonic grin. To hell with the odds.

He rolled onto his back, deciding that Miss Delafield's delicate sensibilities could go to hell too. More important matters demanded his attention. Like the fact that if his muscles stiffened up any further, the injury would slow him down come daybreak—and he and his charming companion would find themselves in more trouble than they needed. He would barely be able to walk, never mind run, much less carry the heavy pack of supplies.

A wave of hot needles stabbed down his back and arm as he moved, but he shifted his weight until he found a relatively comfortable position, easing his shoulder up onto the pillow.

He closed his eyes and let his body go slack, gingerly flexing his arm until the stiffness and burning ebbed. The wound still pained him and would for some time, but he could live with that.

However, the bed was so narrow that his right shoulder, arm, and side now pressed against the girl's back . . . and he wasn't sure she could live with that. He half-expected her to jump to her feet, cursing him.

Instead, she remained deeply asleep, her breathing slow and even, her body warm against his.

Warm . . . and soft. Softer even than the honey-and-rain scent that clung to her skin. He could almost taste that fragrance with every breath he drew, instinctively turned his face toward it. He could not see her in the darkness, but he could feel her hair, tangled across the pillow, a tickle of silk against his bearded cheek.

At the same time he was aware of the long, sinuous

curve of her spine, the feminine roundness of her buttocks against his hip . . .

The heat pooling in his gut.

An instant later he no longer noticed the ache in his shoulder—because another part of him stiffened swiftly and painfully.

Damnation. He clenched his teeth to stop a groan. His body hadn't responded so quickly since he'd been a randy lad chasing doxies in Jamaica. All it took was one breath of this woman's scent, one brush of her body against his and he was ready for her. Aching to have her. More than he'd ached for any female he'd encountered in his life.

Even fatigue, whiskey, and a bullet wound failed to quell the longing he felt—for a treacherous, troublesome lady thief. A woman who would sooner scratch his eyes out than grant him a single kiss. The feeling made no sense. It was a hunger that went beyond explanation, beyond reason.

So why not satisfy it?

The words shot through his head like a bolt of lightning, unexpected and white-hot, burning him.

Why not ease his hunger? Why not seduce her?

Aye, she was haughty and distant and all but dripped disdain for him. She acted as if merely breathing the same air as him would give her some dreaded disease. Even in sleep, she remained stiff and unyielding.

For all he knew, she might even be a virgin.

But none of those were true obstacles. Not to a man of his experience. He knew what women liked. A smile or two, a couple of caresses, a few words he didn't mean, the right kiss . . . and he'd have her in the palm of his hand. All of her.

So why not?

The heat in his belly began to spread, sizzling through his blood. It had been far too long since he had given in to his natural male needs. Back in South

Carolina, he had only rarely visited the brothels in
Charles Towne, always coupling in the darkness and
leaving before dawn, to prevent anyone from seeing
the mark on his chest that revealed his past.

But he didn't need to conceal the brand from her.
She'd already seen it. With her, he could indulge in
pleasure as he hadn't indulged for years.

His heart began to beat faster, images sweeping
through him like a fever. The two of them together.
That slender body responding to his touch until she
melted in the same fire that seared him. Those ripe, full
lips opening beneath his. The sharp cries of her need.
Or would she utter soft whimpers of pleasure?

He didn't know. Wanted to know. Needed to find
out. All he knew, instinctively, in a way he could not
explain, was that she would be different from any female he'd ever bedded. Never in his life had he dared
contemplate having a woman like this—not only beautiful, but exquisite as fine porcelain. Precious. Perhaps
even untouched.

So why not?

The flames consumed him, need blazing into decision. He lifted his hand to touch her.

Just as dawn slipped in.

Daybreak glimmered around the edges of the windows. He froze, his hand an inch from her cheek. The
meager light barely penetrated the fabric he had tacked
over the glass, illuminating the pitch-dark cabin only
to dusky gray. Yet it struck him like a jarring blow.
Stopped him. Slapped him awake.

He blinked, dazed. What the devil had he been
thinking?

The light carried the answer to the question *why not?*
Because there wasn't time. He had to leave this place.
Run. Stay one step ahead of the law.

As the light grew stronger, it also brought back his
reason. What the *hell* had he been thinking? He
couldn't let himself get distracted. Not even for a min-

ute, never mind hours. He had to keep his mind clear. Concentrate on staying alive.

And bedding her would change things. He'd never met a woman yet who could accept that sex was merely a simple, natural act. They always wanted to turn it into something complicated and "meaningful."

And the last thing he needed right now was more complications.

He could see her in the gray light, a soft outline beside him. So close . . . impossibly far. His body still afire, his hunger unabated, he moved his hand, tracing just one fingertip over her cheek, regretting what could not be.

She jumped as if he'd struck her and came awake in a burst of movement, jamming an elbow backward, straight into his ribs.

He grunted in surprise and pain. She shouted a wordless cry of protest and leaped out of the bed— apparently forgetting for a critical moment that they were shackled together.

The cuff yanked hard against his ankle. Cursing, he stood just as the shackles brought her up short. The chain went taut and she went tumbling. She landed on her shapely backside.

"Don't touch me!" she cried, lashing out with her free foot, trying unsuccessfully to scramble backward. "Stay away!"

"I'm not coming anywhere near you," he assured her in an annoyed growl. "Calm down and—"

"Stay back!" Somehow her little knife had ended up on the floor; she grabbed it and struck out in a swift, slashing arc.

Aiming toward a particularly vulnerable spot.

Dodging the blade, he swore vividly. "That's bloody well enough of that." He reached for her, grabbing her wrist. "What the hell is wrong with you, woman? I wasn't doing a damned thing to hurt you."

"Blackguard. I knew I couldn't trust you!" Rising to

her knees, she struggled against his hold. "Let me go!"

"Just as soon as you stop trying to slice me in half." He squeezed her wrist with expert pressure until she dropped the knife. It clattered to the floor.

"No!" She was sobbing and gasping for breath at the same time, almost hysterical.

"I'm not going to hurt you."

"Don't touch me! I don't want you to touch me!"

Before he could muster any kind of reply that might quiet her, he heard a sound in the distance. From somewhere deep in the woods.

"Shh!" He put his other hand over her mouth and went utterly still, listening.

She kept struggling. His palm smothered what he knew must be a colorful string of epithets.

Then she froze too as the sound grew louder, unmistakable—a pack of hunting dogs, baying in full voice. Coming this way. Straight toward the cabin.

They'd been found.

Chapter 10

Nicholas uttered a short, vicious oath. He instantly released the girl, their argument forgotten in a single pounding beat of his heart. He bent down, scooped up his pistol from beneath the bed, turned on his heel. What else should he take? He grabbed the fishing creel he had packed with supplies.

The girl remained frozen, wide-eyed as the barking of the hounds echoed through the forest. "Maybe they're hunting deer," she suggested tremulously. "Or fox?"

"Hunters only come into Cannock Chase after one kind of prey." He slung the fishing creel over his good shoulder. "Outlaws."

"But we don't know that they're after *us*."

"Do you want to wait here and ask?" He tucked the knife that he had reclaimed from her into his boot. Then he took her arm and tugged her to her feet. "*Move*, your ladyship."

The chain rattled against the floorboards as he hurried her toward the exit. Keeping the pistol in his right hand, he opened the door, just a crack.

Outside, pale shafts of morning sunlight spiraled through the trees, glistening on bright leaves and evergreens and grass wet with dew. It all looked deceptively peaceful. He didn't see anyone. No riders. No dogs. Not so much as a single pup.

But he could hear the howling, yelping pack. No more than a half-mile away.

"How could they have found us so quickly?" the girl whispered.

"Must've been searching all night," he replied curtly. "With torches. And I left a nice blood trail for the dogs."

He railed at himself silently. They shouldn't have rested so long. Shouldn't have rested at all. What chance did they have now? Staying in the cabin would be suicide. But they couldn't hope to outrun the dogs. Not for long. Not at this distance. And what use would one pistol be against a score of armed lawmen?

Defeat assaulted him for one hopeless second. *Finished*. They were finished.

Then an image flashed through his head: of himself being dragged into the Old Bailey in London. And handed over to the admiralty.

"Not yet," he vowed under his breath. Stepping out into the daylight, he glanced around at the trees, mind racing, then looked at Miss Delafield.

She shook her head, the hopelessness in her eyes matching his own. "What are we going to do?"

He clenched his jaw and answered with one word. "Run."

Turning left, he led her away from the cabin as fast as their weary legs and the clanking chain would allow. Which was faster than he would've thought.

They fled into the woods, ducking under branches, dodging tree trunks. The pack of supplies thumped against his back with every step, but he put the pain and the burning in his muscles out of his mind. He kept only one image in his head—of the gibbet cage on Execution Dock.

It spurred him to speed he hadn't known he possessed.

And the girl stayed right beside him, keeping up stride for stride. The drag of the heavy shackles slowed them down but didn't stop them. Yesterday's experience had taught them well, and they managed to match their steps with only a few stumbles.

The howling of the dogs sounded louder than before—like the wail of demons from hell coming for him. The girl looked back over her shoulder.

"Don't," he ordered. "Just keep going!"

She obeyed without question for once, turned her face forward and kept running, arms and legs pumping. He could hear her gasping with fear, with exhaustion. But they didn't waste any more breath on words.

The sun streaked through the trees, rising on their right. He kept heading north, at a sharp angle to the easterly direction he had followed yesterday. He didn't bother zigging and zagging or doubling back on their trail, knew there was no hope of losing their pursuers that way. Distance. They needed distance.

Side by side they ran, faster, twigs and leaves crunching under their feet, branches whipping at their clothes, hair, faces. They somehow found their way between, around, through stands of trees and clumps of bushes. They sprinted across clearings. Splashed through puddles. The forest became a blur of sunlight and shadows.

They ran until he thought his lungs would burst, until all he could feel were his boots pounding the ground and air burning his throat. The chain caught on roots and stones, tripping them, like the long arm of the law reaching out to grab them and hold them fast. But each time they stumbled up and kept running. Faster.

His mind worked as swiftly as his blood raced. The dogs would stop at the cabin, certain they had run their prey to ground. The lawmen would approach cautiously. That might gain them some time. A few minutes, maybe more. Maybe enough.

Trees, branches, leaves flashed by. Sweat plastered

the ragged remains of his shirt to his chest and back. His shoulder burned and hurt but he didn't care. It was a reminder that he was still alive. At least for the moment.

He kept thinking that the girl would give out. Knew she couldn't take much more. Waited for her to fall and not get up. But she didn't. Whether it was fear or guts that kept her going, she never faltered.

Their tortured breathing and the jangling of the chain that bound them became the only sounds he could hear.

That and the howling of the dogs. So close it sounded as if the animals were biting at their heels.

Then a pistol shot cracked through the woods. Distant but too close.

"Sweet Jesus!" the girl cried in terror.

Nicholas darted a glance over his shoulder. Saw the lead dogs of the pack—brown and white flashes of color bounding through the green undergrowth.

They hadn't stopped at the cabin.

Why the hell hadn't they stopped?

Damn it. "Don't slow down," he shouted. "We can make it."

But he knew he was lying. Knew it was futile. His legs were practically numb, his battered body threatening to give out. The girl had to be spent. And there was no cover. Nowhere to hide. No chance of losing the dogs. And his only weapons were a pistol, a knife.

The image of the admiralty's gibbet cage loomed. Inescapable.

And then he saw a glimmer of something ahead, through the trees. A thread of blue and white that widened, sparkling in the sunlight. Water. A river.

Hope surged in his chest. If there was a footbridge— and if they could cross it and destroy it before their pursuers could follow . . .

But even that thin hope was quickly crushed when the river came fully into view.

This wasn't any peaceful woodland stream. It was a raging torrent, at least fifty yards wide. They broke through the trees and raced toward the muddy bank. But there was no footbridge. No conveniently fallen trees, no stones, no narrow ford. No way across. They stopped at the water's edge, gasping, breathless.

Miss Delafield glanced behind them, at the trees. At the dogs—which were rapidly closing the brief lead the two of them had gained.

Nicholas looked desperately up and down the bank. They had nowhere left to run. And they couldn't turn back.

Instead of being saved, they were cornered.

He stared down at the water churning and leaping over rocks. It looked deep. Treacherous. Alone, he might jump in and try to swim across. But with the chain, the girl . . .

It would be certain death.

"We'll have to swim across," she said calmly.

He turned, stunned by her cool declaration. "We'll never make it."

"I'd rather drown than be torn to pieces!"

They both looked over their shoulders again. The dogs were so close Nicholas could see fangs flashing in the sunlight. And now he could see riders in the distance. A dozen at least, fanned out through the trees.

He glanced down at the slender girl, at the rushing water. She'd never survive it.

And if she drowned, he would drown with her.

"I can *do* it," she insisted urgently.

A canine snarl behind him—just a few yards away—made up his mind for him.

To hell with the odds.

He jammed the pistol into his waistband, took hold of the rope that secured the creel across his chest. He slung it around his neck and grabbed the girl with his other hand. "On three," he said tightly. "One . . .

two . . ." Her arm seemed impossibly fragile in his
grasp. "*Three.*"

They leaped forward in an ungraceful dive. Hit the
water with a jarring, painful impact that he felt through
every inch of his aching body. And instantly went under.

The chain would kill them; he knew that the minute
the surface closed over his head. He could feel the
shackles dragging them downward, heavy, murderous
links of iron. He kicked and fought, struggling to get
to the air—but he didn't have the strength to battle the
forceful current and the chain too.

He felt the girl torn from his grasp, saw her struggling beside him, a blur of yellow skirts and golden
hair. Thrashing and swimming for all she was worth.

After what felt like an eternity, he made it to the
surface, broke above the rushing water, sucked in a
breath—only to be pulled under again.

The rain-swollen torrent was stronger than both of
them, sweeping them downstream.

He managed to break the surface a second time.
Found himself in a hail of bullets that rained down
around him, striking the water like darts. The metal
pings sounded strange amid the liquid rush of the river
and the yowling of the dogs.

He opened his mouth, inhaled more water than air.
Wondered whether it would be his last breath. Choking, fighting to stay above the drowning torrent, he saw
the riverbank flying past. The surging waters carried
them downstream faster than they could've run. As if
they weighed no more than the sticks and leaves riot-
ing around them.

The current pulled him under again. He didn't know
if the girl had managed to get to the surface at all.
Couldn't see her anymore. His vision seemed to be
turning gray; his muscles started to go weak, his limbs
numb. He couldn't feel the shackle around his ankle
anymore. Couldn't feel anything but the water, every-

where. Around him, above him, below him. Filling his nose, his mouth, all of him.

Darkness hovered at the edges of his awareness, threatening to close in. Urging him to stop fighting its seductive pull.

But somehow he attacked his way to the top one more time, spat out a mouthful of water. Fought for the air he needed to survive.

They had been carried toward the middle of the stream, more by the force of the current than by any effort of their own. The far bank was closer than before. They might even reach it. Sweet Jesus, by some trick of fate they might actually reach it!

But he heard another strange sound—so loud it blotted out even the dogs.

A roar. A deafening roar made entirely of water.

He heard the girl scream. Turned his head to find her right beside him. But he also saw what she did.

A spew of froth and spray and waves breaking over the edge of a precipice. Just a few yards downriver.

A waterfall.

All the breath, all the power, all the life in his body seemed to rise up through his chest in a yell of denial. But he never got the chance to voice it. Just as quickly as the river had given him hope, it snatched it away— and spat him right over the edge of a cliff.

The force of tons of water behind them rushed them into the waterfall like a pair of rag dolls, sent them tumbling out into nothingness beyond. For an instant he found himself weightless. Flying. Falling helplessly, in a pounding curtain of water that carried him down ... down ... down ...

They hit the surface far below, slammed into the depths of a whirlpool that yanked him straight to the bottom, hard, as if the current above had been only a game.

Pain wracked his body. Several feet of swirling, roiling water closed over his head.

And sudden fury rose in him. A shaft of sheer rage at being toyed with by fate. Teased by God.

His stamina, his will, his body may have failed him. But his rage did not.

Kicking, reaching, he rose against the driving power of the whirlpool. Against the column of river water that hammered down from above. The more it tried to beat him senseless and drown him, the more strength he seemed to find.

But he felt a drag on his ankle. The girl—below him, sinking. He turned, felt for her, grabbed for her, caught a fistful of her hair. She was limp, unconscious. Perhaps even dead.

No, damn it. If you die, I die. He grabbed for her again, with his left arm. Caught her.

And felt a horrendous agony rip through his shoulder. Like a slicing blade of pure hellfire. Like he was being torn in half.

Awash in pain and the burning rush of rage, fighting for consciousness, he struggled upward once more, his arm looped around the girl's middle. He made it to the surface only to get a pounding faceful of spray for his reward. He lurched out of its way.

And found air. Blessed air. Life-giving, life-restoring air. For a moment that was all that mattered. It cleared his head, kept him from sinking into unconsciousness, from sinking to the sandy bottom of the river and staying there. And at least for one critical minute, he could think. He realized that the whirlpool wasn't pulling at him as strongly anymore; he seemed to be behind the falls.

And just to his left he could make out a relatively calm place—a pool separated from the waterfall by a half-circle of rocks.

With the weight of the girl and the chain pulling him down, it was a struggle just to stay afloat. But he lunged for the rocks with one last life-or-death burst of strength. He saw a root sticking out from between two of the boulders and grabbed for it, clinging.

Cool shadow blotted out the sun; he realized they were beneath a stone overhang. A canopy of sorts, soaring several feet overhead, that protected them from the tumbling, roaring rush of water beyond.

The girl came awake, coughing, sputtering. Struggling. She was alive. Somehow he hung onto her. But he felt a strange, sticky heat flowing down his back. Blood. In a haze of fiery agony, he closed his eyes and clung to the root and knew that was all he could do. Saving the girl had sapped the last of his strength.

Hang on. *Hang on*.

After a time, he opened his eyes. Blinked as his vision adjusted to the darkness. He glanced back toward the whirlpool. No way in hell he was going back through that again.

He looked in the other direction. A few feet away, cut into the rock, he could make out a crevasse. An opening of some sort. Less than two feet wide. It might be a trick of his vision. A shadow. Or another little joke being played by God.

Or it might be a cave.

It might save their lives.

But it was at least ten feet away. And ten feet had never looked so impossibly distant.

The girl was shaking, limp in his grasp. He squeezed her hard to get her attention, nodded desperately toward the crevasse.

"Can you make it?" he shouted.

She followed his gaze, shook her head weakly.

"Damn it, don't you give up on me now, lady!"

His anger seemed to ignite whatever embers of grit she had left. She lifted her head. "Yes," she choked out in a watery sputter.

It seemed the only word she was capable of. He took it as an assent. And didn't bother counting to three this time.

In a headlong dive, he let go of the root and threw

himself toward the crevasse. They struggled across the ten feet of water together, swimming, kicking, reaching for it in one long ungraceful splash. It felt like he would never get there.

But then he touched it with his right hand, grabbing the edge of the stone with some last reserve of stamina, pulling himself up. She grasped the opposite edge and hung there, breathless.

It took some maneuvering, but he made it out of the water, levering his body into the tight opening, helping her scramble up behind him. The fissure opened to a gap several feet wide.

Then it broadened into a cave.

They collapsed on the cool stone floor, gasping for breath, choking on all the water they had swallowed, spitting up mouthfuls of river. The cave was small, dark, clammy, and contained nothing but wet stone.

And it felt like heaven.

The closest to heaven he had ever been in his life and the closest he ever expected to get.

He lay flattened, on his stomach, his cheek resting against the cold granite, jaw slack, every muscle in his body shivering, weak, twitching spasmodically. He felt as waterlogged as a soaked sponge, wanted nothing so much as to have someone bunch him up and wring him out.

But breathing felt almost as good as that. Bloody hell, he had never appreciated breathing before. In, out, in, out, a smooth flow of air punctuated only by his frequent tortured coughs.

Over the roar of the rushing water, he could hear the faint barking of the dogs. Bloody damn accursed dogs. Yelping at the top of the falls. Probably a good thirty feet above, he guessed. Standing right over their heads.

Howling in outrage because their prey had abruptly disappeared.

A satisfied grin lifted one corner of Nicholas's

mouth. He opened his eyes. The only light came from the crevasse they had squeezed through, but he could see the girl sprawled on her back nearby. She lay utterly still, only her chest rising and falling as she breathed.

Pushing himself up to a seated position, he ignored the blaze of pain down his back and slid the soaked fishing creel from his shoulder. Most of the supplies in it were probably ruined. And his pistol was gone. Lost somewhere at the bottom of the river. He muttered a curse; they were left with only one weapon. He found the knife still tucked deep in his boot. He took it out and flung it down beside the creel.

Then he studied the shackles, briefly hoping, just for a second . . .

Still intact. Of course. No force of man or nature seemed capable of breaking the blasted things.

He sank back down to the cool stone floor and lay there, too weak to do anything more at the moment.

The girl began sobbing.

Nicholas lifted his head. "What are you crying about?" he croaked in disbelief. "We're alive."

She didn't respond, only crying harder, throwing an arm across her face.

"A while ago you were *willing* to drown," he reminded her lightly.

That didn't seem to help at all. She only sobbed more desperately, her whole body shaking with the force of her tears.

He frowned at her, utterly perplexed. Somehow he always managed to say exactly the wrong thing in situations like this. "What the devil is wrong with you, woman?"

"I'm frightened!" she shouted, shooting the words at him like bullets. "Haven't you ever been frightened?"

That struck him dumb. The way she said it, as if the words had been torn out, as if it were a deep admission she hadn't wanted to make, brought the odd, squishy sensation back to his belly. The one he had felt yesterday while she talked about being so hungry that she would steal. It was an utterly unfamiliar feeling. He couldn't even name it.

All he knew was that he had felt the same way. Many times in his life. Aye, he had been frightened.

"We're safe now," he said gruffly.

"No, we're not." She sat up, the expression on her face desperate, angry. "We're not safe! We're not safe at all. We're going to *die!*"

The dogs kept up their incessant baying overhead, competing with the thunder of tons of water plunging into the lethally deep whirlpool outside. She pressed her hands over her ears, bending over and drawing her knees up to her chest, sobbing.

The vulnerability in that pose sent the uneasy sensation traveling upward from his belly to his throat, tightening it. For all her bravado, all her guts, she was still very young. Sitting there dripping river water all over the floor, with her hair and dress a soaked, matted mess and tears adding to the wetness on her pale cheeks, she looked . . . utterly lost. Alone.

And that, too, was something he had felt before.

"There's no need to be scared," he said quietly, not allowing himself to move closer as some impulse urged him to do. "For now, we're safe."

"No, we're not." She kicked at the chain helplessly, furiously. "I can't run anymore. I can't *fight* anymore. There's nothing left in me. Don't you understand? Nothing! I'm not strong enough. I'm sick of running and being shot at and chased and drowned, and I'm sick of these damned shackles, and I'm sick of *you*. I just want to be safe and I'm never going to be and I'm going to *die*."

Nicholas reached out and took her firmly by the shoulders. "No, you're not," he told her flatly. "You may be a lot of things, lady, but a quitter isn't one of them."

He drew her close, held her tight against his chest—and only realized he was doing it a moment later.

But against his better judgment, against all his instincts, he didn't let her go.

He hung on.

And strangely enough, she didn't fight his touch for once. In fact, she went slack in his arms, sobbing out all her fear.

"Shhh," he whispered, letting her cry into his shirt. "You're going to be all right, Miss Delafield."

After a moment, he lifted his right hand and ran his fingers through her wet hair. "We've thrown the law off our trail. The cave entrance is hidden—we never would've seen it ourselves if we hadn't been right on top of it. And the dogs won't be able to follow our scent in the water. The lawmen will think we either drowned or were carried downriver. They'll start looking for us downstream."

None of this sounded particularly reassuring, even to him, as the dogs continued to bay overhead.

She shook her head, clearly not believing him, shivering in his arms. "We're not going to get out of this alive, are we?" she whispered tearfully.

"We have so far. We just have to stick together and . . ."

When he didn't finish, she raised her head.

He looked down into her eyes, into those golden pools he could so easily drown in. "Trust one another."

The words came out in a whisper. He could barely believe he'd thought them, much less spoken them aloud.

A second later she seemed to realize—at the same moment he did—that they were locked in an intimate embrace, her breasts pressed against his chest, their bodies radiating warmth, their lips an inch apart.

He also realized he was holding her not with sexual intent, but gently. Reassuring her. And he had been freely using the word "we" for some time. That wasn't part of the bargain. He only had to keep her alive. Not comforted, just alive.

But he couldn't seem to make himself let her go.

And an instant later, without thinking, he dipped his mouth toward hers.

She suddenly broke the embrace, lurching backward out of his arms. "Yes . . . well . . ." she said stiffly, clearing her throat, hurriedly wiping her damp cheeks. "I guess you're right. I . . . I should be glad we've at least confused the law for now." She brushed off her wet sleeves, as if dusting away some invisible lint. Or ridding herself of his touch.

The law weren't the only ones confused, Nicholas thought dazedly, shaking not from pain or cold, but from the force of something more powerful that seemed to keep robbing him of his senses.

"And I thought I asked you to keep your hands to yourself," the girl added frostily.

He replied with a glare, unable to summon words at the moment. He had liked having her in his arms. Not merely because of the sexual hunger he had for her, or because of any joy or relief he felt at finding himself still alive. The effect she had on him was more complicated than that.

And it made him uneasy.

"But I . . . I suppose I should thank you for saving me," she continued quietly, wringing some of the water out of her skirt. "I would've drowned out there."

"If you die, I die, remember?" he tossed back.

"Yes, of course I remember," she replied, meeting his eyes and matching his sharp tone. "And that brings up another question. Now that we're in here . . ." She looked around the dark cave, paused for a moment. "How on earth are we going to get out?"

Chapter 11

~~~~~⁀◯◯⁀~~~~~

Their cautious footsteps sounded louder than a hundred pairs of shoes dancing across a marble floor. Sam stared ahead, eyes wide, afraid that her next step might carry them straight down some bottomless pit. Or worse, into an impassable wall of solid rock.

The rogue followed behind her, silent but for his labored breathing.

They had yet to find the rear of the cave. Or a way out. Even though they had been walking for over an hour.

The damp, confined space seemed to play tricks with every sound, every drip of water, every skittering of pebbles beneath their feet. Sam practically jumped out of her slippers each time the chain caught on a rock or stalagmite. She had thought herself used to the metallic jangling of the shackles by now, but in here it seemed eerie, ghostlike.

Ominous.

Leading the way, she held her torch high—if a whiskey-soaked petticoat stuffed into an empty biscuit tin could be called a torch. The flame cast a glimmer of light that barely penetrated the crush of darkness around them.

Her heart pounded in her water-ravaged throat. She kept coughing, felt as if she had inhaled so much of the river that she must've grown gills. She edged forward, feeling her way across the uneven ground, her slippers encountering rocks, sand, sticky mud, sharp pebbles.

She shifted the heavy fishing creel on her shoulder, her bruised muscles protesting at the motion. Cuts and scrapes on her arms and legs stung like the devil, adding to her misery.

The waterfall and the rocks had left their mark on her. In more ways than one.

In some spots, the passage narrowed so tightly that they could barely squeeze past. In others it became more like a tunnel, forcing them to stoop down or crawl through on their hands and knees. For the last several yards, it had broadened into what felt like a vast cavern.

But it didn't end.

Now and then she could feel a gust of wind, a hint of fresh air that made her feel certain there *must* be an opening somewhere ahead. She strained her eyes for any speck of daylight. Prayed that they would find an exit that would spare them another encounter with the falls and the whirlpool. Neither of them wanted to risk that again.

So they kept going, deeper and deeper. Didn't dare stop.

They'd lost their pursuers for the moment. But for how long? When the lawmen didn't find them downstream, they would double back to search the forest above. She didn't relish the idea of exiting the cave only to find themselves in the midst of a swarm of hounds and marshalmen.

The sooner they found a way out of here, the better. Time was not on their side.

Please, she thought, looking around her as the flames painted flickering orange shadows on the craggy walls of rock. *Please, there must be a way out. Please, God, help me find it.*

"Let's take a rest."

Startled by the rogue's voice, Sam almost dropped the biscuit tin. She stopped and looked behind her. It was the first time he had asked to stop. Ever. She was usually the one who didn't want to go on.

Then again, he had given her a number of surprises today—including his request that she take the lead as they explored. And the fact that he hadn't protested or made any mocking comment when she offered to carry the heavy pack of supplies.

"Are you all right?" she asked, wishing her heart would stop pounding so hard.

He sank down to the cave floor, leaned his good shoulder against the rough wall, nodded. But he was breathing hard, as if they'd been running for an hour instead of walking at a snail's pace.

The chain rattled as Sam sat across from him, her stomach knotted with worry. Sliding the fishing creel from her shoulder, she set her makeshift torch-in-a-box on the ground between them.

Looking at her invention through slitted eyes, the rogue grinned for a fleeting second. "Sometimes, your ladyship, you amaze me."

She met his gaze, but just as quickly glanced away. She hadn't been able to really look him in the eye since . . .

Swallowing hard, she tried to banish the memory of his arms around her, holding her. She was doing her best not to think of that.

She poked at the burning petticoat with the knife, stoking the fire. Wondering how much longer it would last. "Sorry I had to use up so much of your whiskey." The bottle, wrapped in a length of cloth and cushioned between the sack of sugar and a rolled-up sheet, had survived the river intact. "How's your shoulder?"

He lifted the flask of water he'd been carrying all morning and took a long swallow. "Fine."

She studied him from beneath her lashes. He didn't

look fine. He looked like hell. And he must feel even worse.

Saving her below the falls, he had torn his stitches—and opened what had been a fairly small wound into a jagged gash. But he hadn't told her, hadn't mentioned it at all the whole time they had sat at the cave entrance discussing what to do next.

Only when she had lit the fire and noticed the wound herself, practically fainted at the sight of him bleeding so badly, had he explained.

She had done her best to stitch it again, but he had lost more blood. Too much more.

And now, observing him in the low light, she felt her stomach clench with concern.

His face looked as pale as the fresh white bandage around his shoulder. His hair, his beard, his brows seemed blacker than raven's wings against his skin. Those cynical green eyes had drifted closed, and even his lashes looked darker than onyx against his pallid cheeks.

The heavily muscled arms that had fought so hard against the current and the whirlpool now lay limp at his sides. His ragged, blood-stained shirt hung open; he hadn't bothered to button it again after she had re-stitched the wound in his back.

And though the air was cool this deep in the cavern, rivulets of sweat trickled down his neck, across the matted hair of his chest . . . over the pitchfork brand in the center.

But his expression worried her most of all, because it was a measure of just how much pain he was in; she could see agony etched in the lines that bracketed his mouth, his eyes. His body might be slack, but his face was a mask of effort. He looked like he was ready to give in and collapse, but he was fighting the weakness for all he was worth.

Sam felt an unexpected rush of emotion sweep through her. Something even stronger than concern or worry. Something she hadn't felt for him before. Admiration, perhaps, or respect, for his courage, for his unflagging tenacity. She wasn't sure exactly what the feeling was.

All she knew was that the man couldn't endure much more. Courageous or not, he needed time to heal. Time and sleep. But he kept insisting he was well enough to travel, had muttered something about learning his lesson, that he wasn't going to rest for more than brief periods from now on. They had remained near the cave entrance only a short while, just long enough to be sure their pursuers had moved downstream, before setting off.

She turned and opened the fishing creel, determined now. He had to get some rest. That was simply that. She didn't like the idea of staying in one place too long any more than he did.

But one look at him told her they had no choice.

And since he wouldn't listen to reason—and clubbing him over the head wouldn't exactly help his condition—she would have to try something else.

"Do you want anything to eat?" She unwrapped the whiskey bottle, spread the length of cloth on the cave floor, and started arranging a soggy luncheon on it. "I'm sure even water-soaked salt beef is still edible. And the raisins and figs are probably fine—"

"Not hungry."

His terse reply wasn't encouraging. "Well, I'm starving." She opened the bag of smoked pork, carved a chunk from a wheel of cheese, and started to nibble. The mushy food was somewhat less than palatable, but it was filling.

Unfortunately, it didn't tempt him at all.

She glanced around them in the darkness. Though she couldn't see much, this section of the cave felt airy and cool. The light, steady breeze must be coming from somewhere. There had to be a way out.

"It's fairly comfortable in here." She spoke around a

mouthful of nuts. "A little drier, at least, than some of the other parts we've been in. Why don't we stay here for a while? Get some rest?" She hurried to bolster her argument with logic. "The dogs will be busy downstream for hours, so we've got a little time—"

"And we're not going to waste it." His lashes lifted just a fraction. "Hurry up and finish your luncheon, your ladyship. We have to keep moving."

Sam frowned. Words were clearly useless where this obstinate male was concerned. Action was the only thing he understood.

So, ignoring his suggestion, she took the remains of the ripped sheet out of the creel. Bunching it up to serve as a pillow, she placed it on the cave floor near him.

Then she reached out, put her hand in the middle of his chest, and tried to push him down toward it.

But he was like a rock, unmovable.

He lifted one brow. "What exactly do you think you're doing, Miss Delafield?"

"Keeping you alive."

"I can keep myself alive." He pushed her hand away.

"You've got to get some rest," she said in exasperation. "You need—"

"What I need is to find a bloody way out of this bloody cave. Preferably before that bloody army of marshalmen comes back."

She flinched away from him, startled by his sudden burst of anger.

"What I do *not* need," he continued, glaring at her, "is some female fussing over me."

She held her tongue, biting back her own anger, hearing a clue to his surly mood in the word *fussing*. For some reason, this man found it difficult, perhaps impossible, to let someone care for him in even the smallest way.

And he seemed confident that the matter was closed. Slowly, he got to his feet, though the effort obviously pained him. He was having difficulty breathing, was visibly unsteady on his feet.

She remained seated, kept her voice mild. "I think you'd better sit back down before you fall down."

"You're forgetting who's in charge here."

"No, I'm not." She met his gaze squarely. "You're looking at her."

His expression hardened. "The mutiny's over." He bent and grabbed the fishing creel. "Now let's go."

"Your stubbornness is going to kill you," she retorted. "And if it kills you, it'll kill me."

"I'm not being stubborn. I'm being rational."

"You're being stupid."

"Move your derriere, Miss Delafield."

She stared straight into his furious eyes. And didn't budge. "No."

"It's not a request."

"I don't care. You can take your orders and stuff them. I'm not moving. And the chain is too short for you to pick me up and haul me off, so unless you intend to drag me out of here by the hair"—she flipped the tangled blonde mass over her shoulders, out of reach, just in case the idea appealed to him—"we're staying put."

His emerald gaze glittered with outrage at her defiance. His jaw clenched. And his fists.

But despite the ready violence apparent in every taut line of his body, she stared up at him without flinching this time, though her heart was pounding.

Long moments passed before she found enough breath to speak. "I don't understand," she said softly, shaking her head, unable to make sense of his attitude. "You're only human. Why are you pushing yourself so hard?"

He grated out a clipped, vivid oath. "On your feet, your ladyship. *Now*."

She didn't comply. Silent, she looked up at him, her question lingering in the cool, dark air between them.

And she realized something in that moment: he wasn't going to hurt her. Despite his threats and menacing glares and fierce stance, despite his cold demeanor and his repeated insistence that he didn't give a damn about anyone except himself . . . he wouldn't cause her any harm.

Something in him wouldn't allow it. Beneath scars that bespoke a lifetime of violence beat the heart of a decent man.

Their silent battle of wills lasted one minute. Another. She could practically feel the seconds ticking by.

Finally, she dropped her gaze, deciding to give in.

After a moment, slowly, she glanced up again, and held out her hand. "Let me help you."

The hard line of his mouth curved downward into an expression that was cynical, mocking. After a moment, he sighed, flicked a glance heavenward, shook his head. "Cursed," he muttered under his breath. "I am cursed."

She wasn't sure what he meant, and he ignored her offered hand, but his anger had passed. He sat down again.

Then, stretching out on his stomach, he pillowed his head on his crossed arms and the bunched-up sheet, and closed his eyes.

"No more than an hour," he growled. "Don't let me sleep for more than an hour."

"All right," she agreed quietly.

Without a watch, she thought with a smile, how could she be expected to know exactly how long an hour was?

After only a few minutes, his tense muscles relaxed.

Looking down at him, Sam felt . . . satisfied. That was the only name she could put to the feeling. Satisfied. That she had prevailed, that he had finally listened to reason.

Reluctant to examine her emotions any more closely than that, she turned away and busied herself by bundling up the foodstuffs and putting them back in the creel. Then she took inventory of their other supplies: a few stubby candles, two cups and some eating utensils, the fishing lines and some hooks, a length of rope, and the horn of gunpowder and a dozen bullets taken from Leach and Swinton—ammunition that was useless now, since they had lost the pistol.

What she wouldn't give for some medical supplies and some real food, she thought with a frown. And a blunderbuss. Unfortunately, they had no such help in facing their enemies. All they had was . . .

Each other.

Sam closed the fishing creel and pushed it aside, wishing she could push the thought away as easily. With the inventory done, she had nothing else to occupy her attention. She glanced around the cave, trying to avoid looking at the rogue.

Because every time she did, she found herself thinking of what had happened between them at the cave entrance. Her humiliating emotional outburst. The way he had tried to comfort her.

That was the last thing she had expected from him.

Even now, she could feel her cheeks burning. She felt horribly embarrassed to have shown such weakness in front of anyone—especially a man. Especially him. But for once, he hadn't mocked her. Instead, he had held her. With a gentleness she hadn't suspected he possessed. Just when she thought she had figured out exactly what kind of man he was, he had surprised her.

But what surprised her even more was the fact that she had liked the feeling of his arms around her.

The thought made her shiver. It was an outlandish idea. A dangerous idea. The man was an outlaw. A veteran of the prison hulks. Arrogant. Unpredictable. Not to mention hostile. And impossible.

And she had liked the feeling of his arms around her.

For a moment, just a moment, she had felt safe, warm . . . protected.

That disturbed her in a way she couldn't begin to explain. Nervously, Sam swept her damp hair around her, busied herself trying to unknot the dozens of little tangles.

But even as she did so, she couldn't help sliding a cautious, sideways glance at the man who lay stretched out on the cave floor.

How could she have felt safe in his embrace? She didn't even know his name, for Heaven's sake! Had she lost her mind? Had the tumble over the falls scrambled her senses?

She kept thinking of the words he had whispered, the ones that floated so innocently through her memory: *We just have to trust each other.*

Could she do that? Trust him? Hard experience had taught her that she *couldn't* trust men. Especially not men like him, those of the criminal element. And not even men like her uncle, who had *seemed* so respectable, honorable, and kind at first.

Since fleeing London six years ago, she had remained wary, cautious when it came to the matter of men. Trust meant weakness. Vulnerability. And to be vulnerable was to become a victim.

And Samantha Delafield was never going to be a victim. Never. She had made that promise to herself six years ago—and she intended to keep it.

Tossing her hair over her shoulder, she turned away from the rogue, sighing in relief. There was no mystery here, no cause for alarm. Her emotions had become momentarily confused, that was all. It was perfectly understandable, after the ordeal she had been through the past two days.

If she felt anything toward this man, it was merely gratitude. Ordinary gratitude that he had saved her life in the whirlpool, at great cost to himself.

Nothing wrong with that. Her gratitude, he could have.

Her trust she could not give him.

Dark shadows flickered around them, and Sam realized that her makeshift torch had burned low. Grateful for something—anything—to claim her attention, she tried to think of a way to keep the fire burning. She had kept her eye out for twigs or brush as they had walked through the cave, but she had seen precious little growth of any kind.

They had no fuel but what they had brought with them. Opening the fishing creel, she took the whiskey bottle out, uncorked it, and poured a bit over the biscuit tin. The flames crackled and sizzled and leaped so high that they almost singed her hair.

"Are you trying to incinerate us, or is that merely a creative way to dry your hair?"

Sam shot a glance behind her, the bottle still in her hand. "I'm trying to keep the fire going. And you're supposed to be asleep."

"Can't." The rogue lay on his side, watching her through half-closed eyes. "Do you have to use up *all* the whiskey that way?"

She recorked the bottle and put it back in the creel. "I'm sorry if the noise kept you awake." She wasn't about to let the fire burn out; the prospect of being deep in a cave in total darkness was not something she wanted to contemplate.

"It's not the noise."

His voice was low, almost a groan. Sam frowned in puzzlement, then understood what he meant, what he would not say: the pain was so bad he couldn't sleep.

Her stomach gave an uncomfortable little twist. "Is there . . . anything I can do?" she asked softly.

"You could hand over the bottle."

She hesitated a moment, then took it out again and gave it to him. There was less than two inches of the precious liquid left inside, but she couldn't deny him.

He levered himself up on one elbow and took a long swallow.

The torch flickered again, and the scant circle of light

surrounding them shifted and danced. Uneasily, Sam picked over the items in the creel, looking for something she might use as fuel.

Her fingers touched the powder horn. In a sudden burst of inspiration, she poured a few granules into her palm. Then she sprinkled them over the fire.

"Your ladysh—"

A loud pop and a puff of black smoke interrupted his warning. Caught in a miniature cloud of soot, Sam scurried backward, fanning the air in front of her face, wiping sticky black stuff from her cheeks. The chain pulled her up short.

An amused male chuckle filled the cave. "You may be a talented thief, Miss Delafield, but your knowledge of armaments leaves something to be desired."

She shot him an aggravated look. "It was worth a try." She dabbed at her watering eyes. "And I'm *not* a talented thief," she muttered. "I'm a quite ordinary thief."

"Not according to the bounty on your head."

That made her grimace. "Well, I never set out to be a talented thief. It's merely the fact that I'm a woman. It seems to work in my favor."

"How so?"

She shrugged. "Most people look at a young woman who appears well dressed, well bred, and well versed in the ways of polite society and think, 'How much of a threat could she be?'"

"Indeed. I can see how most people would think that . . ." Those deep-green eyes of his studied her, tracing over her face. "How much of a threat could she be?"

The slow, thoughtful timbre of his voice seemed to resonate through her entire body. She didn't like the way he said those words. Or the way he was looking at her.

Resisting the urge to scoot away a few inches, she

glanced down into the torch flames and fell silent for a moment.

Then she remembered that he was supposed to be trying to get to sleep—not making irritating conversation. "Is the whiskey helping?"

"Some." He lay down again, on his side, not quite managing to hold in a sound of pain.

Instead of closing his eyes, he kept observing her in that penetrating way. "Assuming we make it out of here alive, Miss Delafield, and assuming we somehow manage to get these blasted shackles off"—he gestured at the hated things with the whiskey bottle—"what *are* you going to do? What fiendish plans do you have for spending your ill-gotten gain?"

His voice was becoming slurred. The whiskey was taking effect faster than she'd hoped. Doubting that he was fully lucid, she thought about telling him the truth for a moment.

But then she shook her head. "You'll laugh."

"I won't." He lifted his free hand and crossed his heart. "Promise."

The traditional gesture wasn't very convincing—not when made over that pitchfork brand.

"Yes, you will," she replied softly. "You always laugh at me. You constantly mock my plans, my intelligence—everything about me."

"Not this time, angel," he murmured. "Not in the mood."

Watching him, she realized what he meant, though again, he wouldn't say it aloud. Wouldn't perhaps admit it even to himself.

He needed something to distract him from the pain.

She turned her face away, not wanting him to see in her eyes what she was feeling.

Sliding her long hair over her shoulder, she began weaving the damp strands into a braid, thinking. She decided there was no harm in revealing this particular piece of the truth. "Eventually, I want to book passage on a ship to Italy. To Venice."

He sounded surprised. "Venice? Why Venice?"

"Because . . ." She looked up at the cave ceiling overhead, imagining blue Italian skies stretching out over fields of green and gold. "Because it's everything that England isn't. Clean, open, warm, beautiful . . ." Her voice softened. "Pure." She looked down into the strands of her hair as she twined them in, over, around each other. "I've never seen it, but I've read a lot. Ever since I saw a production of Shakespeare's *Much Ado About Nothing* at a fair one summer, I've wanted to go to Italy. I'm going to buy a small villa in Venice, and live on the Adriatic."

She finished her braid, tied the end with a length of yellow silk torn from her tattered sleeve, and waited for his laughter to begin.

"I can just picture you in Venice."

To her amazement, his tone wasn't mocking . . . but reflective.

She turned to find him regarding her through half-closed eyes.

"In the sun," he murmured, "beside the Adriatic. Dressed in silks and velvets, glittering like gold. Surrounded by jewels and art and glassware." A hint of a smile curved his mouth, but it wasn't sarcastic. "You'd fit in there."

His voice was more than serious; it was almost . . . wistful.

Sam hoped he couldn't see her blushing in the firelight.

His lashes finally lowered completely, as the whiskey or fatigue or both took their toll. "So why haven't you gone there already? Why stay in England?"

It took her a moment to summon a reply. "Because I didn't want to simply leave England impulsively only to wind up in the same dire straits somewhere else. If I'm going to be a thief, better to do that here, where

I'm at least familiar with the language and customs. It would be impossible to try and start a new life in a new country with no money."

"True," he agreed solemnly. "Very true."

"I think it's always better to plan ahead. When I get to Venice, I'm never going to break the law again. I'm never going to *have* to break the law again. I'll take a new name, start a new life—"

"Leave the past behind?"

"Yes."

"Excellent idea. A very good plan." There seemed to be some amusement creeping into his voice. "I wish you luck, your ladyship."

"One *must* leave the past behind," she said firmly, irked by the change in his tone. "Better to live for the future. I'm going to buy a villa and I'm going to open a business of my own. I've even been studying Italian. I'm actually rather fluent. *Sei uno sciocco insopportabile.*"

"*Posso direlo stesso di te,*" he replied. "I am not an insufferable oaf. You are rather fluent."

She blinked at him in surprise. "You know Italian?"

He opened his eyes, grinning. "You're not the only one with hidden talents, angel."

Sam noticed that the word "angel" had lost its sarcastic bite.

But she also noticed that his words were becoming more slurred—more than could be attributed to the small amount of liquor he had consumed.

She picked up the torch and moved closer, leaning over him, her heart thudding against her ribs. His skin was no longer pale but flushed with color. His eyes were glassy in the firelight.

"Oh, *no,*" she whispered.

"Oh, yes," he chuckled.

"I'm not commenting on your hidden talents." She put a hand to his forehead. "You've got a fever. You're burning up!"

A shiver went through him. "Been wondering about

that. I thought your little fire was getting hotter."

He might be joking about it, but a shaft of pure, icy fear went through her. She had no blankets, no fuel to keep the fire going, precious little water, no medicines.

No way to help him.

And with the shackles binding them together . . .

She would be trapped here, unable to move more than two feet in any direction.

For the first time, genuine terror struck her heart. He might actually die. And she beside him. It had merely been a frightening possibility before. Now it seemed to close in around her as cold and inescapable as the darkness.

"No," she choked out. "No! You're going to be all right. You've *got* to be."

He blinked up at her, his eyes glazed, unfocused. "Of course I am," he murmured dazedly. "And I told you before, I don't need any female fussing over . . ."

He passed out before he could finish the sentence.

Chapter 12

London

Prescott Hibbert reclined against the plush velvet cushions of his coach, lazily nudging off his boots and resting his stockinged feet on the seat opposite him. He loosened his cravat as the carriage rolled through the cobbled streets of Picadilly, and unbuttoned the brocade waistcoat that stretched too tightly over his rounded stomach.

Cool night air drifted through the curtained windows, carrying the scent of roses from nearby Hyde Park. Settling comfortably, Prescott smiled as he listened to the familiar sounds of the city that he loved and served: the shouts of hackney drivers cursing at one another, the laughter of evening revelers on their way home from the latest plays at Haymarket or Covent Garden.

Protecting all these people from the criminal element was a burdensome job, but it had its rewards. He flipped open his silver pocket watch—a gift from the Lord Mayor—and checked the time. Almost midnight.

He frowned with regret; he hated to return home from his club this early, but he needed to be at the Old Bailey at seven on the morrow. He had an important felony case to present before the King's Bench, and he wanted to look his best. Snapping the watch shut, he slid it back into his coat pocket.

With a sigh of bittersweet pleasure, he savored the memory of this night and the tastes that still lingered on his lips: rare roast beef, fresh oysters, quince pastry, fine port, and an expensive girl.

The chit he had enjoyed tonight had been a fetching little thing freshly arrived from the countryside. Dark hair, a lovely full mouth. About thirteen years old.

The procurers at his club, the Laikon Society, constantly amazed and delighted him with their offerings. The society catered to men like him, men of importance and responsibility who needed and deserved the very finest in recreation. They had an eye for the best feminine flesh, selecting only the freshest and loveliest girls from the scores who flocked into London every week. Operating with the utmost discretion, they lured the new arrivals with promises of employment and lodgings.

After the first month or so, most of the girls adjusted to their new circumstances. For those who did not, there was always opium.

The truly troublesome ones were handed over to those society members who had unusual tastes. Which had resulted in more than a few unfortunate incidents.

Which was why membership in the club was unspeakably expensive and absolutely secret, operating entirely on passwords and pseudonyms.

And it was worth every pound sterling he paid.

Prescott lit a long, slender cigar, smiling. Tonight's brunette had been brand new; he customarily requested the most recent acquisitions. She had fought him, of course, kicking and struggling. He always enjoyed that. Added a pleasant bit of sport to the evening's entertainment.

Inhaling deeply of the cigar, he rested his head against the velvet seat and blew a ring of fragrant smoke toward the coach's ceiling. Life was good. Life was very good indeed. He didn't see how it could get much better.

The coach rolled to a stop before his town house. Pulling his boots on, Prescott settled his tricorne on his head and picked up his silk cloak and ivory-topped walking stick.

His driver opened the door. " 'Ere we are, Your Honor."

"Very good, Cragg." Prescott lowered himself carefully down the steps to the ground. Years of indulgence had brought him a great deal of pleasure, but unfortunately they had also taken a certain physical toll.

"Same time tomorrow night, sir?"

"Of course, Cragg." Prescott slipped him a guinea and headed for the door.

This was the only part of the day he hated: returning home to his wife. If he was lucky, the old cow would already be asleep upstairs, having half-drowned herself in sherry as was her daily custom. Sometimes, entire blessed weeks went by when he didn't see her at all.

As usual, his valet opened the door, waiting with a silver tray that held a glass of warmed brandy.

But for some reason, tonight the butler was there as well. "Good evening, sir."

"Good evening." Prescott eyed the man curiously as he exchanged his hat, cloak, and cane for the brandy. "What are you doing up at this hour?"

"You have visitors, sir. The Honorable Mr. Lloyd and the Honorable Mr. Eaton. I explained that you weren't expected back until late, but they insisted on awaiting your return."

"Lloyd and Eaton?" The two were his closest friends, colleagues from the high court, and he saw them almost every day. What could be so pressing that it couldn't wait until morning? "Where are they, Covey? In my study?"

"Yes, sir."

"Thank you, Covey. You're dismissed for the night."

"Yes, sir. Thank you, sir." The butler headed off for the servants' quarters.

"You can retire as well." Prescott dismissed his valet with a flick of his hand, then started down the marble-tiled corridor that led to the rear of the house, swirling the brandy in his goblet. Damn and blast, he hoped this didn't concern the case he was presenting in the morning.

He opened the door to his study.

His two friends waited inside, seated before his desk, enjoying glasses of port. Before the hearth stood two other men he had never seen before—lower-class types, one a portly chap with his arm in a sling, the other a young lad with a shock of red hair and nervous, darting eyes.

"Hibbert!" Eaton came out of his chair. "We were beginning to think you'd never get here."

"Eaton." Prescott went forward to shake hands. "Lloyd." He kept looking at the two strangers, his curiosity becoming puzzlement. "What's this about?"

Lloyd pumped his hand enthusiastically. "News that couldn't wait until morning, old man."

"We knew you'd want to hear straight away."

"News?" Prescott walked around his desk and sat down. "What news?"

Lloyd gestured to the two men who stood by the hearth. "A spectacular escape, Hibbert—"

"Near Cannock Chase in Staffordshire a few days ago," Eaton put in. "These two marshalmen were part of it."

"A pair of criminals were being transported here for trial," Lloyd continued, "when they killed two of their guards and escaped into the Chase. These two brave marshalmen barely escaped with their lives. The entire Old Bailey's been abuzz about it since they arrived this afternoon."

"Gentlemen, I'm sure this will all make thrilling fodder for the newspapers, but Staffordshire is not my district," Prescott pointed out, not understanding his friends' excitement over such a mundane matter. "I really don't see why you—"

"One of the fugitives was a woman, Hibbert."

"And we think she might just be someone you know." Eaton turned to the two marshalmen and summoned them forward. "Come, my good man. Tell Magistrate Hibbert what you told us."

"Well, Squire," the fat one began, gingerly holding his arm, "we put up a 'eroic struggle, we did. Dangerous pair, these two. One's a footpad by the name of Jasper Norwell, a big 'ulking bloke, and 'e turned out to be a tricky sort. Nasty cove. We 'ad 'im shackled to the lass, but 'twas all fer naught—"

"Yes, yes, enough about him," Lloyd said impatiently. "Get to the part about the girl. Tell him about the girl."

"Oh, aye, the girl. She was ... well ... she was ..." He seemed to struggle to find words.

"Extraordinary," the lad said at last, turning his hat round and round in his hands. "Like the most perfect porcelain doll, sir. With a beautiful smile, and golden hair, and eyes of gold. I've never seen a woman like her. She didn't look like she belonged in gaol at all. A real lady, she was."

Eyes of gold. Prescott's hand tightened around his brandy glass. *It couldn't be. Samantha? Alive?*

"Tell him how old she was," Lloyd urged.

"I would say about twenty-two or twenty-three," the lad guessed, turning to his companion, who nodded in agreement.

"We thought at once of your long-lost niece, Hibbert," Eaton said excitedly.

"She disappeared five years ago, wasn't it?" Lloyd asked.

"Six," Prescott corrected, his mind racing. "She was sixteen at the time."

Samantha alive and in Staffordshire? He couldn't believe it, barely heard the rest of the conversation that continued around him. Despite all the lovelies he enjoyed at his club, he had never quite forgotten his beautiful, troublesome niece. The one female—the only one he'd encountered in his entire life—that he hadn't been able to bend to his will.

He had tried numerous times. Had actually come quite close on that last occasion . . . but he had never gotten the opportunity to sample her. She had refused him. She had defied him.

She had tried to kill him.

". . . Which would make this girl just the right age," Eaton was saying.

"Yes," Prescott choked out. "Yes, but I haven't seen her since the night she left here. This girl sounds like my Samantha, but there's no way to be sure."

It was impossible. A girl like Samantha could *not* have survived on her own! A gently bred, naive innocent, without a guinea to her name or a practical skill in the world, with no man to protect her?

She had been doomed from the moment she set foot outside his door. He had tried for a year to track her down, even calling upon the resources of the procurers from his club, but she had vanished.

Eaton turned to the marshalmen with a triumphant smile. "Tell him what else you remember about her."

"Yes, speak up," Prescott said impatiently. "There's a reward in it for both of you, if this is indeed my missing niece."

The portly lawman's face lit up at the mention of money. "She was arrested for thieving, sir. Stole some silver from a lady's 'ouse during an assembly—and when the lady turned 'er in, she said the girl's name was Miss Delafield. Miss *Samantha* Delafield."

Prescott almost dropped his glass. It was almost too good to be true. What had he been thinking earlier tonight? That life couldn't possibly get any better?

Well it had just improved, beyond even his dreams. After six years, he might finally have a chance to get his hands on Samantha. A chance to pay her back for the trouble she had caused him. To exact revenge for the attempt she had made on his life.

A revenge that would be both sweet . . . and slow. His retribution would be beyond anything she could possibly imagine.

He realized he was trembling, but it didn't come from fear. He was even more powerful now than he had been six years ago. Samantha's untimely demise had left him in full, legal possession of every last farthing of her inheritance. He had been financially comfortable before, but she had made him very wealthy indeed.

She posed no threat to him. She knew the truth about his taste for young girls, but that didn't bother him in the least. Who would believe the mad, desperate ravings of a wanted felon?

No, he was trembling with excitement. With anticipation.

"Hibbert? Hibbert, are you all right?"

Prescott nodded, realizing that his friends were staring at him. "Yes, yes. Forgive me, gentlemen, I'm . . . I'm overcome." He sat back in his chair, fanning himself. "To learn that my niece is *alive* after all these years . . ." He took a drink, felt the brandy burning through him, almost as hot as the blood lust sizzling through his veins. "It's quite a surprise."

"We knew you'd want to know right away," Lloyd said. "So that proper precautions can be taken."

"Precautions?" Prescott echoed.

"She may be a danger to you, Hibbert," Eaton pointed out. "She's an outlaw. And two marshalmen have been killed."

"The fugitives are being hunted down even as we speak." Lloyd looked concerned. "But if she somehow manages to make her way here to London . . ."

"Yes, I see what you mean." Prescott rose from his desk, pacing over to the window, looking out at the city lights. She wouldn't come to London. She wouldn't dare. "Indeed, precautions must be taken, but not the kind of precautions you mean."

He doubted the lawmen of Staffordshire would be lenient with her. And it would be a cruel twist of fate to have his revenge snatched away just when it was so close at hand.

He turned to look at his friends. "She must not be harmed, gentlemen."

"That's very Christian of you, Hibbert," Eaton said with an expression of disbelief, "considering she tried to kill you."

"You seem to have forgotten that she's quite mad." Prescott thought it best to start reminding everyone of his version of events, lest anyone take her seriously when she started spouting her version. "My two nieces never recovered from their parents' horrible death," he explained sadly, glancing at the marshalmen. "Despite all we did for them, the younger girl, Jessica, took ill the first winter and died. After that, the older girl, Samantha, went quite mad. She tried to kill me one night with a knife. And she escaped before I could have her committed."

"She *did* fight like a madwoman when we tried to lock 'er up in gaol," the portly marshalman said. "Kicked and bit and swore at us like a she-devil."

"There, you see?" Prescott nodded. "She belongs in an asylum, where she can't harm anyone. Where she can be properly cared for . . ." An idea occurred to him and he turned toward the window again. "Somewhere private. Discreet." He looked at his own reflection as a slow smile crept across his mouth. "I know just the place."

"So how shall we proceed?" Lloyd asked.

"We thought you'd want to keep this a quiet, family matter," Eaton said. "Wouldn't want any embarrassment. No one outside this room need even know she's your relation."

"No." Prescott shook his head, turning to address them using his best courtroom voice. "On the contrary. Gentlemen, it is my sworn duty to protect the people of England. If this Delafield girl is indeed my niece, we must bring her in and quickly. In fact, I shall go to Staffordshire at once to join the search personally." He looked at the two marshalmen. "If your men kill the male fugitive, so be it, but I want the girl alive. Do you understand me?" His fingers tightened around the fragile stem of his glass. "I want her taken alive and brought to me."

Chapter 13

⟨decorative flourish⟩

*F*lames. *Burning.* He had always known it would end here. In hell. *He was in hell.* He opened his mouth and could not cry out, opened his eyes and saw only darkness. A cavern of darkness with dancing flames all around, a blur of fire and agony. He shut his eyes against the truth he did not want to see. He was burning alive, could feel the devil's touch searing him through, body, bones, soul all ablaze, melting. Twisting and melting into a shapeless mass of pain without end.

Deeper and deeper he slid into the abyss, unable to fight his own inescapable, eternal damnation. He was falling falling falling into a corrosive pit that swallowed him whole. *Pain heat fire.* And he knew that the torment would never end never end never never never . . .

"Nicholas!"

And he was ten and he turned in the daylight, the bright, piercing daylight of Execution Dock, and saw his father on the scaffold, saw his tall, proud father standing there helpless with his hands behind his back and the rope around his neck.

"Father!" he shouted in horror, struggling against the hands that held him, against the men in their blue-and-white uniforms who had taken him from his father's ship and brought him here. He fought with all his strength but they would not let him go.

Helplessly, he watched as they forced his father up onto a stool—the navy officers he had worked for, the friends he had fought beside in the war against Spain. Why had they betrayed him? Why why why?

One of them tightened the rope around his father's throat. Nicholas called out to him, his hoarse, small voice lost in the growing roar of the crowd.

His father was calling back to him, something important, but Nicholas couldn't hear and he began crying and looked away but one of the men who held him grabbed his chin and forced his head up, forced him to watch.

"Remember this, lad. Remember English justice. This is how the admiralty deals with pirates."

And then all he could hear was screaming, his own voice screaming no no no his father wasn't a pirate never a pirate. James Brogan was a privateer, fighting for the king, a good man, an honorable man.

And he was all Nicholas had in the world. All they had was each other.

And then Captain Eldridge, who was his father's best friend, very best friend, knocked the stool from beneath his feet.

And his father was kicking, struggling . . .

Dying.

And they forced Nicholas to watch until he stopped moving.

Until James Brogan's struggles grew weaker and weaker and finally ended and his body swung back and forth in the breeze.

Back and forth on the rope as the crowd cheered.

Nicholas went limp, sobbing brokenly, collapsing in the navy officers' grasp, his body wracked by heaving, pitiful sobs that were larger than he was.

And they let go of him and he fell to the cobbles and lay there, weeping.

And he was alone.

Talons of fire clawed at him. Pain that burned and ravaged and consumed him until he was ash until he was nothing and still he hurt. Oh God let the hurt end let it end he could not bear any more he was nothing but agony and fire and there was no one to hear him no one to help him.

Lieutenant Wakefield stood over him, smiling, brandishing the glowing iron rod in his hand.

"Be grateful, boy." He spat a mouthful of tobacco onto the deck. "You're to be spared."

Nicholas did not reply, did not fight. Not because he was brave, but because he was too terrified to make even a sound. He did not understand what was happening, what ship this was or why they had brought him here. They had stripped him to the waist. One burly sailor held his arms pinned to the deck, another his legs.

And the one named Wakefield towered over him. "Welcome aboard the Molloch."

He pressed the white-hot metal against Nicholas's chest, pressed it down hard.

Nicholas screamed, a high-pitched scream like a bo'sun's whistle. The sky went spinning, turned black as he felt and heard the sizzle, smelled the acrid scent of his own flesh burning, felt the branding iron bite deeply into him.

He begged them to stop, but his cries and his tears made the navy men laugh.

And when they were done they picked him up and threw him into the hold.

Into a place beyond imagining, a place of darkness and ovenlike heat and the stench of too many bodies packed too closely together. And he cried and he hurt and he prayed, prayed for God to help him. For weeks.

Then he stopped.

Because God had abandoned him. The loving God his mother had told him about would not have done this to him. He came to realize that in this world, there were only devils and hell. Devils in blue uniforms, hell without end.

And he would never cry again.

Because he hated them all hated them all hated them all . . .

He opened his eyes and saw only darkness, saw that the flames had died down but he could still feel them.

Pain heat fire stop but God had abandoned him and he was alone and it would not end would never end never end never . . .

"Seventy-nine . . . eighty . . ."

The lash fell rhythmically, slicing into his skin. They had tied him to the Molloch's mast, stretching his arms tight around it. Splinters pricked the skin of his bare chest, stabbing at the mark they had burned into him five years ago.

"Eighty-one . . . eighty-two . . ."

He did not flinch, did not care. The first ten or twenty were always the worst. After that, a hazy numbness blunted the rest. He didn't feel pain anymore. Or anything at all. He pressed his cheek against the rough wood and stared at Wakefield as the lieutenant counted rhythmically.

"Eighty-three . . . eighty-four . . ."

Blood ran down his back, dripped onto the deck. He had killed a fellow prisoner. In self-defense, but that mattered to no one. His keepers needed little excuse to use their cat-o'-nine-tails. They beat him, fed him barely enough to keep him alive, tried to drain every bit of spirit and fight and feeling out of him.

"Eighty-five . . . eighty-six . . ."

But his hatred was enough to keep him alive. His hatred and his thirst for vengeance. One had become his food, the other his drink.

They nourished him, helped him grow stronger.

"Eighty-seven . . . eighty-eight . . ."

He kept himself alert, always. Never let the other prisoners corner him. Defended and stole every scrap of sustenance he could get his hands on. Trusted no one. Cared about no one but himself.

"Eighty-nine . . . ninety . . ."

Many who were older and stronger than him had died aboard this reeking, disease-infested scow. But not him. His wits and his hatred sustained him.

"Ninety-one . . . ninety-two . . ."

And at night when the darkness closed in, he dreamed.

"Ninety-three . . . ninety-four . . ."

Dreamed of cutting throats.

"Ninety-five . . ."

Lieutenant Wakefield would be the first. Then all the "friends" who had betrayed and killed his father. Especially Captain Eldridge. He would devise something special for Eldridge.

"Ninety-six . . ."

He dreamed of a sea of blood that would slake his thirst for vengeance.

"Ninety-seven . . ."

He ached for blood and planned the best way to obtain it.

"Ninety-eight . . ."

And the plan became a vow. He would become the one thing they feared. What they had made him. What they had branded him.

"Ninety-nine . . ."

A pirate.

The most fearsome pirate that England had ever seen.

"One hundred."

He swore, lashed out, trying to force the sound away, but it came again.

"You're not alone."

He could barely hear it, that whisper, so distant. Knew he must be dreaming. A voice like that did not belong here, with him, in hell. It angered him to hear a voice so sweet speaking words of reassurance, of hope.

Pain he could endure. Hope he could not.

"Shh, I'm right here," it persisted. "You're not alone."

No. No, he was alone and always would be and did not care.

Something touched him, a hand. A cloth. Featherlight against his cheek, his brow. Dampness. Water. So cool, so impossibly good.

A soft touch to match that concerned voice. Gentle water to cool the devil's fire.

A dream. It must be only a dream. Because he could not

*change what must be and he was where he belonged and here
he would stay.*

*Thou shalt not kill thou shalt not kill. Bless me, Father,
for I have sinned.*

No, the goodness could not last. He did not want it
did not want to hope for it. He surrendered to the fire.
Let it have him let it take him he would not fight anymore there was no point.

This was the end. His inevitable end.

Here he would stay, alone for all eternity.

Darkness closed in with the last, feeble flickers of
their last candle, bringing despair that cut through her
as sharply as a blade.

Sam hung her head, pressed a hand over her eyes,
tried to hold back the tears. But she could no longer
deny the truth.

He was dying.

Her shoulders started to shake, her whole body to
tremble as she sat there, crouched over him in the silent
cave that had begun to feel like a tomb. There was
nothing more she could do. Her best efforts weren't
good enough. She had failed him, failed them both.

And they would pay with their lives.

Her breath seemed to leave her body in one long sob.
She had done everything she could think of, stayed
awake hour after hour, tending him until the days and
nights had become a sleepless blur. She didn't even
know how long they had been in here—three days,
maybe four.

She had tried to cool the fever with water, giving him
all that remained in the flask, saving only a few drops
for herself. When that was gone, she had started using
rags to capture the scant trickle of moisture that
dripped down the cave wall, painstakingly soaking the
cloth as full as she could and then wringing it out over
his lips.

She had used the blade of the knife to cauterize his

wounded shoulder, hoping it would stop the bleeding better than her stitching. Then she had stripped off the tattered remains of his shirt and bathed him, again and again, cooling his body as much as she could.

But nothing helped. For a time, he had seemed to improve, only to take a turn for the worse.

And now his breathing had become a labored rasp, so faint she could barely hear it. His body lay utterly still, ravaged by the fever that burned out of control. He no longer called out or groaned or made any sound at all—nothing but that low, fragile whisper of breath.

She pressed her fingers against his wrist . . . but felt only the slightest trace of a pulse.

Shaking her head in denial, she held his hand in hers, wrapping her fingers around his broad, calloused palm.

"Please," she whispered. "*Please.*"

But there was no response. None. She closed her eyes, thinking of all the times she had witnessed the power in this man's hands. She had seen him grasp a pistol, wield an axe, strike out at his enemies; she had known the strength of his embrace when he held her fast, when he saved her in the waterfall . . .

When he comforted her at the cave entrance while she had been so frightened.

Now all of that strength had been stolen away, all of his power taken from him. She threaded her fingers through his, squeezing hard, willing him to fight. But he remained silent, still, unable—unwilling, it seemed—to strike back at this enemy.

He had surrendered. He had given up his grasp on this world, and she was powerless to hold him here.

Trembling, she stared down at him in the last, glimmering light of the candle. His hand looked so large and dark and rugged against hers. She could not believe that something unseen, something insubstantial, could kill a man of such strength and toughness.

But she could feel the fever taking him . . . could feel

the last tentative pulsations of life draining from him.

"*No.*" She wrapped both her hands around his, stubborn enough for both of them. "No, you can't quit. Not now. Not after all we've come through. *I won't let you.*"

But even as she said the words, her tears began to fall, one after another sliding down her cheeks, hot, unstoppable. All the stubbornness in the world would not help him. Nothing could help him. How could she hope to save him? Her own strength was utterly spent.

She was too weak even to hold back her own tears.

A rush of terror and despondency overwhelmed her, stole her breath, her hope. For days, she had resisted despair, refusing to give in, enduring to the limits of her endurance and beyond . . . only to come to this.

Death. Slow, brutal death in the darkness.

The shattering thought tore through her and she slumped over, still holding his hand, barely aware when her forehead came to rest against his rib cage. She closed her eyes and let the hot, choking sobs take her, let the tears cascade down her skin and down his. She was beyond caring, could not bear anymore, could not pretend to be brave anymore.

He had given up his will to fight . . . and extinguished hers.

Part of her wanted to strike him or shake him or yell at him but instead she lay there crumpled beside him, crushed beneath the sheer weight of futility and frustration and helplessness, worn out from too many days without sleep or water or food.

The depth of her feelings stunned her. Because she was not only crying for herself.

That fact struck her with the jarring, painful impact of a pistol shot—she was not simply crying for herself, for fear of her own fate.

She was crying for him.

Him.

She didn't even know his name. She shut her eyes

tighter, tried to stop the sudden, surging flood of emotions.

And failed, utterly. As she had failed at all the rest.

It was undeniable. She felt not only desperation and futility but sorrow. More than anything else, sorrow. For a stranger.

For a man who had come into her life like a thunderbolt straight out of a storm cloud, startling and unexpected, striking hard, changing everything.

She felt astonished, huddled next to him there in the darkness. She could no longer dismiss what she felt for this unpredictable rogue as simple gratitude, or admiration or respect. Her feelings were far more confusing and complex than that; and they were not merely the result of exhaustion. She knew better now.

She knew *him* better now.

Far better than she had when they entered the cave three or four days ago.

He had been delirious for hours, calling out in pain, thrashing until she had to hold him down with all her strength, afraid he would injure himself further. For much of that time, he had been talking, calling out names, cursing, uttering garbled gibberish . . .

And sometimes speaking quite clearly.

Speaking of things so chilling, so horrible, she could only hope he was hallucinating.

But she didn't think he was.

Sam pushed herself up to her knees, wiping at her damp cheeks, gazing down at the brand on his chest through a blur of tears. She didn't know *what* to think anymore, much less what to feel. Before, she had been curious about his past.

Now she almost wished she didn't know.

Because between his fevered ramblings and the little she did know about him, she had managed to piece together a wrenching picture of his childhood.

In his delirium, he had cried out "Father" several times, and spoken of a rope. A scaffold. He had stared into the darkness as if watching it all unfold before his eyes—an execution.

His father's execution. He had been forced to watch his father hanged for some offense.

And that was when he had been consigned to the prison hulk.

Sam looked down at him, still holding his hand, unable to make herself let go. He had been orphaned at a young age . . . an experience she understood all too well.

She swallowed hard, her throat painfully tight. Seeing him now, with his full beard and broad chest and chiseled muscles, it was hard to imagine him as a boy.

But she could imagine how he had felt. Fresh tears slipped from her lashes as she thought of a small boy with bright green eyes, so alone, so terrified, sentenced to a fate that must have been a living death—jailed for a crime not his own, lost among strangers, beaten and lashed and tormented for God knew how many years.

She didn't understand how he had escaped the hulk or what had happened to him after that; she had only been able to puzzle out fragments of his fevered ramblings. It seemed bitterly ironic to know more about who he had been, decades ago, than about who he was now.

But was it any wonder he had become a hardened man, hostile and sarcastic and cold toward a world that had treated him so coldly?

She finally let go of his hand, bitterness and regret rising in her chest. She would never have the chance to understand him. Would never know anything more about him. He had come into her life a stranger, less than a week ago.

And he would die a stranger.

Kneeling at his side in the silent cave, listening to what could be his last breaths, she covered her face with her hands. Tried to find some shred of courage or wisdom or hope that could help him.

"Please," she whispered. "Please, God, help me." Clenching her fists, she lifted her head, staring desperately up into the darkness. "*Help us.*"

The fire chose that moment to flicker out, leaving her in complete darkness.

There was no sound but the liquid drip of water down the cave wall.

And the labored, tenuous breathing of her companion.

She began to tremble, first her hands, then her arms, then her entire body. A new emotion overpowered all the others; perhaps it came simply from the feeling of her own nails digging into her palms, but a sweeping tide of raw determination poured through her.

She would not give in. Not as long as there was breath left in his body and a heart beating in his chest. She would not admit defeat. And she would waste no more time on tears.

"I am not going to give up on you," she said fiercely, staring down at the man she could no longer see. "Do you hear me? I am not going to give up!"

She shouted it so loud, her own words echoed back to her from the depths of the cavern. *I am not going to give up . . . not going to give up . . . not going to give up.*

Turning, she felt for the rag she had been using earlier and crawled on her hands and knees over to the cave wall, pressing the cloth to the trickle of water. As soon as it was wet, she moved back to his side and started bathing him again, sweeping the damp cloth over his chest, his arms, his face. Cooling him as best she could. Trying to return life to his battered body.

They had endured worse than this—both of them. Somehow they would survive this as well.

Together, they would survive.

Clenching her jaw, she uttered the same words he had shouted at her in the whirlpool. "Damn it, don't you give up on me now!"

*   *   *

A flutter of wings passed overhead, close enough to brush her cheek.

Startled awake, Sam sat up, heart pounding. What was happening? What was that sound? Had it been a dream? Disoriented, blinking, she rubbed her eyes, trying to right her whirling thoughts.

The cave was silent, empty.

She must have been dreaming, must've fallen into an exhausted sleep . . . though it couldn't have been for long. The glow of a fire still shimmered in the biscuit tin; earlier, she had gathered some moss from the cave walls, scraping it off with the knife, in the hopes that it might burn. It had not only burned, but it burned slowly. It gave off an unpleasant, sour odor, but at least it provided some light, however meager.

Fully awake now, her eyes adjusting to the blackness, she turned to look down at the man beside her, reached out to touch his forehead.

And found his skin no longer ablaze beneath her fingers.

She started to smile in relief, but as she bent over to study him more closely, she realized he was still deathly pale, his breathing shallow and unsteady. And his pulse . . .

Pressing her fingers to his neck, she could feel it, but just barely.

The fever had finally broken.

But it might have already broken him. Relief might have come too late.

He made a low sound, a weak groan. She almost shouted with joy. A sound was a sound, a sign of life, no matter how faint.

Then a shudder went through him, followed by another. He began shivering, as if he were cold, freezing.

And her spirits fell almost as quickly as they had lifted. For hours—days—she had battled against the fever that had threatened to burn him alive, and now it seemed he might freeze to death instead. Her meager fire would not heat him any more than the candle had. Nor did she have any blankets. And the thin cotton sheet would be useless. The only way she could keep him warm would be to . . .

She moved away from him, instinctively. The idea of his almost-naked body pressed against hers—

The chain brought her up short. She couldn't get away. From him, from what he needed.

Or from her fear. The fear that had been indelibly marked on her soul in that night of violence when she was fifteen.

She had seen the hunger in his eyes. Knew that he wanted her, the way a man wanted a woman. Whenever he had looked at her that way, she had ignored it. Changed the subject. Brushed him aside with some haughty comment. It was that hunger in his eyes that made her reluctant to trust him.

He groaned again, the sound so pitiful, so filled with pain.

Sam stared down at him, torn between the need to help him . . . and the caution that had been her shield, her protection, her way of life for so many years.

But he would not survive without her help. She could not turn away from him now.

And for Heaven's sake, he was unconscious! Wounded. Ravaged by days of fever.

She breathed deeply, tried to slow her racing heart and her spinning thoughts. By all the graces, she knew what she had to do. If only she had—

The flutter of wings swept past her again.

Sam whirled. Eyes darting, she turned one way and another. It *hadn't* been a dream. That sound was real. Bats. But it was ridiculous to feel afraid of a bat after everything else she had faced in the past few days.

Then she saw a small shape, just beyond the edge of the firelight.

And it wasn't a bat.

It was a bird.

She stared, unable to breathe for a moment. *A bird.* A small, brown, ordinary sparrow. It hopped closer, pecked at the pile of moss beside the biscuit tin.

Sam blinked at it. How had it gotten inside? Through the crevasse behind the falls? She doubted a bird could navigate the twisting tunnels and low openings they had squeezed through—not in the darkness.

It must have come in through another entrance.

Another *exit.*

One not far from here.

Almost as soon as she had the thought, the bird hopped away and took flight, into the darkness—heading away from the direction they had come, away from the falls.

Sam's heart pounded, and she realized she was shaking. Not with fear this time, but with hope. Despite everything, there was hope.

A way out, a way to freedom!

She turned back to the rogue, summoning her courage.

Her trust.

If she gave in to her fears now, it would mean certain death for both of them. She had no choice. Swallowing hard, she edged closer.

And lay down beside him.

And felt instantly, uncomfortably aware of every muscled inch of him. Of every shiver that went through his angular frame. Of the way her body fit perfectly to his, even when she merely pressed against his side. As if she'd been made to fit there.

Her stomach in knots, she slid one arm across his midsection . . . slowly . . . and rested her head on his chest. And felt the matted hair, bristly against her cheek.

And the brand.

And she did not dare close her eyes.

Chapter 14

Floating. He felt himself floating. Strange that he could do that, when his body felt so heavy. Weighted down. As if he were made entirely of lead. Yet he drifted, carried by a warm tide. One made not of water, but of fog . . . soft, dusky, pleasant . . . just like the scent that drew him to awareness.

A familiar scent. As captivating as it was delicate. A whisper of warm temptation. It enticed him out of the darkness, but he felt so weak, so heavy . . . so drowsy . . .

With a monumental effort, he lifted one eyelid, halfway.

Then the other.

His head spun dizzily. He couldn't see anything but darkness . . . and the unsteady glow of some kind of light on his left. He wondered where he was. He should know, he thought. But he could not remember. How had he come to be in this place? And where exactly was he?

Everything looked remote, hazy, blurry, as if he were viewing it through the reverse end of a spyglass.

What, for example, was this unfamiliar tangle of blonde hair just beyond the end of his nose?

He blinked once, twice, until it finally came into focus.

A woman. It was a woman.

Miss Delafield, his memory supplied.

He almost smiled, found he didn't have the strength. But what a pleasant surprise. Well worth the effort of opening his eyelids.

Miss Delafield. Yes, of course. Other bits and pieces started clicking together in his mind. *Shackles. Bullet. Forest. Waterfall* . . .

But none of those held his attention at the moment, not compared to the woman wrapped intimately around him. She lay curled beside him, half atop him, her head resting on his chest. Asleep. Soft . . . warm.

She brought his senses awake one by one—the irresistible dusky-sweet scent that was uniquely hers, the silky feel of her hair against his bare skin, the delicate warmth of her breath caressing his chest . . .

He liked having her here. Liked it very much. They fit so perfectly together. He had known they would.

But by God, he had never known that just having her here with him could feel so good. He had been waking up alone for so many years. This felt . . . right. In a way that went beyond explanation. Impossibly, achingly right.

He tried to lift his hand, longing to touch her, but it required too much strength.

That frustrated him. Blast. It seemed incredibly unfair.

Just keeping his eyes open required more effort than he could manage. He resisted . . . but the fog enfolded him again, slowly pulling him down . . . warm, soft, silky. Like the lady who held him close . . . so gentle, so innocent.

And somehow he found the strength to smile.

Sam came awake all at once, startled by a loud sound. She remained where she was, disoriented. She couldn't see in the complete blackness that surrounded her.

She couldn't believe she had fallen asleep. Deeply,

peacefully . . . easily. Even as she tried to adjust to that surprising fact, she recognized the sound that had awakened her.

His heartbeat, beneath her ear.

Steady, strong.

Gasping, she listened for a moment. There was no mistake. She could feel his heart thudding with a regular, powerful rhythm. And he was no longer shivering. The chills had passed; his skin felt warm beneath her cheek, her arm, her hand. His chest rose and fell evenly. His breathing had returned to normal.

He was going to be all right.

She couldn't move for a moment, swept up in a wave of emotions that washed over her all at once. She whispered a prayer of thanks, closing her eyes, the worry and despair pouring off her like rain, leaving behind relief. Joy.

And something more. That unfamiliar feeling she had first noticed last night. Like sympathy, but stronger, mingled with a sort of . . . She couldn't define it. Fellowship, perhaps; the kind soldiers must feel after going through battle together. She had no word for it, but words did not matter at the moment.

He was going to live.

Her muscles went slack as her tension drained away. They would be able to leave the cave, perhaps soon. There were things she should do. Find more moss. Rekindle the fire in the biscuit tin. Get more water.

But at the moment she didn't want to do anything but stay right where she was, beside him. Listening to the sound of his heartbeat.

A moment later, she opened her eyes, lifting her head, feeling uneasy. *What was she thinking?*

She *wanted* to stay beside him?

Unsettled by thoughts she could not untangle, she turned away and busied herself relighting the fire. With a scrape of steel against granite, sparks became flame, and after a few minutes, a scant pool of light encircled them.

Setting the little knife aside, she watched the golden glow warm his features, realizing that her own breathing had become unsteady. She stared down at him, wishing she could make sense of these uncomfortable, unfamiliar new feelings. For so many years, she had carefully kept her distance from men—but now, all of that caution seemed to have vanished.

He remained peacefully asleep, blissfully ignorant of her plight. He looked as blameless as an angel.

A dark angel.

She frowned. Angel, indeed. He was just what he had been all along: a rogue. A stranger.

But instead of feeling wary of him, she felt . . . curious. Drawn to him by some powerful force she had never felt before in her life, could not explain.

Without thinking, she reached out to touch him. As if in a trance, she let her hand move slowly over the broad expanse of his chest, tracing the massive curve of shoulder into bicep, the veins that stood out on his arms. Even his wrists were large, heavy. It seemed he had been made with no softness at all, every part of him rugged, angular, hard.

Whatever gentleness he possessed was well hidden. Perhaps so deeply that even he didn't know it was there.

Fascinated, she couldn't make herself stop as her fingers encountered one unexpected texture after another. He was so different from her in every way. The roughness of the dark hair that blanketed his chest and narrowed to a fine line down the center of his body. The ridges of muscle that sharply defined his ribcage.

But somehow the differences didn't seem threatening at all. They seemed . . . intriguing.

Sam went still, her hand coming to rest over the pitchfork brand. Her heart was pounding. And an unfamiliar heat spread through her middle, pooling deep in her belly.

Now what was happening to her? This sensation was utterly foreign, yet it seemed to come from the very depths of her being.

Oddly, she noticed that *his* heart seemed to be beating much faster than it had before . . .

She froze. Unable to move, to even lift her hand, she turned her head, slowly, as if in a dream, to look at his face.

And found him staring up at her.

Their gazes locked. She felt as if she'd been struck by a bolt of emerald lightning.

She snatched her hand back, her senses and her thoughts scrambled. "You're awake."

She immediately felt like a fool for stating the obvious. A blaze of color heated her cheeks. How *long* had he been awake? While she had held him in her arms? While she had looked at him, touched him? *What in the world had she been doing?*

He blinked at her, slowly, drowsily.

And the smallest hint of a smile curved his mouth.

A thoroughly devilish smile.

The brigand. The rogue! He *had* been awake. Perhaps the entire time. And he hadn't let her know. Hadn't stopped her. He had let her . . . let her . . .

Sam wished the cavern floor would split open and swallow her whole. She started to explain, then realized she couldn't.

What possible explanation could she offer? She didn't understand herself. None of her thoughts, feelings, or actions lately were the least bit rational.

Besides which, she seemed to have completely lost her ability to speak.

But perhaps he wasn't fully conscious yet. Perhaps he was still a bit delirious. Perhaps he wouldn't remember.

He struggled to speak, said something she couldn't

make out. She leaned closer to hear what he was saying. Hoped it would be something feverish. A nice hallucination would do.

"How . . . long?" he rasped.

That sounded completely lucid.

Damn.

And she wasn't sure exactly what he meant. How long had they been in the cave? Or how long had she been holding him and . . . ?

She chose to answer the former. "You've been unconscious a long time." She turned to pick up one of the rags she had used earlier to soak up water, suddenly wanting something to occupy her attention. And her hands. "Three or four days, I think."

He winced, lifted his head, tried to get up.

"No, don't," she said, concern instantly replacing her other emotions. "You're not ready for any kind of acrobatics just yet. Are you in pain?"

He lay down again, blinking as if to clear his vision. He flexed his left shoulder experimentally. "Not bad."

Satisfied, she moved away from him, grateful for whatever distance she could get at the moment. Making her way over to the cavern wall on her knees, she repeated the now familiar, painstaking process of gathering water.

When she had enough to fill the cup halfway, she moved back to him. Supporting his head with her hand, she brought the cup to his lips.

He took a slurping, greedy swallow and almost choked.

"Slowly," she cautioned. "Take it slowly."

With a low sound of impatience, he drained the cup in seconds then lay back on the bunched-up sheet that pillowed his head. He looked exhausted merely from the effort of drinking. He closed his eyes.

And didn't ask anything more.

She turned the battered goblet round and round in her fingers. "I took out the stitches and cauterized your wound to stop the bleeding," she explained. "It'll make an awful scar, but I didn't think you'd mind. That is, you have so many." She barely paused for a breath. "I'm afraid there's no food left. And hardly any water. Just what I've been able to soak from the wall. And I had to use up all the candles. But I kept the fire going with some moss. I know it smells awful, but it burns slowly."

She was babbling. Why was it suddenly important to fill up the silence with words?

Those dark lashes lifted and he gazed up at her, eyes gleaming darkly in the firelight. "You saved my life."

He said it curtly, gruffly. No doubt because speaking taxed his strength—not because her saving him had made him feel any emotion. She found that too hard to believe.

Unsure how to respond, she simply nodded.

"Thanks, angel," he murmured.

She blinked down at him, speechless. He had just expressed gratitude toward her. Gratitude. *Thanks* was not a word that had ever found its way to his lips before now.

And that one simple, mundane word, that expression of genuine human feeling, warmed her heart beyond reason.

"I think there's a way out," she said brightly. "Maybe just ahead. I saw a bird, a sparrow. It flew that way." She gestured, turned to search the darkness. "The exit can't be far. Maybe only a few yards . . ."

Turning back to him, she saw that he had fallen asleep again.

". . . and here I am talking to myself like a fool."

She blushed profusely. The word *fool* described perfectly how she felt. Somehow, between the time she had entered this cave and the moment he had awakened to gaze up at her with those jewel-bright eyes, she had been transformed into a flustered featherwit.

She closed her eyes, rubbed at her temples. "Get

ahold of yourself, Samantha Delafield," she whispered. "This is no time to lose your mind!"

There had to be a logical explanation for what was happening to her. She was tired. She'd been under a great deal of strain. She'd been living in a cave, for Heaven's sake! What she needed was to get out of here. Then she'd be fine. Then she would feel like herself again.

Yes, she would feel like herself again. Soon.

The sooner, the better.

The chain scraped the stone floor with a metallic jangle as they walked—but for once the sound made Sam feel happy. Almost exhilarated. It was good to be moving again. Moving toward freedom.

A cool breeze on her face made her pause. "Do you feel that? Fresh air." She turned to look over her shoulder. "The exit must be just ahead."

"Well then, keep walking," her companion urged, panting for breath. "Don't wait for me. Something tells me I won't be far behind."

She smiled ruefully. He was regaining his sense of humor—sarcasm and all. A few extra hours of sleep had helped him immeasurably, but he was still very weak.

Once they had started out, he had refused to stop and rest, perhaps fearing that he might not get up again. Though, of course, he would never admit that.

She hadn't argued with him this time. She was just as eager as he was to get out of here. Perhaps more so. She never wanted to see another cave as long as she lived.

She hefted the fishing creel on her shoulder and kept walking.

The creel was much lighter minus the foodstuffs and whiskey bottle. They had precious few supplies left— just the utensils, the sack of coins, the fishing lines and rope. He held the biscuit tin, its glimmering fire illuminating their footsteps. Whenever she spotted a patch of moss, she scraped it off with the knife and added it to the tin.

They turned a corner and she saw a gleam of light ahead.

She stopped in her tracks. "Oh, thank God!" she breathed.

"That doesn't look like sunlight," he said dubiously.

As her eyes adjusted, Sam realized he was right. The light that spilled across the rocky floor a few paces ahead wasn't bright and golden like sunlight; it was a muted glow. Almost unnatural.

"Almost like a lantern," she whispered. "Or—"

"Listen," he said sharply. "What's that sound?"

She strained her ears. There could be no mistake.

They both said it at the same time.

"Waterfall."

She felt her stomach drop to her toes. No, it couldn't be! The thought of having to go through another bout with the river . . .

They looked at each other. His expression held the same reluctance and dread she felt.

But a moment later, he clenched his jaw. "Let's go," he said grimly.

"Right." She echoed his determination. They had survived days of the worst kind of suffering in this place. After all that, she refused to be daunted by any obstacle placed in their path.

Quickly, without another moment's hesitation, they walked toward the light, side by side. The cavern floor sloped downward, and the walls closed in around them, narrowing until they were forced to stoop over. The sound of the water grew louder, the wind stronger.

An opening appeared ahead, blocked by branches. Her pulse raced. They might find themselves at the top of a cliff or some awful precipice.

They pushed the branches aside. Cautiously slipped through the exit, bracing themselves.

It was like stepping out of the cold pits of hell straight into heaven.

Into a lush, green Eden.

Sam gasped in awe as they straightened and looked around. The light they had seen was not sunlight but *moon*light. And starlight. Gleaming on a carpet of grass that stretched before them. They had exited into a small glade, tucked into a corner of the mountain of rock that formed the cavern. Craggy walls of stone protected it on three sides, while the fourth opened into the forest.

The waterfall they had heard was little more than a gentle shower, spilling over the hillside on the opposite side of the clearing, into a stream that wound through the pines and oak and ash trees of the forest.

Silently, they walked forward, out into the fresh air. She inhaled deeply. The scent of summer flowers, grass, leaves met them like a warm welcome and she knew she would never forget this particular fragrance as long as she lived. She had never smelled anything so sweet in her entire life!

The silver light, the clear night air, the sound of the wind in the trees, even the waterfall—they all seemed ordinary yet new, familiar yet exquisite.

They were *alive*.

She wanted to fall to her knees in gratitude and dance across the grass at the same time. Joy welled in her heart and flooded through her, so overpowering it brought tears to her eyes, so refreshing she swore she could taste it.

Then her eyes fastened on the stream, and she glanced at the rogue, and she didn't need to express the thought they were both thinking.

Water.

They rushed, stumbled, ran toward the stream, and fell onto the bank and slurped up handfuls of the fresh, cool, clear liquid. She didn't bother to dig out the cups from the fishing creel. Didn't care. She splashed her face, her hair. Her relief bubbled up in her throat and came out as laughter.

A small, furry creature dashed away from the opposite bank to take refuge in a nearby shrubbery.

"A rabbit," she exclaimed in delight, breathless, falling onto her back. "I don't think I've ever seen anything so wonderful in my whole life."

"Forget wonderful—he looks like supper to me." The rogue studied the spot where the rabbit had disappeared. "Where there's one, there are probably more. Maybe a whole warren."

"But how can we catch them? We don't have the pistol anymore."

"We've got fishing lines. I'll make some snares." He stretched out beside her, looked up at the night sky.

And suddenly cursed.

"What?" Sam followed his gaze, but saw nothing threatening in the cloudless black sky spangled with stars. "What's wrong?"

"The moon is wrong," he choked out, sitting up. "The night we stayed at the cabin, it was a quarter full. Look at it now."

"It's half full." Sam shrugged. "What does it matter?"

"It matters because we weren't in there for three or four *days*. We were in there for a week. I've lost an entire *week*." He uttered a short, vicious oath. "I'll never make it to York in time."

Chapter 15

"I don't understand why you are in such a foul mood."

Nicholas didn't reply to Miss Delafield's annoyed comment. He was busy trying to retrieve a fish bone from between his teeth, and he wasn't about to apologize for his swearing, his table manners, or his temper.

They had settled beneath a stand of trees a few yards from the small waterfall. The moon and the firelight shone on the remains of their supper, scattered around them on the riverbank; they had roasted two rabbits and a fish, fried a half-dozen eggs—gathered from a nest near the water's edge—in the biscuit tin, and made short work of a score of wild strawberries found growing beneath the evergreens.

But even a hot meal in his belly hadn't improved his humor in the least.

One week. He had lost an entire week. Which left him only five days to get to York before Michaelmas. Impossible. Food and rest were helping to restore his strength, but he would never make it in time. Not on foot. He needed a horse.

And how the devil was he supposed to obtain a horse in the middle of Cannock Chase?

"I honestly don't see what difference a few extra days makes." Miss Delafield lay on her back, her head

191

pillowed on the fishing creel, as she contentedly munched a strawberry. "Surely whoever you're meeting in York will understand the delay."

"Not bloody likely," Nicholas muttered, sitting near her feet, his back against a pine tree. He finally dislodged the fish bone and flicked it toward the stream.

"Well, we're alive. That's something to be grateful for."

Rubbing at his irritated tooth, he slanted her a glare. Her cheery attitude had grated on his nerves all night, ever since they had left the cave. He had had enough. "Why?" he snapped. "What's there to feel grateful for? That the inevitable has been postponed? It may have slipped your mind, your ladyship, but we're still facing a few problems. Like these for one." He shook his right leg, jangling the shackles. "Not to mention a few dozen lawmen out there somewhere"—he jerked a thumb toward the far end of the glade, where it opened into the forest—"who want to put a bullet or two or ten into us. It's a little early to be holding a victory parade."

She levered herself up on her elbows, her expression as calm as her voice. "I think the fact that we were in the cave for seven days instead of three or four is a good thing. It works in our favor. The lawmen obviously gave up searching this part of the forest a long time ago. Maybe they're looking for us in the towns by now. Or maybe they think we're dead. Or—"

"Or maybe they're still out there somewhere. Waiting for us to fall into their snare just like Mr. Bunny here fell into ours." He nodded toward the blackened carcass impaled on a spit over their open fire.

She glanced at the rabbit, then back at him. "You're right. We have plenty to worry about. And as soon as you're strong enough to move on, we'll worry about it." Lying down again, she sighed wearily. "But do I have to think of all that right this minute?"

Nicholas muttered an oath. He couldn't *stop* thinking

about it. He had wanted to press on the instant he realized how much time they'd lost. But he wasn't strong enough for a grueling trek through the woods. Not yet.

Which aggravated him more than anything else. The pain in his shoulder had ebbed to a dull throb that he barely noticed, but the fever had sapped his energy, left him weak when he most needed to take action. The feeling was intolerable. It seemed as if his own body had joined the conspiracy against him.

And he already had enough to contend with: time quickly running short, marshalmen somewhere hunting for him, no weapons on hand.

And this stubbornly cheerful lady chained to his ankle.

Who vexed him in ways he didn't want to think about.

Nicholas picked up the flask by his side and drank a long swallow of clear, cool water, wishing it were fiery, bracing whiskey instead. "You're right. Why worry?" He wiped his mouth with the back of his hand. "It's only a matter of life and death. *Ours.*"

She gazed up at the night sky, her expression still unconcerned. "My point exactly. Don't you think that if we were meant to die, we would have died in that cave? Or been cut to ribbons by the rocks in the whirlpool? Or been caught by the dogs on the riverbank?"

"I don't believe in fate, Miss Delafield."

"Neither do I," she said adamantly. "There aren't any guarantees in life. I know that. Believe me, I know that." She closed her eyes, just for a second, and her voice was softer when she continued. "But we *didn't* die. We're alive. For now, for this moment, we're all right. Isn't that enough? Do you always have to look at the dark side of things?"

"I'm not looking at the dark side. I'm looking at the only side. The realistic side."

"Fine." She raised her head and shot him an icy

golden glare. "You go right ahead and be realistic. I am going to lie here on the grass and listen to the wind and look at the stars and be grateful and happy that I'm still alive. Because for the last few days—"

"*Seven* days."

"For the last *seven* days I thought I might never see any of this again!" She lay down once more, folding her arms over her chest. "I'm rather enjoying getting reacquainted with the moon and the stars, and when the sun rises in an hour or so, I'm going to enjoy that, too. And I would greatly appreciate it if you would shut up and stop ruining it for me."

Nicholas clenched his teeth, bit back a hot retort. He normally wouldn't sit still while anyone chastised him—least of all a woman. But arguing with this lady was clearly a waste of breath and logic.

He took out his frustrations by tossing pebbles toward the stream, testing the strength of his injured left arm.

Silence fell between them, as heavy as the chain that bound them together, as vast as the night sky overhead, broken only by the crackle of the fire and the liquid rush of the waterfall a few yards upriver.

A warm breeze ruffled his hair. Somewhere off to the left, a small animal ambled through the underbrush. The stream burbled over smooth stones as it flowed past, and silvery pinpricks of starlight reflected off the shallow waters.

If not for the ocean of troubles facing him, he thought sourly, still tossing pebbles, he might have found this little glade peaceful. Even pleasant. There was a great deal a man could make of a moonlit night, a soft carpet of grass, and a lady in a good mood . . .

He switched to his right hand, trying to cut short that line of thought. Ideas like that could prove dangerous to his health.

He didn't have time for any kind of pleasure. He had

to concentrate on getting his strength back and getting the hell out of here.

"We've been given another chance," Miss Delafield said, suddenly breaking the silence. "And I think we're going to be all right."

He paused in mid-throw. "By what logic do you reach that conclusion?"

"Not by logic at all. By faith."

He sent the pebble sailing off in a long arc, uttering a short, sharp sound of derision. "To think I had started to consider you intelligent."

"Pardon me," she retorted, sitting up. "I should have guessed. You're too *realistic* to believe in anything or anyone but yourself."

"You've got that right, lady."

"You've got it all figured out, don't you? You're in charge and nobody else."

"Right again."

"What you are is arrogant. Too arrogant and cold-hearted for a concept like faith. Or even simple human caring." Her gaze locked on his. "You might give *one* of them a try sometime."

He caught that less-than-subtle jibe and purposely let it pass without comment.

When he didn't say anything, she turned her back on him. The chain pulled taut. Shoulders rising and falling, she fumed silently and stared at the river.

Nicholas knew what she was angry about, and tried to ignore her.

Which was bloody difficult when he couldn't get more than two feet away from her.

Just looking at her slender back, he experienced the stab of a too-familiar feeling: guilt. He was being a real bastard, taking out his problems on her. He owed her his life. He would've died in that cave if not for her.

Alone, he would've died.

His time in the cavern was nothing but a blur of pain and heat. He remembered none of it . . . except her, always beside him, cooling his brow, whispering encouragement, comforting him.

He had been lost, alone, beyond the bleak edge of darkness.

And she had brought him back. She had cared for him, cared *about* him, in a way that no one else had for years.

And now he was acting as if none of it had ever happened.

He glanced away, looked at the waterfall, told himself there was no reason to feel guilt. Or anything else. Aye, he would not have survived the fever without her; but she would not have survived the whirlpool without him. They had agreed at the start that they would keep one another alive. A fair trade. Simple enough.

At least it had seemed simple, just a few short days ago. He had even thought that he might have to kill her because she could be a danger to him.

And she still could be a danger to him.

But killing her, hurting her in any way, was utterly out of the question.

You've got it all figured out. He shut his eyes. Hellfire and damnation, he wished that were still true. He didn't know how everything had become so blasted complicated. He didn't want things to change between them, didn't want to feel anything for her. He had to think of himself, as he always had in the past.

That was the only way to survive. The kind of simple human caring she talked about could prove dangerous to his health.

And so he said not one word to her about what had taken place in the cave. He had told her thanks; what more did she want?

What did it matter to him if she felt angry and hurt? He didn't care. He did not . . .

He glanced her way, and somehow the word *care* stuck in his throat. It got all tangled up with the guilt and almost choked him.

Swallowing hard, he glared resentfully at her back. No woman he had ever met in his life had made him feel so confused. No woman had ever made him feel anything at all, beyond simple lust.

What the hell was she doing to him?

At the moment, she wasn't doing anything at all, staring off into the darkness, her spine stubbornly straight, her hair a flaxen cascade that fell to her waist. She looked almost regal, warmed by the golden fire, crowned by silver starlight.

Regal and cool and distant.

But he had glimpsed a completely different side of her in the cave. *That* he remembered vividly: the sensation of awakening to the soft brush of her fingertips over his ribs.

It had been worse torture than anything else he had endured. There had been curiosity in that touch, and more—the most innocent, tender desire he had ever encountered in his life, awakening before his very eyes. Directed at him. He had watched it happen . . . and been helpless to do anything about it.

But he wasn't helpless anymore.

The thought flowed through him like a draught of potent wine. Hot. Tempting. He watched her, sitting only inches away. She might be cool and distant at the moment, but her tentative, curious explorations when she had thought him asleep told him a completely different story. One he couldn't forget.

She might not be able to put the feeling into words, might not understand it at all, but he had glimpsed the unfolding passion in her, had seen it in the dark, molten color of her eyes when their gazes met. She wanted the same thing he did.

He felt his breathing deepen, felt the familiar heat uncurl in his gut. Reason warned him not to venture into these waters . . . but the awareness of her desire increased his own to an unbearable level. Damn it, he *wanted* her to touch him, wanted her to look at him that way again—not with haughty disdain or disapproval or wariness, but with longing. The way a woman looked at a man, in that moment of mutual hunger before they came together.

His body, his breath, his eyes burned as he stared at her. Fantasies rioted through his mind. He wanted those sweet lips to part eagerly for his kisses. Wanted that lush body to shiver with need in his hands. Wanted to hear her cry out with wanton pleasure when he thrust into her silken depths. Wanted to watch her shatter with release beneath him—

Nicholas stood up abruptly, turned away, raked a hand through his hair.

He was shaking. Damn him, he was shaking. Like some inexperienced, overeager lad. He had never let any woman rob him of his senses like this. He had better snap out of it before he lost control. Before he did something he might not live long enough to regret.

He was ablaze with a fire hotter than any fever. One that time and rest would not cure. One that only her touch would cool. Desperate for relief, for some kind of distraction, he looked around the glade.

Water might prove helpful. Staring at the pool below the falls, he started toward it.

"Where are you going?" she protested when the chain yanked taut.

"To take a cold bath," he grated out. "Do you think you could enjoy the moon from over here? Or would that ruin your evening?"

Muttering a particularly unladylike word, she rose and trailed behind him. "We already washed up before. And you're just getting over the chills. I don't think this is a good idea."

"I think it's an excellent idea." Under his breath, he added, "It might just save my sanity."

"What?"

"Nothing." He prowled over to the edge of the water. "Just cooperate for once. You can sit here on the bank and dangle your feet. It won't kill you." The pool looked to be only about waist deep, the sandy bottom visible even in the moonlight. He stripped off his shirt.

She reluctantly dipped in a toe. "I don't know. It feels awfully—"

Nicholas jumped in, forgetting for a second how short the chain was.

Caught off balance, Miss Delafield pitched forward and landed in the water with an ungraceful splat.

And went under before he could grab her.

And came up spitting like a soaked cat. "Damn you, you blackguard. You did that on purpose!"

"Oh, please," he snapped, sick of having to defend his every action and explain himself at every turn. "I just wasn't thinking—"

"Of anyone but yourself! You are *the* most thoughtless, selfish—" Shaking with either fury or cold, she seemed to lose her ability to speak.

So she settled for sweeping her arm across the surface to splash him with a wave of water.

Nicholas gritted his teeth. Never had he wanted to turn and walk away from her more than he did at this moment. Never had he wanted a minute—just one bloody *minute*—of peace and solitude more than he did right now.

The fact that the chain made that impossible frayed what was left of his temper.

"Your ladyship," he said silkily. "It was an honest mistake."

"Honest?" she exclaimed. "Honest?" She splashed him again, apparently warming to her newfound sport. "I don't think you know the meaning of the word."

"Listen, *angel*." He splashed her back. "Let me warn you not to start a water battle with me."

"Too late." She struck a third time, undaunted by his threat.

And then it was all-out war.

They locked in watery combat fit for the Atlantic fleet. Barrage after barrage of froth and spray flew back and forth. Standing toe-to-toe, they soaked each other mercilessly, quickly creating a monsoon in the tiny pool. He advanced. She danced away. She sent a tidal wave toward him. He gave as good as he got. Both refused to back down, her righteous indignation easily matching his frayed temper.

Until she started laughing.

The sound was so unexpected, he almost didn't recognize it.

Then a moment later, he found himself laughing right along with her. The situation was so utterly ridiculous. They had nearly been killed a half-dozen times, had little hope of making it out of Cannock Chase alive, would most likely die wearing these damned shackles . . . and here they were splashing around in the river like a pair of mad otters.

Hearty, genuine laughter welled up from somewhere inside him, from some deep, closed-off place that hadn't been opened in a very long time. The sound blended with the silvery music of her laughter.

And the hostilities ended almost as abruptly as they'd begun.

He wasn't sure who stopped first, but they went still, standing there with the choppy water swirling around them, both laughing, drenched, gasping for breath.

"Feel better?" he asked.

Cheeks flushed, eyes sparkling, she couldn't stop giggling. "Yes," she managed at last. "Yes, as a matter of fact, I do. And you?"

To his surprise, he discovered that the tension and frustration that had bothered him all night had abated. "Aye." He wiped his wet hair back from his eyes. "May I beg quarter, or are you taking no prisoners?"

She considered it with a thoroughly serious air for one second. Then she smiled. "Quarter granted."

That smile lit her features so beautifully that it

robbed him of both breath and voice. The pool calmed around them, the glade returning to peace, the quiet sounds of summer reclaiming the night.

But neither of them moved.

Dripping wet, chilled by the breeze, Nicholas stared at the woman before him and found that he did not want to move.

Her hair and gown a mess, face aglow from her latest impetuous adventure, she stood with hands on hips, up to her waist in now-muddy river water, looking like a cross between a glorious sea goddess and an impish hoyden.

Solitude, he decided, was highly overrated.

"You," he said with another warm laugh, "are not to be believed, Miss Delafield."

"Samantha."

"What?"

"Samantha," she repeated softly. "My name is Samantha. Or Sam. . . . And you?"

Her eyes searched his, seeking, urging. Wanting so badly for him to give her this one simple thing.

"James," he whispered. "Nick James."

Even as the words tumbled from his lips, he couldn't believe he had said them. He had just told her his name. Not his real name, but the one he had lived by for six years. The one that kept him safe. The name of a peaceable South Carolina planter, a man who did not belong in England, who could not explain what he was doing in Cannock Chase, shot at, shackled, and on the run.

He had just committed an unforgivable breach of his own rigid code of security.

And he didn't care half a damn.

He knew it was a gesture of trust. Knew he should be alarmed at the fact that he was standing there sharing secrets in low, intimate tones.

But he wasn't.

The happiness that spread across her delicate features, the light in her eyes at the insignificant gift of his name, was worth whatever price he paid. In that moment, he couldn't think, knew only that they were so close together that if he merely took a single step . . .

He took it. One step and the distance between them vanished. He raised his hand to touch her cheek, barely caressing her skin with his fingertips. "It's a pleasure to make your acquaintance, Samantha."

Her lips parted. She didn't reply for a moment, her eyes huge and dark beneath the shadow of her lashes. She looked up at him as if she had truly never seen him before.

And then she smiled, the most tender, lovely smile he had ever seen turned his way. "And I'm pleased to meet you, Nick."

He felt astonished by the sound of his name on her lips, by the way it flowed over him and through him, like the water all around, gentle, sparkling, warm. Life-giving.

More stunning still was the fact that she did not pull away from his touch. Did not utter a word of protest or denial.

Even when he moved his fingers lower, tracing the fine line of her jaw, her chin. She felt as delicate as the wing of an angel, soft as rare Canton silk. Touching her with only the lightest contact of his fingertips, he tilted her head up, held her gaze for a single heartbeat of time.

And then as if it were the most natural thing in the world, he lowered his head and kissed her.

He covered her lips with his, sampling the velvet warmth of her mouth as he had been longing to do.

She shivered, perhaps because his beard tickled her. But she didn't stiffen, didn't pull away, didn't resist at all.

Instead she responded, tentatively at first, allowing the light pressure . . . then welcoming him with a sigh of surprise and wonder in the back of her throat, a sound as soft as the wind in the trees.

And something that had been knotted tight in his chest unravelled. Something that he couldn't explain, couldn't understand, could only *feel*. The night, the glade, all the world fell away and he knew nothing but her. *Samantha*. He slid his hand along her cheek until his fingers tangled in her wet hair, urging her closer. She tasted of strawberries and summer, of night itself, of feminine mystery, fresh and sweet and more satisfying to his body and soul than any food or drink he'd ever known. He deepened the kiss and her palms came up to his chest, but she did not push him away.

Instead, she clung to him, trembling as if she would shatter if he released her now.

And her touch shattered him instead.

She was an innocent. God help him, he had never suspected how innocent until now. She had perhaps never even been kissed before. Certainly not like this. Yet she accepted him . . . wanted him.

Overpowering desire sank white-hot claws into his body, but he fought it. For her, he had to go slowly. Had to give her time to discover the passionate rhythms of her need for herself, even as they set him ablaze.

But it was too difficult to think of how very vulnerable and fragile she was. Too difficult to think at all. Especially when she yielded to him so completely, leaning into him as if her legs would not hold her. His arm slid around her waist and he drew her in tight. Angling his head, he urged her lips to part . . . and to his astonishment she opened to him.

All his hunger, heat, and longing poured forth, met and blended with hers. She was as brash and impetuous in her newfound desire as she was in every other way, holding nothing back. His tongue stroked along hers in a deft glide, exploring, claiming her satiny heat, and a moan came from deep in her throat, a sound of discovery. Of unmistakable pleasure.

It was the sound he had heard in his fantasies. A groan tore from deep in his chest. An explosion of need glittered through him like sparks from the stars overhead. As the dark water swirled around them, his hand slid down her back, pressing her closer. Through the wet fabric of her gown he could feel every curve of her body, could feel her shivering with heat, with passion, could feel the pearls of her nipples hardening against his chest.

Suddenly she jerked as if lashed by fire and broke the kiss. She blinked up at him, dazedly, as if awakening from a dream. For one instant she remained in his embrace.

Then her lips parted on a wordless sound of denial and she pulled away.

He didn't let her go. "Samantha—"

"No," she cried, struggling in earnest now. "No!"

He released her and she stumbled away a step. Her gaze darted around the glade as if she didn't know where she was. "I can't...I..." One shaking hand came up to touch her mouth. "*No.*"

"Samantha." He stepped toward her, unable to understand how she could change so quickly from sweet fire to cold fear in his arms.

"Stay away from me!" She rushed backward, almost falling in the water. The chain stopped her flight and she went still.

Unnaturally still.

Like a fawn facing a hunter, eyes wide.

Nicholas froze, confused by her reactions. "It's all right." He raised his hands in a gesture of reassurance. "I am not going to hurt you."

She had gone pale. "I've heard that before!"

"I'm not forcing anything on you," he retorted, stung by her words. "You were melting in my arms, lady. You wanted that kiss as much as I did. You wanted—"

"No! I didn't. I don't! I don't want anything from you. I certainly don't want you to ... to ...."

He wrestled to gain control of his desire, his frustration, his temper. "Samantha, you don't have to be afraid," he said more gently. "I *know* this is new for you—"

"But it's not. It's not new at all!" Still trembling, she laughed.

An unpleasant laugh, too high-pitched, almost hysterical.

Nicholas felt a cold tingle down his spine, realized something was wrong here. Horribly wrong. "What do you mean?"

"I mean I know all I need to know about men and their lust," she spat. "I know that it makes them take and hurt and do *anything* to satisfy it. I know all I need to know!"

Her words struck him with the impact of a fist in the gut. He couldn't believe he hadn't guessed the truth before—the way she pulled away every time he came near her, her terror at his slightest touch. "Someone hurt you, didn't he?" Inexplicable fury poured through him. "Someone *made* you afraid. When you said, 'I've heard that before,' you didn't mean from me—you meant from someone else. Who was it, Samantha? What happened to you?"

Shaking, she covered her face with her hands, turned away. "Just leave me alone. *Please.* Just ... just ...."

Go away. She didn't say it, but he knew that was what she wanted. Bloody hell, it should be what he wanted too. Faced with a delicate, emotional situation like this, his usual tactic was to turn on his heel and make a speedy exit.

But this time, that was impossible.

Even without the chain, something inside him made it impossible.

He couldn't walk away from her. Couldn't stand by and watch her torn apart by the pain, by whatever some heedless bastard had done to her.

"Tell me, Samantha," he urged quietly. Driven by some force he could not name and could not fight, he moved toward her, slowly. "Tell me."

"No!" She hunched her shoulders as if she wished she could disappear. "I don't want to talk about it. I don't want to think about it. I'll be all right if you'll just leave me alone. Just—"

"Tell me."

"No, damn you!"

Ignoring her anger, her stubbornness, her curses, he turned her toward him and drew her carefully back into his arms. She struggled but this time he ignored that, too. He wanted to pick her up and carry her ashore, but he couldn't. The shackles wouldn't allow it.

So he stood there hip-deep in water, holding her close, and simply refused to let her go. After a time, she stopped fighting him but she remained stiff, unyielding, angry. Frightened.

He stroked her hair, her back. Patiently showing her what he had already told her: that he had no intention of hurting her.

Gradually she seemed to understand, to believe, for she relaxed against him, yielding as she had before, but in a different way this time, a way that was more than physical. And then he led her out of the water, back to their place beneath the trees. Drawing her down beside him, he sat with his back against a tree and pulled her into his arms again.

"Tell me," he whispered, holding her tight.

Trembling, breathing hard, she shook her head against his chest, remained silent for a long time.

But then the words began to spill out.

"It was summer," she said, so quietly he had to

strain to hear her. "The most beautiful summer night. A night just like this. I was asleep. I didn't know anything was wrong until I ... until I heard the first scream."

"Where?" he whispered.

"*Home.*"

That single word, so wistful, so bitter, choked off her voice for a moment. Nicholas had to swallow hard past a lump in his own throat. He shut his eyes, kept moving his hand along her back, slowly, waiting.

"I was sixteen," she continued in a raw whisper. "The screams woke me up, and then a man was grabbing me from my bed. Me and my sister. They dragged us downstairs. Outlaws. They were everywhere. Like wild dogs. Yelling and shooting off their pistols. They killed all the male servants. But ... but not the women. I saw ... I saw what they did to the women."

Nicholas kept his arms strong around her as the images of horror poured out.

"They were begging for mercy, but the men just laughed. They *laughed*. Even as they were tearing at the girls' clothing and then they ... Oh, God, I saw it all. They were like animals. The girls were screaming. There was so much blood ... and they were screaming in agony!"

Nicholas felt something twist painfully hard in his chest. He had witnessed horrors like that and worse in his lifetime—but for an innocent girl to witness that kind of carnage, at such a tender age ...

"And then the man dragged us into a room—"

"Samantha, did they hurt you?"

"No." She shook her head, repeated it. "No. We escaped." She lifted her head, staring off into the distance as if seeing it all replayed in her mind. "One of the other outlaws distracted him and we got away. We slipped out the window and fled over the lawn, and kept running, and running, and running ..."

He closed his eyes again, feeling such relief, such gratitude that she had been spared. "And that's when you became a thief?" he asked gently.

"No. No, we went to the magistrate in town. He and his men went to our house, and then he came back and told us . . ." Her voice broke. "Told us our parents were dead. He asked me to . . . to go back to the house with him the next day to identify the bodies, because they couldn't recognize my father, be . . . because he'd been shot. In the head."

A shudder went through her slender frame, and her voice and her strength seemed to dissolve. Nicholas drew her in close again, pressing her head to his chest, feeling the hot dampness of her tears on his skin. His throat tightened. He couldn't speak, wished he had words to comfort her, but could find none. So they shared the moment in silence, and he simply held her, letting her pain pour out. Pain and loss that reminded him so vividly of his own.

"My sister and I were left all alone," she whispered after a time. "We had nowhere to go, no one to protect us. And we were so naive, so innocent." Her voice became flat. "But I'm not anymore." She lifted her head, wiping at her eyes. "We had to throw ourselves on the mercy of our only relatives, our Uncle Prescott and his wife Olivia, in London. They took us in. Welcomed us with open arms. He told us not to worry about our inheritance, our land, our money. He took control of everything."

"You mean he stole it from you?" Nicholas guessed.

"Jessica and I didn't care about that. We thought we would be safe with him. I just wanted to be *safe*." Her voice became wavery, fragile. "But we had only been there a few weeks when Uncle Prescott began . . . doing things."

She pulled out of his embrace, shivering, and somehow Nicholas knew not to reach for her, not to touch her. Not now. He let her keep talking, let her spill the rest out. Like poison from a wound that had festered too long and needed to heal.

"He would stand very close to me. Look at me in ways that didn't seem right. Didn't *feel* right. I didn't understand at first. Even when he came to my bedroom one night." She lifted her head, looked at the moon, laughed in that harsh, painful way. "I was *so* naive that it was beyond my ability to comprehend what he could possibly want. He was my *uncle*. I never guessed . . ."

"Samantha," he interjected gently, not sure whether he meant to stop her or urge her to continue. "Hadn't your mother ever told you anything about men and women? Anything at all?"

She shook her head. "No. She always said that when we were older, on our wedding day, she would explain . . . but she never . . ." A splintering sound, not quite a sob, tore from her. "She never got that chance." With a savage motion of her arm, she wiped at her eyes again. "Uncle Prescott told me that he was concerned about me, that he wanted to tuck me in. When it became clear what he really wanted, I fought him. He kept telling me he wouldn't hurt me." Her voice became a whisper. "I fought him so hard that he broke my arm."

Nicholas clenched his fists, filled with a violent urge to kill this son of a bitch.

"It threw him into a panic. He told me to explain to everyone that I had fallen—and he threatened that he would throw me and Jessica out if I breathed a word, to my aunt or to anyone."

"So you left," Nicholas concluded.

She shook her head. "I was sixteen," she whispered. "I was afraid. If I'd had only myself to worry about, I wouldn't have spent another night in that house . . . but I had to think about my sister. Jess was always fragile. I knew she wouldn't survive on the streets. And we didn't have any money—*he* controlled every shilling of it." She ran a hand along a tear in her skirt, over and over. "I was always the strong one. I had to protect my sister."

Nicholas stared at her, stunned at what she had been willing to face for the love of her sister. He had always considered her gutsy, for a woman.

But he had never suspected the true depth of courage and caring she possessed.

"When my arm healed, he started again." She sighed as if wearied by her story, by the telling, by the weight of her memories. "Then that winter, Jess fell ill. I wasn't strong enough for her this time. I couldn't help her." Fresh tears streamed down her cheeks. "She died, so quickly. And I was . . . alone."

The way she said the last word tore through him like a blade. He knew exactly what it was to feel alone, desolate. Somehow her pain made him feel his own more vividly than he had in years. It was as if her anguish, her grief, poured through his blood, his heart.

She didn't protest this time when he reached out and pulled her into his arms. She sagged against him, letting him hold her.

"I-I tried to slip away the next morning, but Uncle Prescott tricked me. He locked me in his library while my aunt was out, and he . . . he cornered me. He had me down on his desk, and he almost . . ." She couldn't speak for a moment. "But I grabbed a pen-knife and used it to defend myself. I stabbed him."

"It was self-defense," Nicholas said adamantly. "You stabbed him in self-defense."

"The warrant," she said bitterly, "reads attempted murder. I was covered with blood. My uncle yelled for the servants and told everyone I had gone mad with grief, that I should be put in an asylum. He tried to have me arrested. But I managed to get away before the marshalmen came. I ran and . . ."

"Never stopped running," he finished for her. He knew the rest.

She was crying again, exhausted, weary, frightened

tears. The tears of a woman who had had her girlhood ripped from her violently, who had spent too many years running.

Too many years alone.

He cradled her in his arms while all the bitterness and hurt flowed out of her. "Shh, angel, it's going to be all right," he murmured. "You're going to be all right."

It was little wonder that she feared men. Feared him.

The truly astonishing fact was that a lady who had been through so much at such a tender age could still believe in things like faith and goodness and human caring.

Could still feel grateful for something so simple as moonlight and a summer wind.

He closed his eyes, grimacing ruefully. Unfortunately for her, she was still too naive, in too many ways. She thought she knew the way of the world, when in truth she knew nothing. Her trust, her faith left her vulnerable to mankind's cruelty.

While her fear, her irrational, mistaken fear, denied her one of mankind's few genuine pleasures.

After a while, her sobbing ebbed slowly to silence. Catching her chin on the edge of his hand, Nicholas tilted her head up. He cupped her face in his palms and gazed down into her eyes, and brushed his thumbs over her cheeks, drying her tears, all the while inwardly cursing himself.

He had been telling himself from the start that he didn't care about this lady thief.

But she had come to mean something to him.

Which was impossible. He had no time for an affair, or a liaison of any sort. They had no future. Not a week, not a day, not even an hour beyond the moment he got the chain off. He had a job to do, an enemy to kill, and she was a complication he didn't need.

But though they could not share a future, he could

share with her one precious gift, now, tonight. Much as she had given to him in the cave, with her soft voice, her gentle touch, bringing him warmth, light, life, he could now give to her.

What had been stolen from her by the outlaws, by her bastard uncle, could be returned.

By one wayward ex-pirate. For once, perhaps Nicholas Brogan could put someone else's needs ahead of his own.

Give without taking.

Experience for himself what simple human caring felt like.

"Samantha," he asked softly, "are you still afraid of me?"

Her lower lip quivered. "A little."

He smiled at the open honesty he had come to expect from her. "Do you trust me, at least a little?"

"Yes."

That made his smile broaden. "The lessons you've learned are the wrong lessons, angel. What happens between a man and a woman isn't supposed to be about pain."

She looked dubious, uncertain.

"You've been made afraid of something that's a natural, vital part of every man . . . and every woman." He stroked his fingers along her jawline. "It's supposed to be about pleasure. Especially for the woman."

That made her look downright skeptical.

"When it's good, when it's right, it's the greatest feeling a man and woman can share." He brushed his thumb over her mouth. "Let me show you, angel." He phrased it as a question, a warm entreaty. "Let me show you."

Chapter 16

❧∽◦◦◦◦∽❧

Sam couldn't summon a reply, couldn't even catch her breath. Gazing into his eyes, tingling at the warmth of his touch, she felt as if she had been swept up into the night sky, spinning among white-hot stars.

Everything seemed to be whirling around her, changing so quickly, leaving her scrambling for something solid to hold on to. But all she could find within herself were new, undefined feelings, too tentative, too fragile for her to depend upon.

Feelings for this man. For a stranger who now knew all of her secrets.

But he wasn't a stranger anymore.

Nick.

She had shared with him memories and pain that she had never shared with anyone. And as he held her so carefully, his broad hands cupping her face so lightly, she chastised herself for being ten kinds of a fool. How could she have told him so much? Why had she trusted him?

She had every reason to feel wary of this man. Any sensible woman would. He was an outlaw. A man who knew too little of gentleness, too much of fighting and recklessness and the hard edges of life. Sitting so close beside him, feeling the heat of his body against hers, she felt an uncomfortable shift in the rhythm of her heartbeat.

The hard, muscular planes of his body, his numerous scars, the pitchfork brand all bespoke a life of harshness and danger. He seemed to be made entirely of steel, corded lengths of steel wrapped around iron. As hard and unyielding as the chain that bound the two of them together. A man crafted from and for violence.

Yet he was capable of gentleness, too. And compassion.

She had experienced that herself.

And he awaited her answer. Would she grant him an intimacy she had never granted any man?

Drawing an unsteady breath, she closed her eyes, unable to bear the heat in his gaze and her own uncertainty. She had no need to fear that he might lose control over his unpredictable male hunger; he was clearly in complete control of himself, as he had been all along.

It was her own reactions that alarmed her.

"Nick," she whispered, "I . . . I haven't been entirely honest."

"I find that hard to believe." He wasn't mocking her; his voice was serious.

"It's true." She opened her eyes, swallowing hard. "When I said I was still a little afraid of you, it's . . . it's not you that I'm afraid of." Confessing brought a cascade of heat to her cheeks. "It's me."

He smiled as if he understood. "What is there to be afraid of, Samantha?"

"Well, when you . . . kissed me, I felt so . . ." She struggled to find words for what she had experienced, felt embarrassed by the memory. Her senses had simply scattered to the winds at the first brush of his lips over hers.

"As if you were hot and cold at the same time?" he murmured, kissing her again, the lightest touch of his mouth this time. "And hungry and thirsty all at once?" He kissed her a third time.

"Yes." The word came out as a sigh, her lashes drifting downward as she experienced the same breathless, almost dizzy sensation she had felt before. "It's like a ticklish flutter in my stomach. And—" Another kiss interrupted her explanation. "A funny ache in my throat."

"And you feel as if you're melting? . . ." His hand moved lower, touching her abdomen, his fingers burning her. "Here?"

Her eyes opened wide. "Yes," she gasped, feeling something powerful unfurl within her, there where he touched her.

"That's all part of it, angel." He brushed a kiss through her hair. "Part of every woman and man, part of you. And me."

The deep, husky tone of his voice sent shivers through her. She gazed at him, felt as if she were seeing him for the first time, found herself noticing things she had never noticed before—the way his beard emphasized the sharp angles of his cheekbones, the deep creases at the corners of his eyes, a small scar on his temple, and that stubborn tangle of hair that always fell over his forehead.

And his eyes. They held hers the way his hands caressed her cheeks—boldly but gently. Staring into those emerald depths, she sought any hint of deception but found none. "You mean that *you* feel these same feelings?"

"Yes," he said huskily.

She looked at him askance, barely able to believe it; in the pool, in his embrace, she had felt herself very close to losing control . . . yet he seemed so in command of himself.

"Whenever you're close to me," he explained when she didn't speak. "Whenever you touch me . . . especially the way you did in the cave."

"Th-that was purely for medical purposes."

"I didn't see a cloth in your hand that last time," he

chided, flashing a particularly wicked smile. "You seemed to be enjoying it."

She dropped her gaze, mortified.

"It's all right, angel." He caught her chin on the edge of his hand, tilting her head up. "It's all right to enjoy touching each other."

"I-I don't . . . I . . ." Even as she said it, she knew it was a lie.

"You think you *shouldn't* enjoy it?"

Was that the reason? For six years, she had lived her own life by her own rules, going and doing as she pleased. The word *shouldn't* had become a part of her past the day she became an outlaw. After so much time on her own, she was used to being in charge of her life, her fate, her feelings; she had come to *like* being in control.

But now it felt as if that control had been snatched away, as if she didn't even know herself anymore. Nick was no longer a stranger, but now she seemed like a stranger to herself.

Even her fear, her wariness, her caution, so much a part of her for so long, was . . . missing.

She felt like the earth had vanished from beneath her feet and she was falling, tumbling through the night.

And the only solid thing she had to hold onto was . . . him.

"Nick, I don't know. It's . . . it's just so . . ."

"New. It's all new to you, angel. But it's a natural, special part of who you are. You're *meant* to enjoy it, just as you enjoy the moonlight and the wind." He smiled. "Maybe more." He leaned closer, nuzzling his cheek against hers, his beard sending a little shiver through her. "Let me show you."

She made a small sound deep in her throat, but even she couldn't tell if it was denial or assent.

"We won't do anything that frightens you," he assured her. "If you want me to stop, tell me and I'll stop.

If you want me to continue..." He brushed his lips over hers. "Tell me and I'll continue."

She was trembling, but the feeling wasn't unpleasant. Not at all. His mouth felt so warm, his hands so strong, so sure when he touched her.

And he was leaving the decision up to her. She had thought him a callous, unredeemable, selfish rogue... but at the moment he wasn't being roguish at all. He was being chivalrous, warm.

Caring.

And that, even more than his kiss, made her heart pound so hard that thinking was impossible at the moment.

"Samantha?"

"Yes," she whispered, realizing that her decision had been made perhaps a long time ago. "*Yes.*"

She barely completed the word when he kissed her again, a soft brush of his mouth over hers that deepened into a slow, hot joining. His arm circled her shoulders and he gently lowered her to the ground, leaning over her in the firelight, his weight on his forearms as his mouth worked tantalizing magic over hers.

She had never known how sensitive her lips could feel. Or how fast her pulse could pound. She reached up to pull him closer, threading her fingers through the dark hair at the nape of his neck. With a low groan, he captured her wrists, lightly pinning them to the ground on either side of her head.

Understanding what he wanted, she relented, allowing him to take command, letting herself surrender control. Stretched out beneath him on the warm grass, she felt the last of her hesitation burn to ashes in the fire of his kiss. She let go willingly, allowing herself to be completely open to his touch, completely vulnerable in a way she had never been before.

Her display of trust brought a soft sound from him, almost a sigh, a sound of deep pleasure. He lifted his mouth from hers, kissing her jaw, her cheeks, her nose.

And when her eyelids drifted closed, he kissed her lashes.

"That's right, angel," he whispered. "Close your eyes and just let yourself *feel*."

He released his hold on her wrists, his hands sliding down her arms, down the sides of her body. Through the thin cloth of her silk gown, she could feel him like a fire in her blood. He nibbled at her ear, began a slow, teasing descent down her throat, his lips and tongue sending a rush of sensations cascading through her.

He caught her skin ever so delicately between his teeth, nipping her in a light, fierce way that drew a cry of pleasure from her parted lips. Arching her neck, she offered herself up to him, to these new feelings that made her feel weak and yet strong all at once.

The night air around her, the leaves overhead, even the ground beneath her seemed to crackle with electricity. Like the heat of a lightning strike. Like a summer storm that drenched the earth with hot rain.

Her heart pounding, she kept her eyes closed as her senses came vibrantly alive, engulfed by his musky, masculine scent, the hardness of his body. By his fingers tracing over her, leaving tendrils of fire in their wake. One of his hands shaped her breast and she tensed, but only for a moment.

Because his touch was tender, careful, almost reverent. She could feel the peak drawing tight beneath his thumb, caught her bottom lip between her teeth to keep from crying out. The barrier of silk and lace between his skin and hers created a dozen different, exquisite textures. A restless heat began building deep within her. He traced his thumb around her nipple in a slow circle, coaxing until it rose to a hard pearl, and her breathing became ragged.

When his hand left her, a low moan of protest slipped from her throat. But then he slid her gown from her shoulder, slowly, inch by tantalizing inch, tugging the lacy bodice lower . . . baring her to the warm night wind.

And she felt his rough, calloused fingertips against her skin, touching her in a way no man had ever touched her before. Her lashes lifted but she managed to remain still, trusting him, her palms upturned on the warm grass. Breathless, she watched him. Watched his dark fingers moving over her, caressing the pale swell of her breast.

And the intimacy felt not threatening but glorious.

His eyes were ablaze as he gazed down at her, stretched out beside her, his every muscle taut, his own breathing rough. It was only then that she realized how powerfully this simple act of touching her affected him. *He wanted her.* Wanted to do more than kiss her and touch her—but he was holding himself in check. Denying his own need, his own pleasure.

For her.

She closed her eyes again, not wanting him to see the tears that welled there, not wanting him to misunderstand. His generosity, his tenderness, surprised her utterly . . . and touched her deeply.

A second later he rendered all rational thought impossible as his mouth followed the path his fingers had blazed. His tongue found the sensitive pearl he had coaxed forth, darting out to tease it again and again. When the peak was wet, tight, his lips hovered over her and he blew softly, dragging a low cry from her throat. She arched beneath him, shivering, shimmering. Wanting. Every part of her ached and tingled, both where he kissed and lower.

And then his arm slid behind her back and he drew her up against him, drew her in tight as his mouth closed over her in the most shocking kiss. He took her deeply into the warm, liquid velvet of his mouth and the feeling was like . . . *hot rain.*

Some hidden, secret part of her, at the very center of her being, trembled and tightened in response as he lavished attention on her, kissing and teasing, gentle and fierce by turns. She felt as if she were soaring into the clouds, swept upward to a stunning, dizzying height she had never experienced before. The sensation was so new, so intense, so unbearably good.

She gave herself over to it, shuddering, mindless. She was lost in the sensations, her senses so scattered that she barely felt it as he lowered her back to the ground, didn't realize he had moved his hand.

Until she felt the heat of his fingers on her thigh.

Her breath broke. She trembled beneath him, sensing that she had barely begun to taste the intimacy he meant to share with her. His palm slid downward in a slow caress, seeking the hem of her skirt. Finding it.

And then the sound of silk in his grasp, sliding upward, baring her calf, her knee, her thigh, was louder than the crackle of the fire.

"Samantha?" he whispered, his voice odd, rough.

She opened her eyes, not understanding his question, until she realized that she had her legs pressed tightly together.

"Do you want me to continue?" he rasped.

She couldn't answer for a moment, struck by the tension in him—the knotted muscles of his arm around her back, the sheen of sweat on his bare chest, the strain etched in every line of his body, his face.

"Yes." Unable to resist, she lifted her hand to stroke his bearded cheek, her heart thundering. "Oh, yes."

He trembled, actually trembled, at the light contact of her fingertips. "Samantha, *please*." He choked out an oath. "Don't."

"You don't want me to touch you?"

"No, that's not—" As she moved her fingers lower, along the corded muscles of his neck, he groaned. "Oh, God."

"I like touching you."

"But this time is just for you, angel." He grabbed for her hand and lightly pressed her arm back to the

ground beside her head. "You can . . ." His breathing
was so harsh in his throat, it sounded as if he were in
pain. "You can touch me later."

He didn't give her a chance to argue, stealing her
words and her breath with another deep kiss. Then she
felt his hand on her hip, sliding her skirt out of the
way.

She felt no fear, no resistance, no hesitation. As easily
as his fingers had parted the silk and lace of her gown,
his tenderness had parted the defenses around her
heart. She trusted him. She was safe with him.

Safe.

In that moment she realized she had been a fool to
think that safety would ever lie in living apart from the
world, in being alone. *This* was what she needed. To
share, to trust, to hold and be held. This feeling of being
cherished and sheltered . . . in this man's arms.

She parted her lips and deepened the kiss, welcoming the slow, languid penetration of his tongue. Liquid
heat poured through her, flowing into her heart, her
mind, her body. She felt as if she were made entirely
of sun-heated water, of melting honey. His fingers
traced along her thigh in slow circles as he waited for
her, patient, letting her decide.

And with a soft, deep sound of acceptance, she relaxed, letting her thighs part, feeling no more need to
guard any of her secrets from him.

He lifted his mouth from hers, nuzzled her cheek.
"*Yes*," he whispered in her ear. "Oh, yes." He brushed
his fingers along the inside of her thigh. "Open for me,
sweetheart . . . that's right."

A storm of sensations rocked her when he sought
and found that most feminine center of her being,
touching her so gently, so softly. She felt as if she'd
been struck by a bolt of white-hot electricity, felt a liquid heat flowing forth to meet his hand, as if his touch
filled her with so much light, warmth, life, that her
body wept fire.

She cried out his name, her hips lifting from the ground as a new, almost violent wanting twisted through her. He stroked the downy triangle with exquisite care, his fingertips unfolding the soft petals that concealed her innermost core, finding the hot flow of honey within.

"Oh, sweet angel," he rasped.

She was writhing beneath him now, swept up in a storm of sensation, of yearning. Even as she knew she couldn't bear any more, he found a small bud within those damp curls, teasing it lightly with his thumb. A pulsing wave of pleasure rocked her entire body. Her breath broke on a ragged cry.

He stroked that swollen, sensitive part of her, again and again, until she thought she would go mad. The wanting, the tension wound so tight she knew she would shatter and did not care. It was a wildness. An all-consuming need. Tendrils of fire that lashed her with sweet torment. But the more she ached for his touch, the more lightly he grazed the delicate bud, building an unbearable storm of excitement and longing within her. She wanted . . . wanted . . .

His mouth covered hers and he kissed her again in that spellbinding way, a slow stroke of his tongue against hers, like hot, liquid velvet, matching the glide of his fingers below as they delved into her silken core. She moaned, shivering with shock and pleasure at the fierce, gentle claiming. The tension spun tighter, faster, winding through her. His thumb whisked over the swollen bud, urging her onward, lifting her beyond earth, *higher*—

Suddenly all the tendrils of fire snapped at once.

Her entire body convulsed and a wordless cry of revelation and release tore from her throat. She was shuddering, falling through the heavens, through a drenching shower of flame, her entire body shattered in a blaze of ecstasy just as the sun broke through the trees.

The first light of dawn bathed her and she was sailing, floating down . . . down through the clouds, utterly spent, more alive than she had ever been. She felt like the light itself, hot, clear, new. Felt as free as the wind, soaring and cascading over all the earth.

She didn't come back to herself until she felt the sun warming her face, wasn't sure how long she had lain trembling in his arms. Opening her eyes, she blinked, half-expecting to find herself still floating through the clouds with angels.

Instead she was here on earth.

With her dark angel.

He looked down at her with a smile, eyes sparkling, and she noticed a softness in his expression that she had never seen before.

Her heart pounding, she smiled up at him, wanting to touch him as he had touched her, to learn every texture, every taste, every breath of him. To wrap her arms around him and never let go.

But she felt strangely sleepy, her body heavy. "Nick, I—"

He stole her words with a kiss. "Shh, Samantha, don't try to understand it. Just let yourself feel it."

With a drowsy murmur of assent, she closed her eyes and leaned into him as he settled back against one of the trees. She wanted nothing more at the moment than to stay right here, with him. It seemed so natural, to fall asleep with her head pillowed on his chest. So comfortable.

So perfect.

This wasn't how she had expected the day to end at all, she thought, smiling sleepily.

Then again, nothing had been as she expected from the moment she met Nick James.

The afternoon sun beat down on Nicholas's bare shoulders as they trudged alongside the river. He had finally abandoned the tattered, blood-stained remains of his shirt. Samantha had used what was left of the sheet to wrap a bandage around his chest, covering the brand. It would have to do for now.

They had been on the move for hours, heading upstream, figuring that their pursuers—if they were still anywhere in Cannock Chase—would be focusing their search downstream. He wanted to get to a town as quickly as possible. He had five days left to make it to York, which meant he had to do two things as quickly as possible: get a horse . . . and get free of the lovely lady at his side.

A thought which no longer held any appeal.

He shook his head in amazement. Only yesterday he had wanted nothing *but* to get away from Samantha Delafield. Now the idea of being separated from her brought a strange ache to his chest. One that had nothing to do with the sensual torture he had endured this morning, the arousal still running through his blood like a river of fire.

He had never experienced this peculiar longing before. He rubbed at his chest, wishing he could wipe away the feeling as easily as he brushed off the perspiration that dotted his skin.

The chain caught on a root and he stumbled.

He recovered before he could fall, but Samantha caught his arm. "Are you sure you're strong enough to keep going?"

"I'm fine."

She let go of him at once.

Realizing he had snapped at her, he repeated it more gently. "I'm fine."

She didn't look convinced, but he wasn't about to explain that it hadn't been physical weakness that tripped him, but thoughts of her.

Which was becoming a weakness in itself. As she looked up at him, as their gazes met and held, a blush suffused her cheeks. He couldn't help smiling; she had been blushing all day, every time she glanced at him. Reaching out, he touched her face. She smiled shyly, her lashes sweeping downward. He would have sworn he saw a shiver go through her.

"It seems I've put a permanent smile on your face," he said wickedly, enjoying the way his teasing made her color deepen. He lightly caressed her cheek. "There's nothing to be ashamed of, angel."

"I'm not," she said quickly, raising her chin.

Her reaction pleased him. He saw no trace of shame or guilt in her eyes. She had embraced passion the same way she embraced all of life. Simply and completely. With warmth and enthusiasm and her whole heart.

She kept surprising him with her conflicting facets, each more intriguing than the last. Miss Samantha Delafield was a woman of delicate sensibilities and steely strength; a refined lady and a talented thief; a sweet innocent who could unabashedly enjoy her sensuality.

Before he knew what he was doing, Nicholas bent his head and kissed her. Her mouth met his warmly, softly. Already she was learning to kiss him back, meeting his passion with her own. His hands came up to her shoulders and he pulled her close. He couldn't seem to get enough of her. He had known so little tenderness in his life and she had so much to give, shared it so willingly, that he drank it in like a man cast adrift.

His lips molded to hers and her sweet feminine fire seared him, sending a riot of sensations careening through his body, his mind, his soul. His response to her seemed to grow stronger every time he touched her.

Abruptly he lifted his head, his body taut, his heart pounding. "You are dangerous, lady."

He said it with a grin, kept his tone light, but knew he was only half-joking.

She was breathing as hard as he was, her eyes a deep, molten gold. "Are you going to keep your word later?" A mysterious smile played at one corner of her mouth.

"My word?" he echoed, confused.

"You said I could touch you," she reminded him softly, "later."

Nicholas felt her voice flow through him like a potent draught of whiskey, felt as if every nerve ending in his body had just been set ablaze. "Right," he choked out at last. "I did, didn't I?" Desperately trying to think of a way to back out of that agreement, he turned her away from him, still holding her by the shoulders, and nudged her forward. "But right now, we need to keep our minds on the trouble we're in, or else we're going to find ourselves back in gaol. Or worse."

She flashed him a look over her shoulder and started off, leading the way.

Following behind her, he tried to gather up the scrambled pieces of his reason.

Which was bloody difficult. Especially when she looked at him as she just had—with a glance that held sweet sensual promise, eyes that shimmered with . . .

He didn't know what to call it. Didn't want to think about it. Tried to put it out of his mind.

Later. He felt his gut twist into a knot tighter than a Spanish bowline hitch.

No. Absolutely not. There would be no later.

Nicholas frowned. Until this morning, he had been convinced there would be nothing wrong with taking his pleasure of her and then taking his leave. Why should she be different from any other woman he had known? It wasn't as if he'd never had a virgin before; he'd sent more than one maiden on her way with a few new skills in her feminine arsenal and a smile on her face. Never had he hesitated in bedding a willing lady.

Until now. Until Samantha. It seemed important to him, somehow, to protect her innocence. To avoid taking the treasure she offered.

That was a first for Captain Nicholas Brogan, he thought with a rueful twist to his mouth—protecting a treasure instead of taking it.

No one would ever believe it.

He watched her walking just ahead of him, infinitely fascinated by the way she moved, the way her hair caught the light. He couldn't puzzle out his reasons, but he intended their first moment of physical intimacy this morning to be their last.

He didn't dare trust himself to touch her that way a second time, to hold her lush, naked body in his arms and not take her.

His gaze lingered over her, his thoughts drifting back to the glade. He still could not believe what had happened between them. Not the way she had responded to him so perfectly. That didn't surprise him.

No, what baffled him was that her dazzling release had been as pleasurable for him as it had been for her—even though he had been in torment, raked by claws of need, longing to bury himself in her depths. It had taken every ounce of will he possessed not to claim her. She had been like melted honey in his arms, yielding, open, ready. And he had restrained himself.

This had been the first time he had ever given pleasure without taking some in return. And it had made him feel unbelievably . . . good. More than good.

Happy.

He shook his head, reminding himself that more pressing matters required his attention. Matters of life and death. He needed to concentrate. York. The blackmailer. Five days left.

Less than five days.

Damn it, Brogan, concentrate.

They kept walking, each lost in their own thoughts, the forest passing by in a monotonous parade of tree after tree, branch after branch, evergreen after evergreen.

The afternoon sun slanted low through the canopy of leaves when he thought he heard a sound up ahead.

"Wait a moment." He stopped Samantha, coming up to stand beside her. "What's that noise?"

They both stood still, listening. The wind carried the sound toward him: voices.

"Bloody hell." Grabbing Samantha, he darted into the underbrush.

"Who do you think they are?" she whispered.

He didn't reply, knew what they were both thinking. *Lawmen.*

But the sound didn't grow louder. Whoever it was, they apparently weren't moving. And he heard no dogs or horses.

And some of the voices were undeniably feminine.

"I'm not sure," he whispered. "Care to take a closer look?"

She nodded. They crept forward, cautiously, staying within the shadows of the trees.

A few yards further on, they could see them: a group of people camped in a clearing ahead.

Nicholas stopped and slipped behind the broad trunk of an oak, pulling Samantha with him. Cautiously, he peered around the curve of the tree, wishing he had a spyglass.

He could hear her breathing rapidly. "If they aren't lawmen," she hissed, "then who are they? Who else would venture into Cannock Chase?"

He studied the camp. There were at least forty people—men, women, and children. Travelers of some sort; their camp was made up of a motley assortment of carts and wagons, many brightly painted.

"Gypsies," he said at last. Outcasts, like all the other people who sought sanctuary in this forest.

Samantha seemed to relax. "We should probably go before any of them see us."

"Not so fast, angel." He was still studying the camp. Where there were carts, there were bound to be horses.

After a moment, Samantha made a sniffing sound. "Can you smell that?" She crowded in beside him to get a better view, inhaling deeply of the wind. "Oh, I wonder what they're cooking."

The spicy scent made his stomach growl. "Some kind of stew." There was a large cookfire at the center of the circle of wagons, and a pair of women were tending a large black iron pot suspended over the flames.

But even more tempting to him were the horses. He spotted them on the far side of the camp, about two dozen of them, picketed at the edge of the clearing.

He smiled. "How careless of them to put their horses where someone might sneak up and steal one."

"You've got to be joking. How are we going to pull that off without getting caught?" She jangled the shackles. "Not to mention the fact that riding might be a bit difficult. How are the two of us even going to get *on* a horse?"

"We'll figure that out when the time comes."

"But the lawmen who were searching for us might have talked to these people. Might have offered descriptions and a reward. Going into their camp is too dangerous."

Nicholas contemplated that for a moment. She was right. They had no way of knowing how long the gypsies had been here. It would be risky. "I'll go in under cover of darkness while you stay—"

He cut himself off.

"Sorry," she said wryly. "Wherever you go, I go."

Glancing down at her, he remembered that he had made the same mistake before, but for a completely different reason. Last time, it had been because he wasn't used to being half of a pair. This time . . .

It was because he wanted to keep her safe.

That fact rendered him speechless. The strangest feeling coursed through him. A feeling of . . . rightness. A powerful urge to protect her.

"Besides, I can take a little danger, if you're determined to do this," she continued, oblivious to the real reason behind his silence. "I'm not all that fragile."

He could argue that point, he thought; she had shattered quite completely in his arms this morning. "I know," he told her instead, tracing a finger over her cheek, regretting for the first time that she was so brave. So willing to put herself in danger.

"So what are we going to do?"

He was wrestling with an answer to that question when a new noise came from the far end of the camp. One that seemed out of place in the forest. A familiar clang of metal striking metal.

A sound that changed everything.

The unmistakable clatter of a hammer on a blacksmith's anvil.

Chapter 17

⁓⁓◠◠◡◡⁓⁓

Moonlight trickled through the interlaced tree branches, falling in shimmering pools, dancing across the forest floor. The silver-blue glow faintly lit their way as they crept closer to the gypsy camp. Sam could barely breathe past the fear that clamped around her chest like a band of steel. Nick led the way, stealthy, silent. She couldn't believe he could be so calm. So coolly assured that this insane plan would work.

Midnight's hush had fallen over the woods, broken only by the flutter of wings through the leaves over-head as a bird took flight . . . an occasional cough or snore from one of the wagons . . . the bark of a dog. The chain made little noise; she had sacrificed the remains of her petticoat to muffle the shackles, braiding the cloth in and around the iron links to render them silent.

Or at least as silent as possible.

If the gypsies had appointed sentries, or if one of their dogs caught a scent, or a sound, she and Nick could quickly find themselves facing a group of sus-picious people, questions they could not answer. And loaded pistols.

The vividly painted wagons loomed out of the shad-ows like a handful of jewels scattered across the clear-ing. Only a few more yards and they would reach their target.

Still within the cover of the forest, Nick halted, his voice scarcely a whisper as he pointed at one of the wagons. "That one?"

"I think so."

They moved toward it, along the edge of the trees, both glancing around, cautious. All afternoon, they had circled the camp, studying it from every angle, engaged in a heated debate. As evening fell, they had snuck closer for a bit of careful reconnaissance, and finally faced the facts: stealing a horse would be useless because they couldn't hope to ride—not wearing the chain. And they couldn't exactly burst in and hold the camp's blacksmith at knifepoint, demanding that he remove the shackles.

So they had come up with a different strategy. One that would free them from the chain once and for all *and* net them a horse or two.

If they didn't get killed first.

They stopped in the shadows at the point where the forest gave way to the clearing. At least ten yards of open ground lay between them and their destination.

"That's the one," Sam whispered, crouching beside Nick in the underbrush.

He shook his head. "No guards, not even a dog." His voice was no more than a faint, warm breath against her ear. "I still say they would have some kind of security around the thing if it contained any valuables."

Sam shivered—not from anxiety, but from the feelings that poured through her when his lips brushed against her earlobe. "Sometimes people do the opposite of what you would expect. Hide their best jewelry in a linen drawer instead of their safe. Or tuck several thousand pounds in cash between the pages of a tattered old book. They tend to think they're smarter than the average thief."

His teeth flashed white in the moonlight. "Luckily for us, you're not the average thief."

"Trust me, they've got something valuable in there.

No one's gone near that wagon all day. There have been people coming and going from all the others, but not that one. And if you'll notice," she said a trifle smugly, "they *do* have a lock on the door."

He peered through the darkness, then nodded. "Forgive me for doubting you." His grin turned to a frown as he studied the lock and the chain attached to it. "How much of a problem is that going to be?"

She withdrew the golden needle case from her bodice, clutching it in her hand. "There's no way to know until I see it up close."

They observed the camp a moment longer, watching for any movement. It was essential to their plan that no one know they had been there, or even suspect anyone had visited the camp.

They intended to pay generously for the blacksmith's services, and his silence—and they didn't want the man to guess he was being paid with the gypsies' own money.

Nick took her hand. "Let's go."

They broke from the trees, crouching low to the ground, moving swiftly, covering as much distance as quickly as they could while making as little noise as possible. Nick's hand felt strong and warm around hers. Almost strong enough to make her ignore the icy-hot tingles of fear chasing through her.

They made it to the wagon and flattened themselves against the side, standing in its shadow. Sam was puffing, gasping more from fright than from the exertion. She tried to control her breathing, tried not to make any sound at all. Nick seemed unruffled; she had been worried about his condition, feared he might be attempting too much too soon, but he seemed fine.

She marveled at how cool he was in the face of danger, didn't know whether his attitude came from courage or recklessness or something else.

And there wasn't time to think about it. He was gesturing toward the door. Nodding in assent, Sam extracted one of the lockpicks from her needle case.

They darted around the edge of the wagon and up the short steps that led to the door. Nick gave her as much room as possible, pressing flat against the door, glancing around the camp. Sam grabbed the lock and went to work.

It was a difficult design, one she had encountered only once or twice before. But she had done this dozens of times, she reminded herself. Tonight was no different from all the other nights she had plied her trade.

But her fingers seemed slippery. The pick didn't work. The lock refused to budge.

Her heart began to pound. Perhaps she was simply out of practice. Or perhaps she was having trouble because there wasn't enough light.

A minute passed. Another. Somewhere a baby cried.

She bent closer, deftly turning the pick one way and another, trying to feel her way into the lock's secrets. Her very life depended on success. And his as well.

Why wasn't this working?

She heard the soft cooing of a feminine voice as the mother went to comfort her child.

"Hurry," Nick whispered in her ear.

She was about to protest that the tickle of his beard against her neck was distracting—but just then the lock finally gave way.

Almost shaking, she unhinged it, slipped it free of the chain, opened the door. They moved inside swiftly, quietly, drew the door closed behind them.

The moon offered just enough light for them to see a jumble of goods inside: bolts of cloth, lamps, cooking implements.

Nick swore. It was a supply wagon.

Sam muttered an oath under her breath. Quickly, they rifled through the merchandise piled on shelves along the walls, on the floor, in the corners. And found nothing.

At least, nothing of value.

Her heart fell. They had taken a terrible risk . . . for this?

Somewhere in the camp a door creaked open, then shut—and she heard footsteps outside. Coming closer.

Ice shot through her veins. Both of them spun toward the door. They were trapped!

Before she could speak or even think, Nick stepped in front of her, drawing her behind him, the knife raised in his hand as he faced the door.

She blinked at his broad shoulders, astonished. He was protecting her. Had done it as if without thinking, as if it came naturally all of a sudden—when he had always insisted he didn't give a damn about any life but his own.

Before she completed the thought, the footsteps came to their wagon. She inhaled sharply, braced herself.

But the footsteps passed by hurriedly, headed for the forest.

Both of them let out a long breath. Sam felt like sinking to the floor. She unfastened her fingers from Nick's arm, realizing only after the fact that she had grabbed onto him as if grabbing for life itself.

"Hell of a time for some fool to go relieve himself." He tossed the knife in the air with a flick of his fingers and caught it by the blade before sliding it back into his boot.

"Let's get out of here."

"Can't. Not until he comes back."

Sam realized that was true. For the moment they were stuck in here. Sitting on a sack of grain, she looked around forlornly. She had been so sure of herself, her head filled with tantalizing images of stolen treasure, ropes of pearls, gold, jewels—and it was just a supply wagon. Why the gypsies had put a lock on the door, she didn't know.

All she knew was that she had failed. And they didn't dare linger in camp long enough to investigate any of the other wagons. They had been here too long already.

"This is my fault," she said apologetically.

"Doesn't matter now." He poked around in some sacks piled in one corner.

He didn't seem angry, wasn't chiding her for the costly mistake she'd made, wasn't mocking her in any way.

Which only made her feel worse.

He found a pile of garments behind the sacks. "At least we'll get some new clothes out of it."

"Those are probably cast-offs," she murmured absently, looking down at the shackles that gleamed dully in the moonlight. "Gypsies buy them from wealthy landowners in the countryside and sell them as they travel from town to town."

He picked out a shirt and some breeches. "There are even some decent shoes down here."

"Those should prove useful," she said miserably, "since it looks like we're going to be walking through Cannock Chase for the rest of our lives."

They both quieted as they heard the footsteps draw near again. Sam held her breath, struck by a sudden, terrifying thought. If the person happened to glance the right way, see the chain hanging free on the door . . .

The steps grew louder.

And passed by.

Shaking, she stood and turned to leave. She had endured all the danger she could stand for one night. But Nick was still poking around in the corner. Beneath the mountain of clothing, he had discovered what looked like a small barrel. "Hello," he said with soft interest. "What might this be?"

"Nick, we should go."

He wasn't paying attention, too intrigued with his new find; using the knife, he tried to pry off the lid.

"Nick," she repeated urgently, tapping him on the shoulder. "We don't have time."

He lifted the lid and both of them inhaled sharply. "Oh, my God," Sam whispered.

Nothing but the silvery spill of moonlight illuminated their place beneath the trees, a mile from the camp. They hadn't risked a fire, hadn't wanted to draw any attention to themselves.

Sam hunched over a lustrous jumble of deep green French silk piled in her lap, her needle flashing in the moon's glow. There hadn't been time to check the sizes of the garments she had grabbed in the wagon; the white cotton chemise she had taken, with its ruffled bodice and billowy sleeves, would fit, but the skirt was much too large. Taking the last few stitches in the waistband, she glanced up at Nick.

She had teasingly offered to sew him into his new breeches, since the chain made it impossible for him to get them on, but he had rejected the idea instantly. Hadn't seemed to find it the least bit funny. He would change into them, he'd said, after the shackles were removed.

He had been in an odd, quiet mood ever since they left the camp. At the moment, stretched out in the leaves, he barely paid any attention to her at all.

He was too busy counting coins.

The barrel in the wagon had been full to the brim with guineas, shillings, farthings—a treasure chest worthy of a pirate, overflowing with gold and silver. They had taken handfuls, scooping them into his stolen shirt.

A second barrel beside the first had contained the kind of jewelry Sam had imagined, chains and pearls and gems, but she had argued that they shouldn't take any of it. Each piece was unique, all of it too easy to identify.

But Nick had helped himself to a single jewel. A ruby the size of a small egg.

He held it up now in the moonlight, admiring its delicately cut facets.

"I still say it was a mistake to take that," Sam said in disapproval, tying off a length of thread with an expert knot. "If anyone happens to check that barrel and notice it missing—"

"We'll be long gone by then."

"But we can't even use it to pay the blacksmith. He might recognize it."

"I have no intention of offering it to him." He tossed the jewel a few inches into the air and caught it, smiling as if he savored the feel of it in his palm. "This one's for me, angel. Me and no one else. This little bauble makes up for some of the hell I've been through on this trip." He slipped it into the pocket of his worn, ripped black breeches.

"It was a risk we didn't have to take," she said quietly as she put away her sewing supplies.

"Your ladyship, some people are satisfied with moonlight and sunshine." He sat up, stuffing gold guineas into his coin purse. "And some people prefer shiny things of a different kind."

"You act as if you've never seen money before."

His head came up sharply, and he started to say something . . . but then he just smiled. "Not for a lot of years," he said coolly, chuckling. "Not for a whole lot of years." He patted his pocket. "This little trinket is going to make life at home better than it's been in a long time."

He returned his attention to the coins he had been sorting. Sam folded her new skirt and set it aside, questions tumbling through her mind as she watched him. *Home? Where is your home? What do you do there? Are you a tradesman? A criminal? A military man? A tavern keeper?*

What became of that small boy after he survived the prison hulk?

Who the devil are you?

Even after all they had been through together, all they had shared, she still didn't know the answer. He had hardly been forthcoming about his past. Or his present. He seemed intent on keeping his secrets.

"Besides," he concluded flatly. "I'm owed."

She didn't ask what he meant by that comment either. Because she suspected he would not tell her. "How much money do we have? Is there enough?"

"Over five hundred."

She whistled softly. "I would say that's enough."

"Enough to make one blacksmith fat and happy and set two fugitives free." His eyes met hers. "Within a few hours, your ladyship, we'll be miles from here."

"Free to go our separate ways. At last."

An awkward silence fell, broken only by the clink of the coins he was counting.

Free at last. She should be ecstatic.

So why did the thought make her feel so . . . wretched?

She pulled up her legs, wrapping her arms around them, resting her cheek on her knees, observing him in the scant light. The silvery glow played over his features, made his new white shirt gleam, his black hair seem all the darker. With a gem in his pocket and gold at his fingertips, he looked happier than she had ever seen him, his eyes alight, his smile easy and broad. It seemed he was in his element, somehow. And it made him appear so relaxed, so confident . . . so undeniably handsome.

Even though she didn't approve of his reckless little ruby theft, she liked seeing him happy.

A now-familiar warmth unfolded within her, that feeling she had never been able to name. Except that this time it brought an ache as well.

Only a week ago she had been ready to send this man to the gallows to save her own neck. But that was before he had saved her life, comforted her when she thought her whole world without comfort, laughed with her . . .

Touched her in a way no man ever had.

With his tenderness and warmth, he had banished her fears. Taken them away as easily as he had plucked that blood-red gem from the gypsies' treasure.

Free? She had never truly been free until she was shackled to him.

And the thought of leaving him, of never seeing him again . . .

He lifted his head—and some of what she felt must have shone in her eyes, because he stopped counting abruptly.

The silence stretched out between them.

He broke it first. "So where will you go tomorrow, once you're finally free of me?"

Straightening, she stretched and yawned and somehow managed to keep her voice casual. "Merseyside." She had shared with him all her other secrets, saw no sense in withholding that one. "I'll go to the room I keep in Merseyside, pack my things, leave the country."

"Off to Venice, then?"

"Yes." Somehow the thought of Italy's blue skies and sparkling Adriatic wasn't as appealing as it had once been. "And what about you?"

"I have that business appointment in York."

"I meant after that."

She kept her tone light, not demanding, though she longed to know more about him. Everything about him.

He glanced away, and she knew she had made the right decision when they had left the cave: she hadn't told him about his delirious ramblings, had kept the knowledge of his painful childhood to herself, not knowing how he would react. Hoping he would volunteer more information himself, without any prodding.

For some reason, it was important, achingly important, that he trust her.

"I'm a planter," he said slowly, "from the American colonies. I'll be returning there as soon as I conclude my business in York."

"I see." Part of her felt pleased that he had trusted her with that much information.

And part of her did not. A *planter*? Of all the possible occupations she had imagined for him, that wasn't one of them. He didn't seem like a man who belonged in the fields, worrying about crops and weather and weevils.

She wondered whether he was telling her the truth.

And she hated how much it hurt, that he might be lying to her. What right did she have to expect the truth or anything else from him? They were two strangers who had been thrown together by chance. Outlaws who fiercely guarded their independence. Who cared only for themselves.

That had been their bargain all along.

She wondered exactly when that bargain had been broken.

And why it hurt so much.

"I've never been to the Colonies." She refused to let the hurt show in her voice. "What's it like there?"

Again, he hesitated.

And again, he told her. "Very different from England. Hot. Humid. The . . . uh, place where I have my plantation is mostly salt marsh. More water than land. I grow indigo, rice, tobacco. There are plenty of fish, and some good hunting. Quail and deer, mostly. It's not much, but I've got a damn fine wine cellar, all the rum and brandy a man could drink, and it beats the hell out of . . . some of the other places I've lived."

"It sounds nice."

He choked out a little self-deprecating laugh. "Not quite as nice as Venice."

She shrugged.

They held one another's gazes a long time. Then he turned and fished around through the leaves for the creel that held their supplies, and took out the flask. They had filled it with water from the stream before leaving the glade. "Well, in any event, here's to getting out of England in good health." He poured water into two cups and handed her one, raising his in a toast. "Here's to America, to Venice, to freedom."

"Freedom," she echoed, with a smile she did not feel.

They clinked their cups together, and their fingers touched.

A tendril of fire shot through her hand, whirled straight to the center of her body, made her catch her breath. "Nick . . ."

He withdrew quickly. "We don't have time for . . . uh . . . That is, we should get some sleep, your ladyship."

She noticed that he had been calling her that again, instead of using her name, and wondered whether he was doing it on purpose. "Nick, I just . . . I want to . . ." She sighed in frustration. "I wanted to say . . ."

"What?" he asked tightly.

She wasn't sure. What was there to say? *Freedom doesn't mean the same thing to me that it did a few days ago? I don't want to leave you?*

I care about you?

The thought stunned her. It was overpowering, undeniable.

True.

She cared about him. And she couldn't simply walk away as if he meant nothing to her.

"It doesn't matter, Samantha."

"It does matter," she returned evenly. "You matter."

He stared at her as if in shock.

"You matter to me," she said simply.

"Don't say that."

"It's true."

"It shouldn't be."

"Why?" She reached out and touched him, laying her hand lightly on his arm.

He flinched as if she'd burned him with a hot iron. "Because," he ground out. "Damn it, it's not right. You're . . ." He swore again, shutting his eyes. "You're a lady. The kind of lady who deserves better than—"

"Better than a planter from the Colonies?"

"Better than a man like me," he finished fiercely, opening his eyes, those emerald depths ablaze.

"Well, that's too bad, Mr. James. Because I've been living my own life and making my own choices for too long to change now. I know what I want." She slowly curved her fingers around his arm, realized how taut his muscles were beneath the smooth, white cotton. "I know what I *feel* inside."

He stared at her with that dangerous fire in his eyes. "You have no idea what you're saying."

"I think I do." She leaned closer, breathed against his lips the way she had learned from him, asking without words for his kiss. "I know what I want."

"Samantha . . ." He said it like a warning, his body rigid. "*No.*"

"Yes. Nick, *yes.*"

She felt him tremble. Heard him groan, a wrenching sound that seemed to be ripped from the very depths of his being.

Suddenly he circled her with his arms, pulled her against him. His mouth covered hers, plundering, hot.

And she abandoned herself to the fire in the moonlit darkness of Cannock Chase.

Chapter 18

$\sim\!\!\curvearrowright\!\!\curvearrowright\!\!\curvearrowleft\!\!\sim$

Sam fell with him down into the leaves, her mind and her reason no longer in charge. Her heart made the decision, carried her away on a wave of emotion stronger than any she'd ever felt. She met his kisses eagerly, returned his caresses with her own. Leaves crushed beneath them, filling the night air with the smells of earth and pine.

The worn fabric of her gown gave way beneath his questing fingers. She had saved her new clothes to wear on the morrow; the dress did not matter. With a groan, he tore the bodice from her, baring her to his kisses. Hot, open-mouthed kisses that set her afire. Impatiently, he rent the skirt as well, and then she was free of the last of her lemon silk gown.

She lay naked beneath him. Naked on the leaves. And felt no shame, no shyness. The wind caressed her, warm and damp with the promise of rain, a summer wind that made the branches and the moonlight dance around them. His broad shoulders almost blocked the light, his powerful arms bracketing her body. He tore off his shirt, sent it sailing into the shadows. He remained poised over her for a moment, his breathing harsh.

She drew him back down to her, stroking his back, feeling his scars beneath her fingers . . . so many marks of suffering. So much pain. She wished she could take

245

them all away, erase them with only a touch.

His hands were everywhere, his caresses rough and gentle, quick and unbearably slow. She sought his mouth, his kisses, more. He cupped her breasts, his thumbs and fingers working magic that sent sensations spiraling through her.

She kissed his throat, his chest, the sprinkling of dark hair tickling her lips. She gently kissed the brand, feeling his heart pounding beneath her mouth. He brushed his cheek against her, the rough silk of his beard an extraordinary sensation against her sensitive skin. Then he bent his head and stroked one hard nipple with his tongue, taking the hard peak into his mouth, suckling, teasing. Fierce ribbons of heat whipped through her.

She felt tingling, alive, burning all over. Her lips felt swollen and sensitive from his kisses, yet her mouth was eager for more of the taste of him. Musky, spicy, warm.

He slid one hand down her ribs, her waist, over the curve of her hip . . . lower. He touched her thigh. Her fingers dug into the taut muscles of his arms. Anticipation whipped through her, for she knew what to expect this time.

And then he touched her as he had before, that first time, that first magical night that had been like no other in her life. He found the warm place at the very center of her being, his fingers sliding over her . . . and then into her.

She gasped at the intimate touch, her voice no more than a soft cry of wordless yearning. He slowly explored the soft petals that concealed her most feminine secrets, and she could feel the rain of warm honey flowing from her, heard his low sound of approval as he felt it too.

His thumb found the tiny bud hidden there, made it bloom with fire. Fire and rain. He swept her upward to the heights she had experienced before in his arms, and this time she wanted to take him with her. This time she did not want him to hold back. For she did not fear him. She wanted him, cared for him.

Loved him.

The thought flitted into her mind and out again before she had a chance to react, for he was gathering her beneath him, his body covering hers. She whispered her assent, wanting to be wrapped in his strength, his hunger, his dark masculine heat. Instinctively, she tilted her hips upward.

"*Angel.*" His voice sounded like he was being stretched on a rack of agony. "Wait—"

"No more waiting," she whispered. "No more holding back."

"There might be pain for you."

"I don't care." She moved her hips against him and he lost the rest of his warning in a groan.

The intensity in his eyes was so vivid she could see the color even in the darkness, the burning emerald green. "I don't want to hurt you."

She could tell that he meant it in ways that went beyond physical pain.

"Nick," she whispered, putting all she felt in her heart into her voice, her eyes. "I trust you."

He buried his head against her shoulder, muttering indecipherable words, curses, something that almost might have been a prayer. She slid her hand down his back, in a slow caress, feeling how he was rigidly controlling himself. How he was shaking with the force of his need. The same need she felt for him.

"No more holding back," she whispered again.

He went still.

Then with one last oath, he reached down, unfastened his breeches.

And slid into her with a single thrust.

She felt the pain he had warned her of—but it was only a momentary twinge as he parted her deeply, embedded himself within her.

And became part of her.

*   *   *

Nicholas struggled for control and could not find it.
For the first time in his life, he lost his hard-won self-
mastery. He felt himself shatter and knew that only she
could put him back together again.

He withdrew, stunned by the mind-numbing pleasure he felt, then surged forward again, sinking deeply,
losing himself to the ancient, primitive rhythm. Losing
himself to her.

She was a gift greater than he deserved, but that
didn't stop her from giving herself completely, generously, joyously. Nothing stopped her. Instinctively, she
raised her hips to meet his long, slow strokes. The sleek
heat of her was like hot silk, yielding to him, clasping
him deep inside.

He threaded his fingers through her hair, tangling
his hands through the golden mass. The sound of their
breathing was harsh and hot. Their mouths came together in a joining as fierce and hard as that below.

And then a shattering explosion of pleasure shook
them both. He was drowning in sensations, and her
with him. Their voices blended, her soft cries a tender
contrast to his low groans. They clung to one another,
surrendering to the storm.

And to each other.

The distant sky had turned to gray, the stars fading
with the moon, and still they did not stir. Nicholas reclined against a tree, one knee raised, Samantha dozing
in his arms. She lay naked against him, her arm draped
across his midsection, holding him as tightly as he held
her. Her passion-bruised lips curved upward in a smile
that it seemed nothing could erase.

She looked so young, so sweet and trusting.

Too young. Too trusting.

You matter to me.

Her words rang in his mind. It had been a very long
time since he had mattered to a woman. To anyone.

Longer still since anyone had mattered to him.

He couldn't remember the last time someone had been this important to him. He couldn't deny it any longer.

Even as he wished it wasn't true.

She stirred, but neither of them said anything, both loath to break the peace. The two of them had spent so long in battle—with each other, with the world—that peace felt rare and special.

After a time, though, he became aware of moisture sliding down his ribs . . . from tears on her cheeks.

"Samantha?" he asked softly, hearing the concern in his own voice as he reached down and tilted her head up. "Damnation, I—"

"No, no, it's not you. You didn't hurt me," she assured him, tightening her arm around him. "I'm not crying because of that. It's because I . . ." She hid her face against his chest. "You've given me such joy, Nick. I can't even put it into words."

Her gentle admission made that strange ache unfurl through his chest again. Her words filled a place inside him that had been dark and empty for a very long time. Filled it with warmth and light and . . . *life.*

"Even with a shackle around my ankle and lawmen on our trail," she said with a little laugh, tracing lazy patterns along his chest with one finger. "I'm happy. For the first time in years . . . I'm happy."

He circled her with his arms, tightening his hold on her. He could feel her happiness seeping into him, melting through him. It was a completely new experience. One of many he'd had in the last few days.

Never, in all his innumerable liaisons, had he ever made a woman happy. He'd made love to them, made light of them, even made room for them on his ship now and then . . . but mostly he had made them miserable.

But Samantha was different. Unique. Unlike any lady he'd ever met. Her intelligence, her courage, and her

impetuous enthusiasm for life all captivated him as
much as her beauty. And her sweet innocence and gentle heart affected him in ways he had never imagined
possible.

Made him yearn for all the things he had denied
himself these past six years, he thought with a painful
tightness in his throat. Warmth, kindness. Caring.
Things he had thought he didn't need to survive.

Samantha made him see—as if a blindfold had been
ripped from his eyes—that he'd been living only half
a life.

That in every way that mattered, he *had* died in that
fiery wreck six years ago.

And he realized as he held her in his arms that he
didn't want to give her up. Didn't want to send her off
to Venice.

Where she would no doubt attract suitors by the gon-
dola load. She might think she'd enjoy an independent
life there, but with her beauty, wit, and charm, she
wouldn't be alone for long. Some rich baron or count
would snap her up the way he had snapped up the
gypsies' ruby.

He could picture them sniffing around her villa, each
intent on taking her for his own and making her his
wife—

He cut that thought short as a surge of possessiveness shot through him. The image of Samantha with
another man, lying in the brocade-draped bed of some
Italian count . . .

"Nick?"

"Sorry." He had to forcibly relax his hold on her,
realizing he was squeezing too tight.

Possessiveness. Yet another new experience. He had
never been possessive with a woman before; he cherished his own freedom too much to interfere with anyone else's. He had never expected or demanded
exclusive relationships with his mistresses.

But now he found himself entertaining reckless

thoughts: thoughts of taking Samantha with him.

Keeping her with him.

"Nick?" she asked hesitantly. "There's something I've been wanting to . . . to tell you."

He shifted his weight and looked down at her, smiling, glad for a distraction from his bewildering thoughts. "Tell me." He wondered if there was something else about her past she wanted to share.

Sitting up, she reached for her yellow silk gown— only to have it fall apart in her fingers. She blushed profusely. There wasn't much left of it.

"Sorry about that." With a grin that betrayed his lack of remorse, Nicholas handed her his new shirt. Her new clothes were out of reach under one of the other trees. "You were saying?"

She slid her arms into the sleeves. "Well, when we were in the cave, during your fever . . ." She paused while he helped with the buttons. "You . . . you were delirious for a while, and you . . . said some things."

His fingers froze. He felt as if a load of lead ballast had just been dropped on his head. "Things?"

She covered his hand with hers, looking at him with concern in her deep golden eyes. "About how you came to have the brand."

He stared at her, mute, horrified.

"It's all right," she said quickly. "You talked about how you . . . you saw your father hanged. And the prison hulk, and a man with the branding iron. You said the name Wakefield."

Nicholas remained utterly still, his every nerve ending on edge. He didn't confirm or deny the truth of what he'd apparently let slip. "What else did I say?"

"That was all." She brushed her fingers along his hand, his arm, smiling. "It's all right. I understand."

"You understand?" he repeated on a dry throat.

"Yes. You were thrown in gaol for a crime your father committed. It wasn't your fault." Her eyes held concern . . . and curiosity. "And I think I can guess the rest."

He withdrew his hand from her touch, feeling as if he was suddenly, entirely made of ice. "Can you really?"

"I don't think you're a planter."

A riot of curses tumbled through his head. But he had no voice.

"You fight as if you're used to fighting," she continued. "And you tell directions nautically. You've always checked which way we're going by looking at the stars. You haven't been finding our way, you've been *navigating* it. Then there's the way you work with rope—those knots you used to secure the fishing creel. And the brand . . . and your scars. It looks like you've been flogged."

He felt as if he was splintering into painful glass shards.

"I'd say you're a seafaring man," she said triumphantly. "Perhaps an officer in the navy? You're certainly no planter. Or if you are now, you haven't always been. And you wouldn't be an ordinary seaman. You're not an ordinary anything. You're too used to giving orders and having them obeyed." Smiling, she reached out, caressing his bearded cheek with her fingertips. "Won't you tell me the truth . . . Captain?"

Chapter 19

~~~⌒◯◯⌒~~~

"No."
His curt reply seemed to take her completely by surprise. She stared at him in confusion, the warmth slowly melting from her expression. "But—"

"No," he repeated more forcefully. "No, I don't care to tell you the truth. Do I need to make it any clearer for you?" He untangled himself from her, stood up, wanted to walk away.

And hated that he couldn't. The chain pulled taut before he moved two paces.

He couldn't move. Trapped, he went still, left with no outlet for the furious energy coursing through him, the disbelief. He had told her. Damn him, he had told her about his past—not all of it, but far too much. He stood in the shadows, breathing hard, unable to even look at her.

What a tale she had spun from the few strands that she knew! Hellfire and damnation. She thought he was some kind of bloody naval hero? *Him?*

She thought *he* was the innocent one, that his *father* had been guilty of a terrible crime?

She was so naive, so eager to believe the best about him—when the truth was completely the opposite.

The truth was that his father had been an innocent man wrongly accused.

While he, Nicholas Brogan, had committed terrible

crimes that could never be forgiven. Had spent fourteen years in a mindless quest for vengeance. Spilled an ocean of blood. Heedlessly hacked down whoever stood between him and his quarry.

Including a child. He had taken the life of a child.

He shut his eyes, clenched his fists, choked by guilt. How would *that* compare to her image of him as some kind of noble navy captain?

He didn't have to guess. He knew that a woman as gentle and innocent as Samantha would never be able to forgive such a senseless act of violence.

"Nick." She sounded as if he'd knocked the breath from her. "I don't understand. After all we've shared ... after..." She struggled to speak. "You *still* don't trust me?"

He could not make himself turn and face her. "The less you know, the better off you are," he said tersely.

"But I thought ... I thought you ..."

He whirled. "What?" he snapped.

She gazed up at him, looking perplexed, mystified. Hurt.

He knew what she wanted to say. *I thought you cared.*

The word was like a knife in his gut, and she hadn't even said it aloud.

She couldn't possibly understand. And he couldn't make her understand. A man like him *couldn't* care. Not about her, not about anyone. The crimes he had committed all those years ago had doomed him forever. Sentenced him to a life of secrecy.

A life alone.

For a few idiotic, reckless moments, he had forgotten that. Had allowed himself to entertain the idea of being a man like other men, with softness and comfort in his life. The softness and comfort that only a woman could offer. One special woman.

But there was no way to change what he was—a pirate with years of sin branded on his soul.

He had made his choice when he was barely more

than a boy, with no thought for the future, no concern but vengeance. And never had he regretted it.

Until now.

"Nick," she whispered, her eyes full of pain.

"Don't," he bit out. "Don't ask questions you don't really want answered, Samantha. And trust me," he added darkly, "you don't want that one answered."

"I don't understand."

"Well, I can't explain it to you."

"You mean you won't."

He turned away. How the hell had this gotten so complicated? Once, he had intended to take his pleasure of her and take his leave. Then he had thought to merely initiate her into the pleasures of her passion . . . and again simply walk away.

But she had made mincemeat of all his intentions. This lady possessed the most unfathomable, annoying ability to turn his mind and his motives to mush. He couldn't simply shrug her off as he had every other female who had shared his bed.

But he had to walk away from her. *He had to.* He couldn't take her with him. Couldn't tell her the truth. It would be better for them both to send her off to Venice, to her dreams.

He felt another blade in his gut, twisting this time, ripping upward to his throat. Frustrated, he fell back on a phrase that had served him well in the past. "I never offered you any promises."

"I never asked for any."

Swearing, he turned to face her again. "Then what's the problem? I thought we both knew what was happening. What we shared was"—he forced the word out, his voice sharp as a knife edge—"pleasure, nothing more."

She flinched as if he had slapped her.

And he wished that the darkness of Cannock Chase would close in and swallow him whole.

"Yes, of course." Her voice remained cool and even,

as if she were making a great effort to control it. "Pleasure and nothing more."

She looked so small and fragile, swamped by his shirt, the cuffs engulfing her hands. It made his heart ache just to look at her. "Then what is it you want from me?" he asked.

"The truth."

He shook his head, shut his eyes.

The truth that she wanted would be the end of everything. The truth—his past, his real name and identity—would turn the hurt in her eyes to shock, horror.

And hatred.

Because Nicholas Brogan, scourge of the Atlantic, terror of the Caribbean, despised by every law-abiding, God-loving Englishman, was exactly the sort of man that a good, sweet woman like Samantha Delafield would utterly loathe.

And it would do no good to try and explain that his infamous reputation had far exceeded his actual deeds.

Because his actual deeds were more than enough to merit her hatred.

And if he told her even a *hint* of the truth, he would have to spend the rest of his life wondering whether she had mentioned his name to someone else. To anyone else.

He already had one blackmailer to worry about. He didn't want to live the rest of his days looking over his shoulder for a few dozen more.

His life was going to be bleak enough as it was.

The force of that fact hit him like a physical blow. On their first night in gaol, he had suspected that this lady would have some part to play in the divine retribution God had in store for him—and now he knew that was true.

She had been a brief taste of Heaven. Of genuine happiness. The only one he would ever know.

He opened his eyes, tried to harden his voice. "Sorry to have to disappoint you on that score, your ladyship.

If it's truth you want, you've got the wrong man. If you had rules and conditions, you should have spelled them out before you and I—"

"Stop it."

"I just wanted to make it clear—"

"It's clear," she said icily. "Everything is clear. I understand you perfectly."

The sun broke through the trees. She rose and walked past him, the chain clanking, and scooped up her new clothes. Turning her back, she started unbuttoning the shirt she wore, her movements slow and steady.

Then she passed it to him in a calm, civilized manner that twisted the knife in his gullet all over again. He almost wished she would throw it at him. Curse him.

Instead she simply started to dress in her new clothes. Didn't say another word.

Nicholas turned his back. Partly to give her some measure of privacy, partly because he didn't want her to notice that he couldn't keep his own hands steady. Pulling his shirt on, he tried to ignore that her warm, delicate scent permeated the cloth. He buttoned it to his throat with quick, savage motions, covering the brand on his chest, as he had so many innumerable times in the past. The mark of the *Molloch*. The indelible evidence of who and what he was.

What he would always be.

Samantha would be better off without him. Soon, she would be on her way to Venice. Which was for the best, he told himself. She already knew too much about him; he would be safer with her out of England. And perhaps when he put some miles between them, all of these blasted *feelings* would start to fade.

Besides, she would be happy there. She would have her villa by the Adriatic, her lacemaking business ...

And some rich Italian count or baron for her husband.

Bile burned its way up his throat. He clenched his

hands, wanting to throttle the bastard—whoever he would be. The vision of Samantha showering her sweet passion on some other man made him want to put his fist through the nearest tree.

And of course, now that he had shown her she had nothing to fear from lovemaking, she would be less reluctant to accept another man in her bed.

He muttered a curse.

"Are you ready, your ladyship?" he asked curtly. "It's time to go."

The sun, Sam thought, had the most awful way of revealing things. Everything that had seemed dreamy and magical and special last night had been exposed by the glaring light of day.

Transformed into something common and real and painful.

And the worst part was that she could see her own foolishness now, with agonizing clarity.

As she followed Nick through the trees, heading back toward the gypsy camp, their shackles jangling, she kept hearing his biting, cynical words. *I never offered you any promises.*

It was true. He hadn't said a word about caring, or any feelings at all. Clearly, he didn't *have* any feelings for her. She had been a pleasant distraction to him, nothing more.

And she couldn't even hate him for it. He had shared with her exactly what he had offered: physical pleasure. He hadn't hurt her. Hadn't taken anything by force. She had given it all willingly.

She had given him her innocence.

She had given him her heart.

The first he had accepted gladly.

The second he didn't want.

If she had misinterpreted his soft words and gentle touches, had seen behind them a meaning that wasn't there, that was her own stupid mistake. Obviously there was a lot she still didn't understand about love-making.

She had thought it involved the heart, not merely the body.

The morning sun felt unseasonably hot, beating down on her, plastering her stolen chemise to her back and shoulders. The coins in the deep pocket of her green silk skirt bumped against her leg now and then; Nick carried the bulk of their stolen money in the coin purse, but he had insisted on giving her a few guineas. She would need to buy food on her way to Merseyside, he had pointed out—after they were separated.

She stared at his broad back as he trudged ahead of her. Those were the last words he had spoken to her. He had barely even spared her a glance since they set out at dawn.

Which was just as well, she thought gratefully; she had come perilously close to tears during their last exchange. If nothing else, she wanted to get out of this with some shred of her pride intact. At least she had one saving grace: she hadn't humiliated herself completely by telling him that she loved him.

If he insisted on keeping his secrets, at least she still had one of her own.

Though that didn't make it hurt any less.

She could hear sounds coming from the gypsy camp: women chatting as they prepared the morning meal, the laughter of children playing.

And the metallic, clanking rhythm of the blacksmith at work.

Nick led the way as they crept closer. They remained within the trees, cautiously circling around until they were positioned a few yards from the smithy's wagon, and stopped.

He slanted her a measuring glance. "This is it, your ladyship. Remember, if anything goes wrong—"

"I remember the plan," she bit out. "Let's get on with it. I want this chain off as much as you do."

"Snapping at each other isn't going to help."

"I promise I'll put on a convincing performance. I'll be a picture of ladylike sweetness and light."

"Samantha," he growled.

"Don't worry about me. You just do your part."

"Just remember to let me do the talking."

She gave him an icy stare. "*Trust* me."

If her barb stung him in the least, he didn't show it. Nothing seemed capable of penetrating his armor to pierce his heart. She was beginning to wonder if he had one at all.

But then, he had trusted her with his life before; he didn't seem to have any qualms about that. His life, he would willingly place in her hands . . . but not the truth.

"Fine." He hefted the coin purse in one hand. "Let's get on with it."

They left the concealing forest behind, heading straight across the clearing toward the blacksmith's workplace.

Boldness was a key element of their plan.

"Good day to you, sir," Nick called out. "I wonder if you could help us with a small problem."

The man straightened, squinting at them in the bright morning sunlight. Sam felt her heart pounding, but pasted a friendly smile on her face.

This was the crucial moment. If the lawmen had passed through here, told the gypsies about a pair of fugitives on the run, mentioned a reward . . .

"And who might you be, *machao*?" the smithy asked suspiciously, his voice thick with an accent that sounded vaguely Spanish or French to Sam's ears. "On *vacances*, on holiday?"

"Not exactly," Nick said smoothly. "Merely some fellow travelers fallen on a bit of bad luck."

They stopped a few paces away. The man's gaze fell to the shackles. "Travelers." He chuckled mockingly, muttering something to himself in his native tongue. "Ah, *sim*. Of course. Travelers."

"You can see we're in need of a man with your skills." Nick lifted the heavy coin purse. "And we're ready to reward you handsomely."

Sam felt a knot travel from her stomach up to her throat, tried to remain outwardly calm. There was little to prevent the gypsies from surrounding them and taking the money if they chose. The two of them had no weapons but the knife.

And Nick's impressive fighting skills. She had seen him in hand-to-hand combat . . . and didn't care to witness a repeat performance.

The blacksmith looked them both over from head to toe, especially Nick, sizing him up. "I might be able to help you, *ami* . . . for the right price."

They were starting to attract attention—a few curious children, some women walking by with baskets of laundry. Most of the men were apparently still in bed.

"I'm sure you can appreciate," Nick said quietly, "that we'd prefer to keep this a private matter." He nodded toward the gathering onlookers. "Unless of course you'd like to share your fee with your companions?"

The smithy glanced around, then eyed the coin purse greedily. He waved away the interested parties, shouting at them in that strange language, including what sounded like a few curses.

Whatever he said, his words and surly glares took care of even the most curious; the women and children obeyed him quickly.

Apparently the smithy was not a man to be toyed with.

"Told them you were old friends come to visit," he explained. "Follow me." He led them around to the back of his wagon, where an array of tools hung from the side—all manner of picks, axes, hammers, and

many wicked-looking implements Sam couldn't identify.

Nick got right to the point. "How difficult will it be
to get these off?"

"Difficult." The smithy crouched down on his
haunches, studying the shackles with an expert eye. "I
would say at least . . ." He shifted his gaze to the coin
purse. "A hundred pounds difficult." He spat in the
dirt. Then he stroked Sam's ankle. "Unless you like to
pay your debt in another way, *senorita*."

She almost kicked him—but Nick's hand was on the
man's shoulder before the smithy could draw another
breath. "The lady's not part of the bargain."

Nick didn't hit him, didn't draw the knife; she heard
no threat in his voice.

But something about his grip on the blacksmith's
shoulder made the man release her. Instantly.

"All right, *ami*, all right. Old Ramon, he thought you
might want to save yourself the money, is all."

"Try not to think, old Ramon. You've got work to
do."

"Show me the money first."

Nick counted out one hundred in gold guineas.
"And how much might it cost to throw a pair of your
fine horses into the deal?"

"Another . . ." Ramon eyed the coin purse, as if mentally weighing it even as Nick emptied it. "Two hundred."

Sam struggled to hold her tongue. Two hundred! It
was highway robbery, but they were in no position to
argue.

Besides, she reminded herself, it wasn't their money.

She fought the urge to glance at the wagon they had
robbed last night, subdued the grin that tugged at one
corner of her mouth.

"Luckily for you, I'm a generous man." Nick handed
over the demanded price. "And there might be more.

A little something extra for your silence. If anyone happens along asking questions—"

"I never saw a black-bearded *machao* and his blonde *senorita* in all my cursed life."

"Exactly."

"How much more?" Ramon asked with a greedy smile.

Nick closed the coin purse and tied it to his belt again. "After you've done the job."

The smithy nodded in agreement. Transferring the money to his own coin purse, he slid it down his shirt. "Who the devil are you, *ami*?"

"Someone you're better off not knowing," Samantha put in dryly.

They were perhaps the truest words Nick had ever said to her.

The blacksmith chuckled. Taking one of the strange-looking implements from the wall, he bent down over the shackles. "Give me your foot again, *senorita*."

Sam cautiously inched her foot toward him.

This time he didn't touch her with anything other than professional intent, apparently keeping either his fee or Nick's towering presence in mind. He worked at the cuff around her ankle, but gave up after a few minutes, tossing the tool aside.

"*Morbleu*, whoever put these on you, they did not want them to come off!"

Sam's heart started pounding. She was half-afraid that the shackles might be permanent after all. That she might really be chained to Nick forever.

And some stupid, reckless part of her was thrilled by that thought.

But Ramon was already choosing other tools from the wall—a small hammer and a sharp-looking chisel. Returning to her side, he lightly placed the chisel against the bolt that fastened the cuff around her ankle.

"Now be very still," he warned, lifting his hammer.

She bit her lip, looked away, frightened that she was about to lose a foot.

Her eyes locked with Nick's.

Then she heard and felt the blow all at once—a metallic clang that reverberated through her very bones.

The cuff fell open, slid to the ground.

And the chain was off. They were separated.

She was free.

Chapter 20

~~~~~~

Separated. Sam could hardly believe it. She stared at the chain, lying harmless on the ground, gleaming dully in the bright morning sunlight. Already Ramon was working on the cuff around Nick's ankle.

Free. The moment they had been waiting for, working for since that first morning in gaol, when fat Bickford had laughed as they were linked inseparably together. Had it been only a matter of days? It seemed like a lifetime.

But instead of bringing relief or happiness, freedom brought . . . numbness. It didn't feel as if she had just been relieved of a burden.

It felt as if she had just lost some part of herself. Some vital, important part.

Sam released a long, shuddery exhalation, realizing she had been holding her breath, that she was trembling. She bent down and rubbed at her sore, bruised, reddened ankle, chastising herself for such outlandish thoughts.

The shackles had brought her only pain. And a mark that looked like it might be a permanent scar. To mourn their loss was foolish—and she had been a fool too often of late. No more, she vowed.

She would waste no more time on emotions that only brought hurt.

"Which horses?" she asked the blacksmith.

"Eh, *senorita*? What's that?" Ramon was still crouched on the ground beside Nick; with a second sharp blow of his tool, they were both released from the shackles. Both free.

"We just paid you two hundred for a pair of horses." She pointed toward the line of bays and blacks and chestnuts and dappled grays picketed a few yards beyond his wagon. "Which ones are ours?"

"Ah, *sim*. The two bays on this end." Rising, he gestured with the chisel. "They are mine. I hate to see them go."

"With two hundred pounds," Nick commented dryly, "you'll be able to buy yourself a whole herd."

"True. True, I will," the smithy conceded with a greedy grin.

"How much for saddles and tack?" Nick asked in that same cynical tone.

"*Ami*, you mentioned some extra when the job was done, no?" Ramon held out his palm. "I would say . . . another hundred will cover the rest. I have no saddles, but their *cabedals*, their halters are there." He indicated some leather harnesses draped over the traces at the front of the wagon.

Nick opened his coin purse again. Sam didn't waste another minute watching the transaction. She walked over to pick up a bridle—and almost stumbled. Moving freely felt so odd, so unfamiliar.

She hadn't realized how much she had gotten used to the heavy restriction of the shackles, to matching her stride to Nick's. Without the cuff, her ankle felt strangely light, her steps almost weightless. Unnerved by the awkward sensation, she tried to ignore it, grabbing a bridle and heading for the horses.

"Wait."

She heard Nick's imperious command behind her and ignored it as well. She didn't have to take his orders. Not anymore.

Reaching the bays, she chose the smaller of the two;

they were draft horses, meant for pulling wagons, not
carrying ladies. It took her a few minutes to figure out
which part of the halter was meant for the animal's
mouth; she had often gone riding as a girl, but had
always had a groom to handle this sort of thing.

"You're doing that wrong," Nick said.

She glanced over her shoulder to see him walking
toward her.

It struck her as utterly strange to view him from a
distance. She had never seen him any way but up close
before. He strode across the grass, all confidence and
muscle and overpowering energy, his broad shoulders
straining against his shirt, the sunlight accenting the
angles and planes and shadows of his body.

She ignored the little flip her heart made and turned
back to her task. "I know what I'm doing," she lied.

"You're going to end up on your arse in the dirt
before you get ten yards." Reaching her side, he took
the halter from her hands.

"I do *not* need your help," she protested, piqued at
the way he just took over. "You have no right to . . .
to . . ."

He ignored her ire, deftly bridling the horse for her.
"Were you planning to just ride off, your ladyship? No
goodbyes?"

"How about good riddance?" She congratulated herself on how cold that sounded—because her pulse was
fluttering wildly. She reached for the leather reins, but
he held them back.

An odd expression played around his chiseled
mouth, not quite a smile, not quite a grimace. "I'm going to miss you, angel."

He sounded like he meant it. Which only confused
and infuriated her further. "You'll get over it, I'm
sure." Every fiber of her being urged her to leave. Now.
She moved to the side of the horse, intending to mount.

Nick leaned against the animal's flank, blocking her
way.

She clenched her fists, glanced uneasily toward Ramon. The smithy wasn't paying them the least attention; he was sitting on the steps of his wagon, counting his earnings. "Mr. James," she said under her breath, "you've got that pressing business appointment to keep in York, remember?"

Nick still didn't budge.

She stared at his chest. "Goodbye, all right? Are you satisfied?" Her throat seemed to close off and suddenly she knew why she wanted—needed—to get out of there and fast.

Not because she was angry with him but because she was dangerously close to revealing her real feelings for him. Her voice had already turned quivery with emotions that threatened to swamp her, with words that threatened to spill out.

Words she refused to speak.

She lifted her gaze, trying desperately to pierce him with a cold, uncaring look. "Goodbye. Is that what—"

His arms circled her, drawing her in hard, possessively, as his lips covered hers in a hot, deep joining that was just as hard and possessive. The feel of his mouth on hers sent tendrils of fire snapping through her, but this time she resisted. She pressed her fists against his chest, tried to break free, couldn't.

An instant later, she didn't want to. The sound of protest in her throat became a sound of longing. She didn't want her freedom. Didn't want to say goodbye. Didn't want to leave him. Her resolve, her anger, her facade of cool control melted in the heat of his arms. She surrendered to the spicy, male taste and scent and feel of him. He held her as if he meant to brand her body with his, bending her backward, kissing her deeply until the world swirled around her dizzily and the earth seemed to vanish from beneath her feet.

Then he broke the kiss just as suddenly, set her upright, steadied her until she regained at least some of her balance. She felt breathless, flushed, speechless. He looked down into her eyes, for a long time.

For the last time.

The thought raked through her like talons of ice. Then his hands were catching her by the waist, and he scooped her up easily, lifting her onto the horse's broad back.

"Stay away from the main roads." His voice sounded taut, strained. "Keep your guard up. If you see any . . . if . . ." He seemed unable to finish the sentence. "Damn it," he said roughly, "just be careful." He handed her the reins and stepped out of the way. "Go and find your dreams in Venice." He squinted, perhaps because the bright sun blinded him. "Go and forget me."

Sam could feel her lower lip quivering. "Don't ask for any promises."

She couldn't say any more. Couldn't bear any more. *She would never forget him. Never.* Touching her heels to the horse's flanks, she wheeled the stallion and set off toward the east, into the dazzling morning sunlight. Hot tears made the forest nothing but a blur of dark shadows and emerald green.

And she did not allow herself to look back.

Clouds rumbled in the night sky overhead, obscuring the moon and stars. Lightning flashed in the distance, and the wind that tangled her long hair carried the threat of rain. Sam thought of stopping and seeking shelter. She had left Cannock Chase behind an hour ago, and now followed what must be a sheep or cattle trail across open fields.

Her ruffled cotton chemise and silk skirt would offer little protection from a downpour, but she couldn't seem to make herself care whether she got drenched or not. She kept going, slowing from a trot to a steady walk. The stallion didn't seem the least bit weary; she was the one who felt sore from hours of riding.

And from last night. One delicate part of her body felt particularly tender, bringing a constant memory of the innocence she had given away, the sweet intimacy she had experienced.

The closeness she had lost almost as quickly as she had learned to cherish it.

She blinked away the dampness in her eyes, couldn't believe she had any tears left. Dear God, she couldn't remember the last time she had felt this miserable. Too miserable and tired to worry about rain or anything else. Everything was so different from the way it had been last night. It felt so odd to be alone.

Once or twice while she was still in the forest, she had heard movement behind her on the path—and even as she had concealed herself in the trees, her heart had fluttered with hope. Was it Nick? Had he changed his mind and followed her? . . .

The first time it had been a deer, the second time a wild goat.

And both times had made her feel like a fool. How could she *still* be so naive, so witless as to think he might come after her? Nick James was not the type of man to chase after a woman. He had enjoyed her, shared pleasure with her for a brief time, and that was that, in his view. She would never see him again.

The sooner she got used to that idea, the better.

Rain began to spatter down from the black sky, matching her bleak mood. The horse nickered softly as the fat drops splashed his sleek brown coat.

"Sorry, old boy." She sighed. "I promise when we get to Merseyside, I'll sell you to someone who has a nice warm stall for you."

Hunching her shoulders against the rain, she decided that perhaps it would be wise to stop somewhere. A hot meal and a roof over her head might do wonders for her spirits. A farm would suffice.

Or perhaps she should even splurge on herself and go to an inn. Order a hot bath sent up. And some scented soaps and a pretty nightshift.

The idea made her sigh; a touch of civilization could

be just what she needed, after so long in the wild. But she wasn't sure what kind of indulgences she could afford at the moment. Shifting her weight, she reined the stallion to a stop and slipped her hand into her pocket.

And felt something lumpy.

Frowning, she glanced down. With the clouds blocking the moon, she could barely see, but there was definitely something other than coins in her skirt pocket. What the devil had she . . .

As soon as her fingers closed around the object, she knew what it was.

She gasped, pulling it out and holding it up. A flash of lightning lit the sky, striking brilliant sparks from the red facets that sparkled and winked at her.

The ruby. It was Nick's ruby!

She stared at the jewel in open-mouthed astonishment. He must have snuck it into her pocket when he held her in his arms. And she had been so swept up in his kiss, she hadn't even noticed.

But why? Why would he give it to her?

Suddenly she remembered what he had said after he kissed her. *Go and find your dreams in Venice.*

A wrenching, hot wave of emotions suddenly overwhelmed her, a rush of surprise and love and tenderness. The jewel would buy her passage to Italy. It would bring more than enough money to complete her journey to Venice. Enough for a small villa as well.

Awash in disbelief, her heart melting, she barely noticed as the storm gathered strength around her, the rain pounding down in a drenching cascade. She closed her eyes, closing her fingers around Nick's ruby, his gift. This gem had meant so much to him. He had been counting on it to buy him a better life. And after paying the blacksmith, he couldn't have even a hundred pounds in coins left.

He had sacrificed his own comfort, perhaps more . . . for her.

Pressing the jewel to her chest, she felt warmth radiating through her even as the storm soaked her clothes and hair and skin. She looked over the rain-swept fields, west, toward York.

Nick James had stolen her heart as easily as he had stolen this gem.

Yet he was still very much a mystery to her.

And always would be.

Tears joined the raindrops that clung to her lashes. Nick was part of her past. She couldn't change that. If one thing was clear, it was that he did not want her in his life.

Wiping at her eyes, Sam turned her horse back onto the road. She had to seek shelter. Had to gather up her scattered wits and the fractured pieces of her heart and keep moving.

She slipped the ruby back into her skirt pocket . . . but could not make herself let it go.

In another two days, she would reach her flat in Merseyside. And then, thanks to Nick's gift, she would be on her way to Venice.

Chapter 21

~~~⌒◯⌒~~~

The Black Angel.

Clearly, this was not one of York's finer establishments.

Sitting astride a spirited gray hunter a few yards down the street, Nicholas studied the pub that had been his destination for weeks, his heart pumping a fiery satisfaction through his veins that he could only call triumph.

He flicked a glance into the clear night sky, sending a defiant glare heavenward.

He had made it. Despite all the insurmountable obstacles thrown into his path. Despite the physical torments he had endured—and the other, more painful retribution God had meted out. He had made it, with three days to spare.

Keeping the horse under control with one firm hand on the reins, he reached up to raise the collar on his greatcoat and pull his tricorne low over his eyes. It wouldn't pay to let impatience get the better of him now. The streets were almost deserted at this late hour, most of the night's revelers having already stumbled home, but it was still wise to be cautious. He nudged his mount forward.

The pub huddled in the middle of a row of cheap gin shops and bawdy houses. A pair of grimy oil lamps on either side of the door spilled light onto the street and illuminated the wooden sign that hung from an iron stanchion.

The Black Angel. The tavern's name was spelled out in bold lettering, above a picture of a winged creature with a fierce expression—and a pitchfork in one hand.

Nicholas couldn't hold back a grimace, certain now that the blackmailer was someone who knew him. Someone who had seen the brand. This place had not been chosen by chance.

Anger and resentment sizzled through him, made his heart pound harder against his ribs. He did not like the feeling that his unknown, unseen adversary held all the cards. Did not like being here at all. He had never asked to be forced into this game. Whoever the blackmailer was, he was about to discover that gambling carried risk.

That he'd made a grave, greedy mistake the day he'd sent that note to South Carolina.

Dismounting, Nicholas tried to appear calm and casual as he led his horse toward a hitching post. Tried to blend in to his surroundings. Fortunately, at the moment he looked more like a member of the house of commons than a vicious pirate.

He had stopped at a town after leaving Cannock Chase, where he traded the sluggish draft horse for the fastest animal he could afford, wolfed down a hot meal, and bought himself a new set of clothes. In addition to the greatcoat and tricorne, he now wore a waistcoat and breeches of navy blue brocade, a ruffled shirt with a fancy ascot that was choking him, and a frock coat with wide cuffs.

Appearances could be deceiving. And helpful.

Tying his stallion to the hitching post, he pretended to be loosening the cinch on the animal's saddle while he surreptitiously glanced around, wariness lifting the fine hairs on the back of his neck.

He didn't see anyone. No one crouched in a doorway, no one peered from nearby windows. No one had been posted on watch.

Of course, the blackmailer was not expecting his arrival. The cove would come here three days from now expecting to find a package—not Nicholas Brogan himself.

With a grim smile of anticipation, Nicholas opened his saddlebag, pausing to light a cheroot, a daily indulgence that he had missed for too long. The smoke curled into the cool night air as he exhaled. A few days and several drenching downpours had made a marked difference in the weather, the long, humid summer finally giving way to the first chilly bite of autumn.

As he tucked the box of cheroots back into his saddlebag, his fingers brushed the white cotton shirt stuffed into the bottom ... the shirt he'd stolen from the gypsy wagon.

The one that carried a light trace of Samantha's scent.

He went still, then withdrew his hand, glaring at the rumpled garment, telling himself he should just get rid of it. Leave it behind with everything else he'd brought out of Cannock Chase.

But somehow he couldn't. He'd had ample opportunity over the past couple of days to dispose of it, yet he kept carrying it around.

He frowned, beginning to realize that time and distance were not going to dull these blasted feelings. He couldn't stop thinking about Samantha. He couldn't even get used to the strange feeling of *not* having the shackle around his ankle.

Every step he took reminded him of her.

And while riding in the rain, he had found himself thinking about her thin chemise and skirt, wondering whether she had bought a coat or cape to protect herself from the weather. Or stopped somewhere to seek shelter.

Was she safe and warm? Was she taking care to avoid the lawmen who were almost certainly still searching for the two of them? Was she all right?

He closed the flap on the saddlebag with a sharp motion, reminding himself that Samantha had survived on her own for six years before meeting him; she didn't need his protection. Inhaling deeply of the fragrant cheroot smoke, he blew a blue-gray cloud into the night air . . . but he barely tasted what had long been one of his favorite pleasures.

He was wondering what Samantha had thought when she found the ruby in her skirt pocket.

Wishing he could have seen the expression on her face.

He abruptly realized he was gazing up at the moon with a smile tugging at his mouth. He shook his head, tried to come back to his senses, clenching his jaw, clamping the cheroot tighter between his teeth.

It had been a senseless act of generosity, giving away that jewel. One he would no doubt live to regret. But there was no sense in tormenting himself over it, or anything else concerning his ex–traveling companion. Samantha was no longer his responsibility, no longer . . . his.

She was never *meant* to be his, he reminded himself ruthlessly, tying the saddlebag shut. She had been a brief respite from the hell that he lived in, a taste of Heaven that would haunt him the rest of his days. All he had left were memories, images that kept him awake at night.

And a rumpled shirt.

He turned and headed for the pub door, trying to force Samantha Delafield from his mind. There were only three days left before Michaelmas. He couldn't allow himself to get distracted at this critical point.

He walked swiftly toward the Black Angel, his shiny new boots barely making a sound on the wet paving stones. Reaching the door, he pushed it open and stepped inside.

A haze of smoke washed over him, carrying the pun-

gent scents of ale and wine and male sweat that thick-
ened the air. The only illumination came from an iron
chandelier filled with flickering candles; it cast a dull
glow over the hand-hewn tables and benches scattered
haphazardly around the room, some filled with
drunken patrons and men holding conversations in low
tones.

He saw that there were no cheery groups of locals
sharing gossip and ribald jokes and tavern songs. And
there was only one other exit: a door at the back. This
was a place well-suited to clandestine meetings and nefarious goings-on.

The blackmailer had chosen well, he noted, his
respect and caution growing.

He moved toward the long counter that filled the
right side of the room, and summoned the yawning
tavernkeeper with a flick of his hand.

But before he could place his order for an ale and
ask a few questions, a hand landed on his shoulder and
a quiet voice sounded behind him.

"I've been waiting for you."

Sitting with his back to the wall, his tricorne on the
bench beside him, and one booted foot resting on the
bench across from him, Nicholas studied his companion, shaking his head. "Damn it, you are the last person
I expected to find here."

Manu raised his mug of ale in salute, his grin unre-
pentant. "Glad to see you, too, Cap'n."

"You never could follow orders worth a damn." Still
scowling, Nicholas took a long swallow from his own
glass. "I should have had you keelhauled years ago."

Manu nodded with a mock-serious air. "Might've instilled the value of discipline in me."

"I suppose it's too bloody late now."

"That it is, Cap'n." The African's grin broadened.
"That it is."

Nicholas fell silent, studying his glass, running his

thumb over a chip in the rim. There was no sense in sending Manu away, now that he was here. And to tell the truth, he was glad to have the company. It was good to see his quartermaster, to have loyal help at hand.

A loyal friend, he corrected, the thought coming into his mind unbidden. He frowned, surprised at the word. He had long refused to grant any man his trust, let alone his friendship.

But Manu had stuck by him through a lot of rough seas—steadfast despite all of his captain's failings and surly ways, always there when needed. Even during the times when Nicholas Brogan had insisted he didn't need anyone.

Nicholas glanced up, unable to think of a better measure of a friend . . . or a man more deserving of the word.

He noticed the way Manu even respected his long, moody silences. His frown slowly turned into a grin that matched his friend's. "So how long have you been here?"

"Two days. Been keeping an eye on the place."

They both shifted easily to a low, conspiratorial tone.

"Has the package arrived yet?" Nicholas lit another cheroot.

"Aye. The barkeep's got it. Says no one has inquired about it yet. Other than me."

Nicholas glanced at the fat man dozing behind the counter on the opposite side of the smoke-filled room. "Glad to see we've entrusted something so valuable to an alert, dependable sort."

Manu chuckled. "Aye. I thought it best to be here whenever the place is open. Though I've practically pickled myself. His pub may be a piss-hole but his ale is good."

Nicholas took another long swallow from his glass, laughing. "It would take more than two days of ale to pickle you, you old sot. So tell me, why aren't you in South Carolina?"

"I only meant to take a small detour. After I dropped you off on the coast, I decided to sail down to London to have a little talk with a certain lady."

"Clarice." Nicholas lifted an eyebrow, curious and a little bemused. "You still think she's involved?"

"I admit I thought she was. A woman scorned, and all . . ." Manu shook his head. "But she said she hasn't given you a single thought in the past six years, and I believe her. Took me a while to track her down—she's not in the East End anymore. Got herself a town house in Cavendish Square. Paid for by a pox-faced merchant banker who thinks the sun rises and sets in her dainties. She's not wanting for money."

"So she finally hooked herself a big fish, did she?" Nicholas blew a puff of cheroot smoke toward the grimy ceiling. "Always knew Clarice would land on her feet."

He felt not a twinge of jealousy. Clarice had been a pleasant distraction during a time when he'd been single-mindedly devoted to vengeance. He had never been able to give her what she'd wanted—what she'd demanded. Money, security, devotion, a future. He and Clarice had spent as much time at each other's throats as they had in each other's arms. And after two years together . . .

A sudden, jarring thought struck him like a belaying pin between the eyes: even after two years together, he had found it easy to leave Clarice. He'd found it easy to leave *every* woman he'd ever had a liaison with.

Until Samantha.

Somehow, in a little more than a week, Samantha had become as much a part of him as the life's blood that flowed through his veins and the heart that beat in his chest.

"Clarice's feet are traveling in very well-to-do circles these days," Manu continued. "She wasn't exactly happy to see me. Her gentleman friend doesn't know about her past associations."

"With less-than-savory characters like us." Nicholas tried to force his mind back to the topic at hand.

"And she'd just as soon keep it that way." Manu drained his glass. "She isn't involved in this business, Cap'n. She swears she never told a soul that you survived that fiery wreck."

"But no one else knew," Nicholas muttered. "No one but the three of us."

"Perhaps we were wrong about that. Someone else must have known."

"Someone who decided not to do anything about it for six years." Nicholas glanced at the other men seated at the tavern's tables. "Which makes no sense."

"Aye," Manu agreed. "That's why I decided to make another little detour once I left London. Figured York wasn't all that far away. Besides, our ship wasn't in any shape to leave port."

Nicholas frowned. "Problem with the mizzenmast again?"

"No, the mizzen is fine. Problem with the patch job we did below the waterline a few years back. She was taking in water amidships."

Nicholas swore.

"It's nothing that can't be fixed, Cap'n. I just didn't have the money. Had to leave her in dry dock in London."

"How much do we need?"

"About fifty, maybe seventy-five."

"Terrific." Nicholas felt for his coin purse. Evidently, he was going to leave England every bit as poor as he had arrived.

But better that than not leave England at all. He contemplated sending Manu straight back to London with the money. "Manu, as soon as this business is over," he nodded toward the counter at the far end of the room, "I've got to leave the country and fast. I . . . uh, ran into a little trouble with the law on my way here."

"I wondered about that."

The lack of curiosity in his voice surprised Nicholas. "You aren't going to ask what's been keeping me?"

"I know, Cap'n. Everyone in England has been talking about little else for a week."

Nicholas felt ice slide through his veins. "What the devil do you mean?"

Manu slid from the bench and crossed to the bar, scooping up a pile of newspapers and bringing them back to the table. "It's been in all the papers." He pushed the newspapers across the scarred tabletop. "Thought the description of the 'scurrilous male fugitive' sounded familiar. Especially the sound of the way you . . . uh . . . took care of the guards."

"Bloody hell," Nicholas groaned, reading the blaring headlines:

DARING DAYLIGHT ESCAPE IN STAFFORDSHIRE.
MARSHALMEN KILLED. TWO FUGITIVES SOUGHT.
MAGISTRATE HIBBERT OFFERS REWARD.

Publicity was the last thing he wanted. It could be decidedly bad for his health—and Samantha's.

"It's really not bad news, Cap'n," Manu said with a chuckle. "No one who doesn't know you could guess it was you. *I* wasn't even sure. They list you as some footpad by the name of Jasper Norwell. You're not the one they care about." He opened one of the papers to an inside page, pointing. "The articles are all about *her*."

Nicholas stared at the story beneath Manu's finger—and every sound, every movement in the pub seemed to stop for a frozen moment of time.

It was a pen-and-ink sketch of Samantha, perfect in every beautiful detail.

He grabbed the page, his fingers so tight, they crinkled the paper. "What the devil—"

"The law has that picture posted on every wall in the north of England. You, they couldn't care less about. *She's* the one who's big news."

Nicholas wasn't listening. He was reading. He felt as if he'd been struck in the chest with a battering ram, as if all the air had been knocked from him.

Though he was mentioned once or twice, Samantha was the focus of all the stories. There were descriptions of her in every paper—detailed descriptions. All supplied by a young marshalman by the name of Tucker.

Nicholas ground his teeth, suddenly saw the paper through a red haze. He should have killed Tucker while he had the chance.

Samantha's uncle, well-known London magistrate Prescott Hibbert, claimed to be deeply concerned about his "mad" niece. He was in the area to join the search personally. And he had offered a substantial reward for any information on her whereabouts. Anyone who had seen her anywhere in the vicinity in the past few months was asked to contact him.

Nicholas felt bile rise in his throat as he read Hibbert's sentimental pleadings. It was all lies. Bilge water. Hibbert was the one who had hurt her.

And the bastard would no doubt do worse if he caught her.

"I don't think you have anything to worry about," Manu was saying, sounding jubilant. "There's very little mention of you at all. It's *her* they're after. Really rather comical, isn't it? That they think you're merely a footpad?"

"Hilarious." Nicholas shoved the paper aside. He didn't seem to have enough breath for more than that one word. Samantha was in far more danger than he was—and that irony wasn't the least bit amusing.

A feeling slashed through him unlike any he had known before, one that cut far deeper than worry or concern.

Cold, stark, overwhelming fear.

Had Samantha stopped at a town on her way to Merseyside? Had she seen a newspaper?

"Cap'n?"

Manu sounded confused, but Nicholas barely heard him. His heart was pounding, his hands sweating. Damn it, what could he do? There was no way to warn her, no way to get to Merseyside and back before the blackmailer arrived here in York.

He had to stay here and kill whoever showed up to collect the package. It was the whole reason he'd come to England. Risked his life. He couldn't walk away now.

What the hell was he going to do?

Samantha was alone.

And she was riding straight into a trap.

Chapter 22

Trudging through the dark streets of Merseyside, Sam felt so exhausted she could hardly keep going. The night wind bit through her thin garments and she rubbed her arms, heading toward home, her legs aching with every step.

After three days of riding, her entire body felt sore. She had sold the stallion at the first stable she'd come to upon arriving in the village—and if she never saw another horse again, that would be just fine with her.

Shivering, she tried to cheer herself up by thinking of how good it would feel to sleep in a real bed tonight. She had avoided all the towns between here and Cannock Chase, deciding that an inn would be a dangerous indulgence, since she couldn't know where the lawmen might be searching. She had stopped to rest only once, at a farmhouse, trading a few coins for food and shelter. But she had barely been able to close her eyes for long.

It felt so strange to be on her own . . . to have no one watching over her while she slept. She missed that feeling.

She missed Nick. So much that she could barely eat, let alone sleep. Whenever she did manage to slip into unconsciousness, he even invaded her dreams.

The first time she had seen her reflection, in a mirror while washing up at the farmhouse, she had been shocked by how different she looked. Beneath the dust and grit from the road, her skin looked wan, pale, her eyes red from crying. She had also discovered marks on her neck that no amount of soap and scrubbing would remove—and realized they were tiny bruises from Nick's passionate kisses.

He had marked her, body, heart, and soul.

Swallowing hard, she tried to banish the thought, as he had banished her from his life. But without thinking, she slipped her hand into the pocket of her green skirt, her fingers closing around the ruby, as if seeking its warmth.

The instant she realized what she was doing, she forced herself to let it go. She squared her shoulders and kept walking. It was time to face facts, to stop wishing for what could never be. In time, she would grow used to being alone again. The days and nights would get easier. Eventually.

She hoped.

The moon was almost full now, shining on the rain-splashed streets of Merseyside, but her mood remained as cold and bleak as the worn, wet cobbles underfoot. Usually when she arrived here, it was with a feeling of relief, happiness, satisfaction; whenever she completed her work in a given district, she would travel here to add the money to the cache concealed in her room.

She had always looked forward to the time she spent here. This place offered her brief glimpses of a normal life, a respite from her outlaw ways. She usually rested a week or two between jobs, living peaceably, visiting the marketplace, chatting with neighbors. Her favorite activity was to make a picnic supper and eat in the town square, watching the local children at play.

But tonight she felt no joy, no relief.

She was just tired, she told herself. Spent from her ordeal. What she needed was a good night's sleep. Everything would look better in the morning.

Finally, she came to the ramshackle building that

housed her room. Glancing up at her window, at the cramped space in the attic that she had called home for five years, she couldn't even summon a smile. Trudging up the steps in the dark, she realized she was going to have to pick the lock on her own door. Her small purse, containing her keys, had been confiscated by Bickford when she'd been arrested.

There was little space to move and less light at the top of the stairs. By memory alone, she felt for the lock, and went to work. She had it open in a matter of seconds. Sighing, she pushed the door open, stepped inside, and closed it behind her.

Moonlight spilled in through the window. She moved forward in the darkness, squinting as her eyes adjusted—and tripped over something.

"What in the world . . ."

It was her little hall table, lying on the floor. Stumbling, she froze.

By the scant silvery light, she could see a vase lying smashed on her threadbare rug. Chairs broken. Her few clothes and belongings strewn across the floor.

Her place had been robbed. Ransacked! Whirling, she realized that in her weariness, she had forgotten to check her one security measure—a thread that she always placed carefully in the door.

A prickle of danger went down her neck. *Lawmen.*

Remaining utterly still, she didn't even breathe, wondering whether she was alone.

She didn't hear a sound. Not a footstep. Not a breath. Nothing but her own terrified heartbeat.

She was alone. But perhaps they were watching from outside. It might be only a matter of minutes before they rushed in to arrest her.

Whispering oaths, pulse racing, she turned and ran to the far corner, to the hiding place where she kept her money. She had to get out of here and fast.

Pushing her dresser out of the way, she felt for the box hidden in the wall behind it. She bit her lip, straining for it in the darkness. Was it there? Had they found it? Taken it?

Her fingers closed on the smooth walnut jewelry case. She clutched it in shaking fingers, yanked it free, ripped it open. Her money was still there.

With a sob of relief, she shut it and whirled toward the door.

And noticed the movement behind her an instant too late.

As if time itself slowed, she heard the footstep and the click of a pistol being cocked in the very second that a heavy, masculine arm grabbed her from behind, clamping over her mouth, cutting off her scream.

The box slid from her numb fingers and hit the floor as the man's other arm circled her waist.

"Good evening, my dear niece," a familiar voice growled in her ear as the cold barrel of a pistol jabbed into her ribs. "So nice to see you again."

Shock and terror catapulted through her mind. It was her worst nightmare came to horrifying life. *Her uncle had found her*. The room seemed to spin, every fiber of her being screaming in denial.

No! She struggled, kicking, fighting his hold on her with all her strength.

"Now, now, Samantha. Don't make trouble for yourself." He subdued her easily, shifted the gun until the cold metal pressed against her throat. "It will go easier for you if you cooperate."

She went still, breathing in shallow gasps, shutting her eyes. *God, please, help me*. This was impossible. How had he found her?

"I must say, I'm surprised to find you still alive," he whispered in that soft voice that had haunted her nightmares. "And pleased. It didn't even cost me very much. The people of this poor district were pitifully eager to trade information on your whereabouts for a few coins. I'm sure you'll be worth every shilling." He shifted his hold on her, squeezing her breast. "We have such a lot of catching up to do."

A white-hot flash of panic rendered her momentarily blind and immobile. Moonlight and darkness swam around her, tumbling as her stunned senses reeled in disgust and disbelief. Unconsciousness threatened to swamp her. *No, no, no!*

"But not here and not now, unfortunately." He loosened his hold on her just long enough to stuff a rag in her mouth, tying the gag behind her head. "As you can see from the remains of your room, the marshalmen are rather overzealous in their quest to bring you to justice. They might return before long, and hanging is not what I have in mind for you, my dear." He jerked her hands behind her back, binding them tightly with a length of rope. "I've a lovely place awaiting you in London. A private suite where you'll be available to me whenever I please." He chuckled, a low, unpleasant sound. "We'll have ample time to get reacquainted at my leisure. Years."

The roar in her ears was like the rush of a waterfall. She was drowning. *Helpless.*

Oh, God, please.

Nick, help me.

"The marshalmen might spend the next several weeks chasing their tails, but they're never going to find you, my dear. No one's ever going to see you again. Now, off we go." He shoved her ahead of him toward the door. "We mustn't waste any time."

"You're not taking her anywhere, your honor."

Sam froze in the middle of the room, staring in shock at a dark silhouette that filled the entryway.

"Who are you?" Uncle Prescott demanded belligerently.

"Call me a concerned bystander." The man stepped inside, closing the door behind him.

Sam didn't recognize the voice, and she couldn't see him very well in the moonlight. Her rescuer was a tall, slender young man with dark hair, dressed in a black frock coat and breeches. A man she had never seen before.

And he was brandishing a gun.

A second later she realized with a shock that the right sleeve of his coat hung empty. He had only one arm.

"See here," Uncle Prescott snarled, "*I* am in charge of this investigation. If you're with the marshalmen—"

"Wrong guess."

"Do you have any idea who I am—"

"Oh, I know who you are." The young man chuckled. "It's been in all the papers."

"Then you know I could have you arrested for pointing a gun at me. Assaulting a magistrate is a serious offense. I advise you to leave here before I call the marshalmen."

"You're not going to call anyone. It would ruin your plans. Now, I'm afraid I can't let you take the lady with you. Step out of the way, Miss Delafield."

She started to move.

"Stop right there, Samantha." Uncle Prescott snarled, aiming his pistol at her. "I'd hate to damage one of your lovely legs—but you know I'll do it."

Sam froze, trapped in the line of fire between the two men.

The stranger advanced fearlessly toward Uncle Prescott. She could see him better now. He had blue eyes, hard, angular features. And he couldn't be much older than she was.

"I don't mean to be unreasonable," he said calmly, "but I need to ask the lady some questions. And I can't do that if you take her to London."

"Fire one shot and this place will be swarming with lawmen."

The stranger slid the gun smoothly into the waistband of his breeches at his back. "We can do this quietly, if you prefer." A blade suddenly flashed in his hand.

Fear gleamed in Uncle Prescott's eyes. "Do you think I'm afraid of a *cripple*?" he sneered.

A muscle twitched in the young man's tanned cheek. "I think you'd be a fool to underestimate me," he returned smoothly.

Uncle Prescott laughed at him—a cruel, familiar sound that made Sam shudder.

The stranger's eyes narrowed, his voice taking on a hard, angry edge. "I'm offering you a choice. You can leave here right now and live, or stay and die. Which will it be?"

Uncle Prescott sobered. After a moment, he slowly began to lower his pistol.

But then he suddenly turned it to use as a club and attacked.

The stranger dodged out of the way with surprising, fluid grace. He aimed an agile kick at Uncle Prescott's hand, knocking the gun from his grasp. Sam couldn't tear her eyes away, looking on in horrified shock as Uncle Prescott lunged in again and the two men locked together, wrestling for the blade, grunting.

The struggle went on for a taut, quiet, terrifying minute. Uncle Prescott had a clear advantage. Already he was pressing the blade toward the young man's neck. But then the stranger used his strength and evident experience to fight back, kicking, twisting.

And their struggle ended as suddenly as it began. With a quick, sideways thrust of the knife, the stranger jammed it into Uncle Prescott's throat.

Clutching at the hilt, Uncle Prescott sank to his knees, his bulging eyes turning desperately to her. He reached out one hand as if to plead for help. A second later, he fell forward, gurgling as he drowned in his own blood.

Sam staggered backward, tripped over something,

and fell to the floor. She lay there stunned, numb with shock.

Looking up at the stranger who stood over her uncle's dead body, she didn't know whether to feel thankful . . . or more terrified than ever.

He kicked Prescott onto his back, staring down into the sightless eyes for a moment. Sam almost thought she saw remorse in the young man's face, just for an instant. Then he knelt, yanked out the blade, and moved toward her.

She tried to scramble backward, but with her wrists bound, she was helpless.

He smiled grimly at her. "Miss Delafield, there's nowhere to run. And don't bother to thank me. I'm not here to be gallant. I don't give a damn about you or your fat uncle or anyone else who preys on the innocent." Bending down, he set the knife aside and used his hand to open the box she had dropped. "He was nothing but a corrupt scum, and from what I've read, you're nothing but a thief." He counted the money with a low sound of pleasure. "It's money that I'm most interested in."

She stared at him in confusion, trembling. Was he a bounty hunter of some kind? A thief-taker?

He picked up the knife and the slender box, sliding both into the pocket of his worn frock coat as he stood. Then he hauled her to her feet. "Sorry that there was no time for proper introductions. My name is Foster. Colton Foster. But that's not important. I'm here for a little information."

Hooking his foot around a straight-backed chair that the marshalmen had knocked to the floor, he righted it and pushed her into the seat.

Then he drew the knife again, holding it in front of her eyes. She could see her uncle's blood still on it.

"Now, you wouldn't scream for help, would you?" he asked coolly. "Because you don't want a dozen

marshalmen in here any more than I do. We're agreed
on that, are we not? Just nod."

She nodded.

"Very good. We're getting off to an excellent start."

He leaned closer. She squeezed her eyes shut as she
felt the cold touch of the blade against her skin.

But the chill against her cheek lasted only a second.
He cut off the gag.

However, he left her hands bound. Her arms were
tingling, going numb.

She spat out a mouthful of fuzz, tried to speak.
"W-who . . . what? . . . "

"Let's not waste time, Miss Delafield. I have precious
few hours to spare. Just to expedite this matter, let me
explain a few things." He pulled up another chair,
turned it around and sat in front of her, folding his arm
over the back. "It was the stories in the papers that
caught my attention—"

"What stories? What are you—"

The tip of the knife touched her chin. "Please don't
interrupt. And please don't waste my time by playing
innocent. As I said, I'm in something of a hurry." He
withdrew the knife, but dangled it in his fingertips only
inches from her face.

Sam strained at the ropes that bound her wrists, hating that she was helpless, glaring at him in furious silence.

"Better," he said. "Now then, after I noticed the stories in the papers, I located your uncle and followed
him out of London, figuring that he would lead me to
you. I had hoped to find the answers I seek still attached to your ankle . . . but unfortunately, it seems
that you and your nefarious companion have parted
company."

Nick, she thought with a sudden rush of understanding and an equally strong rush of fear. He was
after Nick.

"After the marshalmen ransacked your room and

found nothing," he continued, "your uncle decided to wait for you. I thought he might know something I didn't, so I decided to wait, too. I was about to give up and leave, when you finally arrived and . . . well, you know the rest." He toyed with the knife, turning it deftly in his fingers. "All I want, Miss Delafield, are the answers to a few simple questions. Give me what I want and you can be on your way."

"Not without that box in your coat pocket, I can't."

Her answer seemed to surprise him. "You should be grateful that I'm letting you escape with your life."

"You expect me to believe that, Mr. Foster? Killing seems to come pretty easily to you."

His eyes darkened to a deep, stormy sapphire. "*I* don't kill without reason. I've merely learned a few ways of defending myself over the years. As I said before, it's not you or your fat uncle I care about. Now are you going to answer my questions?"

Stony silence was her only reply.

"Let's start with a simple one. In fact, this question is so simple it might make the rest unnecessary. Maybe I'm wrong. Maybe I'm jumping at shadows. You'll have to tell me."

She shrugged.

"Ah, a hint of cooperation." He leaned forward. "The man who was arrested with you—was he in fact a footpad by the name of Jasper Norwell?"

Sam just stared at him. She didn't know what sort of man this Colton Foster was, what he wanted with Nick, or what he might do once he found Nick. So she held her tongue.

"We can do this the easy way," Foster said icily, "or we can do it the hard way." The knife came up to brush her cheek in a slow, lethal caress. "I'm very good with this blade. I could have you *begging* to answer my questions in a matter of seconds."

Sam debated frantically, terrified. For herself, and for

the man she loved. Every beat of her racing heart demanded that she protect Nick.

And she didn't know if Foster would actually carry out his threat against her. Hadn't he said something about not hurting innocent people? Yes. Yes, he had.

On the other hand, he didn't seem to consider her innocent.

"I'll ask again," he said. "Was your companion the footpad Jasper Norwell?"

He drew the knife downward, pressed it against the hollow of her throat.

Another hairsbreadth and he would slice open a vein.

"No," Sam whispered, glaring at him, hating him. "He wasn't."

The young man's blue eyes went cold, piercing. "I see." His mouth tightened to a hard line. "The descriptions in the papers mentioned dark hair and green eyes. Did he also happen to have a scar—a brand on his chest, right here?" He drew the symbol over his own chest with the blade. "A downward-pointing pitchfork with three tines?"

Sam squeezed her eyes shut. "I . . . I don't know."

"Don't lie to me, Miss Delafield," he said angrily. "Judging from those marks on your neck, unless there are rather large mosquitoes in Cannock Chase these days, you and your traveling companion became quite friendly. Now tell me the truth. Did you see a brand?"

She resisted for one more desperate, frightened moment.

Then she nodded.

Foster erupted in a sudden fury, cursing, pushing away from his chair. "I can't believe it!" He paced across the room. "I can't believe Brogan would risk coming back to England."

"Brogan?" Sam asked in confusion.

"If he thinks I'm going to walk into his trap, he can think again. He should have simply paid up. I could have demanded forty or fifty thousand. I only asked for a pittance!"

"I think you've got the—"

"Damn it, I never asked for a confrontation. This is exactly what I didn't want." He turned, stalking back toward her. "All I asked for is what he owes me. That bastard robbed me of a brilliant naval career. Of everything. Of my *life*." He struck at the empty sleeve hanging from his coat. "He *owes* me. And one way or another, I'm going to collect."

"You've got the wrong man!" Sam managed to interrupt at last. "The man with me was not someone named Brogan. He was a planter from the Colonies, a man named Nick James. Not—"

The glare turned on her cut off her words and her breath. "I told you not to waste my time. Don't try to protect him."

"I'm telling you the truth."

"The truth? The truth is I've got a problem here, Miss Delafield." He strode toward her and stabbed the knife he still held into the seat of the chair he had occupied. "You see, I don't have nearly enough proof to go to the authorities. Just my own suspicions and a few notes gathered from years of investigation. I've been bluffing. Never thought he wouldn't pay." He turned away again, raking his hand through his hair. "I can't go to the Old Bailey empty-handed with a wild story about Nicholas Brogan rising from the dead. Not only will they *not* pay me the ten-thousand-pound bounty, they'll have me committed."

Sam's mind was spinning with confusion at the name he had just mentioned. "W-what . . . what did you say?"

"What I need is a new plan." He paced again. "Brogan's going to pay for this bit of treachery. Thinks he's outwitted me, does he? Bastard. I'll take his money *and* turn him in for the bounty."

"*Nicholas* Brogan?" She gaped at Foster in disbelief.

The legendary Nicholas Brogan had been a pirate. One of England's most ruthless pirates. The very name belonged in the same infamous ranks as Henry Morgan, Captain Kidd, Blackbeard.

She started to shake her head, slowly at first, then more quickly. This was madness. A mad, ridiculous, horrible mistake.

Foster turned toward her again. "Don't tell me you don't know. You were shackled to him for almost two weeks, day and night, and you don't know?"

"Don't know what?" she cried desperately. "I think you're insane! The man with me was named Nick James."

"Stop lying. How many men has he brought with him?" He drew his pistol, aimed it in her direction. "What's his plan?"

"I don't know what you're talking about!"

He stalked toward her with a look of fury. For a moment, she feared he would actually shoot her from sheer frustration.

But when she didn't flinch, he backed off a step, lowering the pistol, looking down at her with astonishment.

Which rapidly turned to amusement. "You really don't know, do you?" He laughed. "After all these years, the old blackguard must have become skilled at keeping his secret."

"His name," she insisted doggedly, "is Nick James."

"Of course it is. Why not. A perfectly bland, ordinary name. One he no doubt picked for exactly that reason." He stepped toward her, leaned down until his face was level with hers. "Let me tell you exactly whom you've been spending time with, lady. The real name of the man who's been nibbling on your neck is Nicholas Brogan. As in *Captain* Nicholas Brogan."

Samantha stared at him in open-mouthed horror. "You're lying."

"Why would I lie? You think I'm lying about that

brand? I can even tell you exactly where he is at the moment. He's in York."

She felt all the breath leave her body. It all made a horrible kind of sense.

Someone you're better off not knowing.

Oh, dear God!

And the lash marks on his back, the way he had navigated by the stars—she had guessed he had been a seafaring man. Even that he had been a captain.

No wonder he had refused to tell her the truth about his past!

The entire room started spinning, pivoting around her in a blinding whirl of darkness and light until the broken furnishings on the floor seemed to go skidding across the rug. Pieces of Nicholas Brogan's infamous reputation cartwheeled across her dazed mind. It was said that he had been driven by greed. That he would sink any ship without regard for human life.

She had thought of Nick as dangerous—but she had never truly known just how dangerous he was.

And here was young Colton Foster standing in front of her, telling her that Nick—Nicholas—was responsible for his lost arm.

That was the man she had fallen in love with? A man who would heedlessly kill and maim? That was the man she had shared her heart, body, and soul with?

She shook her head in denial. "No! No, it's not true. It *can't* be true. Nicholas Brogan died years ago. He went down with his ship, burned to death in a fire. The authorities held a great celebration when it happened. I-I was in London then. They had a procession, a victory parade—"

"Yes, he fooled everyone. Almost everyone," Foster said angrily. "As for the admiralty, they couldn't exactly *check* that sunken hulk for his charred remains, could they? But they wanted the public to believe that they had done their job, wanted to reassure the citizenry that the last notorious menace had been removed from the high seas." Yanking his knife out of the chair seat, Foster sat down again. "The truth is, he's alive and well. And he's very good at fooling people."

The truth of those words hit her with the impact of an explosion. She fell forward, feeling as if her heart had just been torn from her chest. *She had been such a fool! He had misled her completely. And she had believed him, fallen right into his hands, accepted every lie.*

Loved him.

"He and I are old . . . acquaintances," Foster continued, oblivious to her pain. "And we had an arrangement. A business arrangement. But apparently he decided to change the rules." He reached out and grabbed her chin, tilting her head up. "But if he can change the rules, so can I. I've decided on a new plan, Miss Delafield. There's a certain package I need picked up, and I believe I'm going to send a courier to fetch it for me. Someone expendable."

She gaped at him, then jerked her chin from his grasp. "You don't expect me to—"

"Yes, I do. And I'll accompany you, because frankly, lady, I don't trust you. It seems to me that Brogan worked his charms on you and turned that pretty head of yours completely to fluff. In case you get it into your mind to try and warn him, I'll be right there with this pointed your way." He brandished the pistol. "And even if Brogan has men with him, no one will be able to recognize me. No one knows who I am, not even Brogan himself. It's the person collecting the package who'll be in jeopardy."

"What gives you the idea I'm going to help you?" she spat.

"Three reasons. One, your uncle's dead body is about to be found in your home. The marshalmen were keen on arresting you before—try to imagine how they're going to feel about you now. You'll be facing murder charges by morning. I don't think you want to remain in England any longer than necessary. Two, since I'm not an unreasonable man, as soon as you hand the package over to me, I'll give you back some of this"—he tapped his pocket, where he carried her box of money—"so you can be on your way. And three—" He waved the pistol under her nose. "I'm not giving you any choice."

Sam stared at him, thinking frantically, trying to make sense of what was happening. But her mind was whirling, her heart pounding. She didn't know what to do, where to turn. All of her plans had been smashed to pieces. She was right back where she started the day she fled London: alone, terrified, hunted.

Except that this time, her heart was in pieces as well, shattered like the fragile porcelain vase on the floor, all the love she had felt for Nick spilled, wasted.

She shut her eyes, feeling hollow inside, as if every drop of light, warmth, life had drained out of her.

Nick.

No. No, that wasn't his real name. He had lied to her. Used her and discarded her. No wonder he hadn't wanted her in his life—she had been nothing but a brief amusement to him.

She was shaking, with hurt, with anger. Opening her eyes, she stared at Foster. What could she do? She needed time to think. To plan. The only safe choice was to play along with him for now. Look for an opportunity to get away from him.

All she wanted was to curl into a small ball and sob out all the pain in her shattered heart.

Instead, she lifted her chin and met his gaze evenly. "Very well. I'll do what you ask—"

"How wise of you."

"*If* I have your assurance that you'll give me my money back once you have your blasted package."

He smiled, putting the gun away. "Agreed. You've made the right choice, Miss Delafield." Rising, he helped her to her feet. "You're working for me now."

Chapter 23

❦

This was absolutely without question the most insane thing he had ever done.

Wind and rain whipped at Nicholas's clothes, his hair, his face as he bent over the stallion's neck, urging him to more speed. Hooves pounding, the gray hunter galloped over the fields, his gleaming coat flecked with foam.

It would take another two or three hours to reach Merseyside. If he didn't break his neck first. And he wasn't even sure how he was going to find Samantha's place.

And the entire town would no doubt be swarming with lawmen.

But he did not care. The disturbing thing was how little time he had spent debating with himself. Samantha's life was in danger, and that was enough to make him change his plans.

He had spent all of five minutes explaining the situation to Manu before he left the pub—entrusting his friend with the vital mission that had brought him to England. Ordering Manu to kill whoever came to pick up the package, without questions, without hesitation.

The wind drove raindrops into his face like needles, but he barely noticed. He couldn't live with himself if something happened to Samantha while he had the power to prevent it. He couldn't walk away, spend the rest of his life wondering, never knowing if she had escaped or not.

She mattered to him . . . more than he mattered to himself.

And by hell, if her uncle had laid a hand on her, he would have the bastard's guts for garters.

The hunter sailed over a rail fence and Nicholas spurred the horse onward, faster. When he found Samantha, he intended to escort her to London personally. He didn't give a damn whether she wanted his protection or not. He wouldn't be able to think straight until he knew she was safe.

He would put her on the first ship bound for Venice. Then he would rendezvous with Manu at Clarice's, and once their ship was repaired, they would leave for South Carolina.

Nicholas wasn't sure how he was going to endure that—to see Samantha again, touch her, hold her in his arms, only to send her away a second time.

God, apparently, wasn't through with him yet.

He shot a glare heavenward, beginning to suspect that God had a cruel sense of humor. At least where ex–pirates were concerned.

Only one thought cheered him as the stallion raced across the hills: by nightfall tomorrow, the blackmailer would be dead.

Manu had promised that, this time, he would not disobey orders.

After days of rain and fog and miserable gray weather, Michaelmas dawned bright and clear, the blinding sun and blue skies dazzling by contrast. The change in weather seemed to have drawn every inhabitant of York into the streets, Sam noticed as the hackney coach carrying her and her "employer" jounced over the cobblestones.

Perhaps she could escape, slip away in the throngs, she thought with a feeble glimmer of hope.

The hard metal gun barrel jammed into her ribs ended that thought almost before she finished it.

"We'll be there in a few more minutes," Foster said tightly. "Now remember, Miss Delafield, follow your instructions to the letter, and you'll be on your way as if none of this ever happened. It'll all be over, like a bad dream."

She swallowed hard. A dream? More like a nightmare. She was trapped in a nightmare that seemed to have no end. "I'm not going to cause any trouble."

Not unless she saw an opportunity to get away from him without catching a bullet in her back.

Sitting next to her on the upholstered velvet seat, Foster didn't reply and didn't relax a muscle. He clearly didn't trust her, despite her best efforts to put him at ease. The journey from Merseyside had taken two days. Two of the longest, most trying days she had ever endured. She hadn't slept or eaten, and kept shivering with chills despite the charcoal-colored riding habit she now wore; the snug, woolen layers of the waistcoat, full skirt, and hooded cape were useless against the cold fear inside her.

Foster had allowed her to change clothes before they'd left her room, but he had searched her for weapons before cutting the rope that bound her wrists—and he had found the jewel in the pocket of her green silk skirt and confiscated it.

In the midst of all the violence, she had forgotten about Nick's gift. But when Foster had taken it, she had started thinking. Remembering.

And she felt more certain than ever that Nick James couldn't possibly be Nicholas Brogan.

How could a man supposedly driven by greed have given away that jewel?

And not everything he'd told her had been a lie. What about the awful images of his childhood that had slipped out during his fever—his father's hanging, the horrors of the prison hulk? Those hadn't been concocted to win her sympathy; they had been the truth.

"I still say this could be a case of mistaken identity," she insisted quietly as Foster looked out the coach window. "Nick James is no pirate. Surely there could be any *number* of men in England with that pitchfork brand. They can't all be Nicholas Brogan."

Foster shook his head and muttered something under his breath; she couldn't quite make it out, but the tone sounded insulting and she caught the word *blondes* followed by *witless*. "Miss Delafield, you are grasping at straws."

"And you're blinded by your thirst for vengeance."

He turned to glare at her, eyes blazing. "You live my life for just one day, lady, and then tell me I'm not entitled."

She looked from his youthful face to the empty sleeve that dangled from his shoulder, then dropped her gaze. "I know your life must be difficult," she said quietly, "but you're not the only person in the world who's ever suffered."

"Suffered?" he asked sharply. "What do you know about suffering? Do you have any idea what it's like to live as a *cripple*, Miss Delafield? To have people stare at you everywhere you go? To see nothing in their eyes but pity and revulsion? To be only half a man?" He shot the questions at her, his voice harsh. "Do you know how a man who's only half a man earns a living? He scrapes out an existence, survives on the fringe of society, resorts to begging to survive, spends every day and every night of his life alone—"

He cut himself off abruptly, turned to look out the window again.

Sam pressed herself back into the plush cushions of the coach, stricken by Foster's outburst . . . and by his pain. She felt a wave of sympathy and pity that she knew would enrage him. His life must indeed be terrible, she thought—not because he had lost an arm, but because he had given up on life at such a young age, had allowed anger and bitterness to turn his heart to ice.

"Mr. Foster, you may not believe this," she ventured softly, "but I know what it's like to be alone—"

He spat an oath. "Save your sad tales for someone who cares. Whatever you've suffered is nothing compared to what I've suffered. Especially at the hands of Nicholas Brogan." He said *Brogan* like a curse, as if the very name were responsible for all his pain. "You, he merely seduced and discarded like a cast-off garment, the same way he's always treated his doxies." Foster turned to her again, his eyes cold, his voice casually cruel. "Would you like to know how many mistresses he's had? I could give you a rough estimate—"

"No, thank you," she retorted, her voice brittle. "I can live without that particular piece of information."

"Suit yourself. But believe me, Miss Delafield, this is not a case of mistaken identity. I've spent years tracking Brogan down. I've learned a great deal about him. And it's not vengeance I'm after," he said flatly. "It's justice. That murdering bastard has been living a merry life filled with wealth and women. He can spare a few thousand pounds for one of his nameless, faceless victims. I only want what I'm entitled to."

He glanced out the window again, then rapped on the ceiling of the coach with the butt of his pistol. "This is the place." His voice hardened as he pointed the gun at her. "Cling to your illusions if you like—just remember to do as I've told you."

Her eyes on the gun, Sam could not reply. She was in a great deal of danger no matter what she did.

If she tried to warn Nick, she could be guilty of aiding and abetting one of the most notorious criminals in English history.

But if she did as Foster ordered, she could be signing a death warrant for the man she loved.

The coach rolled to a stop. Foster got to his feet, concealing the gun in the pocket of his frock coat. "Time for you to earn your freedom, Miss Delafield."

He pushed open the door and stepped down from the carriage, glancing left and right along the crowded street before motioning her out. He flipped the hackney driver a coin, but even before the coach rolled away, Sam felt the barrel of the pistol jammed into her ribs again.

"In case you feel the urge to get creative with the instructions I've given you," he said as he pushed her toward a tavern a few yards down the street, "I want you to keep one thing in mind."

"And what is that?" She tried to sound utterly cool and composed.

He nodded to the tavern sign overhead. She gazed up at the scrawl of letters spelling out the pub's name, the Black Angel, and the picture below—a demon with a menacing expression and a pitchfork in one hand.

"He's not worth dying for," Foster finished.

Sam's throat tightened painfully. "A brand and a few lash marks," she insisted, "do not make a man Nicholas Brogan."

Foster chuckled, a low, mocking sound. "We shall see." They were only a few feet from the door. "Now then, I'll go in ahead of you. Count to twenty before following me in. I don't want it to appear that there's any connection between us."

"I understand."

"And remember, I'll be watching. I'll have my eyes and my gun on you . . . and your money in my pocket."

With one last stern look, he went inside, leaving her in the street.

Sam stood in the shadows beside the door while the crowd moved and flowed around her. She began counting. *One . . . two . . .*

She still didn't know if she was doing the right thing. Some of what Foster had told her rang true. She had seen Nick fight, had seen him kill with brutal efficiency.

And why would he refuse to tell her about his past—
unless it was too horrible to reveal?

Three . . . four . . . five . . .

But how could Nick, the man who had made love to
her so tenderly, who had held her so gently, who had
comforted her and saved her life and made her laugh
. . . how could that man possibly be Nicholas Brogan?

Six . . . seven . . . eight . . .

And if Foster was lying, shouldn't she give Nick a
chance to explain himself? Shouldn't she try to warn
him?

Nine . . . ten . . . eleven . . .

Yet if Nick *was* Nicholas Brogan, and she let on that
she knew his real identity, she could be risking her life.

Twelve . . . thirteen . . . fourteen . . .

Oh, hellfire and damnation! If she had any sense at
all, she would run. Run from this blasted place. From
York. From England. Leave right now and forget she
had ever met Nick—or whatever his real name was.

Fifteen . . . sixteen . . . seventeen . . .

But she couldn't. She wouldn't get far without a shilling in her pockets.

Eighteen . . . nineteen . . .

And despite everything, she could not leave Nick to
his fate.

Foster might be lying. He might be wrong. Nick
might not even be here.

Twenty.

Steeling herself for whatever lay ahead, she pushed
open the door and stepped into the pub.

With a single, swift glance, she scanned the room.
Coughing on the thick cigar smoke and the smells of
ale and sweat, she sought that black hair, those green
eyes, the broad shoulders and hard, sun-chiseled face.
The Black Angel was crowded—but she didn't see
Nick.

And he was not the sort of man who blended easily

into a crowd. Even disguised, she would recognize him.

He wasn't here.

Smiling in relief, she shot a look of triumph at the tense-looking young man who sat on the far side of the tavern. He was wrong. Foster had had it all wrong! The man he was after was *not* Nick James!

He merely nodded toward the counter, reminding her of her job.

Awash in relief, she moved to comply. The sooner she fetched his accursed package, the sooner she could be on her way. Eager to get this dreadful business over with, she elbowed her way through the crowd, heading straight for the tavernkeeper.

Manu sat in a dark corner at the rear of the pub, hat pulled low over his eyes, a newspaper concealing his face. He peeked over the top edge now and then, glancing toward the tavernkeeper, awaiting the signal they had agreed upon.

The crowd in the Black Angel was unusually large today—farmers, townspeople, travelers all out enjoying the holiday and the good weather.

So far, there had been no sign of his quarry.

But he was a patient huntsman. Smoking a cheroot, he easily divided his attention between the task at hand, the paper before him, and the disbelief that careened through his head.

He still could not understand what he was doing sitting here alone. Could not believe the way Cap'n Brogan had left so abruptly.

Because of a woman.

He kept shaking his head, still stunned even two days after the Cap'n's mumbled explanation and sudden departure. Manu never would have believed it possible, would have laughed himself stupid if anyone had even suggested it—but it was clear that Nicholas Brogan, scourge of the high seas, terror of every good

English heart, had fallen in love with a woman. And fallen hard.

After a couple of decades spent resisting the wiles of the fairer sex, the captain was completely besotted. Not that he would ever admit it, of course. Couldn't see what was right in front of his face. He had sputtered some bilge about honor among thieves and owing the lady his life and then he had gone to rescue her.

Almost more mystifying was what he had said as he left. Two words Manu had never heard from him before.

Be careful.

An expression of concern. A casual sort of thing one might say to a friend.

From a man who had always sworn that he had no friends.

Glancing over the top of his newspaper again, Manu sat up straight. The tavernkeeper was signaling him, surreptitiously gesturing toward a cloaked figure at the far end of the counter.

Manu nodded, and the tavernkeeper carried the package toward the person who had come to claim it. Tension and ready violence flooded through Manu's veins. So this was the blackmailer, at long last . . .

He froze, staring at the unmistakable curves beneath that woolen cloak. It was a woman!

The momentary surprise faded a second later. Hadn't he warned the Cap'n, time and again? Hell truly had no fury like a woman scorned. He grimaced. The blackmailer's sex didn't change a thing. Not with his captain's life at stake.

She was the one who had chosen to play this dangerous game.

And Hell was exactly where this woman was headed.

The tavernkeeper handed her the package. There was no time to waste.

Say your prayers, you blackmailing wench.

Rising from his seat, Manu slipped his hand into his coat pocket, his fingers closing around a knife that fit perfectly in his palm. The small, lethal blade would do the job quickly, quietly.

He would slit her throat and be out the door before anyone knew what had happened.

Before her body even hit the floor.

Chapter 24

London

Fog descended with the gray light of evening, swathing the streets of Cavendish Square in a damp, misty cloak punctured only by the occasional bright gleam of a streetlamp. Most of the homes lining the elegant avenues already had curtains drawn for the night, as the families inside gathered for supper. Smoke billowed from every chimney, thick tendrils rising to curl greedily around the sun, which hung suspended like a burnished gold pocket watch over the rooftops.

Nicholas rode alone through the empty streets, paying little attention to the wealth displayed all around him, even less to the half-finished cheroot smoldering between his fingertips. His stallion plodded along at a walk. Now and then, a carriage clattered past or a harried servant, arms laden with packages, crossed the street in front of him, but he barely noticed. Though he felt a clammy chill in the air, he did not bother to button his greatcoat.

The cold and darkness closing in around him matched his mood perfectly.

It had been two days since he'd left Merseyside. Alone. Samantha had been long gone by the time he located her room. She hadn't needed his help after all, had apparently taken care of her problem herself. All he had found were a swarm of lawmen and her uncle, dead. Evidently she had killed the lecherous old sot herself and escaped.

His gaze fell to the worn cobbles beneath his horse's hooves. By now, she was no doubt on her way to Venice.

And no matter how many times he'd told himself he should feel happy and relieved, he did not.

Because it meant he would never see her again.

That inescapable fact had ripped a hole through him, deeper than he ever could have imagined. It left him feeling as dark and empty as one of the sooty chimneys that spat smoke into the gathering twilight. He hadn't realized the truth until it slapped him in the face: part of him had been racing to Merseyside to save her . . . but part of him had been racing there, risking everything, just to see her again.

And now she was gone. Out of his life. Forever.

He scowled, hating the pain that idea brought. He lifted his head, watched the red-gold sun melt over a distant church spire. Damn it, he had never *wanted* to feel anything for Samantha Delafield. What was the point? What was the bloody point in learning just how much he could feel for her, now after it was too late?

Except to drive home a lesson he'd already learned decades ago: that God took from him whoever he cared about.

And to exact further payment for the sins he had committed, remind him that he would never be forgiven.

Closing his eyes, he stuck the cheroot between his teeth again, inhaled deeply, exhaled the hot smoke. "I get the point already," he muttered under his breath.

He opened his eyes, watching the sun pierced by the church spire. The hell of it was, he knew he had no one but himself to blame. Knew he did not deserve the gentleness and caring and warmth Samantha had brought to his life. A woman like her had not been made for a man like Captain Nicholas Brogan.

And he never could have revealed his secrets to her, told her the truth about his past, his crimes. Could not have asked her to forgive the unforgivable.

Could not have endured seeing hatred in her beautiful golden eyes.

It was better this way, for them both. A clean break. Clean and final.

He kept telling himself that as he arrived at the town house on Sussex Street, noting with only fleeting interest that Clarice had indeed done well for herself. The place all but reeked of money, from its polished windows and soaring brick facade to the neatly landscaped yard complete with a dozen red rosebushes. He rode around to the back and stabled his horse, then headed for the rear entrance, doffing his hat to rake a weary hand through his matted hair.

It surprised him somewhat that no one was waiting to meet him; he had thought Manu would be keeping watch.

Unless Manu hadn't arrived yet.

He knocked at the back door. No one answered. Leaning against the door jamb, he knocked again, frowning, wondering where the servants were. Clarice was not the sort to endure menial labor, especially not in a place this size.

The cheroot in his hand made a tiny red beacon in the fog and gathering darkness. He had to use the polished brass knocker several times before the door was opened—yanked right out from under his fingers.

"If you expect me to bid you welcome," a familiar feminine voice snapped, "you'll be waiting the rest of your miserable life."

The greeting was almost enough to make him smile despite his bleak mood. Some people never changed. "I can see you'll make a most pleasant hostess, Clarice."

"Well, don't stand there attracting attention." She grabbed him by the arm and pulled him inside, closing the door only after she looked around to make sure nobody had seen them.

"You don't appear pleased to see me."

"Oh, I'm thrilled." She locked the door and rounded on him. "Absolutely thrilled."

The years had been kind to her, he noticed by the light of a crystal chandelier glowing overhead. There wasn't a dark curl out of place in her elaborate coiffure, her figure was still perfect, and whatever lines time might have drawn on her skin had been artfully concealed with cosmetics. Clarice could still outshine half the beauties in London.

What surprised him was that he felt not a single stirring of the old fires that had burned between them, all those years ago. Time, it seemed, had permanently banked those flames.

Time and a golden-eyed lady who had branded him forever.

"Correct me if I'm wrong," Clarice said with exaggerated politeness, folding her arms over her chest, "but I don't *remember* inviting a bunch of stray fugitives to take a holiday under my roof. What makes you and that arrogant friend of yours think you can just stroll in and take over after all these years? I am *not* running a home for wayward ex-pirates here!"

Nicholas removed his tricorne and greatcoat, tossing them over a nearby chair. "Manu and I just need a safe place to hide for a couple of days until our ship can be repaired. Is he—"

"This is *not* a safe place. And give me that foul-smelling thing." She snatched the cheroot from his fingertips just as he was about to take another puff. "I have enough trouble on my hands without having to explain why my house smells like the back room of a Spitalfields tavern. I've got myself an arrangement with a rich widower—"

"A merchant banker, I'm told." He watched with

dismay as she disposed of his last cheroot in a pretty lacquered dustbin. "Congratulations."

She ignored his sarcasm. "He's a very kind, generous *gentleman*." She drew out each word, especially the last one, her hazel eyes boring into him. "Who likes to visit me frequently. Sometimes daily. I've had to go through all sorts of hell—"

"Watch it, Clarice. You've been around me less than five minutes and already your language is slipping."

"—to explain to him why he can't call on me at the moment. He doesn't know anything about my past."

"And I sure as hell am not going to tell him," Nicholas assured her. "I have no intention of interfering with your affairs, Clarice. I'm sorry for the inconvenience, but I thought it wise to get off the streets and out of the public eye before I end up full of bullet holes. I've made the papers, you know."

"It's not the first time." Her voice and demeanor softened—so imperceptibly that someone who didn't know her well wouldn't have noticed. "And that's the whole point. You're not safe anywhere in England. Certainly not in London. Not even here."

He raised an eyebrow. "So you do still care."

She scowled at him. "Blow it out your scuppers, Brogan. All I want is exactly what I wanted six years ago— you out of my life. As quickly as possible."

"We'll be out of your way just as soon as the ship is ready. Now then, can I talk to Manu?" He turned and headed down the corridor. "I assume from your pleasant good humor that he's arrived ahead of me."

"Upstairs." Taking a candelabra from a polished table, she followed him. "He arrived this morning."

"Well, why didn't you say so?"

She pushed past him to lead the way up a curving, gilded staircase. Nicholas couldn't help noticing the richly appointed rooms, the gleaming marble floors. Despite all the verbal daggers he and Clarice always threw at one another, and all the past wounds inflicted, he felt genuinely glad that she had found the happiness she had always sought. "I take it the servants have the night off?"

"Servant. I can only afford one. My housekeeper manages to do the work of ten women. And yes, I sent her on holiday." She cast a glower over her shoulder. "Since my third floor has been converted into an inn for outlaws."

They went past the second floor and up to the third. At the top of the stairs, she turned a corner and stepped aside.

And there sat Manu, in the hallway, asleep in front of a door.

Nicholas looked down at him in bewilderment. Clarice woke him unceremoniously with the toe of her slipper. "Wake up, Manu. The prodigal pirate has returned."

Startled from his sleep, Manu rubbed at his eyes and stood up. "Cap'n. Glad to see you at last." His voice sounded odd, as if he were either exhausted or drunk. "We were getting worried."

"*You* were getting worried," Clarice corrected. She shoved the candelabra into Nicholas's hands. "Now, if you'll excuse me, I've had enough of the good old days for one day. I'll leave you lads to hash this out." Turning, she headed back down the stairs.

"Hash what out?" Nicholas glanced from Clarice's retreating figure to Manu. "What's going on? Are you all right?"

"Fine, fine." Manu rubbed at his temples as if he had a headache.

Nicholas waited a moment. "So?" he prodded impatiently, when his friend didn't say anything more. "What happened? Did you take care of the blackmailer?"

"Aye, Cap'n. That I did. Just follow me." Manu led the way down the corridor to another room.

Inside, he picked up a package from the table beside the door.

Nicholas breathed a long, slow sigh of relief as Manu placed it in his hands. It was the package he had sent from America, addressed in his own hand, with South Carolina tax stamps on it.

And one side was soaked with blood.

He closed his eyes, shook his head in disbelief. It was over. It was finally over. "You killed him, then."

When Manu didn't reply, Nicholas's eyes snapped open.

His friend stood there in silence, his expression uncomfortable.

A sense of foreboding spread through Nicholas. "Don't tell me you disobeyed orders again."

Manu blew out a breath. "Aye," he admitted at last.

"Damn it, Manu. You—"

"Let me explain, Cap'n—"

"Explain what?" Nicholas demanded angrily. "Why the devil didn't you kill him? If he's still alive, where—"

"You'll understand in a moment, Cap'n. I . . . uh, wanted to try and explain first, but . . ." He muttered a curse. "Maybe it's best if you just see for yourself."

"See *what?*"

Manu led him out the door, down the hallway, and back to the room he had been sitting in front of. "Brace yourself, Cap'n. This may come as a shock."

He opened the door.

And Nicholas felt the package slip from his suddenly numb fingers. *Shock* didn't begin to describe the stunning feelings that slammed into him, the deafening roar of his pulse in his ears.

Sitting on the bed on the far side of the room, Samantha glared back at him.

Samantha Delafield.

It took a moment for the room to stop spinning, for the fact that she was here to stop crashing into the fact that she didn't belong here. In this situation. In this house.

Because the fact was, she *was* here, bound and gagged, her golden eyes ablaze with fury.

And in the middle of all the shock and confusion pouring through him was another feeling.

Absolute, undeniable pleasure. Something frighteningly close to joy. His heart was beating so hard, he couldn't catch his breath. He hadn't realized just how deep a gash losing her had torn in him.

But he felt it now. Felt just how wide and empty it was, now that he saw her again. He had to grab hold of the door jamb to steady himself.

When he finally could speak, his voice sounded dry and strained even to his own ears. "What the hell is she doing here?"

"She's the one who picked up the package."

Nicholas looked from his friend to Samantha sitting on the bed and back again, feeling as if he were in a dream, as if Manu had just spoken a foreign language he couldn't understand. *This wasn't real. It couldn't be.* He slowly shook his head, uncomprehending. "That's impossible. It's insane. She was in Merseyside. She couldn't have anything to do with—"

"She was the one, Cap'n. I was about to do what you ordered, but she turned around just as I was coming up from behind her. And when I saw her face . . ." He shrugged helplessly. "She looked exactly like the description of the girl in the papers, the girl you're in . . . uh, that is, the girl you were with."

Dazed, Nicholas could barely make out what his friend was saying, listening with only half his mind, the other half reeling. He felt as if the roof had just come crashing down on his head at the same time the floor disintegrated from beneath his feet. *Was she in league with his enemy? Had she been from the beginning? Had it been no accident that she'd been placed in the cell next to his that dark night in gaol?*

No, he thought furiously, staring into her eyes, hating how the possibilities tore him apart. *By God, no.*

"I asked her name and she refused to tell me," Manu continued, "and then she started making a fuss—and I thought it best to get her out of there. I didn't know whether she was the blackmailer herself or somehow working with the blackmailer, so I figured it was best to just hang onto her. At least until you got here and could decide what to do with her."

What to do with her? That was one of a dozen questions Nicholas couldn't begin to answer.

"She fought like a hellion," Manu noted ruefully, pulling up his sleeve to reveal a bandage around his arm. "Afraid the blood on the package is mine. I ended up getting cut with my own knife, so I finally knocked her out, loaded her into a hackney coach . . . and brought her here."

"And what was her explanation for all this?" Nicholas asked sharply.

"She wasn't very forthcoming with any information, Cap'n. But I think she knows more than she's let on."

Nicholas could barely see her anymore, his vision blurred by a haze of confusion and hurt and betrayal.

Manu was silent a moment, shifting uncomfortably. "So what are your orders?"

Clenching his jaw, Nicholas held out his hand. "Give me your knife." As soon as Manu slapped it into his palm, he headed for the bed, gripping the hilt in his fingertips. "And leave us alone."

Chapter 25

~~⌒◯◯⌒~~

Sam stared at him with her heart in her throat as he stalked toward her. Her entire body had gone cold, as if she had been drenched with shards of ice.

Captain, the African had called him.

She's the one who picked up the package.

The pain and horror slashing through her were unbearable. Until the moment he stepped into this room, she had been able to deny, to doubt, to hope. Until she heard those words, she had stubbornly refused to believe that Nick James had any connection to that tavern in York, to Colton Foster and his package and all the bitter, angry claims he had made.

But everything Foster had told her was true.

The man she had fallen in love with wasn't a navy captain or a merchant captain. And he wasn't a peaceful planter from the Colonies.

He was Captain Nicholas Brogan.

No. God, no, please. She shut her eyes as he came to stand beside the bed. Feeling the cold touch of the blade against her cheek, she thought it would almost be less agonizing if he would simply slit her throat.

Instead, he cut off the gag.

She coughed, gasping for breath, straining against the cold misery that squeezed her chest like an iron band. When she was finally able to force herself to open her eyes and look up at him, all the pieces snapped into place. The last of her confusion vanished. Everything became perfectly, horribly clear. In the tavern, when the African had accosted her, she hadn't had the most distant idea who he might be or what was going on.

But he was a member of Captain Brogan's crew.

A fellow pirate.

She flinched away when Nick reached for her hands, and he hesitated . . . then apparently changed his mind. He did not cut her free.

Instead, he turned on his heel and moved away from her, raking a hand through his hair.

"Nick," she whispered on a painfully tight throat. "Tell me it's not true! Nicholas Brogan died years ago. You can't be—"

"Stop it," he choked out, his voice hoarse. "Stop denying the truth that's right in front of your face. Damn it, there's no use pretending anymore."

His admission was like a sword slicing through her. Hot tears welled up in her eyes. "No," she whispered. "No, it can't be."

God help her, she *wanted* him to lie to her. She would believe him. She would believe anything. Anything but *this*.

He turned to face her, his face an unreadable mask as their eyes met and held.

She was shaking, opened her mouth, could not speak, could find no words, no breath, nothing inside her but a cold, vast emptiness deeper than any physical wound. "I . . . I thought you were a . . . a planter. Or—"

"Some kind of naval hero?" he asked bitterly. "Sorry to disappoint you, angel." He tore his gaze from hers, paced to the window.

"But Nicholas Brogan was a vicious murderer! They said he killed heedlessly, wantonly. That he would sink any ship in his lust for riches."

He stared out into the last light of sunset, his back stiff. "I don't suppose it would help to point out that 'they' are not always accurate. Or that the navy spread a great many lurid, exaggerated tales about my exploits," he said in a taut, strained voice. "The admiralty wasn't overly fond of me—"

"Are you saying it was all lies?"

There was a long pause.

"No."

A chill rippled through her. Followed by a shock of hurt, betrayal, fury. "How many people have you killed, *Captain*?"

"Do you think I kept count?"

"An estimate will do. A hundred? Two hundred?"

His hand came up to savagely grip the velvet curtain that hung beside him. Even from where she sat, she could see that he was shaking. Yet his voice held no anger when he finally answered; he spoke so softly she could barely hear him.

"It doesn't matter now, does it?"

"It does matter! How could you . . . how could I . . ." She shook her head, unable to continue, wanting only to bury her face in a pillow and sob out all the pain that was tearing at her heart.

She had believed in him. Trusted him. She had revealed everything to him—all her secrets, all the agony of her past, sharing with him her heart, her body, her soul. She had loved him.

Loved a man who had killed and maimed without conscience.

"I hate you," she blurted, unable to hold back the anger and hurt. "I hate you for what you've done!"

His whole body jerked as if she'd struck him with bullets instead of words. His fingers dug into the curtain like talons.

Then he stopped shaking. Slowly, he turned to face her.

And there was no fire in his eyes when he looked at

her. No warmth at all. No light, no life. His gaze was cold, distant. Heartless.

He looked at her the same way he had when she first met him.

It was as if Nick James, the good, decent man she had known, the tender lover who had won her heart, had vanished. As if he'd never existed, been nothing but a dream. A romantic fantasy who had come to life only briefly, in the imagination of a foolish, naive, innocent girl.

No. No, she wouldn't believe that. She lifted her chin, refusing to flinch from his icy glare. "Your friend Manu told me you were in Merseyside. That's why you weren't in that pub in York." She swallowed hard. "You were trying to save me, weren't you?"

He wouldn't reply.

"You risked yourself to save me."

"I told you once before, I'm not in the business of rescuing damsels in distress."

"Then what were you doing in Merseyside?"

"Honor among thieves," he retorted. "I thought I owed you at least a warning. And it was a mistake. Look where it's gotten me. If I had been in that blasted pub, this business would be ended. But no, like a fool, I trusted someone else to take care of it for me." Jaw clenched, he strode toward her. "You, Miss Delafield, have caused me nothing but trouble and pain from the moment we met."

"Our acquaintance hasn't been particularly enjoyable for me, either," she replied, concealing her hurt beneath glacial formality. "And why—"

"I'm the one who's supposed to be asking questions here. Starting with where *you* were. You were supposed to be in Merseyside. What the hell were you doing in that pub in York? How are you involved in this blackmail scheme?"

"I'm not involved. I don't know anything about a blackmail scheme."

"Then what were you doing collecting that package?"

"It's a very long story, Captain Brogan."

"I appear to have time, Miss Delafield." He sat on the edge of the bed. And still made no move to untie her.

He didn't trust her at all. He never had.

She glared at him, her words as sharp as the pain inside her. "When I got to my flat in Merseyside, I found it had been ransacked. My uncle was there. He . . . he said he was going to take me with him to London. Lock me up in some place where he would . . ." She couldn't continue.

A muscle twitched in his cheek, but other than that he didn't react. His voice remained cold, steely. "Get to the part about the blackmailer."

His callous attitude tore the wound inside her even deeper. She had to fight just to draw a breath, feeling as if all the air had been knocked from her. "I'm getting to that. The blackmailer said he had followed my uncle. He said he had seen the stories in the papers—"

"What's his name?"

"Foster. Colton Foster. He blames you for making him a 'cripple,' as he calls it. His right arm was missing. He said you and he were old acquaintances."

Nicholas was silent a moment, his brow furrowed in thought. "I don't remember anyone like that. And I don't know anyone by that name." His mouth curved downward.

She could tell that he doubted her story. "Damn you, I'm telling you the truth! He said he had followed my uncle to Merseyside because he wanted to question me. He was suspicious that you were trying to change some business arrangement you had made with him. He ended up fighting with my uncle, and he killed him, and then he . . . he told me who you really are."

Nicholas gazed at her stoically.

Sam felt her throat tighten, her mouth turn dry and hot. "And I didn't believe him," she choked out, unable to bear her own foolishness. "I tried to convince him that it must be a case of mistaken identity."

His face remained expressionless. "You still haven't explained—"

"Let me finish," she snapped. "He took all my money, and he took . . ." Her eyes suddenly swam with tears. "He took the ruby you gave me." She blinked quickly, desperate to keep her tears from falling, refusing to raise her bound hands to wipe at her eyes.

Nicholas whispered a curse and suddenly rose from the bed, pacing to the window.

She felt even colder and more alone when he withdrew from her, almost wished they were shackled together again. Wished it wasn't so easy for him to walk away from her.

"Why?" she asked, struggling to keep her voice calm. "Why did you give that jewel to me?"

One of his broad shoulders rose in a casual shrug. "Payment for services rendered. I always leave a woman with some token after she's shared my bed."

The pain that lanced through her was white-hot. She clenched her fists until her nails dug into her palm, willing it away.

He did not care for her. She meant nothing to him.

She never had.

"So he robbed me blind," she continued quickly, desperate to finish her story, to tell him what he wanted to know so she could get out of here. "And he ordered me to pick up the package for him. He suspected he was walking into a trap."

"So you were simply to act as his courier? He was just going to trust you?"

"No. Of course not. He was there, in the pub. He was right there with a gun pointed at me."

Nicholas jerked around to face her. "He was there and you didn't tell Manu?"

"I didn't know the African had anything to do with you—he was just some stranger accosting me. I certainly wasn't going to tell him who I was. As soon as he grabbed me, I could see Foster coming across the pub toward us, but then Manu was dragging me outside, and then he knocked me out . . . and I woke up in a coach on the way to London."

Nicholas's voice dissolved in a string of particularly vivid, heated oaths. "And what did this Foster look like? Besides the missing arm?"

"He was about my age, maybe a little younger. With brown hair and blue eyes. Rather ordinary, really."

"In other words, he could be anyone."

"Any one of dozens of people who want revenge against you? One of the nameless, faceless many you hurt during your career as a pirate?"

He glowered at her. "Did he say anything else that might prove helpful?"

She paused, remembering. "He did mention something about . . . about you robbing him of what should have been a brilliant naval career."

"Which still doesn't narrow it down." Throwing himself into a nearby wing chair, Nicholas covered his face with his hands. "Damn it, I thought this blasted mess was finished. I should have known better. What the hell made me think I could sail out of London and leave it all behind?" He propped one elbow on his knee, resting his forehead on his palm. "I should have known better."

He looked and sounded so weary, so tired, Sam felt a sudden longing to reach out to him, to smooth the hair back from his forehead, to ease the lines of tension around his eyes, his mouth.

But of course, she couldn't move a muscle with her hands tied.

It destroyed her to realize that she felt something for

him. That she still cared for him, even knowing who he was and what he had done.

Even knowing that he felt nothing for her in return.

"Are you going to untie me?" she demanded, fighting the tender feelings that had her heart pounding. "I've told you all I know. I'm of no further use to you. Let me go."

He raised his head, looked at her. "Tell me one thing," he asked wearily. "Since you suspected my real identity, why did you walk into that pub at all? Why didn't you just go to the local authorities, try to claim the ten thousand pound bounty on my head for yourself?"

Because, you idiot, I'm in love with you. She had to bite her tongue to hold it back. "Honor among thieves," she retorted.

His eyes turned cold again. "I see."

"Are you going to untie me?"

"No, your ladyship," he said slowly, leaning back in the chair, "I'm not."

She went very still, blinked at him, confused. "You can't keep me here."

"I can't let you go. There's no telling how long honor among thieves will hold out against the temptation of ten thousand pounds."

"Do you seriously think I'm foolish enough to go within a hundred miles of the authorities? *My* face is the one that's been in all the papers."

"No, I don't think you're that foolish. But I don't trust honor among thieves. Never have."

"And you don't trust *me*. You don't . . ."

Care about me. She couldn't finish the sentence.

"No, I don't trust you," he said bluntly, rising from the chair. "Every single time I've trusted anyone in the past, it's proven to be a costly mistake. And one thing about getting older—you learn from your mistakes."

"I don't think you've learned anything in your whole accursed life, you blackguard!"

Ignoring that cold appraisal, he walked past her, toward the door, leaving her there with her hands bound.

And her heart broken.

"I wish I'd never met you, Captain Brogan," she called after him.

He paused at the door, glancing back over his shoulder, his expression one that she hadn't seen before. She couldn't, wouldn't believe that it was hurt she saw in his eyes.

"The feeling, Miss Delafield, is entirely mutual."

He slammed the door behind him.

Sam awoke to find the room doused in shadows of dark navy and midnight black; moonlight spilled in through the windows. She wasn't sure how long she'd been asleep, or what had jarred her awake. Sitting up, she winced at the kink in her neck, blinking in the darkness.

A sound came from outside the door, a soft knock.

"Come in," she said hesitantly, hoping whoever it was wouldn't notice the hoarseness of her voice.

Her throat was parched, raspy from crying.

Instead of Manu or his captain, it was the woman who entered. "Miss Delafield?" She peeked around the edge of the door, whispering. "Are you awake?"

"Yes. Please, come in."

"I brought you something to eat." Wearing an elegant purple dressing gown, the woman crossed the room carrying a silver tray in one hand, an oil lamp in the other. "That pair of pirates wouldn't think of it, but I guessed you'd be hungry after so long."

"Thank you, madame," Sam said politely, though she had no appetite.

"Clarice. And I don't think this is necessary, either." Setting the lamp and the tray on the bedside table, she untied Samantha's hands. "You're not going anywhere, not with Manu parked outside your door. And the drop out these windows is about thirty feet, straight down."

Sam flexed her fingers and rubbed her wrists, giving her hostess a grateful smile. "He'll be angry with you."

"Hell, it won't be the first time." Clarice picked up a china cup filled with steaming, spice-scented tea and thrust it into Samantha's hands. "Besides, no matter how much he blusters, no woman really has anything to fear from Sir Nicholas." She handed over a piece of roast chicken.

Sam accepted both the food and drink, deciding it was best not to argue. She had had enough arguing for one day. "*Sir* Nicholas?"

"That's what they called him, in the old days. For his chivalrous treatment of captives . . . especially the ladies. Despite all the stories spread about him, he never abused prisoners taken in raids. He never let his crew touch them, either."

Sam blinked in surprise. "But I thought . . . I mean, according to his reputation, Nicholas Brogan killed without conscience, and all he cared about was money."

Clarice laughed. "Tall tales invented by people who didn't know him at all. I never met a man in my life who cared *less* about money. When I knew him, Brogan's one and only goal was vengeance."

Sam dropped her gaze, staring down at her own reflection in the dark surface of her tea, remembering what Nick—Nicholas—had said earlier.

"They" are not always accurate.

"Vengeance against whom, Clarice?" she asked softly. "And why?"

"It was mostly the navy he was after. I don't know why. He never talked about his past. Not to me, not to anyone. All I know is . . ." She paused, sighing. "He got the vengeance he wanted. It almost killed him, but he got it. And as soon as he did, he quit. Left England, gave up piracy. He was never the greedy murderer the admiralty made him out to be."

Sam took a sip from her cup, her hand trembling, the hot liquid burning its way down her throat. What Clarice said contradicted everything she had heard about the infamous Captain Brogan. Had she judged him too quickly?

She wasn't sure *what* to believe anymore, couldn't make sense of all the conflicting stories. But bits and pieces of what she knew about Nick—Nicholas—were starting to fit together in her mind.

Like the brand, the lash marks, his horrific childhood aboard a prison hulk . . . a ship run by navy overseers.

And the image that had wrenched at her heart once before: that of a small boy with bright green eyes, alone, terrified, subjected to torture. Orphaned, as she had been orphaned.

There was so much she didn't know about Nicholas. So much that, perhaps, *no one* knew about him. For him, keeping his secrets had meant staying alive; it couldn't be easy to let down his guard.

And earlier tonight, when he had finally begun to share his past in even a small way, how had she reacted? Instead of listening, instead of offering the sort of understanding and comfort he had once offered her, she had cut him off with angry, hateful words, so wrapped up in her own hurt and betrayal that she hadn't given him a chance to explain.

"Miss Delafield?"

Startled from her thoughts, Sam lifted her head, realizing that she'd been staring down at her reflection again, oblivious to everything but memories of Nick. "I'm sorry." Glancing down at the chicken leg she still held in her hand, she set it aside on the tray. "And it's Samantha. Or Sam."

"Samantha . . ." Clarice began, studying her with a pensive expression. "I really didn't come here to talk about Brogan's sordid past. I wanted to . . ." She glanced at the abandoned chicken leg, frowning. "No appetite," she said under her breath. "Staring off into nothing in the middle of a conversation." She began counting on her fingers, as if ticking off a checklist. "Definite moony look in the eyes. Oh, hell, I think I'm already too late."

"Too late?" Sam echoed, watching her in puzzlement.

With a rueful curve to her lips, Clarice pointed a lacquered fingernail at the rope she had tossed on the bedside table. "I don't think you need that or a guard on your door to keep you here. I don't think you want to leave him."

Sam clutched at the fragile teacup in her hands. "That's . . ." She swallowed a quick gulp of the hot liquid. "That's—"

"The truth. Don't bother denying it, sweetie." Clarice sighed. "You're not the first pretty young thing to fall victim to the charms of Sir Nicholas. I came here to warn you about that." She shook her head mournfully. "Samantha, that man can't even say the words 'I trust you,' never mind 'I love you.' If that's what you're hoping for . . . you could spend the rest of your life hoping."

Sam's cheeks burned. How could her feelings be so transparently clear when she barely understood them herself?

She also realized suddenly that Clarice spoke as if from experience. She felt foolish for not seeing it earlier. "You and he . . ."

"Let's just say, a very long time ago, I was one of those pretty young things who fell victim to the charms of Sir Nicholas." Clarice grimaced. "One of many."

"Many," Sam repeated in a whisper, remembering what Foster had told her about Nicholas Brogan having numerous mistresses.

"I have no regrets," Clarice continued with a shrug.

"I've learned my lesson. That's what I wanted to tell you, Samantha. Love is a wonderful fantasy. It makes for pretty fairytales to amuse children. But it's not something that we adults find very often in the real world. Learning that lesson is part of growing up."

"I see," Sam said, not seeing at all.

"It's better to be realistic." Clarice rose, carrying the lamp to the mantel opposite the bed, using it to light another lamp there. "Take me, for example. I've got myself a lovely house, lots of rich friends, a man who takes care of me."

"A very nice life," Sam said hollowly.

"Very nice," Clarice agreed. "And my gentleman friend is quite kind. He's sweet and thoughtful. He pays for my home, gives me gifts—"

"But he says nothing about caring or love? This benefactor of yours doesn't love you?"

Clarice laughed, a sophisticated, sparkling sound. "I've never asked. I'm too old for that sort of thing, sweetie. And too smart."

But something in Clarice's voice and her laughter sounded forced. It made Samantha wonder whether any woman could ever truly give up on love.

And made her suspect that Clarice wasn't following the very advice she was trying to give. "And do you love him?" she asked softly.

Clarice didn't answer at first. She ran one finger over a porcelain figurine of a dancing lady on the mantel. "He's . . . he's a member of the peerage, Samantha. I was born gutter trash in a hovel in the East End the likes of which is beyond your imagination."

"But that shouldn't matter if—"

"We're from two separate worlds," Clarice said more forcefully. "And even though I can play at being part of his world, I'll never truly belong in it. It's impossible." She walked back toward the bed, her smile a bit too bright. "I've accepted that."

Sam felt a surge of empathy for this woman she

barely knew. She knew exactly how it felt, to love the wrong man.

And to know that he did not return that love.

"I'm happy with what I've got." Clarice indicated the lavishly decorated room with a sweep of her hand. "This is the best I could hope for. I've not done too badly for myself."

"No," Samantha agreed, not feeling it. "You haven't."

In a purely financial sense, it was true. But without love, she felt, all the riches in the world would be worthless.

"But I didn't come here to talk about me," Clarice chided gently. "I came here to help you." She sat on the bed and placed a hand on Samantha's arm, the gesture almost sisterly. "Take some advice from someone older and wiser, sweetie. Put this behind you as soon as you can. Learn from it. Find yourself a man who will treat you *right*. Someone stable and reliable."

Sam sipped at her tea, not tasting it.

"A nice merchant or a barrister or an apothecary," Clarice advised. "He won't set you on fire, but so what? A rogue will set you on fire, all right—and burn you to a cinder and be gone before your ashes cool. Without so much as a by your leave." She gave Sam's arm a gentle squeeze. "Do yourself a favor, sweetie. Take it from me. Stay away from sailors, soldiers, actors, musicians, and outlaws of all sorts. It's a rule of thumb to live by: Never love a rogue."

"I'll try to remember that."

"Good." Standing, Clarice set the dishes of food on the bedside table, picking up the tray. "Now try to eat something, Samantha. He's not worth losing your appetite over." Taking her lamp, she headed for the door, but paused with her hand on the latch. "And Samantha?"

"Yes?"

"Even when you find yourself a nice barrister, guard your heart," she whispered, opening the door. "Lock it up tight, like a safe. And never give any man the key."

Chapter 26

Nicholas had already drawn the curtains and turned the lamps down low. Now he prowled the room, looking at the gilt-framed pictures on the walls, the vase of flowers on the dressing table in one corner. He rearranged the collection of glass bottles on another table. Wasn't sure why, except that it gave him something to do.

Something other than stare in bleak pain at the woman who lay sleeping on the bed.

Stopping before the hearth, he braced one arm against the mantel and hung his head, gazing down at the hot coals in the grate, unable to feel their warmth. For hours now, he hadn't been able to feel or think or even see. He could only hear—a single voice that ripped through his memory, his mind, his heart.

The sound of Samantha declaring her hatred for him.

He shut his eyes, his fingers closing tightly around the edge of the mantel, gripping the cold, polished marble. He had always known she would hate him if she ever learned his true identity. But the fact that he had anticipated her reaction so accurately hadn't cushioned the blow in the least.

Unable to sleep, he had found himself drawn here, to her, to the source of his pain. It made no sense, this power she had over him, this connection between them. Nothing seemed able to break it. The force was almost magnetic. As if he were a compass needle and she were true north.

Straightening, he turned to look at her. It was strange to discover that, without the shackles, he felt more bound to her than ever.

He noticed that someone had untied her. Clarice, no doubt; a plate of food sat on the night table. Untouched. Samantha had fallen asleep fully clothed, still wearing the blouse and woolen waistcoat and skirt of her riding habit. But she had taken off her shoes . . . and he noticed the mark around her ankle. The shackles had left what might be a permanent scar.

The same mark they had left on him.

His heart thudding in his chest, he walked back to the wing chair he had placed beside the bed. The huge, velvet-draped four-poster made her slender form seem so small, so . . . alone.

He sat down, listening to her soft breathing, watching her while she slept. The way he had watched over her during so many long nights in Cannock Chase. And the ache inside him widened and deepened.

He reached out and let his hand rest on the blankets, near hers, but he did not allow himself to touch her. He hadn't intended to come here until morning, to tell her the decision he had made. A decision that would make her furious—if it were possible for her to be any more furious with him than she already was.

He didn't look forward to fighting with her again. He was so bloody tired of fighting.

And so he did not wake her, wanting simply to look at her, to hold onto one last, peaceful moment.

His gaze traced over her, memorizing her in the gentle glow of the lamplight—from every flawless curve of her face to the way one of her hands clutched a corner of the pillow, while the other lay upturned on the rumpled covers. Her fingers looked so delicate, so pale next to his.

Breaking the chain hadn't changed anything, he

thought, his throat constricting. Time and distance had only made him more aware of how important she was to him, had only made his feelings for her more powerful. Conflicting needs to possess and protect, to ravish and cherish. Samantha Delafield was the most precious treasure he had ever held in his hands. The only one that had ever really mattered to him.

The only one that was utterly beyond his reach.

She stirred, making a small sound—and opened her eyes. Their gazes met and held.

Both of them went still. Neither of them spoke or even breathed.

She glanced at his hand, so close to hers, and then she sat up, withdrawing as if afraid he might burn her. "W-what are you doing here?"

It took him a moment to summon an answer—at least, one that he was willing to speak aloud. "Couldn't sleep."

She drew her legs under her, perching in the middle of the bed as if she might make a dash for the door.

But she didn't. In fact, a moment later, strangely enough, she relaxed a bit. And though her gaze remained wary, he didn't detect any of the blazing fury he had seen earlier. Perhaps because she was tired.

He looked down at his hand still resting on the covers. And decided with bleak resignation that there was no sense in delaying the inevitable. "I've made a decision."

"Oh?" she asked cautiously. "About what?"

"You."

She didn't say anything for a moment. "I wasn't aware that there was a need to make a decision about me," she said mildly. "I'm not a threat to you, I promise."

"But if I let you go," he replied quietly, bracing himself for the inevitable explosion, "you might change your mind about that someday. A year from now. Two years. You might leak my name to the authorities."

When she didn't respond, he glanced up—to find her eyes sparkling with some emotion he could not name.

Still, she remained calm, quietly waiting for him to continue his explanation. Which knocked him off balance; he had come prepared for another heated argument, not for this . . . this . . . he wasn't even sure what to call it.

"The way I see it," he said, regarding her uneasily, "I have two choices. I can either kill you—"

"Not my favorite choice."

"Or keep you."

She blinked at him. Once. Twice. "Keep me?" she echoed as if he had spoken a foreign language. "What do you mean by that?"

Her cool question stretched his nerves even tighter. Rising from the wing chair, he walked to the end of the bed, waiting for her to erupt in outrage and hatred. "I don't like the idea, but I don't seem to have any other satisfactory option." He toyed with the velvet drapes that hung from the canopy, his fingers destroying a delicate golden tassel that held them in place. "If you're with me, I'll know you're not blathering to the authorities."

"I see."

"It's the only solution."

"It's kidnapping."

The way she calmly pointed that out made him laugh, a dry, choked rasp that hurt his throat. "Not the worst crime I've ever been accused of."

"All right. I'll go."

"Besides, you have no choice. It's not safe for you to stay in England, not with your face in every newspaper and a murder charge hanging over your head and . . ." He stopped, his gaze on the tassel in his fingertips, as her words finally made their way to his brain. He slanted a glance toward her. "What did you just say?"

"I said all right. I agree to your 'satisfactory option.' I'll go with you."

He stared at her, stunned silent by her quick acquiescence. He could detect no sarcasm in her voice, no anger in her expression.

No hatred in her golden gaze.

Suspicion instantly replaced his surprise. "Don't think I'm handing you a chance to escape," he said harshly. "You'll be leaving with Manu in the morning. He'll see you aboard our ship and take you to South Carolina." He paced away from her before he could wreck any more of the bed curtains.

"Wait a moment, what do you mean *I'll* be leaving?" she protested, her voice taking on a sharp edge for the first time. "What about you?"

"I'm staying in London."

"You can't stay here." Her air of calm vanished, suddenly and completely. "If you haven't noticed, there are a large number of people here who want to kill you."

He stopped in front of the hearth, keeping his back to her. "That's exactly why I'm staying. I'm not leaving until I've taken care of the blackmailer once and for all. I'm not going to trust it to anyone else this time."

"But he might already be telling the authorities about you. He wants the bounty on your head. He'll do anything to get it."

"Exactly. Which is why I intend to go out in the open and make it a little easier for him to find me."

"You're going to get yourself killed."

It almost sounded as if that mattered to her. He turned to look at her, but she glanced away before he could read the emotion in her eyes.

And he abruptly realized what—or rather, who— might have changed Samantha's attitude toward him; the dishes on the nightstand offered a clue.

He frowned, renewed suspicion glittering through him. The last thing he needed was a pair of scheming females allied against him. "Why do I get the feeling there's something going on here that I don't know about? Did Clarice say something to you?"

"Yes." Samantha kept her gaze fastened on the covers beneath her. "She told me all about rogues and locks and safes and fairytales."

"What?"

"And she said that you're not worth losing my appetite over."

This wasn't making the least bit of sense.

"And I don't care." Her head came up, her eyes blazing now. "Why can't you just leave with me and Manu?"

He folded his arms across his chest, realizing he was about to get the argument he hadn't wanted. "Because I am not going to spend the rest of my life on the run."

"You're not going to *have* a life to spend if you insist on this insane plan!"

"I'm not asking for your opinion. I'm telling you where you're going to go."

Her anger finally ignited. "Well, let me tell you where *you* can go, Captain." She grabbed a pillow and threw it at him with a frustrated oath, aiming for his head.

He sidestepped neatly and it landed on the hearth. "No sense condemning me to Hades, angel. I'm already halfway there."

"Damn it." She added a few more curses as she looked around for something else to throw at him. "I wish I'd never fallen in love with you."

"Before you damage any more of Clarice's—what?" he sputtered in shock. "What did you say?"

She went still, bent over the side of the bed, one hand reaching for her shoe.

Frozen in that position, she turned her head to gaze at him, hanging there half upside-down. "Uh . . . I said . . . that is . . . I meant . . ." Closing her eyes, she gave up and let herself go limp, her hair falling in a cascade around her and trailing on the floor. "I said I wish I'd never fallen in love with you."

He remained rooted in place, not allowing himself to take one step toward her. Not one step. "You can't love me."

"Well, I do," she said from beneath that tangle of golden curls.

"You shouldn't."

She finally righted herself, sitting up with a sharp toss of her head, her golden mane gleaming in the lamplight. "I don't care." She lifted her chin in that mutinous little gesture he'd come to know so well. "I love you."

He remained silent, struck dumb, unable to bear the joy pouring through him. Hatred, he could endure. Pain, he could endure. But not this.

Every fiber of his being urged him to cross the distance between them, to sweep her into his arms and kiss her breathless. But he didn't. Couldn't.

He knew he could only bring her misery. Knew her love for him wouldn't last.

Because God had not made a woman like her for a man like Nicholas Brogan.

"Nicholas?" she murmured, a smile tugging at her lips. "I think the pillow is on fire."

"Blast the pillow," he choked out. "Let it burn."

He couldn't move toward her, couldn't make himself turn away, couldn't tear his gaze from her. For one long, glorious moment, he drank in her smile, the look in her eyes, the love—feasted on it like a condemned man devouring his last meal.

Then, in agony, he closed his eyes, committed that look to his memory.

And turned his back on her. "We all make mistakes in life, angel." He tried to sound careless, cool, but instead his voice sounded hoarse. "You'll get over the mistake of falling in love."

With a frustrated oath, she launched herself from the bed. "Listen, you stubborn . . . impossible . . ." She seemed to run out of words to describe him—and fell back on an old one. "*Rogue*. Clarice told me you're not worth losing my appetite over. Foster told me you're not worth dying for. Everyone you've ever *met* seems to have a low opinion of you—"

"Which should make you think twice about what you just said," he retorted.

"It doesn't. Because I've been thinking twice about what *you* said earlier—that 'they' are not always accurate." She stopped a few paces behind him.

He could hear her breathing, rapid and shallow, swore he could hear her heartbeat, pounding wildly. Or was that his own?

"Nicholas," she said more softly. "I don't think they really know you at all. I don't think you've ever allowed *anyone* to know you. Not the way I do."

Her words, so gentle, so caring, lashed him more painfully than any whip that had ever scarred him. And the sound of his name on her lips—his real name, spoken so tenderly—cut deeper than the hot iron that had branded him. "You don't know me as well as you think you do, Samantha," he said roughly. "You don't know the truth."

"I know that Clarice said you gave up piracy. That you quit. That's when you went to the Colonies, isn't it? You weren't lying to me about that, were you?"

"No." He tipped his head back, glared up at the ceiling. "I wasn't lying." Hellfire and damnation, he *wanted* to lie. Wanted to deny, conceal, walk away. Wanted to do anything but tell her what she was forcing him to tell her.

He had never admitted the truth. To anyone. Had never spoken the words aloud.

But he couldn't lie anymore. Not to her. And there was no point. No point in trying to save himself. No point in a futile effort to postpone the inevitable.

"Then I don't understand," she said in that same quiet, gentle, compassionate tone that tore at him. "How can you say—"

"She didn't tell you *why* I quit, did she?" he snapped. It was best to get this over with quickly. Once and for all. Admit what he was. Make her see why she couldn't love him.

"No, she—"

"Of course not. Because Clarice doesn't know. No one knows." He turned on his heel so suddenly that he startled her. "You want the truth? All right. I'll tell you the truth."

He made it swift, sudden, final, like a single thrust of a cutlass, severing everything between them.

"I killed a child, Samantha. That's why I quit and walked away. I killed a child!"

Sam stared at him, her mind reeling, her heart in her throat. She was so shocked at both what he said and the brutal, blunt way he said it that she couldn't speak.

"A young boy," he continued harshly, "only ten or twelve years old. I took his life without even thinking." He took a step toward her, as if inviting her to either strike him in outrage or back away in horror.

She did neither, unable to move or breathe or even lift her hand and reach out to him as she wanted to. Her entire body seemed suddenly made of stone.

"I shot him," Nicholas went on when she remained still, his voice savage and stark, his gaze stabbing into hers. "I killed him because he stood between me and vengeance. That was all I wanted. All I cared about. I spent so many years seeking vengeance that I wasn't even *human* anymore. I was exactly what they'd made me. An animal. So blind to anything but blood and violence that I didn't even realize it until I—" His voice suddenly choked out. "Until I watched that boy falling to the deck and I could . . ." He shut his eyes, as if saying the words aloud brought it back too clearly. "I could see myself in his eyes. I could see what I'd become."

"Oh, Nicholas," she whispered, wanting to touch

him and not daring, hurting inside for what he had done, and for what had been done to him.

"So *that's* the truth about me," he snarled, his eyes piercing her once more. "That's who you *think* you're in love with."

"But, Nicholas, h-how," she whispered tentatively, "why were you seeking vengeance?"

"I was after the men who killed my father," he said curtly.

"But I thought your father was executed for some terrible crime. I thought—"

"That he was a criminal and I was innocent?" he scoffed. "Wrong again. My father was an innocent man, a good man." His voice faltered, then picked up again, angrily. "He was betrayed by his friends. By people he trusted."

Sam kept silent, letting him spill out the words and the pain, knowing they'd been bottled up inside him for years.

"My father was a privateer during the war with Spain," he explained tightly. "His job was to harass and plunder Spanish ships. He *worked* for the bloody navy, called the officers his friends. He took all the risks while his raids helped fatten the crown purse and build the Royal Navy fleet. But after the war was over, the crown decided that the privateers had outlived their usefulness. Some of them had crossed the line and turned pirate—so the navy rounded them *all* up. Decided they were too dangerous to be left roaming the seas. My father was arrested on a trumped-up charge of piracy and . . ."

"Executed," she whispered, shutting her own eyes, remembering how Nicholas had called out during his fever, the horrifying images of his father's hanging.

"Executed," he confirmed, turning away from her. "The rest of us on the ship were spared—"

"But what were you doing on his ship?" she asked

in confusion. "You couldn't have been much older than—"

"Ten." He stopped before the hearth, picked up the figurine of the dancing lady from the mantel. "I was ten." He paused, turning the delicate white porcelain in his dark, calloused hand. In his present mood, Sam half-expected him to break it, or throw it.

Instead, he set the figurine carefully back in place. And when he spoke again, some of the fury had left his voice, replaced by wistfulness. "My mother died when I was eight. My father took me to live with relatives, but I would have none of it. So I slipped away the very next morning and snuck aboard his ship." He dropped his head, staring down at the coals in the grate. "By the time Father discovered me, we were well out to sea. He was furious." The soft sound that escaped Nicholas almost could have been a laugh. "He kept threatening to put me ashore . . . but he didn't want to be apart from me any more than I wanted to be apart from him."

Sam wrapped her arms around her middle, feeling everything inside her wrench with pain. As he spoke of his family, she heard an emotion in his voice that she had never expected to hear from him: love.

The love he felt, especially for his father, shone through his words, clear and strong even after so many years. "So when your father was arrested, you were only a boy," she said softly, understanding fully for the first time, "and that was why you were sentenced to the prison hulk?"

"Aye, they 'spared' me because I was so young." He rubbed at his chest. "And sent me to the *Molloch*. That was where I spent the next eight years, until I escaped during the riots. By then, all I cared about was killing. I wanted to repay the navy for what they had done to me. And to my father."

"And that's when you became a pirate."

"That's when I became what they had made me," he corrected. "And I was good at it—"

"Because you were reckless," she said softly, moving toward him one quiet step at a time, her bare feet soundless on the polished oak floor. "Because you didn't care about your own life."

He kept his back to her, and his broad shoulders rose in a shrug, but his breathing was shallow, his body tense, as if he were waiting for something. "I joined up with one pirate crew after another, and the price on my head went up every year. All I cared about was making as much trouble for the navy as possible. I was a thorn in their side for fourteen years," he said with satisfaction.

"So all the legends about you being greedy and—"

"Rich and having treasure chests buried on every island in the Caribbean? Bilge invented by the admiralty. I never kept a shilling. What the hell did I care about the future? I didn't know and didn't care if I was going to have one."

She stopped when only a few inches separated them. "But you finally got the vengeance you wanted?"

He started to answer, then stiffened, as if sensing how close she was to him. His entire body went taut. But still he did not look at her.

She started to reach out to him, wanting to touch him, to offer the kind of reassurance and comfort he had once offered her, but she stopped herself, unsure whether he would accept her caring.

Her love.

A heartbeat passed. Another.

His breathing and his voice were both sharp when he finally answered her question. "Aye, I got the vengeance I wanted. I don't even remember parts of that fourteen years. Some of it's nothing but a blur. All blood and swords and pistols." He shook his head. "And faces. Sometimes I still see the faces. People I hurt." His voice broke on the word *hurt* and he stopped, breathing hard as if he had run a great distance. The words came faster when he continued. "Then on that last night, when I finally had Eldridge in my sights—the man who had betrayed my father— when I finally found what I had wanted for so long ... I realized I had lost ..."

Yourself, she thought. *Everything of value. Everything that mattered.* Unable to stop herself this time, she reached out and touched him, placing a trembling hand lightly, gently on his back.

He was so lost in his memories of that night, he didn't seem to feel her touch. "The ship was on fire. I was cut off. Cornered. I couldn't reach him. The navy crew were swarming all around me. I was ... sweet Jesus, I was so blinded by rage." His voice started to shake. "I saw what I wanted slipping through my fingers. I turned and fired at the first blue uniform I saw ... and it was only a boy. A cabin boy."

"Nicholas ..." She moved closer, slid her arms around him, tried to offer something more, words of comfort, but her own voice broke.

"I watched him fall," Nicholas whispered. "I was staring right into his eyes, and I watched him fall ..." Tremors shook him, one after another, so strong they seemed to come from the depths of his muscled body, from his very soul. "And I could hear my mother's voice, reading to me when I was his age. Even over the sounds of the battle, I could hear her ..."

He paused, as if suddenly aware of Sam's presence, of her hold on him. But instead of stiffening or pulling away this time, he turned toward her, into her embrace, burying his face in her hair as the words slipped out of him.

"*Thou shalt not kill,*" he whispered brokenly, his powerful arms trembling as they came around her. "*Thou shalt not kill. Thou shalt not kill.*"

She pulled him close and held him tightly, tears sliding down her cheeks. She could feel his hurt like a knife inside her, could see how the guilt tore at him. He had lived with this bottled up inside him for years. Had cut himself off from the world, from people, from anything gentle or caring or kind. Had condemned himself to an isolated prison of his own making. Not merely because he needed to conceal the truth about his identity.

But because he believed he didn't *deserve* to be part of anything good.

"Nicholas," she whispered, a sob tearing from her throat. "Oh, Nicholas."

"So now you know the truth," he said a moment later, his voice still unsteady, though his hold on her was unyielding. "The real truth about who and what I am."

She only held him tighter. "And your name, the one you used in South Carolina?" she asked, her tears dampening his shirt. "The 'James' was for your father, wasn't it?"

He nodded. "His name was James Brogan."

She closed her eyes, feeling as if she was meeting Nicholas for the first time, realizing that she was perhaps the first person *ever* to really know him, to understand him.

He had so much good in him. So much caring and kindness, learned during his childhood; it was so deeply a part of him that even years of abuse and violence hadn't destroyed it.

But he was torn apart by remorse, consumed with pain and guilt over what he'd done during those years—guilt so terrible that he couldn't forgive himself. Couldn't set the good, decent, true part of him free.

Not by himself.

She lifted her head, wiped at her tears with one trembling hand. "So you gave up piracy on that night. And ever since, you've been living by the name of Nick James, as a planter in South Carolina."

"Thinking I could leave it all behind," he said hollowly, unwrapping his arms from around her, letting her go. "Almost thought I'd done it, after six years."

The longing, the defeat in his voice brought a lump to her throat. "Almost . . ." She didn't move away when he released her; she stood her ground, gazing up at him. "But you *have* been living peacefully all that time. You've been trying to live as a law-abiding man. And you succeeded until Foster forced you out of retirement."

"I can't blame him for what I am."

"But what you are now is *not* what you were all those years ago," she insisted. "You're not the same man that you were then. *I* know that even if no one else does. Even if you can't see it—"

"Samantha—"

"You've changed," she said stubbornly. "The good and honorable side of you, the side that the navy guards on that prison hulk tried to beat out of you, is still there. They *failed*, Nicholas. They didn't destroy you. The good . . . the love," she amended quietly, "has been right there, all along, hidden deep inside. Waiting for you to reclaim it."

His eyes gleamed brightly as he gazed down at her, his expression one of astonishment that was very close to awe.

"And now you have," she whispered, sliding her arms around him again. "You have. You *are* a good man. You deserve to be forgiven. And loved."

His arms enveloped her, and she both heard and felt all the breath leave him. "You can forgive what I've done?" he choked out, his hold on her fierce, his voice raw with emotion. "Even knowing the truth?"

"The truth is that you're not a harmless planter. But you're not a dangerous pirate, either. You're a little of both. Innocent and outlaw." Her voice grew softer with each word. "Like me."

Reaching up, she cupped his face in her hands, as he had done so many times with her. "The truth is," she whispered, "that 'they' were wrong about you, Nich-

olas Brogan. And I'm not one of 'them.' I can't con-
demn you. I know you too well." She pulled his head
down to hers, parting her lips for his kiss. "And I love
you too much."

Chapter 27

A rumpled pile of clothes lay forgotten on the floor, skirt, petticoat, breeches, shirt discarded by impatient hands. The sheets felt soft and cool beneath her as Nicholas lowered her to the bed, his touch gentle and strong as his fingers glided along the curves of her body. Her heart pounded with a rhythm as tender and fierce as the kisses they shared, while the lamplight bathed them both in gold.

Balancing his weight on his braced arms, he lifted his mouth from hers, eyes sparkling with what might have been a trick of the light . . . or dampness. Sam felt her heart unravel as she realized he was still trembling, still overwhelmed by the words she had spoken.

Twining her arms around his neck, she whispered them again. "I love you." She pulled him down to her, wanting no distance between them, ever again. "I love you, Nicholas Brogan."

He gazed at her as if he would be content simply to look at her for all eternity. Then his name on her lips became a sigh of desire as his mouth covered hers once more, his hands caressing, claiming. The rough silk of his beard against her jaw, her chin, sent tendrils of fire unfurling through her, the mat of hair on his chest creating delicious friction against the sensitive tips of her breasts.

She opened beneath him, welcoming the satiny glide

of his tongue against hers as she welcomed the heat
and hardness of his body. His weight pressed her down
into the mattress, his fingers seeking and finding her
feminine heat. She gasped as he parted her intimately,
heard his groan of pleasure and wanting as he discovered the hot rain below.

His mouth left hers to close over the tight pearl of
one breast, wringing soft cries from her lips. The heat
of his mouth, the wet touch of his tongue made her
arch beneath him, offering more of herself. All of herself.

With a feather-light brush of his thumb, he sought
and teased the sensitive bud hidden within her downy
triangle, until she was writhing beneath him, pleading,
whispering helpless words of need. She buried her fingers in his dark hair, drawing him back to her, wanting
more of him. All of him.

His arms circled her as if he were embracing life itself, holding on with all his strength. Her lips parted
as their mouths met in a kiss so deep it felt infinite,
their breath and longing joined, pulses racing, hearts
run wild. They had been away from one another only
a few days and it felt like an eternity. *Dear God, she had
missed him.*

She had ached for this, during too many long, empty
hours—for his kiss, his passion, his tenderness, for the
indescribable feeling of having Nicholas with her, beside her, part of her, body and soul, night and day.

Losing him had shattered her heart, but with every
kiss, every touch, every emerald-fired glance, he
mended and healed, restored and renewed. He made
her heart beat wildly and her soul sweep to new
heights with his.

They were both sheened with sweat, shuddering in
the grip of passion before he gave in to her, to them
both, pressing her back into the sheets. He gathered her
beneath him, enfolding her in his strength, his potent
power, every muscle taut as he positioned that steely,

male part of him at the honey-dampened entrance to
her body.

He brushed fevered kisses over her cheeks, her lips,
her jaw, then pressed forward in a long, slow thrust
that dragged a groan from deep in his chest. She instinctively arched her hips, taking him all the way inside her, moaning at the feel of his heat and hardness
becoming part of her in that ancient, mysterious way.

Every part of her felt tingling and alive as he began
to move, withdrawing and then surging forward until
he possessed her completely. The sensation of being
utterly joined to him made time seem to slow, to stop.
The night, the glow of the lamp, the smooth sheets beneath them faded from her awareness and there was
only the two of them, together. The sound of his breath,
the spicy scent of his body, the way they fit so perfectly
together, as if God had made them exclusively, exquisitely for one another.

Each deep, slow stroke sent a cascade of pleasure
through her. Her silken depths yielded and enveloped
him and the tendrils of fire spun tight within the core
of her body. His darkness and strength blended with
her pale softness until each became lost in the other,
giving and taking, surrendering and claiming, loving
and loved.

Together they moved as one. A fullness began building inside her, a sweet pressure that sent her rushing
toward a breathtaking height she had never reached
before. The feelings became so intense she thought she
would surely die of them, knew instead that they gave
her new life.

Suddenly they reached the peak and tumbled over
the edge together. She felt all the heavens shatter
around and within her, her gasps and cries of pleasure
a softer echo of his deep groans as rippling waves of
ecstasy swept them both. Washed by cascades of heat
and light, they kissed, shuddering with their mutual
release, two made one. Now and forever.

Her mind and heart repeated the words as she drifted down through an enchanting, sensual fog of bliss.

Now and forever.

The silence of night still enveloped the house some time later as she lay beside him, resting her head on his chest, tracing the brand lightly with her fingertips. They hadn't moved or even bothered to straighten the rumpled sheets, too languorous from their lovemaking to do anything but hold one another.

"I missed you, Nicholas," she whispered. "Dear God, it almost frightens me, I missed you so much. Without you, I felt so . . . so . . ." Words could not explain the feeling.

"Lost," he finished for her softly. "Alone. Empty. As if some vital part of you had been torn away."

She lifted her head. "You felt the same way?"

A strange, pained smile tugged at his lips. "Every step I took was a reminder that you weren't with me," he explained softly, winding a lock of her hair around his fingers. "I couldn't get used to the feeling of not having you beside me. I even kept that shirt you wore in Cannock Chase, because it carried a trace of your scent."

She smiled at him, then ducked her head before he could see the tears glistening in her eyes. He cared about her. He might not be able to say the words, but he cared. "Nicholas, please don't leave me again."

"You deserve better, angel," he said roughly. "Better than a washed-up, impoverished ex-pirate and a small house on a swampy island, where life will be a daily struggle to wrest some kind of sustenance from the land. You deserve your dream. Jewels and velvets and Venice." He stroked her hair, her cheek. "But I've taken that from you, too. Along with your innocence. And I can't even bring myself to say I'm sorry. Because I'm not. Selfish bastard that I am, I want you with me."

She closed her eyes, sliding her arm around him to hold him tight. If she had to spend the rest of her life trying, she would make him see how worthy he was of the gift of her love. She didn't care how long it might take. "Then come with me. Don't send me away with Manu," she pleaded. "Nicholas, you and I have both spent too many years alone, thinking we had to live that way to survive. Trying so hard to be strong. But strong only takes you so far." She held him fiercely. "Love has to take you the rest of the way. I can face anything as long as I'm with you."

It was true. And she would stay with him for all the days of her life, whether or not he ever said the words she longed to hear.

"I love you, Samantha."

She gasped, lifted her head, gazing down at him in wonder. It was as if he'd read her mind. The words flowed through her like sun and water, warm, sparkling, life-giving.

He raked his fingers through her hair, drew her mouth to his, kissed her long and hard.

"Then come with me," she pleaded when they came up for a breath. "Leave England with me—spare Foster's life." *And save your own*, she thought. "You've proven that you can spare a life. That you can care and give . . . and love."

"But there's no way of knowing when or where or if Foster might show up again. I wanted to get you *out* of danger," he countered, "not take you into danger with me."

"I'm not leaving without you."

"Stubborn lady. You'd think we were shackled together or something."

"We might as well be," she said firmly. "Because you're not getting rid of me. And no blacksmith in the world is going to break that vow."

He smiled at her. But still, he hesitated. "It would mean spending our life running."

"I've always wanted to travel."

"I'm serious, Samantha. If I let Foster go, I won't be able to go back to South Carolina."

"I hear Venice is nice."

His smile broadened. He stroked her cheek. Then he gave in at last. "All right, angel. I'll give you your dream."

London was a shadow on the horizon, a jagged silhouette in the light of dawn, and Sam had already discovered just how little she knew about ships.

She did her best to stay out of the way as Nicholas and Manu worked the rigging and the wheel, trimming the sails, speaking to one another in what sounded to her like a foreign language—made up of words like "leeward" and "spritsail yard," and "thirty degrees on the port quarter."

The ship was barely larger than a fishing schooner. In fact, it might *be* an old fishing schooner, she thought, gazing down into the glassy waters of the Atlantic slipping by. She liked the wind in her hair, and the smells of wood and canvas, the sea-spray in her face.

Clarice had been happy to bid them farewell—and not merely because Nicholas had said she could send word to her rich banker that the coast was clear and all pirates had abandoned ship. She had hugged Samantha, whispering in her ear, "You've got a chance, the two of you. The kind of chance most people don't get in this or any other lifetime."

Remembering, Samantha smiled, her suspicion confirmed that beneath her tough exterior, Clarice was a genuine romantic.

Standing up, Sam grabbed a polelike piece of wood overhead to steady herself—only to have the opposite end connect with something solid.

"Ow!" Manu rubbed his head, looking at her with a mournful expression.

"That's called a 'boom,' Samantha." Nicholas

laughed, standing a few feet away, securing the anchor. "For obvious reasons."

"I bruise easily, miss," Manu protested. "And I try to keep from bleeding more than once a week."

"Sorry, Manu," she said meekly. She glanced at his bandaged arm. "And I really am sorry about that, too."

"All right, all right," he said gruffly. "I'll agree to a truce if you promise to stop apologizing."

"Done." She smiled.

Nicholas came up beside her and kissed her. "Why don't you go below and wait for me in my—in our—cabin."

"Aye, aye, Captain." She gave him a salute and followed orders, though if there were only going to be the three of them manning the ship all the way to Venice, she would have to learn a little seamanship sooner or later.

She clambered down the ladder that led into the dark belly of the ship, heading toward the back. *Aft*, she reminded herself, her mind and heart filled with thoughts of Nicholas and Venice and sunsets over the Adriatic. She opened the door to their cabin.

And didn't notice she wasn't alone until the door slammed shut behind her.

She whirled to find a tall, slender figure stepping forward from the shadows.

A dark-haired young man with only one arm.

"We meet again, Miss Delafield," he said coolly, the gun in his hand glinting in the pale morning light. "Did you think you had seen the last of me?"

Chapter 28

~~~~~⌒◯⌒~~~~~

Sam felt cold terror rain through her. "Foster!"

He smiled. "I was waiting for Brogan to come below—but this is much better. You'll make an excellent shield."

Her eyes on his gun, heart hammering in her chest, Sam backed away, toward the porthole. If she could just call for help . . .

"Please stop right there, Miss Delafield. And don't scream. Even if you're bleeding—if you lose an arm, for example—you'll still be useful to me." He motioned her toward the door. "After you."

She froze. "How did you—"

"I told you once before, I know a great deal about Brogan. Including who some of his old friends are. It wasn't difficult to locate that doxy's house."

"Clarice," Sam gasped.

"Have no fear, Miss Delafield. She's alive and well and she'll stay that way. Though she should choose her friends more carefully. I've been watching the house for several days. I followed the African when he went to the docks one morning, thinking he might lead me to Brogan. Instead he was checking on this ship. Apparently it was in need of repair, which proved fortunate for me. It was fairly easy to sneak aboard with one of the repair crews and stow away. I knew Brogan would show up eventually."

361

"I thought it was money you wanted. Not murder." Moving only her eyes, Sam glanced around quickly, desperately, looking for some weapon she might use.

"The bounty is good for Captain Nicholas Brogan dead or alive—and after all he's put me through, I've decided that dead will be safer. I'm going to do what I should have done in the first place." He smiled. "Rather appropriate, isn't it? A nice funeral at sea for England's most infamous pirate. I think I'll let the African live, so he can testify as to his captain's identity."

"You told me once that you don't kill without reason!"

"I've got ample reason," he snarled. "And you've got your own life to worry about, Miss Delafield. Cooperate with me or you might not live long enough to be thrown in gaol."

"You can't kill us. You'll never make it back to port."

"Don't judge me by appearances." He nodded toward his empty right sleeve. "I spent half my life at sea. I've enough experience to manage a ship this size quite well." He motioned her toward the door with a flick of the gun. "Now move."

"You can't do this," she pleaded. "Nicholas isn't what you think. He never was. You don't know him."

"I know all I need to know."

"But he's no threat to you. He's leaving England because he was willing to spare your life. And the reason he didn't pay your blackmail demand is because he doesn't *have* any money to pay you. He's not rich. He has nothing. Nothing but this ship and . . . and me."

"How sweet. And how creative. Save your lies—"

"But he's not a ruthless killer! He was only a boy—"

He cut her off with a vicious curse. "Shut up." He pushed her toward the door. "Let's go above and find him. And keep your hands where I can see them."

"Samantha?" Nicholas called curiously, glancing up from his work as a familiar blonde head appeared in the companionway that led up from below. He smiled. "What are you doing? Have you come back to—"

"Nicholas, it's a trap!" she cried, scrambling up the last two steps in a rush.

Someone caught her from behind and shoved her aside with a violent push. She struck her head against a boom and crumpled to the deck.

Nicholas lunged toward her.

And froze when he saw the gun pointed at him.

"Hold it right there, Captain." The intruder swung the pistol to encompass Manu. "And you, as well. Nobody move."

"Who the hell are you?" Nicholas snarled, his eyes still on Samantha, his heart pounding with shock and concern. She moaned and sat up, apparently unhurt. *Thank God.*

"I'm wounded that you don't remember me. I certainly know you. I've been tracking you down for years. Step by step. Piecing your life together."

Nicholas finally turned his full attention on the intruder—a slender young man with dark hair.

And only one arm.

"Foster," he spat.

"Indeed. Pleased to make your acquaintance. Again."

Seething with rage, Nicholas grabbed the first weapon at hand—a knife he used for cutting rope.

"Stay where you are," Foster warned. "I've got enough bullets for you and your first mate and your little blonde mistress here." He swung the pistol toward Samantha, who sat very still. "You're not going to leave this ship alive, Brogan . . . but I could let them live. I haven't decided yet."

Nicholas leashed his anger. He slid a glance at Manu. Together, they could take him, but neither of them would risk Samantha's life.

He returned his gaze to Foster. The gunman facing him was barely more than a lad. He could hardly believe that the blackmailer who had made his life a living hell was no more than eighteen or twenty. "If it's money you want—"

"Oh, I'll get money and plenty of it. Ten thousand pounds. And probably a commendation from the admiralty for bringing you in."

"How did you find out I was still alive?"

"I didn't have to *find out*," Foster retorted hotly. "I was there! I was on the ship that went down. I saw you swimming away, your African friend here taking you to safety. And I swore right then that if I survived, I would devote the rest of my life to bringing you to justice. I vowed I would make you pay if it was the last thing I did."

Nicholas frantically searched his memories of that night. "I don't know you."

"Of course not. Why should you? I was only a boy. I was a cabin boy on the navy ship you attacked that night. I worked for Captain Eldridge."

Nicholas stared at him in stunned silence. The deck suddenly seemed to shift beneath his feet, the horizon tilted dizzily, the wind felt unnaturally cold against his face.

Sweet Jesus, it all made horrible sense. That was why it had taken six years for the blackmailer to make his demands . . .

He had been growing up.

But even in shock, Nicholas felt another, unexpected emotion: relief. The innocent life he *thought* he had taken had in truth been spared.

But the final irony was that in order to save himself, he had to kill Foster now.

And he wouldn't do it.

He threw his knife aside. "Go ahead and shoot."

"No!" Samantha cried, scrambling to her feet.

"Stay back," Nicholas ordered her.

Foster looked from one of them to the other, his gun swinging left and right, his expression confused.

"I'm not going to kill you," Nicholas said forcefully. "I won't do it."

"How noble." Foster raised his gun, aiming right between Nicholas's eyes.

"No, please!" Samantha threw herself between them, sobbing. "Don't do this. Don't you see? You're *him* twenty years ago."

"Samantha—"

"Get out of the way, Miss Delafield."

"No. You can't do this! He was just a cabin boy, too. He was as innocent as you were. He spent years seeking vengeance, just like you. You're the same!"

The lad's eyes burned. His jaw clenched.

"When does it stop?" Samantha's voice softened to a whisper. "When does all the killing stop?"

A second passed. Another.

"Foster, I'm sorry," Nicholas said with genuine feeling. "I can't make you believe that, but it's the truth. I can't make up for all the losses and pain I caused, but I can give you what you want—"

"Nicholas, no!"

"You can go ahead and kill me." He raised his hands, palms up, in a gesture of surrender. "Get your ten thousand pounds. It won't bring you peace, and it sure as hell won't bring you happiness. You'll find that vengeance solves nothing."

Foster cocked the gun. "But it *will* bring me satisfaction."

"Then go ahead," Nicholas said, his voice steely. "Destroy your life the way I destroyed mine. I took the vengeance I wanted and it brought me nothing but years of misery and anguish." He lowered his voice to a soft accusation. "Fire that gun and you'll become what I was. You'll *be* me."

The young man swallowed hard. The gun in his hand wavered, unsteady.

"Colton," Samantha pleaded, her voice desperate, "you asked me not to judge you by appearances. Don't judge Nicholas. It's a mistake to judge *any* man by appearances or by his reputation. You can never know what's in his mind." Her gaze shifted to Nicholas. "Or in his heart."

Foster's hand was trembling.

"You can either shoot me," Nicholas said slowly, cautiously, "or you can choose a different way. Let me give you what I didn't have at your age." His voice turned rough with emotion. "A second chance."

"It's too late for that," Foster replied. "I've come too far to change now. It's too late."

"Too late?" Nicholas asked ruefully, hearing the two words that had haunted him for years. "No, Foster, you're wrong. If there's one thing I've learned"—he glanced at Samantha—"it's that it's never too late to change."

Manu cleared his throat. "No matter how far you've gone down the wrong road, turn back," he said quietly. "Old Turkish saying."

Foster's eyes burned into Nicholas's, just as they had in the middle of a blazing deck six years ago.

Then, slowly, his hand shaking, the young man lowered the gun.

Nicholas watched it happen, almost blinded by the light of the sun rising over the waves. He felt a warmth that flowed not only through his body, but through his soul—a sense of forgiveness and renewal, as if he himself were getting a second chance. A chance to regain the years he had lost to violence and vengeance.

"So what the hell am I supposed to do now?" Foster asked uneasily.

"I have an idea," Nicholas said, even as the idea occurred to him. "I have nothing to offer you—nothing that can make up for what I did to you. I can't give you money, and I can't give you back your arm or your lost career. But perhaps I can offer you a better life than the one I've had."

"Meaning what?" Foster asked, eyes full of suspicion.

"Meaning . . ." Nicholas glanced at Samantha and then at Manu for approval. "How do you feel about South Carolina?"

Epilogue

South Carolina, 1743

Bright sunlight filled the streets of Charles Towne with spring's fresh warmth and dozens of townsfolk, many of whom stopped to chat with Sam as she carried a basket along the wharf, heading for a shop in the middle of the thronged shopping district.

She glanced up at the sign overhead as she opened the door. JMF CHANDLERS, LTD. "Excuse me," she said, trying to ease her way through the noisy crowd of ships' captains, sailors, and clerks inside. "I've a delivery for the owner."

She found the owner in his office, booted feet propped on his desk as his two co-owners held a noisy argument from either side of him.

"We can't possibly fill another half-dozen orders by next week," Colton was saying, holding up a sheaf of papers he had filled with figures. "Manu—"

"It's our busiest time of year, lad. We'll manage."

"We'll manage, we'll manage," Colton sputtered. "That's what you always say."

Nicholas looked up at Sam with a smile. "Have you come to steal me away, wife?"

"I've come to bring you lunch." She plunked the basket on the desk.

"I'd rather you steal me away." He slipped out from between his partners. "Besides which, what are you do-

369

ing walking such a distance on a warm day like this?"

"It's a lovely day. And the house is less than half a mile away. Besides, I've been doing this every Friday for a year and a half. It's tradition."

Green eyes sparkling, he took her by the elbow and led her into Colton's adjoining office, closing the door. "It was tradition before you were carrying my child," he said tenderly.

She smiled back at him, still glowing with the news she had shared with him a few days ago. "Nicholas, I'm only two months along. And I'm not that fragile."

"It seems to me we've had this conversation before." He kissed her. "Allow me to remind you . . ." He kissed her again, nuzzling her cheek, whispering in her ear. "Of just how completely you shattered in my arms last night."

She glanced over his shoulder, through the interior window at the adjoining office. "Nicholas, we have an audience," she reminded him.

"Hell, they're enjoying their argument too much to notice if I steal a kiss. And I've missed you," he murmured. "I've spent every blasted hour for the last six weeks in this office."

"That's what you get for owning the most successful ship's chandlery in the South. You've got a reputation for offering the very best merchandise. Not to mention expert advice to go with it."

"Aye." Pulling up a chair, he eased her into it, handling her as if she were made of porcelain. "Manu and I made rotten farmers, but between the three of us"— he nodded toward the arguing pair in the next room— "we manage to make a fair go of this."

"A fair go," Samantha concurred with a grin, knowing he was being modest. The ruby and the cash she'd earned during her years as a thief had provided enough seed money for the three men to start their business. Their seafaring expertise, knowledge of ships, and reputation for being some of the most honest businessmen in town did the rest . . . though rumors about Nicholas persisted.

Some said he had a mysterious past. Now and then, someone in Charles Towne even whispered the word "pirate."

But scores of people in the Colonies had mysterious pasts. And anyone who saw the way Nicholas James doted on his wife couldn't believe he *ever* could have been a dark and dangerous character.

"Now then," Sam said, beaming up at her husband, "are we going to have lunch?"

"We don't dare leave it in there for long," Nicholas grumbled, slanting a glance at the basket in the other room. "As soon as that young pup shuts up long enough to notice there's food in the room, he'll wolf it all down before anyone else can get a crumb."

"He's still a growing lad," Sam admonished, laughing. The relationship between Nicholas and Colton had been cool at first; it had taken months before they even called one another by their first names. But as they had come to know one another, a mutual respect had grown between them, which had gradually warmed to genuine friendship.

"Did you bring me some *gnocchi*?" Nicholas asked, toying with the lace-edged sleeve of her gown.

"And *pesto*." Sam nodded. "Mrs. Cascarelli brought over a whole potful to thank me for the last-minute work on her daughter's wedding veil."

They had discovered a mutual passion for zesty Italian food during their honeymoon in Venice. They had been married in a villa on the Adriatic, at sunset, on a beautiful autumn day.

She wore the wedding present Nicholas had given her pinned to the inside of her bodice, over her heart . . . since it would be rather hard to explain to anyone who saw it.

It was a special piece of jewelry fashioned by a Venetian goldsmith: a tiny pair of shackles, embedded with sparkling rubies.

Nicholas had had it made in secret, instructing the jeweler to select the best cuts from the gem, before selling what was left to raise cash for his new business.

Gazing up at her husband, Sam realized his face had taken on a serious expression. "What?" she asked, concerned. He so rarely looked serious these days. "Is something wrong?"

"No," he whispered, gazing down at her with eyes full of wonder. "Everything's right. It . . . just amazes me sometimes."

"Why?" She reached up to stroke his bearded cheek.

"Because I once thought that you . . ." He closed his eyes. "I thought you were some kind of punishment, sent to make me pay for my sins. But that's not the truth at all. You're a gift," he whispered. "Despite all I did in the past, God loved me enough to . . . bring you into my life. You and . . ." Opening his eyes, he lightly placed a hand on her abdomen. "Our child."

He couldn't say any more, he was so overcome. Sam rose into his embrace, holding him tight. "And you're a gift to me. I love you, Nicholas."

He wrapped his arms around her, burying his face in her hair. "I promise. Dear God, I promise I'll treasure these gifts all the rest of my days."

Sam felt her heart swell with emotion so strong it spilled over as tears. They kissed, a long, slow kiss, and then he swept her up into his arms.

"Nicholas," she protested breathlessly.

"Yes, wife?" he asked, heading for the back door.

"Where are we going?"

"Home."

"But what about your lunch?"

He grinned wickedly. "I've something better to nibble on."

Smiling, she wrapped her arms around his neck as

he stepped out into the sunlight. "I do believe I've married an incorrigible rogue, Mr. James."

"Aye, Mrs. James." He laughed. "I do believe you're right."

Avon Romances—
the best in exceptional authors
and unforgettable novels!